THE STARTING GUN

A knock on the door.

"Don't answer it," the woman said, but Whittaker was already up out of bed. When he opened the door, he found himself looking at a gun.

The killer shot the woman first. Then Whittaker.

Open the door and die, Whittaker thought. Life is like that.

So is death.

Former award-winning investigative reporter **TOM HILLSTROM** worked on the Patty Hearst and Son of Sam cases. Now, he lifts the lid on the workings of the NYPD's Homicide Squad as detectives piece together a baffling global puzzle in . . .

Riddle

RiDDLe

TOM HILLSTROM

A JOVE BOOK

To Margel and Red

RIDDLE

A Jove Book / published by arrangement with
the author

PRINTING HISTORY
Jove edition / January 1987

ISBN: 0-515-08949-4

Prologue

The mysterious Arab woman lying next to him had fallen into a deep sleep, but James Whittaker, although equally exhausted from their marathon of lovemaking, felt as if his eyelids had been tacked to his forehead in some ancient oriental torture.

Anxiety ripped his insides as Whittaker raised himself into a sitting position against the waterbed's stainless steel headboard and reached for a cigarillo from one of the glistening, dandelion-yellow plastic cube sidetables. He depressed a button on a navy blue device the size and shape of a grapefruit, waited a few seconds, then extracted a three-inch metal prod, its tip glowing like an ember, and lit the tobacco. He inhaled deeply, ignoring both the burning in his throat and the sudden nausea that jolted his already smoldering stomach. The tobacco did little to ease the tension, and his legs, spread out stiffly atop the mauve silk sheets, continued to fight the soft swell of the king-sized liquid mattress.

Whittaker gripped the bed's metal frame with his free hand, then commanded aloud: "On light—low." A concealed, voice-activated digital receiver translated his words into the closing of a relay which, in turn, energized the track lighting above him. The lighting, as commanded, was subdued.

Puffing on the plastic tipped cigarillo, he began looking around the distinctly American, high-tech bedroom seventeen

1

stories above Park Avenue. He stared at the stark, silvery frame of the red-cushioned reading chair, its matching table and lamp, and at the floor-to-ceiling bank of electronic consoles. Red and green LED lights flickered to the rhythm of the mellow jazz quartet bathing the room with sound from quadraphonic, man-sized corner speakers. He studied the phallic-shaped, pitted bronze floor sculpture, which twisted Giacometti fashion from the floor, past eye level, to a burnished cap resembling an oddly elongated golden metallic mushroom. Then he closed his eyes and marveled at how the flash, glitter, and excess had met such little resistance from his severe British sensibilities, at how the faddishness of it all had appealed to him so, reaching deep to some inner yearning and fulfilling what his fool doctor—his fool *former* doctor—would most certainly have dismissed as mere emotional wanderlust in a man helplessly awash in the whirlpool of his own lost identity.

Whittaker re-opened his eyes. He turned to his side and began visually caressing the bare back of the Arab woman curled at his side. With uncharacteristic modesty, she had pulled up the sheet. But the fabric reached only to the bend of her hip and there was nothing to hinder his hand as it came to rest on her shoulder. Her perfumed skin had an oaken cast to it, and was youthful and smooth, without blemish until his fingers reached the mysterious pencil-sized scar below her collarbone about which he had questioned her, only to get laughter for an answer. Was it a knife wound, as he suspected? Or some obscure surgical procedure?

Her body shuddered slightly at his touch, but her sleep continued, even as he reached over her and with his fingertips began tracing the contours of her breasts.

"Who are you, love?" he asked in a hoarse whisper. "Where did you really come from? And who sent you?"

There was no answer.

Whittaker left the bed and padded over the white shag rug to the windows. He opened the heavy rust and orange checkered drapes and looked out on the Manhattan skyline. Even double-paned windows and silicone caulking failed to block the city's noise—sirens, horns, and brakes. A sanitation truck screeching and a man yelling. More sirens. More horns. He peered down on Park Avenue. It had the appearance of a moat. A pair of moats, actually, dual arteries of ceaseless traffic. Cars and buses and, although it was unlawful, an occasional truck. Every second or third vehicle, a taxi. Now and then, a dark stretch limousine, and less frequently, the numbered rooftop of a police patrolcar. Across the avenue were other brick, concrete, and granite fortresses, their height their security, weary-eyed, garishly uniformed doormen their sentinels.

How queer, Whittaker thought, this dirty, vibrant, violent city. So many conflicts. And contrasts. He had been in New York, what, nine, ten months? And still the city surprised him. On occasion it startled him, even though, what with Calcutta, Tangiers, Khartoum, and Bangkok, he thought he had seen the extremes of the semi-civilized world. In India, a beggar might paw at your pantleg; in New York, he spat on your shoes.

A strange sound jarred him. A high-pitched, but muted beeping from the bed's sidetable. The telephone! Whittaker still had not become accustomed to the absence of a bell. Whenever he heard the beeping, he gushed adrenaline thinking it was a fire alarm.

He picked up the cordless receiver and carried it to the window. "Hello."

"Whittaker?"

"Yes. Who's this?" he asked, his free hand rubbing the thick lard-white scars disfiguring his thighs.

"You know who this is." A cynical laugh.

The laughter told him. "What do you want? We're finished. I informed you of that."

"You know goddamned well what I want, and I'm right outside your building waiting for it."

"Wait all bloody night, if you wish."

"I'll do just that. You can't stay up there forever. Just don't forget me, Whittaker. I'm not gonna forget you, you fuck."

The line clicked dead. Whittaker replaced the receiver in its cradle. He shook his head. The man was an imbecile. Strictly low-class, with the intelligence of an opium-crazed coolie.

No problem, this one. Still, Whittaker warned himself, he would have to be careful.

He closed the draperies and returned to the bed. He lifted his hands a moment, inspecting them—they were somewhat blanched but steady—then gently nudged his sleeping companion.

"Ohhhh!" she purred in her too practiced fashion, stretching. "Come to me, my Englishman."

Whittaker had no opportunity—from the other end of the apartment came a sharp knocking on the door.

"Don't answer it," the woman said.

But Whittaker was already out of the bed, on his feet, pacing. The knocking continued. Angrily, he flipped off the switch to the tape deck. Perhaps the woman was right and he shouldn't answer it. There was a pause in the knocking; then it resumed. "Oh, fuck it," he said finally, and walked off, still naked, to answer the door and end this annoyance once and for all. Any thug could be bought; this one's price would be low.

Whittaker unfastened the security chain and opened the door, his words already forming on his lips. But he had no chance to speak. A pistol was pointed at his chest. He began backtracking, subconsciously moving his hands to protect his groin. The gun followed him, staying within a yard even as he retreated back into the bedroom.

The Arab woman sat up abruptly, clutching the sheet to her breasts. "What is this?" she demanded.

"Shut up!" Whittaker barked. But he was too late—the shot came instantly and with precision. The woman's body lifted off the bed. A narrow cavern, red and deep, marked the center of her forehead. Death appeared instantaneous.

Whittaker stared disbelievingly at the lifeless woman, then looked back to the gun, now once again pointed at him. Every force within him commanded that he say something to stall his doom, that he somehow distract the steel-faced killer whose unblinking eyes expressed such contempt and hate for him. But he stood paralyzed, demeaned by his nakedness, his words frozen with the thought that he was about to die—a loser.

Then the explosion, piercingly loud, echoing again and

again off the walls of some infinite canyon. The shot on the
mark. His body snapping back, then folding to the floor. His
chest was afire, a searing tunnel of darkness above the heart.
His blood, warm and sticky, spilled in rivulets into the well
of his sternum and down his ribcage to the carpet's spongy
softness. Then the burning began to subside, replaced by a
numbness. He began to grow cold.

The room was quiet now—quiet except for the slow wind-
ing of a tape in the video recorder across the room, beneath
the blank television screen in the electronics bank. The machine's activity puzzled him. Had he left the recorder on?
From the same direction came the sound of breathing. Quick
breathing, but muffled, barely audible. He struggled to lift his
head to look toward the television, but the muscles in his
neck refused to respond. He began to shiver, and a gurgling
erupted deep within his lungs. His mouth grew dry and his
ears began to pound. But his eyes remained open, still seeing
in the bedroom's dim light—focused now on his Gucci's, on
the floor under a grotesque aluminum dresser. Loafers, scruffed
and dull, badly in need of a polish.

Whittaker forced his whitening lips into a thin smile. His
chest was heaving, his spirit ebbing away with the flow of
his blood, and his attention had locked on a pair of thin-soled,
dirt-encrusted, tar-stained shoes.

Life was like that, he told himself.

Then he died.

1

The doorbell rang in three urgent bursts. Ezekiel Patrick Ling, known as "Monk" to just about everyone, lifted his eyes from his book and looked to the loft's streetfront windows—only the soft glow of a streetlight and the red of a neon sign on the bleak residential hotel across West 15th Street seeped through the break in the thick, too short, dark blue drapes he had hung to deaden the outside noise.

A wino, he thought hopefully, and returned to his reading. It was a volume of Kierkegaard, and he had read it many times. He was studying it once more because he was no longer certain many choices in life were either/or. Too many times, it seemed, his missing a third or a fourth route through the maze had defeated him.

The doorbell rang again, longer and more authoritatively, unwelcome evidence that it was not a wino. Nor was it likely that it was Callahan, the artist who lived one floor above, arriving home stoned on a variety of pharmaceuticals, and attempting to muster his fat boyfriend out of bed, to aid him up the six flights of stairs.

Ling lowered the footrest of his reclining chair and swung his feet to the floor. He rubbed his eyes, then forced them to focus on a loud, ticking brass alarm clock atop an oversized mahogany dresser which, despite its bulk, appeared lost in the vastness of the sparsely furnished loft. It was 1:27 a.m.

Ling stood. He rolled his shoulders to loosen a sore, knotted muscle in his back, then shuffled to the lobby intercom, which was difficult to reach on the wall above an unfinished plywood counter in the kitchen nook. But before he could press the call button, there was a heavy-handed knock on the door.

"Who the hell is it?" Ling demanded.

"Johnson. From the Sixth."

Ling remembered him—a tall, young black cop, slightly overweight, who had been cursed with running an identical errand two, maybe three months earlier, sometime in the summer, on a sweltering, humid night. Then, as now, Ling had disconnected his telephone. The patrolman had not welcomed the climb to the fifth floor on that night either.

Ling, wearing only his shorts, opened the door. Johnson was hatless. He was puffing from the climb. He was annoyed.

"They want you, Monk—and fast," he said.

"Who's they?"

Johnson smiled. "About the only fuckers in the world who could get me to come back to this place: the Chief of Detectives and the police commissioner."

Ling showed pain. "What's wrong with this place?"

Johnson advanced inside and closed the door. "Let's put it this way—you get some kind of magic wand to make me single again, give me all that money you inherited, and I'd be a mother if you'd find *me* holing up in a Chelsea loft with bare pipes and concrete walls, in what used to be a factory and still should be, in one man's opinion. Besides, it's only what? Seven blocks from the goddamned Academy, and a whole lot of bad memories."

Ling smiled. "So you're short on class." He began slipping on his pants. "What do they have?"

"A pair of D.O.A.'s. Uptown. Something heavy. And that's all I know."

Ling buttoned his shirt in silence, then strapped on his shoulder holster. He reached under his bed for his service revolver, checked to see if it was loaded, and put it in place. He slipped on a blue blazer, then disappeared into a curtained-off alcove which served as a darkroom. His fingers moved in the darkness through his collection of cameras, until they found his favorite Nikon. He grabbed an extra spool of Tri-X film, and put it into one of the jacket's sidepockets. Returning to the light, he checked the camera's A.S.A. setting and fastened its strap, the wide, heavy-duty style favored by professionals. He collected his trench coat from the back of a chair, then moved to the door. "Let's get it over with."

The patrol car, its lights flashing, sped up Sixth Avenue, Johnson at the wheel, Ling's eyes sweeping the never-deserted streets. The electronic siren wailed, then broke off abruptly and emitted a horribly discordant screech from the bowels of its defective circuitry. Johnson pounded on the dash; the siren resumed its wailing.

"Cheap shit," the patrolman said. "Drives ya batty."

"They plan it that way," Ling responded.

A couple staggered from a bar, the man clumsily attempting to flag a cab. Two cabbies raced to claim the fare. Nearby, a short, round woman in a babushka was picking through a trash basket. A leather-vested teenager rested menacingly against a black steel gate pulled across a florist's doorway.

Johnson slowed at 34th Street, then sped through the intersection, against the red light.

"Ya know, I've heard a lot about ya, Monk, but there's one thing I don't understand," the patrolman said.

"What's that?"

"Your name is Chinese and they say you speak Chinese, but you ain't no Chinaman."

"That's right," Ling said, leaving the question hanging.

Johnson waited uneasily, then finally said: "Hey, look, man, I didn't mean nothin'. Just curious. The Army sent me to Germany. Never got to China, though."

Ling said nothing.

Frustrated, Johnson concentrated on his driving, darting back and forth between lanes. Two glassy-eyed hookers, one white, the other black, spotted the patrol car belatedly at 45th Street. They vainly attempted to fall back into the shadows. A wino lay curled in the gutter a half-block further. The eyes of two slender boys, no older than eighteen or nineteen, darted from car to car as they awaited paying chickenhawks.

Soon they were heading crosstown. Johnson had to hit the

brakes hard and swerve wildly to avoid colliding with an ambulance barreling down Fifth Avenue. The patrolcar's rear wheels spun out as he made the turn at Park Avenue and headed north again.

"Stop," Ling ordered.

"What?"

"This is fine right here. Just stop."

Johnson, bewildered, pulled the patrol car to the curb.

Ling opened his door and stepped out. "What's the address?"

Johnson, doublechecking his notebook, gave it to him.

"I'll walk."

"But jeez, man, the P.C., all the other brass, they want your ass there fifteen minutes ago, and if that don't happen, they're gonna come down on me."

"I'll handle it," Ling snapped. He slammed the door and walked away, then stopped and returned to the open window. "Look, Johnson, I appreciate the lift and I'm sorry about the hassle I caused you, okay?"

Johnson hesitated, then nodded ambivalently. Ling turned away.

Ling rubbed his eyes as he walked. He felt weary. Instinctively, he patted his blazer to check for his weapon. He glanced down to the Nikon. It was bouncing off his chest with each step.

What was awaiting him this time? he wondered. The frantic rush to find him, and the presence of the police commissioner most certainly meant a V.I.P. A diplomat, maybe. Or some political or Wall Street bigwig. Or a show business personality.

How many would this make? How many corpses had he chased? There were over a thousand murders in New York City each year. Three per night. Add to that another thousand suicides, and half again as many heroin and methadone overdoses. As he walked, Ling calculated that he probably had stared into the frozen eyes of at least a thousand murder victims. In at least three hundred of these, there had been no arrests. Perfect crimes.

He was in no hurry, and his slow pace caught the attention of suspicious doormen. With his open collar and unshaven face, Ling was someone to be watched on the gilded avenue of the rich, the powerful, the chic—and the fake.

He began to grin. They needed him—again. A tough case and they called Ling. Later, when it was over, he could go fuck himself. They'd fire him, some of them, if they had the nerve, but few in the pack of bureaucrats who governed the department had any balls. Those who did, once his usefulness had passed, would handily shunt him aside, as they clawed over each other's backs in their fight up the department's ladder, as if, in the end, it mattered. For now, they could wait. He would walk.

Ling liked to walk. Approaching a crime scene on foot had its useful points—he could take measure of the scene from afar, noting details that would be lost in the mad dash of a screeching squad car. He could also get a feeling—a feeling that the killer, too, might have had. Perhaps Ling's feet, right now, were following in the murderer's footsteps. By walking, Ling could also search windows in neighboring structures for the streetwatchers, those loners who filled their empty hours monitoring the sidewalks and pavement below, as if studying tropical fish in an aquarium. Like beat cops, the street watchers could spot the slightest variation in a neighborhood's tempo. But, inevitably, they never came forward as witnesses— unless some flatfoot knocked on their door.

Ahead was what appeared to be half the department's motor pool, marked and unmarked cars double- and triple-parked outside one of the avenue's eyesore, wedding-cake-style highrises. Sitting on the fender of one highly polished sedan was a plainclothesman whom Ling recognized as the P.C.'s driver. Ling's stomach tightened.

The driver called out when he recognized him: "They're waiting for ya, Monk. What the fuck you do, take a bus?"

"What we got, the mayor's sideline?"

"Worse—you can learn it from them."

Ling stepped to the curb and scanned the windows of the buildings across the street. In one, with a light on, was a shadowy figure bent over the sill. Ling noted the floor and the window's position relative to the building's corner, then turned to the commissioner's driver. "What floor?" Ling asked.

"Seventeen."

A uniformed cop, standing beside the doorman, waved Ling into a large, ornate lobby filled with gold-framed mirrors, and expensive, though worn, upholstered furniture. Another patrolman posted near the elevator bank was manhandling a tall, spindly character whom Ling recognized as Charlie Penn. Penn was a one-man broadcast news service, who chased police calls with a tape recorder, and fed interviews to several of the city's radio stations.

"I want you to move now, scumbag," the cop was yelling. Penn spotted Ling. "Monk!" he shouted. "This prick won't let me up."

"They told me no one," the young cop explained, not recognizing Ling but sensing authority.

"I'll handle it," Ling said. The patrolman, irritated, backed off. Ling put his arm around the graying newsman. "How are ya, Charlie?"

"What the fuck's with that kid?" Penn glared at the retreating cop. "I've got credentials."

"I know, Charlie. Just back off a bit. You'll get your fill."

"Here, read the fuckin' thing," Penn said, shoving an orange badge-shaped cardboard press card toward him. " 'Authorized to pass police and fire lines wherever formed.' Plain, simple English. Black ink."

Ling had the newsman headed for the lobby exit. "Look, Charlie. This isn't for you here. Run of the mill crap. A little delicate, that's all. You know, the family."

"But the address . . ."

"Not what you think, Charlie. Believe me."

"You're straight with me, Monk, right?"

Ling pinched the newsman's cheek. "Go find yourself a mugging, something on the street. Stick that mike of yours in the face of some dying wino. Ya know, I still remember the night you did that. The last words this guy hears in this life is you asking, 'What do you feel about the death penalty?' The poor bastard was dying, for chrissake."

"It's my job, Monk, you know that. Three kids I raised."

"So leave now, Charlie. Call me sometime—I'll pop for a drink."

Penn stopped. He stared at the detective a moment, judging him, then headed out the door. The newsman had only reached the sidewalk when Ling called after him. Penn turned. Ling, his expression both conspiratorial and contrite, approached him and bent to his ear. "I don't have the heart to screw ya, Charlie, but you gotta protect me."

"What's up? I *did* smell something here, you know. You guys don't lie very good."

"The heat's on, Charlie. It's going to get worse before the sun comes up, and they don't want press here—not yet. So you've got to disappear around the corner or something and cover my ass. But stick around."

Penn grinned. "You're nice, Monk. I'll put you on the air. Help you make sergeant."

"The chief's here. So's the P.C. You see them, make your move—but you never talked to me."

Penn nodded, then headed for the door.

Ling moved to the elevator bank and flashed his gold shield to an elderly, white-gloved operator. On the ride up, Ling braced himself for the crowd of gawkers he knew would be waiting in the hallway. He also knew, given the address, who it was likely to include: little old widows, some rich foreigners, a young couple or two living off family money, one or more psychiatrists, and maybe a television personality. There would be no children, of course, or very few of them—Park Avenue was not in the business of housing families.

The elevator doors opened. The crowd was there. Most were still in their bedclothes; all of them were chattering. Ling, saying nothing, maneuvered his way through. The apartment door was closed, but through it he heard the troubled voice of Chief of Detectives Julius Golden barking out orders. Ling reached for the doorknob, but a young patrolman posted in the hallway immediately challenged him. The cop's eyes were on the Nikon.

"Goddamn it, I said no press," he barked to the elevator man. Then, to Ling: "What the hell's with you guys, anyway. I see you up here again and you'll spend the rest of the night in a holding pen."

The patrolman's hand went to Ling's chest.

"Hold it, Lopez," came a shout from the apartment door. Detective Second Grade Mickey Triano emerged from inside and pulled the cop's arm off Ling. "I thought you guys were smart. This is Monk Ling, for chrissake."

Lopez quickly backed off.

"I'm sorry, man. I didn't . . ."

"Forget it," Ling said. Then to Triano: "A board meeting?"

"All the yellow braid you've ever had nightmares about."

Ling had not seen the other detective in months. Triano was short and stocky with a well-defined paunch, and a teddy bear quality that had proven a magnet to many women. He had once been a very talented cop.

"They're waiting for you, Monk," Triano said, leading him inside.

Golden spotted Ling immediately. "Where the hell you been?"

"Home."

"So why don't you answer your phone?"

"Bad line or something, chief." Ling smiled. He admired Golden. Short and shaped like a bell, his hair parted in the middle and graying, he was the Department's mascot, the subject of precinct locker room discussions from the Bronx to Staten Island. Much of the talk was conjecture about the logistics of Golden's bedroom groping with his outspoken, Amazon-sized Scandinavian wife. There were more than twenty-eight thousand cops on the force, two thousand of whom Golden commanded in the Detective Division, and not a one of them was unaware of his secret passion for soap operas. In fact, Ling speculated, the chief had probably been catching up with "General Hospital" on videotape when the call came in, summoning him to Park Avenue.

Police Commissioner Hamilton Grambling, a onetime United States attorney, stepped forward and shook Ling's hand. "Good to see you, Ling. Did they tell you what we have here?"

Grambling looked worried. Ling shook his head.

"It's sticky. Looks like your textbook uptown homicide and then it turns out . . ."

"Just a minute, commissioner," Golden interrupted. "Let him soak up the scene first. If he knows who it is, it might color his perceptions."

"Good thinking," said the P.C.

Golden told Triano: "Take him in."

Triano led Ling into the bedroom, glanced back to see if anyone else was with them, and began laughing.

"I must have missed something," Ling said sarcastically, looking toward the bed where the body of a swarthy young woman lay unclothed.

"All this bullshit. You eat it up, don't you?"

"What do you mean?" Ling looked to the thick, white shag carpet and saw the bare feet of the other corpse protruding from around the corner of the bed.

"The deference. The respect. They stand out there like they own the Yankees and here comes their star nine-million-dollar pitcher. For chrissake, Monk, if they had to yank a patrolman out of a sector to find me, they'd have my nuts hanging from the rafters of One Police Plaza."

"If they could find them," came a voice from the floor across the room. Dr. Stephen Jason, deputy medical examiner, rose from the floor where he had been examining the second victim, a male.

The two detectives moved around the bed. The doctor stepped back. Ling stared down at the corpse, which was also unclothed. There was something in the air, some intangible force that lingered at the presence of a murder, and Ling felt it now. He always did. Maybe it was the victim's last, incomplete death gasp. Or some fourth dimension aftershock of the brain's final burst of electrical impulses as it vainly tried to defeat its final trauma. Or perhaps—as Ling considered most likely whenever he thought of Alex, his wife—some spiritual presence, a formless being, a soul, a damn ghost. Whatever it was, it was there, announcing to all willing to feel it that man's ultimate sin had been committed here.

"Shot in the chest. Appeared to sever at least one artery," the M.E. said. "The woman got it in the forehead."

"With what?" Ling asked.

"Small caliber. Probably a twenty-two."

Ling looked to Triano. "Pissed-off husband?"

"Don't think so, Monk. According to the neighbors, this chick had been here for a couple of days. And no ring."

"Mob?" Ling asked, aware of the increasing preference by professional hitmen for small caliber weapons.

"Can't rule it out, but the mob doesn't seem to fit, the two of them being naked and all. Wise guys would have let her dress.''

"A growing trend," the M.E. commented dryly. "Bare-assed homicides. We're up to three, four a week. Sign of the times, I guess."

"You got a time for these, doc?" Ling asked.

"Two to four hours, I'd say. Can tell you with more confidence once we get them on the table."

Ling moved to the bed and stared at the woman's corpse. In the forehead, almost dead center, was a single bullet hole. Small. Bloodless. She was lucky—she never even heard the shot before she was gone. Her hair was coal-black, cut short. Her still-open eyes were wide and deep gray. Her sharp facial features and dark skin suggested she might have had roots in the Mideast. An Israeli, or Arab, perhaps.

"Neighbor said her accent sounded French," Triano said.

Ling turned away from the bed and bent over the male body. The man had not been as lucky as his lover—the chest wound probably meant he had lingered.

Ling studied the face. The eyes were turned upward and only the whites showed. The mouth was frozen grotesquely, its lips seemingly stopped in mid-syllable of a final word, uttered as the shot struck home. Or had it been a smile? The cheeks were sunken, as they usually were in the early stages of death, before the tissue reversed the process and began to bloat. The victim's black hair, incongruously, still showed its luster and remained combed precisely into place. Ling's eyes traveled down the body, noting the lividity, the dark red settling of blood along the victim's back and the extremities, where they touched the floor. The arms were like sticks, the victim's back flat as pasteboard—no manual labor here. A paunch suggested a drinking man. Hands unblemished, fingernails manicured. A gentleman. About forty.

"He hasn't been moved?" Ling asked.

"That's what the lividity seems to suggest—with both of them," Jason replied.

"Anything else?"

The pathologist shook his head. "Nothing more I can do here." He reclaimed his clipboard from the bed. "This is rapidly turning into one of those nights."

"How's that?" Triano asked.

"First, I get this fat bitch, three-hundred pounds maybe, dead in bed up on the West Side. Took two of us to move her just so we could get to the bottle under the covers."

"Pills?" Ling asked.

"Naw. Medicinal alcohol. Guess she was desperate. Three-hundred pounds and a hundred of that was her liver."

"We all got it tough," Triano said, impatiently. The physician's account came too close to his own history.

But the M.E. wasn't finished: "Then up to East Harlem for some junkie two weeks ripe on the top floor of an abandoned tenement. I goddamned near broke my leg when the rotten stairway gave way."

"So quit, if it's getting to you," Triano said. "Take up gynecology or something."

Jason glared at Triano, then turned toward the door. "Check my office tomorrow on these," he said to Ling on his way out.

"What's with him?" Triano asked.

Ling shrugged—but he knew the answer. Jason had been a very successful anesthesiologist until he grew too fond of some of the numbing drugs he administered. Now, collecting corpses on the night shift was all the medical profession would tolerate. Ling always made it a point to check his eyes.

"The brass, Monk . . . ," Triano said.

"I know," Ling answered, returning his attention to the male victim's body. He studied it feature by feature, dwelling on the jutting, square chin, and the bushy dark eyebrows. With the eyes rolled and only the whites showing, their color was unknown. Ling pictured them brown, then gray, then blue. Then it came to him—blue. He had seen this face somewhere. In a magazine, perhaps. Or the newspapers.

"Recognize him?" Triano asked.

Before Ling could answer, a department photographer appeared at the door. "Can I shoot?" he asked.

Ling waved him in.

The flashing of the photographer's strobe gave the death scene a surreal quality, like that of a disco floor. Ling, meanwhile, inspected the room. He moved along each wall, his fingertips grazing the mirrors, the wallpaper, the furnishings. At the bed, he formed a fist and pushed it into the rumpled bedsheets. The linen began undulating. It was a waterbed.

Ling paused at a tall, bronze floor sculpture, its phallic symbolism blatant, then moved to a large, brightly colored mural. He found the artist's signature in the corner—the scrawl was unreadable.

Atop an unusual aluminum dresser were a comb and hairbrush alongside a crystal tray filled with lotions, aftershave, and cologne. Ling opened the top drawer. On one side was a stack of magazines. He lifted one. "Sorority Dreams," read its title. Pornography. Very slick. Times Square's best. The man was a collector. On the other side of the drawer was a collection of vibrators, dildoes, jellies, lotions, creams, and other sexual ointments and paraphernalia.

Triano smiled. "The neighbor said he was a swinger."

"Or a dreamer," Ling said.

Other drawers revealed men's socks, underwear and other clothing, except for one bin that was filled with red, black and pink lingerie—more decorative than utilitarian in their powers of concealment.

Across the room from the bed was a large, rear projection television, surrounded by shelves containing other electronic paraphernalia, including a video recorder, tape deck, turntable, amplifier, various audio and video editing devices, an assortment of audio cassettes, and a large library of videotapes.

"The speakers are in the corners," Triano said, pointing to one of four tall, walnut boxes.

The photographer, having shot the corpses from every direction and angle, began rewinding his film. "Got what I need, Monk—unless you want something special."

Ling said no, and dismissed him. The photographer stopped at the door, watching as Ling flicked on extra lights and began focusing his own Nikon.

"Still after my job, huh?" the photographer asked.

"Only an amateur."

Ling ignored the bodies—he would rely on the photographer's work for that—and instead used a wide angle lens to shoot each of the four walls. Changing lenses, he opened the dresser drawers and closet cabinets and shot close-ups of their contents. Then he stopped—he would return for a more thorough documentation later.

"Ain't no other homicide cop in the entire world does all this camera crap," Triano said.

"My mind's shot—can't remember unless I've got a picture."

Ling placed the Nikon on the bed, then returned to the corpses. Without hesitation, he lifted each limb. He held each of the victims' hands, studying the skin texture, the fingernails. He examined their teeth, then ran his fingers over the cheeks, the woman's smooth as a newborn's, the man's raspy with a day's worth of beard.

"Ain't no cop in the world does that either," Triano said.

Ling didn't respond. He returned the bodies to their original positions and stepped to the center of the room. A strange sensation came over him. The muscles of his face fell lax with numbness, his fingers lost their tension and began to curl and the sounds reaching his ears from the other room grew muted. But his eyes came alive with penetrating power, darting back and forth, up and down, noting the tiniest of details, the subtlest of colors. He began moving slowly around the room, pausing here and there, his eyes wide and, occasionally, unmoving. In that instant he was alone, his imagination struggling to move back in time to the moments before two lives had been taken, his mind locked in a labor of empathy, as he attempted to jump into the personalities of slayer and victims, grasping their hopes and goals, their weaknesses and frustrations, filling the same space that they had, breathing the same musky air, viewing the same furniture, artwork, and silken-papered walls . . .

"You sick or somethin'?" Triano asked.

Ling ignored him for a moment, then offered a smile. "I'm fine."

"All of a sudden, you . . . you began to look pale."

"I'm okay," Ling said impatiently. He returned to Triano's side. "The lab crew ready?"

Triano nodded.

"They can have it. I'm through."

They started to leave, but Triano stopped. "Can I ask you something, Monk?"

Ling looked at him.

"Always wanted to know why you work over the body like that. I mean, that's the M.E.'s thing, not ours."

Ling grinned. "I couldn't decide if I wanted to be a doctor or a garbageman—I chose garbage," he said, deciding that to answer honestly, to explain the importance of getting the touch, of feeling the coldness and stiffness—would sound silly to a seasoned detective like Triano, and would probably be spread through the city's squad rooms by the next payday. "Anything missing?"

"We can't find a wallet. There's a purse here, though. Money in it, but no I.D."

"Some robbery, huh? What about the doorman?"

"Saw nothing."

"Tenants?"

"The guys are working on them now."

Ling led Triano back to the brass awaiting them in the living room.

Golden spoke first. "What d'ya think?"

"Single shot in each with near-professional accuracy. A wallet missing, but nothing else. No defensive injuries or any other sign of a struggle. Doorman knows from nothing. Nobody hears anything. The victims bare-assed. Your ordinary uptown catch-a-thief-by-surprise murder, except . . ."

"Except what?"

"Except it's wrong."

Golden nodded. "Something's missing, all right."

"Who was he?" Ling asked.

The chief looked to Grambling, who, with a somber face, gave Ling his answer: "One James Canton Whittaker—the British prime minister's brother."

2

A young bobby, standing as a lone sentry in the early morning London drizzle, saluted smartly at the door of 10 Downing Street. Breckenridge Collingsworth acknowledged the greeting, then rang the bell. The mansion's longtime butler answered the summons promptly.

"Good morning, sir."

"Good morning to you, George. We have a bit of a gathering today, do we?"

The servant shook his head. "Only you, sir. And Mr. Dunlap."

Collingsworth was relieved—the crises that usually led to his being summoned by the prime minister typically involved dozens of the government's top officials—and government by committee rarely worked well, especially when time was a factor, as it most frequently was.

The butler continued: "Mr. Dunlap is awaiting you in the anteroom, sir."

Whatever would prove to be today's crisis, Collingsworth welcomed Dunlap's presence. Dunlap was the prime minister's top political strategist and adviser. He was usually at her side for most of her public day, acting as a gatekeeper, to separate ally from foe, and as a guardian, to ensure she made no promises or took any action that would jeopardize the party's delicate hold on the government. When Dunlap failed—

and this was seldom—Collingsworth stepped in as fixer, a quiet, young emissary who had smoothed troubled waters from Leeds to Belfast, and Moscow to Buenos Aires. Few people outside of government knew Collingsworth existed, but he had the satisfaction of knowing that his impact in Britain's halls of power had been felt throughout the Commonwealth, if not the world.

Collingsworth, who had made it a point to lease a flat within quick walking distance of 10 Downing, expected he would be dispatched to yet another foreign capital. He brought a small, packed suitcase.

Dunlap, rumpled and unshaven, greeted him gravely.

"What now?" Collingsworth asked.

"Her brother."

"Arrested?"

"Worse—murdered."

"Murdered?"

Dunlap, his face still showing his own initial disbelief, nodded.

The two men sat. Through a closed door they heard the voice of the prime minister.

"She's on the line now with her mother," Dunlap said.

"Where did it happen, the Bahamas?"

"New York. She received word from the President himself. The Mayor of New York just called a minute or two ago."

"Do they have a suspect?"

"No one in custody, if that's what you mean. I expect there's a list of a hundred possibilities."

Collingsworth shook his head. James Whittaker had embarrassed the British government in a half dozen nations. Now, even in death, he apparently would once more taint the remarkable successes achieved by his sister. "How is she taking it?"

"The first words out of her mouth were, 'Damn him!' But I think under that thick skin of hers, she's troubled by it."

"How did he die?"

"Gunshot. Found him on a bedroom floor, a woman in bed—both naked, naturally."

Collingsworth thought a moment, then said, "Labour will find some use for it, no matter how it turns out."

"Of course. She realizes that, and that is why you are here."

The door opened, and the prime minister entered with her customary all-business demeanor and gait.

Her two aides stood. "Please accept my condolences and . . ." Collingsworth started, but she cut him short.

"The simple truth is we were not close. You knew that, Mr. Collingsworth. All of England did."

"Still, he—"

"He was a greedy, unprincipled failure, who would have done anything within his limited reach to topple this government unless we acquiesced to his outrageous demands. An ambassadorship, you might remember, is one plum he demanded. And when we said no to that, he turned to harassing the Americans, all the while hoping it would come back to hurt me."

"You deserved better, Madam Prime Minister," Dunlap said.

She took a seat, motioning the others to do the same. "It started with that wife of his. Then the accident. He was never the same."

"No man would be," Dunlap offered.

She reflected in silence a few moments, then looked Collingsworth in the eyes. "I have no illusions about what we face," she said. "Every political enemy we have will now accuse us of trying to milk the public for sympathy, if they don't accuse us outright of having him killed."

"It *could* work to our advantage," Dunlap said, wistfully. "There *will* be a sympathy factor. The public respond to a death."

The prime minister frowned, rejecting his optimism. "In retrospect," she said, "we should have had him under closer observation. I can see that clearly now. Of course, I did not want to risk a thorough surveillance. My god, can you imagine if it had reached the yellow press—a story of how the prime minister was having her own brother tailed or bugged or whatever else it is that our people do?"

"You had no choice," Collingsworth said.

"I'm not certain I have any choices now but we don't know that yet, do we. That is why I am consulting you."

There was a knock at the door. The butler entered and announced the arrival of Messers. Noble and Tarrant. Collingsworth had had dealings with them both. Noble was from Scotland Yard, Tarrant from a Whitehall bureau, the very existence of which was unknown outside a circle of fewer than a dozen key government and military leaders.

The prime minister thanked them for coming, especially on such short notice, then told them of her brother's murder. Their expressions revealed that they had already heard the news, quite possibly, Collingsworth speculated, before the New York police.

Again fending off any offers of condolences, the prime minister bid them be seated. "It was my decision to hold you back in your activities with respect to my unfortunate brother, gentlemen," she said, "and as I recall, both of you tactfully suggested otherwise. I should have listened to you then, and what I'd like to learn from you now is anything you have learned about my brother."

Noble and Tarrant looked at one another.

"We dropped him, for all purposes, when he left Manila," the Scotland Yard man said, somewhat defensively.

Tarrant spoke next: "We kept up with him with some degree of thoroughness in the Caribbean. Once he landed in New York, however, we began to tiptoe. Sticky situation, that. But he was in regular contact with our embassy in Washington. One of the secretaries handled him, Mr. David Holmes."

"David Holmes," the prime minister repeated. "Hasn't he been standing in for the ambassador?"

Dunlap nodded. The British ambassador had been away from Washington for more than a month, recovering from heart problems at a retreat in the Midlands.

"Anything else?"

"Whittaker . . . your brother, I mean . . . had had social relations with an American," Tarrant said.

She laughed. "I should think the objects of his 'social relations' would number in the dozens, sir."

"This woman is connected with the administration. An

economic adviser. Very influential, by all appearances. Her name is Marilyn Mason.''

"And did *she* arrange an ambassadorship?'' the prime minister asked sarcastically.

"According to the reports, the few reports I've seen, she was truly fond of him,'' Tarrant said, his tone hinting that he, for one, considered this astonishing.

"Perhaps here is a clue as to why we can't talk economic sense to Washington.'' She looked at Dunlap. "They've got some starry-eyed adolescent in control of the dollar. She is so gullible she's infatuated by what can best be described as a power-starved scoundrel.''

"The woman killed with Mr. Whittaker, it wasn't Miss Mason, I gather,'' Collingsworth said.

"No,'' Dunlap answered. "Our reports indicate she was possibly a foreigner, an Arab, perhaps. The American authorities do not yet know her identity.'' Dunlap cleared his throat, then looked to the two security men: "Was there any forewarning that he might have been the target of terrorists, some radical group?''

Noble and Tarrant both shook their heads.

"The Eastern bloc. Any sign that they had an interest in him?''

Tarrant answered: "It would be a reasonable assumption that the Soviets might welcome having the brother of our prime minister in their pocket, although the quantity of sensitive information he could offer would be severely limited. In the event, we saw no indication that this was underway.''

"There was his involvement with the American anti-nuclear movement, but I believe you knew all about that, ma'am,'' Noble said.

"Yes,'' she responded. "He wanted to embarrass the White House, and through that, get back at us here. That much was clear, wasn't it, Mr. Dunlap?''

Dunlap agreed.

The prime minister was silent for a moment, her eyes alternating between Tarrant and Noble. "Please keep all channels open,'' she said finally. "I want to know everything. Hold nothing back out of respect to my emotions or bloodlines.'' She nodded, dismissing them.

She waited until they had left the room, then put a hand on Collingsworth's arm. "Once more, my young Breckenridge, you're going to take care of things for me."

"Whatever your wishes, ma'am."

"I want you there . . . I want you side by side with the FBI, the police, or whatever of those endless American agencies will be at work on this situation. Whatever they find out, I want to know. And if there is a way to—how do they say it?—cut our losses, that is exactly what I want done."

"Stay in contact with Holmes at the embassy. He'll be instructed to serve as your conduit back to London," Dunlap added, revealing his foreknowledge of the plan.

"We have an RAF jet standing by to fly you to New York, and we'll be advising the Americans of your arrival to serve as my personal liaison," the prime minister said. "And of course, our public position must be that we are seeking nothing extraordinary, no special treatment. Fleet Street will be running amok with this as it is. Any questions?"

"I don't think so." Collingsworth already was considering what tactics to use with the Americans: low-keyed and subtle, even a bit naive, capitalizing on any sympathy.

"Be off then. I have a funeral to arrange. And . . ." she stood and pressed close to him. A single tear rolled from an eye. "And thank you, Breck."

"You'll have your answers," he promised.

Dunlap escorted him to the front door. He motioned the butler away, then spoke softly: "Be careful over there. Think everything through. If this is handled incorrectly, it could well be our ruin."

"I've been there before."

"I know you have. And I'll offer only one suggestion . . ."

"Yes?"

"Proceed cautiously with the police—at least until you learn what they know. Until then, I'd be very conservative in the amount of information I shared." Dunlap handed him a thick envelope. "A copy of her brother's file. Thought you'd want to read it." They shook hands.

"We've arranged police transportation to Heathrow. It's a two-man jet you'll be going in. You'll be cleared for Kennedy, and a helicopter will take you on to Manhattan. The

State Department will have a car there. The rest is up to you.''

Collingsworth called for the butler. The servant presented himself, a small suitcase in his hand. Collingsworth accepted it and looked at Dunlap. Collingsworth smiled. "Keep me pie warm, mate," he said in a false cockney, then turned to the door.

Outside, more than a dozen cameramen and reporters had materialized. They gave the young emissary a quick inspection, then lowered their cameras. Collingsworth had no trouble passing through them and into a waiting police car—the press had no idea who he was.

3

The morning rush hour had passed and the subway car was half empty. Stanislas Lubelski took a seat next to a well-dressed couple and watched with interest as a Transit Authority patrolman attempted to rouse an unwashed, rag-covered drunk passed out on the double-seat near the doors across the aisle. Opening his eyes, the drunk mumbled something about Brooklyn. The cop wasn't interested. He ushered the drunk off the train at the next stop. Seeing the derelict, Lubelski thought of the Russian.

Lubelski dreaded his meetings with the Russian. Petrovich was so crude, so stupid. But that was the way of the modern Soviets. Cultureless thugs, at least those in the field. Nothing at all resembling the heroic Russian revolutionaries with whom Lubelski had allied in his youth, an alliance for which he had paid so high a price. Those Russians of the 'thirties and 'forties were thinkers, philosophers. They were committed. But somewhere the heritage had been broken. Their successors, in the pretentiousness of their narrow minds, were of the same ilk as the upper class the revolution had sought to crush. Selfish, power-hungry, would-be despots had infected the system, men concerned only with how much vodka they could horde and how many icons they could smuggle to western markets. Men like Petrovich.

There could be no greater contrast, Lubelski thought, than

that between himself and his Soviet master. As correspondent for the Polish state news agency, attached to his nation's U.N. mission, Lubelski was routinely invited to the diplomatic community's most prestigious affairs. He got around. He met people. He tasted the highest life New York City had to offer. In contrast, Petrovich, in his three years in New York, traveled in a world of grease, underground garages, and mechanics racks—the price he paid for attempting to cloak his KGB status through a ridiculous charade of being the Soviet mission's ranking chauffeur. Drivers, no matter what their concealed authority, waited at curbsides.

The train pulled into the sharply curved station at South Ferry. Lubelski got off, climbed the stairs, and walked past the terminal entrance into Battery Park. Leaning against the waterside iron fence, he studied the harbor for a few minutes, then retreated to an unoccupied bench across the footpath. He sat, facing the water, a banker from Wall Street taking a break, perhaps, or a tourist pondering the meaning of the Statue of Liberty in the distance.

Cyclists and joggers sped by. Mothers and nurses pushed strollers and carriages. A flock of pigeons passed. Two kids on skateboards barreled toward him, turning at the last instant, the wheels of one of the boards scuffing Lubelski's highly polished shoes. He shook a fist at them.

"The sons of capitalists," came a whisper from behind him. Lubelski did not turn. Petrovich. One of the Russian's most irritating traits was that he thought himself humorous. Lubelski could hear the KGB man's footsteps as he moved from behind the bench, then, through his side vision, glimpsed the Russian's short, broad figure skulking toward the terminal. Lubelski waited, searching for signs that either of them had been followed. Seeing none, he went to board the ferry.

They met at the bow, standing side by side against the rail, the huge Pole hovering over the Russian. Petrovich was silent until the ferry was underway. "I'm upset, Lubelski. My stomach hurts. My liver, it's swollen," he said in Russian.

Lubelski had no interest in the state of Petrovich's health. He adjusted his silver aviator glasses, then ran his fingers through his thick, pure white hair. "I'm always intrigued by that statue there," Lubelski said, in English. "The truth is, it came from French leftists, but course they don't tell you that on the tour.''

"Don't waste my time with inanities," Petrovich snapped in Russian. "Moscow has a job for you."

"You know what else intrigues me?" Lubelski continued in English. "Welfare Island . . . in the East River." He looked at the Soviet. "It once had a prison, an orphanage, and an insane asylum. Did you know that?"

"Lubelski, an important mission was blown. They want to know why."

"Charles Dickens once toured Welfare Island and later wrote about it. He very properly condemned the Americans for their barbaric treatment of the children and the insane—only he thought he was on Rhode Island." Lubelski laughed heartily. "The Americans, when they read him, didn't know what he was talking about."

The Russian glared at him.

"You don't know of Dickens, the English author?" Lubelski asked. There was no reply. Lubelski shrugged. He looked out over the water.

"You are very difficult, Lubelski. You are very certain of yourself. This life here—you forget who you are. That is a mistake." The Russian's voice was threatening.

"There are some rocks on the tip of Welfare Island, the residue of what once was a miniature fort. An imbecile constructed the fort over many years. He was convinced that the British navy would invade New York again. The authorities permitted him to do his work." He glanced at the Soviet. His voice lowered into a conspiratorial whisper. "And no one ever told the poor chap he was on the wrong end of the island—the harbor entrance is to the south."

Petrovich slammed his fist onto the rail. He recovered himself, then sheepishly looked around to see if his lapse in control had caused any of the other few passengers at the bow to look at them. It hadn't. "You heard the news about this Englishman—Whittaker, the prime minister's brother?"

Lubelski grinned. "I should have known."

"You should have known what?"

Lubelski's smile broadened. "Your handiwork, was it? All

the blood, the corpses left behind, a building no doubt full of witnesses.''

"We didn't kill him," Petrovich protested.

Lubelski thought a moment, then asked, "The girl?"

The Soviet nodded. "She was ours. Anatole."

Lubelski had known of Anatole. "That little French-speaking whore from Morocco?"

The Soviet's face grew red. "That little whore, as you call her, had already seduced half the power structure of Western Europe.''

"She drank too much. Too many drugs."

"She got the job done."

"But not this time, eh?"

Petrovich looked to the sea. "She was close, that we knew. He was vulnerable, very vulnerable, and Moscow wanted him." His eyes returned to Lubelski. He spread his hands. "Now this."

"What happened?" Lubelski asked.

The Russian shrugged. "I had not heard from her in more than twenty-four hours."

"Did she get anything?"

Petrovich shook his head. "She didn't have time. They had instructed her to proceed slowly, a step at a time."

They were silent for a while. A tug pushing a garbage scow passed off port. In the distance, a freighter was making its way toward the Brooklyn docks.

"Now there is worldwide attention," Petrovich said finally. "We have to keep our distance."

"So you come to me."

"We made you."

"And I'm retired."

"Retired? What do you wish, a pension?" The Russian laughed derisively. "Yours is a lifelong vocation, comrade, like that of a priest."

Lubelski lowered his eyes. Petrovich, of course, was correct. One did not retire. There was an eternal line—and if he crossed it, he would never again see the sun set. With one final indignity: there would be no trace.

"What exactly do they want?" Lubelski asked, submitting.

"Nothing complicated. Just who did it and why."

"Why don't you simply wait for the police?"

Petrovich laughed. "Like on television, huh?" He gripped Lubelski's arm severely. "Think it through, comrade—Whittaker was a fish in a very small pond. Look to his wake and there swims another fish. The other fish, too, can be baited."

Lubelski looked at him in disbelief. "What you're saying is find the murderer and recruit him?"

"It's a possibility."

Lubelski shook his head. "What in the world would Moscow do with a New York mugger?"

"We don't think that was the case."

"Why not?"

"The timing. The setting. Whittaker's ambition. His circle of friends. A peculiar kettle of fish. We have no choice but to look into it. Out of it may come opportunity."

Lubelski stared at him a moment, then pointed to a pair of pigeons pecking at crumbs on the deck. "Look at them. I wonder if they get off at Staten Island? There must be dozens of Manhattan pigeons marooned on Staten Island, don't you think?"

"We want you on this assignment," the Russian said sternly.

Lubelski rested both arms on the rail. "Was her cover blown?"

"I don't think so."

"And if I say no?"

The Soviet stared at him. His thick lips rolled into a grin. "There are some who might consider a certain highly compensated agent too long in the capitalist world, too long in having produced nothing more than dubious grain reports and political gossip . . ." The Russian's words trailed off. He lost his grin.

Lubelski pushed his face inches from the Russian's. "Do you think I need *you* to threaten me? Do you really think I, who was fighting the revolution the day you were born, need some classroom politician from the KGB academy to talk to me in this fashion?" Lubelski eased back. "I will do what has to be done."

They glared at each other, then the Russian stalked away.

"Petrovich!" Lubelski called after him in English. "If you'd come to me first, it would have worked."

The KGB agent, retreating to the passenger cabin, did not respond.

Lubelski turned back toward the sea. The operation had been handled poorly, he concluded. Whittaker surely must have suspected something. Perhaps the Englishman had had something in mind himself, an arrangement to propose, a profitable arrangement. If so, all the Russians probably would have had to do was make themselves known and available. Instead, Moscow, as was its custom, opted for a more aggressive strategy. Two corpses were the result.

Lubelski spotted a newspaper discarded on the deck. He walked over to it and picked it up. It was the late edition of the *Daily News*. The murders of James Whittaker and his unidentified lover had won the double-banner headline. Lubelski skimmed the story, finding that it related little more than he already knew from the radio news. He lowered the paper. Within a dozen hours, the American specialists in the Kremlin would be studying the same edition, along with all the other New York newspapers. They would listen to the tapes of the New York radio and television newscasts. Then there would be more questions for Petrovich. Lots of them. There would be more pressure. And Petrovich would efficiently pass all of it to Lubelski. Moscow wanted answers. It would be a race—a race between Lubelski and the New York police to solve a crime. Lubelski sighed. His body, once so hard, so muscular, so dependable, began to sag. He was sixty-two, tired, weary . . .

He threw the paper overboard.

The ferry tooted its horn as it approached the Staten Island berth. Several yards out, the captain cut his engines to float in. All was quiet, except for a few hushed discussions, the seagulls swooping all around, a bell tinkering on a nearby channel marker, the slosh of water against the ferry's side, and the agonized groan of a rope holding another vessel to its mooring in the face of the sudden and powerful wash of the ferry.

The ferry slammed into the rubber fenders of its berth and was secured. Lubelski watched as the Soviet was among the first passengers to disembark. Lubelski wandered into the terminal. Through a window he saw the Russian climb into a black, featureless Ford sedan.

A bell began ringing, announcing the imminent departure of the next Manhattan-bound ferry. Lubelski boarded. He sat inside on a bench against the wall.

He thought of Petrovich with disgust. They were so simple-minded, these Russians.

4

His wife was calling him, her voice soft and beckoning, and Monk Ling reached out to run his fingers through her satin-like hair, but his hand clutched only the hard oak of a bench in a normally abandoned office on the second floor of the Seventeenth Precinct stationhouse.

He opened his eyes slowly. He looked at his watch. It showed a few minutes past eight. He had not intended to sleep so long. Only an hour or so is what he had intended.

He ran a hand through his own hair, gray-streaked and curly—it was damp. He sat up and attempted to straighten his shirt, which, also wet, was clinging to his back. Sleep had not been peaceful. It rarely was. With nightfall, the pain was deepest, when he sensed the touch of Alex's body against him, when he felt the rhythm of her breathing, heard her whispers, shared her excitement when they were making love. Awakening, he would inhale deeply, attempting to expel the haunting memories, but the intake of night air would only fuel the illusion and he would sense that her perfume was about, that she had left the room for a moment, but was close by, and soon would again be close against his side.

His head ached and his eyes could not adjust to the light streaming past the edges of the window shades and under the closed door. He struggled slowly to his feet and, gritting his teeth in anticipation of the pain, raised his arms and stretched. But no pain came.

He moved to the window and raised a stained shade. Across the street, in a third floor window off the fire escape of a dreary tenement, stood a woman, a fat woman, naked, her huge breasts dangling like deflated balloons. She spotted Ling staring at her and gave him the finger. Ling looked down to the street. At the stationhouse entrance, a mob of cameramen, photographers and reporters had gathered. Two uniformed patrolmen blocked the door.

As he watched the hungry newsmen and photographers, Ling thought of the quarter of a million dollars Alexandra had left him as her legacy. Although minuscule in the context of Park Avenue, that amount could go a long way toward buying his coveted privacy, in the mountains or out in the country. Thus far, he had barely touched it. Maybe now, he told himself, was the time to change that.

Ling left the small office, returning to the large squad room that had been commandeered as temporary headquarters for the Whittaker investigation. The second floor room had once been home to an entire squad of detectives, plus a special unit of vice investigators. But a reorganization, the brainstorm of an almost-forgotten P.C., had left the squad room virtually abandoned. Now, only a small precinct investigative unit, of which Mickey Triano was a member, was based there. Ling's eyes drifted around the room. Like the rest of the stationhouse, it was filthy, every surface covered with a grimy patina betraying years—no, decades—of neglect. The very air was violent, reeking of an infinite procession of criminals, winos, bag ladies and mental cases come to testify to the modern urban condition. On desks and window sills and the floor were the moldy remains of half-eaten takeout dinners and lunches, dozens of crumpled coffee cups, disarranged newspapers, some dated more than a year earlier, empty aspirin and antacid bottles, and yellowing scraps of note paper bearing names, addresses, and phone numbers once relevant, now as meaningless as losing lottery tickets. On the walls were a bank calendar, a yellowing Detectives' Endowment Association handbill and an assortment of pencil and felt pen scribblings, including: "Free the Pigs," "Fire Sale: Truth and

Justice'' and ''Tell it to John Lindsay.'' Sociologists had already turned to inventorying garbage; better, Ling thought, that they look to the floors and walls of a squad room for a measurement of the times.

In a curious way, Ling found the grime and neglect fitting. He had been sent on a case to Los Angeles once, and found the police facilities colorful, clean and modern. The cops were physically fit to a man and the patrolcars tuned. The phones and radios worked, and the files were neat and orderly. But there was something about all the tidiness and efficiency that didn't work. Cleared desktops and antiseptic hallways belonged in hospitals, not big city police stations.

That he was not at the moment in Los Angeles was brought home to Ling by the voice of Chief of Detectives Julius Golden, who had gone home to shower and change, and was now back, booming out orders.

''Mornin', chief,'' Ling said to him, coming up from behind.

Golden looked at his watch. ''Glad you could join us. You see that zoo outside? They want answers. So do I.''

''Several leads are being pursued and the investigation is continuing,'' Ling deadpanned.

''They don't buy that line anymore.''

''Then tell them we don't know a damned thing.''

''Which is probably closer to the truth.''

Golden put his arm around Ling and ushered him to the side. ''You know, I was up watching one of my TV tapes last night when Triano called me with this. And it's bad enough I don't get to see the damn ending but I also got to see two feds running around that Whittaker apartment. You wouldn't want to tell me a little something about that, would ya?''

Two young FBI agents had appeared at the murder scene while Golden and the P.C. were downstairs addressing the press. Ling had recognized neither agent, though they complained they were regulars on the detested night shift.

''Sightseers,'' Ling said. ''They said they'd been told from the top not to step on any toes.''

''What the fuck—I mean this is ours and they've got no goddamned right—''

''They know that, chief. Sightseers. No more.''

"We'll see," Golden said. He released his arm from Ling's back. "I want you at the head of the line on this case, Monk. You and Rosie McKinnon and Jack O'Brien. I've also grabbed Dotty Levine."

"O'Brien?" Ling asked. He had little fondness for O'Brien. O'Brien was tough—too tough. There was, for example, the time he had shot a dried-out junkie full of heroin to inspire him to open up about his pusher. The junkie did talk—and then went right back on the needle. Three months later he was dead from an overdose. O'Brien seemed to enjoy the outcome, and Ling had considered him sadistic. But later, Ling came to understand it was not sadism that motivated O'Brien so much as corruption. Some cops bent rules to fix cases; others, like O'Brien, bent rules to win convictions. Only the currency was different. There was more bad blood between Ling and O'Brien. Ling had once proven one of O'Brien's collars innocent—and O'Brien had never forgotten.

"I'm well aware of the thing between you two, but I want him on this," Golden said. "There won't be any crap."

"Can I nominate another?" Ling asked.

"Like who?"

"Mickey Triano."

Golden appeared shocked. "Triano? Why, in god's name?"

"He's good."

"So's my wife."

"He's got the knack. Taught me a few things once."

"He's unreliable. A drunk. Trouble."

"Jeez, chief, I thought you were a mystic."

"What the fuck does that mean?"

"It's metaphysical," Ling said, his tone serious. "See, Triano—he's you, he's me, he's all of us. He needs this."

Golden shook his head. "You're fuckin' crazy."

"You need him."

"Okay. But he falls, you fall with him."

"What else is new?"

Ling thought of Triano—he, too, had been a hotshot in his first few years as a detective, another Ling, in many ways. Then came the trouble. Burnout, many thought—but Ling sensed it was something else. Maybe Triano simply had had his fill of department politics, department paperwork. Whatever it was, he had personally nailed half the Brooklyn mob, until he was stopped—by himself.

Ling thought of the others: McKinnon. A second-generation cop. Black. Veteran of the detective bureau known for his uncanny sixth-sense knack at closing homicide cases. Someday he probably would land the chief's job.

Dotty Levine. Dorothy, officially. Short, squat, and plain, she had won her gold shield before the term "women's liberation" had been coined.

O'Brien, despite his ethics, was streetsmart, and could occasionally get the job done. He had a special ability to extract information from lonely tellers, purchasing agents, desk clerks, and the other paper-shufflers who run the world. Ling decided to suppress his prejudices and give O'Brien a chance.

The chief was looking at him, inspecting Ling's soaked shirt. "Maybe you wanna run home, Monk, take a shower, shave."

"I'd like to talk to Triano and the others who were first on the scene. Also the dispatcher."

"That can wait."

"Memories fade."

Golden thought a moment. "Okay. I figured you'd want to do that. I kept one of those two uniformeds around. The other, Lopez, I sent home. His wife's pregnant."

The chief threw his shoulders back and strode off to give the press the meaningless release that would tell them nothing, yet satisfy the demands of editors looking only to fill broadcast time or newspaper space with something, no matter how distant it was from reality. Ling watched him leave. Golden would have no trouble with the press—they loved him. He was a character.

Ling scanned the room. The two FBI agents were there, off in the background, ties still tightly knotted, faces grim, eyes taking in everything. Ling smiled—the Bureau's trademark white shirts might be gone, and the haircut standard tempered, but the young agents still looked like products off an assembly line in some Midwestern factory. In contrast, the city detectives scattered about the squad room were disheveled and weary.

Triano, across the room, hung up a phone. Ling went over to him.

"Let's have a talk," Ling said, then led Triano into the office where he had taken his nap. Ling flipped on the lights and they took chairs at a 1950's vintage heavy wooden table, Triano spilling some coffee from a cracked porcelain cup, adding one more stain to the dust-ketchup-ink-grease-tobacco finish.

Ling stared at the other detective a moment. Triano's decline had begun rapidly, on a crazy drunken night when they nailed him firing his service revolver at the old fortress-like Women's House of Detention. A month at the department's secret drying-out camp in upstate New York followed. Then came the rubber gun patrol, sometimes called the bow and arrow squad, Triano stripped of his weapon and assigned desk duties until he could prove himself once again.

"You okay?" Ling asked, noticing a slight tremor in Triano's hands.

Triano lifted his cup. "This poison—doctor says I shouldn't be drinkin' it. But it's this or gin. Figure the caffeine will get me in less trouble." He reached for a cigarette, then sheepishly returned it to the pack.

"It's all right," Ling told him.

"Sure? You quit, didn't you?"

"Yeah—but go ahead."

Triano lit up.

"What I want to know, Mickey, is everything you did from the first moment you got the call."

Triano fidgeted in his seat. His eyes showed suspicion. "Well . . . the call came in and I headed over there. You know the rest."

Ling leaned forward. "Everything, Mickey. Every little thing you said or did or thought until I arrived on the scene."

Triano now appeared irritated. "Why, Monk? What the hell for?"

Ling sat back in his chair. His eyes were on the tabletop. "You take a cop whose wife, say, is a pill-popper, and he goes on some call and there's a subject there that has the same symptoms, the same signs, as his wife. So he sees her as a pill-popper, yet you or I or a hundred other guys might miss it." He paused, looking now at Triano. "Or you take a cop who just found out his wife has been cheating on him and he goes to a murder scene where there had been a triangle. Well, his bias just might be slanted in favor of the person who was cheated. And if that's the case, he's going to miss something. See what I mean?"

Triano hesitated, then answered, almost inaudibly: "I guess so."

"So take me through it, step by step."

Triano straightened. "Actually, I wasn't there when the call came in—I was out getting some coffee. Solloway took the call. Mort Solloway."

"I know him."

"Same shitlist I'm on. Well, he doesn't want to take the run—he doesn't want any call, if he can help it. And besides, he says, it's a chance for me to redeem myself, the Park Avenue address and all, and since I'm half Irish, I have half a chance of getting off the shitlist whereas a Jew like himself is facin' the rubber gun patrol at some pound or somethin' no matter what the fuck he does. That's the way he put it." Triano paused.

"That's bullshit," Ling said.

Triano thought a moment, then said: "Whatever." He cleared his throat. "Well, I take the job, get to the building. The apartment door's unlocked—that's why the porter found them; the door was unlocked and partially open—and I go in. The place is empty, 'cept for the stiffs and the two uniforms. I look down at the male victim, and I know I've seen that guy's face somewhere. Then I remember where and realize who it is. What the fuck do I do now? I ask myself. Blow this one and I might as well retire. I start cursin' Solloway, wondering if that fucker knew all along who it was. And then I think to call the chief, throw it straight in his lap. The lady next door whose phone I'm usin'—one Mrs. Harriet Cunningham—she tells me the victim didn't really live in the building, was some kind of guest. Lot of parties and women, she says. And the guy had a fancy accent. 'What you mean by that?' I ask her, and she tells me he spoke British. Then I know I'm right."

"That's it?"

"No. I ask this Mrs. Cunningham if she knew of any trouble between Whittaker and anyone else. Nothing like that, she says, but of course she'll think about it."

"Then what?"

"Then you and all the brass show up and I go through that apartment inch by inch, like you said. You already know about the coke and grass."

Triano had discovered a small glassine envelope with a few grams of cocaine, and a wooden cigarette box with a couple of ounces of marijuana. Considerably less, Ling concluded, than would have been discovered in a sweep of half the other apartments in the building. "What else, Mick?"

"That's all I can think of, Monk." Triano's hands were still trembling; his face was pale and drained.

"Thanks."

Triano didn't move. His eyes were on the floor. "Say, Monk?" he said finally, his expression sheepish, his voice muted. "I'd like to be with you guys on this one, if you could arrange it. I mean—"

"First man on the scene stays with the case, Mick. You know that."

"Yeah, but with my history—"

Ling gripped Triano's arm. "They want me, they got you, Mick."

"Thanks, Monk. And I won't . . ."

Ling stopped him. "You and me—it's been awhile. That uniformed guy, Sullivan—he around?"

"Outside—and pissed."

"Send him in, would ya."

Triano stood shakily and headed for the door.

"Tell me something, Mickey . . ." Ling called after him. Triano stopped.

"How long you on the wagon?"

Triano stalled, then asked: "Officially?"

"No."

"Off the record, it's been a week. It gets kind of rough." Ling smiled. "I know."

Presently, a heavyset patrolman in his late forties, dressed in a wrinkled uniform, entered.

Ling knew a thousand Sullivans in the Department, maybe

two thousand. Many fancied themselves as rebels, and saw in the maverick Ling a soul brother, unaware how he detested their emptiness and the destruction they caused. Surly, pot-bellied, sneering. Twenty-five years on the force and they never made sergeant or gold shield or even plainclothes. And their wives urging them to put in their papers from the day they reached twenty years on the force, but them putting it off and putting it off, because unlike so many of their buddies from the Academy, they never went to night school, never got that goddamned degree, never made the right connections, so that the best that was awaiting them, the very best, was a uniformed guard's job in some meat market, at just slightly above the minimum wage—and even that was iffy.

"Let's get this shit over with," Sullivan told Ling.

"Where were you when you got the call?"

"On patrol. Where the fuck would I be?"

"Doing what?"

"What's that got to do with anything?"

Ling stood and leaned over the table, placing his face inches from that of the older cop. "You answer me, you fat jerkoff, or your jelly ass'll be sittin' in the P.C.'s office in an hour. Understand me?"

Sullivan raised a hand in a peace gesture. "I'm tryin' to cooperate, Ling. It's just that I've never been through somethin' like this. Like I'm on trial or somethin', ya know?"

Ling relaxed. "Try again."

"Well, me and my new partner—this spic kid Lopez—we're handlin' a little street dispute when the call comes in."

"What kind of dispute?"

"Two fruitcakes. They're working up a lather sayin' some cabbie ripped 'em off, and the hack . . . well, he figures he'll be a mother before two fags get the best of him."

"Then the call comes over the radio."

"Right. Man down. Possible D.O.A. Nothin' about shots fired or man with a gun or anything like that." One of Sullivan's paw-like hands went to work scratching his belly. "Well, it takes me like fifteen minutes to get Lopez to leave the fairies settle it themselves and then we go to the address. Doorman there tells us there's this couple upstairs that look like they're dead. There's some spade maintenance man there. He's about to turn white, he's so scared. He takes us up. Turns out he's a Haitian. He tells us that and I start lookin' at my hands, trying to remember if I touched him. That's all I need is to catch AIDS. What the hell would I tell my wife? And with all the queers in this town, it's a wonder I . . .''

"So the porter takes you upstairs," Ling interrupted.

"Yea. And sure as shit, there's the stiffs, starkassed naked. Fuckin' perverts, probably. And then Lopez starts bitching how this means a body watch for us and he don't like that. But a veteran like me don't mind the smell—I figure it's one way to rest my achin' feet."

"That it?"

"Yeah. We called the squad and they send Mickey Triano over. The poor bastard, what he's been through and he's gotta catch this one."

"Thanks. You can go now."

Sullivan stood. "Listen, Monk, I'm sorry I was so hardassed. Didn't mean to bust your balls. Kinda tired is all."

"Yeah."

The dispatcher, summoned from his electronic console, followed. Ling did not know him but, like Sullivan, he came from a mold—balding, with an unkempt fringe of hair, glasses, ink-stained wash 'n' wear shirt with an open collar, unpressed slacks with a belt much too narrow for its loops. He could walk without attracting notice into any Municipal Building office. His name was Paterno, and he appeared to be in his mid-fifties.

"I'm good at what I do, detective," he began. "I've been doin' it for more than twenty years. Started long before they got all this computer stuff."

"How did the call come in, please?"

"A male's voice on the line, and he's all agitated and excited. I can't understand a word, so I try to calm him down. Finally, I figure he's a foreigner and he's talkin' some kind of creole. 'Oh, christ,' I say to myself. I took this Spanish course they made us take, but creole I don't know. And it would be just my luck, after all these years, to send an ambulance five blocks from the right address or something, and then get hauled before some board."

"He was a Haitian," Ling said.

"Figured it was something like that."

"But you were able to calm him down."

"I guess so. At least so I could make out there were a couple of bodies and get down the address. I send it out as a 'Shots fired. Possible DOA's.' "

Ling thought for a moment, then asked: "That was the only call on it?"

"Yeah—at least as far as I know."

Ling thanked and dismissed him.

"Will I get overtime for this?" the dispatcher asked. "I was supposed to be off at eight."

"Of course. Sign Chief Golden's name to the form."

Ling fought to restrain his smile. Golden had no authority to approve overtime for a civilian dispatcher. Sometime two months from now the bureaucracy would spit the form out on the chief's desk. Ling would have to make it a point to avoid him then.

Golden returned from his meeting with the press just as Ling finished with the dispatcher.

"They want blood—probably mine," the chief complained.

Ling smiled. "Come on, Julie, nobody can handjob the press better than you."

"Don't lay more than two bucks on that. Right now, I want to meet with you and the others."

Golden collected his other key detectives—Triano, McKinnon, O'Brien, and Levine—and herded them off to a corner.

Golden sat on the edge of a desk.

"I want to give you some idea of how big this is," he began. "Mickey here, he has the presence of mind to call me directly, not operations. And then I called the P.C. He, in turn, had the mayor awoke and His Honor proceeds to call the President, who's aboard Air Force One, for chrissake, somewhere over the Pacific. You got that? The President?"

There was no response. Golden didn't seem to expect any. "Now, the first answer I want is just how did that kid reporter get up to the seventeenth floor. This radio guy's crawling all over me how he kept a lid on the case only to get screwed."

No one answered.

"Talk to me, damn it!" Golden demanded.

McKinnon spoke up: "She was this chick from one of the all-news stations, chief."

"I know who she was. And she's got tits and an ass, right?"

"Ah . . . yeah, chief, but—"

"And she started shakin' them around some cop's face and in seconds, the whole fuckin' world knows the score here and we don't even have the stiffs packed away yet." He pulled a cigar from his jacket. "*That* was a fuckup. I don't want another." He removed the cigar's wrapper. "Now, where are we?"

They looked at one another, each unwilling to be first to speak, until Triano offered nervously, "It's like a little bit here and a little bit there but nothing to hang a hat on."

Golden's face showed his impatience. "What we do have is a whole lot of questions, right? Like, anybody seen anything in this that might suggest terrorists?"

"Not me," said McKinnon. The others shook their heads.

"Then what about enemies?"

"From what I know, you could start with his sister," said Levine.

"Okay, Dotty. We'll send you to question her. How's your curtsy?"

"About as good as yours," she responded.

Golden looked at McKinnon. "You got somethin' more to say, Rosie, or you just drawin' a paycheck."

"This Englishman," McKinnon said, "it wasn't his apartment."

"I know that already," Golden said.

"Well, we've got several tenants saying he'd been livin' there for a couple of months."

"Some kind of sublet?" the chief asked.

"More like he was a guest. The apartment belongs to Robert Crayton Samuels III."

"Of Samuels Steel?" Levine asked.

"You got it. The tight-assed little mother that runs all those anti-nuclear rallies."

The anti-nuclear movement. It was in that connection, Ling remembered now, that he had seen the name of James Whittaker in the news. A week or two earlier, Whittaker had written an open letter to the *New York Times* protesting the nuclear arms buildup, and blasting both the White House and his sister's administration for their role in it.

The chief had a gleam in his eye. "This kid, Samuels . . ."

O'Brien interrupted: "He's had the lease for more than four years. The rent checks come in with daddy's signature. Apparently the kid gave the deceased the keys and let him take over."

"Where is he?"

"We're workin' on that now, chief," O'Brien said. "And by the by, this Samuels, he could be a queer."

"Gay," Levine corrected him.

"A gay queer, then," O'Brien deadpanned.

"What else?" Golden asked, impatiently.

It was the woman's turn. "The super gave us the name of a girl. One Samantha Simpson. The super cashed a check for her once. Says she lived there with Whittaker on and off for maybe four, five months. One of the dayshift doormen says she left—with her luggage—a day before the murders."

"One of those strange coincidences, huh?" Golden asked.

"Could be, chief."

"By the way," McKinnon said, catching Golden's attention, "since I knew you'd want me to, I screamed at the M.E.'s people to call in a toxicologist early. They did and he phoned five minutes ago. No surprises. Mr. Whittaker and friend were filled to the brim with booze. Also coke, they think. But they don't want to go on an official limb with that 'til they finish their tests."

"Good work, Rosie."

"Tell that to the chief medical examiner—he'll be after your ass for bringin' the chemist in early. A stroke or two might help. Oh, and that street watcher Monk spotted? It's an old man. Retired accountant. He says he saw all kinds of people comin' and goin' from that building, and about nine of them looked like killers."

"Let's keep him in mind. We get a sketch or photo, show it to him."

McKinnon nodded.

"What's with the lab?" Golden asked.

"Very little," Triano answered. "Confirmed the marijuana and coke found on the premises and raised a thousand prints. They're trying to sort them out now."

"Keep on them. And get our two friends from the Bureau off their asses and ask them to expedite the print matches in Washington," Golden said. Then to Ling: "What'd you get, Monk, you and your famous instincts?"

"I think maybe you ought to have a parking ticket check, like with Son of Sam. Not now, maybe, but if we're lucky, somewhere down the line one of those names is going to jump out."

"Good thinking," Golden said. He looked at O'Brien. "Do it and I don't care how many men it takes, or how long. Get a list of every ticket written within five blocks of that building, then check the registrations and assemble the names."

O'Brien pouted.

"Something the matter?" Golden asked.

"It's Ling's brainstorm. Why can't he do it?"

Golden glared at him. "Cut that crap, goddamnit. I don't have time for it."

O'Brien looked away. "You'll get your ticket check."

Golden turned back to Levine. "And you, Dotty, keep on the trail of this Samuels. Maybe intelligence has a line on him. Wherever he is, we want him."

Levine nodded.

"Rosie, grab whoever O'Brien isn't using and continue to hit the building and the neighborhood. That coke and grass had to come from somewhere. Maybe we can find out where."

"Right, chief."

"That's it for now—and it goes without saying I'm open to anybody's ideas, no matter how wild they might sound. Now get going."

They began to file away. Ling tapped Triano's shoulder. "This girlfriend. We got a name. Do we also have an address?"

"Working on it."

Ling turned to Golden: "Can I have her? If she's not our shooter—and my gut feeling is she isn't—we could use her on our side."

"The Ling magic, huh?"

"They all want to mother him," Triano said.

Ling looked to the floor. He shuffled his feet. "I'm embarrassed."

"As soon as you get an address, Mickey, get it to Monk," Golden said. "In the meantime, I'm off to City Hall to pacify the P.C. and the mayor. And I'm gonna tell them things are going swell and it's just a matter of a few technicalities before we collar some scumbag that did this to the poor English fellow and his church-going girlfriend, right?"

"We're working on it," Ling said.

Golden's expression grew serious. He alternately stared at Ling and Triano, his eyes asking for help. Then he left.

The others broke up slowly. As Ling chatted with McKinnon, another detective came up. "There's a phone call from Washington, Monk. Guy wants to talk to whoever's in charge."

"Give it to the chief."

"He just walked out the door."

Ling nodded. The detective pointed to a telephone receiver on a nearby desk. Ling picked it up. "Homicide. What can I do for you?"

"This is David Holmes, first secretary at the British Embassy in Washington, and, at the moment, acting ambassador. Who is this, may I ask?"

Ling told him.

"We got the news earlier this morning."

"I'm very sorry," Ling said. "We're doing all we can to learn exactly what happened and arrest the person responsible."

"I'm confident of that. I have nothing but respect for the New York Police Department. I saw your work when I was attached to our mission at the United Nations before I came here."

"What can I do for you now, sir?"

"Well, we're in constant touch with London, given the circumstances, and I was wondering . . . I was only curious if we could forward them any word of progress."

"We are attempting to develop leads, sir."

"But nothing definite yet."

"That is correct."

"Well, I thank you, officer. I thank you indeed."

"So long, Mr. Secretary."

Ling took out his small schoolboy's pocket notebook. He entered the name David Holmes as well as the time. The tone of Holmes' voice had changed subtly with the news that the police had yet to develop a definite lead to the killer. Was it genuine concern? Or something else, perhaps. Ling wasn't sure. But they would be speaking again, of that Ling was certain.

5

Marilyn Mary Mason, the most influential economic adviser to the President of the United States, held aside the lace curtains of the living room's tall bay windows and peered out at her Georgetown neighborhood. The one visible patch of sky was an intimidating gray. How appropriate, she thought—Washington was normally beautiful in the fall, but today it was bleak, overcast and unseasonably cool, a portent of the dreary, wet winter months ahead.

She had been checking the window apprehensively every few minutes, but thus far, her fear of callers had been proven unfounded. No one had approached her doorway, not even a messenger from the White House. She was relieved—she was in no condition to see anyone at the moment.

Marilyn released the curtain and extended her hands; they were shaking. She would need another pill shortly. In the meantime, maybe she could do some aerobics—she was wearing her aikido workout outfit and the exercise might calm her down—or perhaps she could call someone, vent her fear and anxiety. But whom could she call? Whom could she trust?

She sat on the floor and began her stretching exercises, but her body protested. She felt weak and her head hurt. Abandoning the calisthenics, she began pacing through the apartment, trying to occupy her mind with plans for the decorating yet to be done. The apartment was small and efficient, perfect for a woman whose career gave her little time for keeping a home. A counter with four stools separated the kitchenette from the combination living room/dining room. The only other rooms were the bedroom and a relatively large bath. The apartment had come furnished, and she had not yet had a chance to give it much of a personal touch. She had hung a display of her diplomas above her small writing desk, and ordered a frame for a bull fighting poster she had bought on impulse in New York. The poster, however, still rested on the floor of the small foyer, waiting to be hung. And the kitchen needed some new wallpaper. But that really ought to wait until the landlord's handyman did something about the water pipe leak behind the sink. Damn him anyway! She already had complained twice about his ineptness.

She moved into the bedroom. The bed wasn't made, but so what? No one was coming. The closet door was open, revealing her pitifully small wardrobe—a half-dozen business suits, blouses, two skirts, a single cocktail dress, jeans, and little else. If only she had time for shopping! The bedroom, like the rest of the apartment, was mostly barren of anything decorative. Atop her dresser was a small, framed photograph of her late father, and a musty, padded-fabric jewelry box that had been her mother's. It carried an embroidered legend: "Niagara Falls—1940." Inside the box were but a few pieces of jewelry, simple earrings and a couple of undistinguished bracelets. Someday, whenever she had a moment to catch her breath, she would have to visit a jeweler, too.

All of that would have to wait, however. Marilyn was not in the mood to deal with any shopkeepers, even at a hardware store. Instead, she went to the refrigerator and removed a can of diet cola—she drank, on the average, a dozen of the caffeine-spiked soft drinks each day, ordering it by the case for her office—and sat at the kitchen counter. She gulped from the can, then stared at her radio next to the toaster. The radio was dialed to an all-news radio station. She had rigged the microphone from her portable tape recorder so that it rested against the radio speaker. Whenever the newscast renewed its cycle and updated its top story—the murders of the British prime minister's controversial brother and a mysterious woman companion—she turned the recorder on. The taping allowed her to play back the report, to doublecheck for any new details she might have missed upon first hearing. Up until now, however, there had been little elaboration beyond the initial report about the killings, the "several possible leads" and the statements from the surviving sister, the President, the New York mayor, and others.

The broadcast had turned to sports. It would be several minutes before the top stories were repeated. As she waited, Marilyn lifted a thick manila envelope from the table. She had been fingering it on and off all morning. She opened the flap, then stopped—no, she was not up to another look at its horrible contents.

The doorbell! Marilyn jumped to her feet. Her hands went to her mouth. She thought she might vomit. "God, who could it be?" she asked herself.

She rushed into the bathroom and looked into the mirror. Her face was worse than she feared, her skin drawn, her eyes sunken and dark. She touched her hair—the strands were stringy; in desperate need of a shampoo. There was no way she would answer that door!

She flipped off the bathroom light. Whoever it was would think no one was home. But the radio . . . She started for the kitchen, then stopped—it was too late. The caller would already have heard it. She retreated back into the bathroom and pressed her back against the wall.

The doorbell rang again. And again. "Go away!" she silently pleaded. Finally, the bell stopped. Marilyn waited for what seemed like several minutes, then tiptoed to the front. She parted the curtains slightly and looked to the entrance. No one was there but a package was on the doormat—a cellophane-wrapped potted plant.

She opened the door just enough to reach the plant and pull it in. The plant was a staked vine, some type of succulent. Expensive, no doubt. There was a small white envelope. She opened it. The note was addressed in a squared-off masculine scrawl to "My wonderful Marilyn."

"Devastated to learn you are ill. Cheer up! See ya Saturday. As always, Bill."

Bill who? Then she remembered. "Oh, god," she said

aloud. Bill. She had not given him a thought. A low-ranking advance man. Round-faced, short, and plump. Dandruff on his shoulders. Tobacco breath. He had been harassing her for a dinner date for months. An evening in the right restaurant with a presidential adviser was, of course, a step up in the White House's pecking order. A date with Marilyn Mason was a special coup. She was the child prodigy of modern economics. Penn State. The University of Chicago. The London School of Economics. She once could have had her pick of prestigious academic appointments. Instead, an unknown in political circles, she had chosen to join an obscure governor's presidential campaign. Incredibly, he had won—and then came her first disappointment. Bowing to the consensus of his other advisers, the new President meekly agreed he could not place a twenty-eight-year-old female in charge of the national economy. A semi-retired California savings and loan executive thus became the chief presidential economic adviser; Marilyn was named a presidential assistant. All of the White House knew, however, that the old man was merely a figurehead, and it was Marilyn who was influencing the President on what strings to pull in manipulating the U.S. economy.

In a moment of distraction, Marilyn had given her consent to Bill, the advance man. Now, she would have to remember to cancel. A repugnant, ambitious, glorified gofer—she didn't need that kind of evening now.

Marilyn crammed the plant into a trash basket next to her desk, then returned to the bathroom. She opened the medicine cabinet and removed one of several bottles containing little green and white pills. She took one, started to replace the cap, then took another. Her hands, they were shaking so—an extra pill wouldn't hurt.

Resuming her vigil in the kitchen, she concluded she had been very wise to call in sick. They would have noticed the tremor. Someone might have asked questions. And although it was her very first sick day since joining the administration, nothing much would be lost—she had had no appointments with the President scheduled for today and she . . .

Marilyn suddenly had a nightmarish thought—the President might summon her for an impromptu meeting. Although rare, such unscheduled conferences had occurred. She would have to think of a contingency plan, in case he did.

She brushed back her hair and considered, for a moment, a shower and shampoo. But that could wait. And anyway, the newscast was returning to the day's top stories.

Marilyn flipped on the recorder but almost immediately stopped it when the report from New York was no different from that delivered a half-hour earlier. Damn! What she needed was information. Maybe she could call . . . No, she wouldn't do that.

Her hands had steadied, and a calmness began to soothe her insides. Those wonderful pills were having their effect. She could try it again now, do what had to be done.

She removed a large stewing pot from her cabinet and placed it in the kitchen sink, then balled up a few pages from the day's *Washington Post*, saving, of course, its front section with its account of the Whittaker murders. She lifted the manila envelope and this time found the courage to remove its contents, seventeen eight-by-ten glossy color photographs and a packet of negatives. Holding the stack of photos face-down, she ignited the crumpled newspaper. One by one, she ripped the photos into pieces and fed them to the flames. The film strips followed. The destruction did not take long and as the flames began to die, she stared into smoldering ashes, smiling.

She thought of Whittaker. He was so different from the men who normally made plays for her, the hungry climbers who saw her as a doormat to the inner circles of Washington power, and all the cowardly nothings who populated the halls of government like eunuchs gawking at a harem and who accomplished little more than to occupy space and waste air. Whittaker had been of neither group. There had been something electric about him; he communicated a certain sensitivity that showed he understood what it meant to be consumed by a quest for something, the desire to make a mark, the compulsion to take life to a higher plane. He had recognized her special intelligence and understood her assertiveness. He had fulfilled her need for tenderness, yet also answered her occasional lust for raw, physical release. In fact, he had helped tap a dark side of her womanhood that she previously had not known existed, liberating her from the falsehoods that had been instilled in her from birth. Making love with James Whittaker was not filled with the pain, boredom, humiliation, and revulsion which had been the rule in her earlier, infrequent attempts at achieving sexual ecstasy. She had learned from him that the same heights she assigned to her brain and her career could be the standards for other areas of her life as well. He had introduced her to the joys of good food, and they had made the rounds of Manhattan and Washington restaurants together. He had taken her to discos and they had danced for two, three hours at a stretch, the pounding of the bass and the drums and the flash of strobes energizing their spirits. And they had dreamed together.

One night in particular remained as vivid in her memories as when it had happened. They were eating a late dinner at Windows on the World, atop the 110-story World Trade Center, with New York spread below them as if it was a play city on a child's electric train table. In the distance, like a string of pearls, were the lights of the George Washington bridge, and nearer, making her way slowly toward the harbor's mouth, was the *QE II*, the last of the world's great ocean liners. "We'll be aboard her, someday," Whittaker had told her. "You and I together. I promise." The mere thought of crossing the Atlantic with this gentle, charming Englishman touched something deep inside Marilyn, the same kind of feeling she got from dollhouses and white picket fences and lace. But then Whittaker had changed, then he . . .

The phone rang, startling her. She stared at it. Was it the office? God, what would she do? Perhaps it was a wrong number. Stop ringing, please, she pleaded. But the ringing continued. She considered pulling out the cord. Or locking herself in the bathroom. But maybe it was the White House, and the President was facing an emergency. She hesitatingly lifted the receiver.

"Yes?" she said timidly.

"Hi, babes. It's me, your big sister."

Marilyn exhaled deeply. "Sally! Where are you?"

"Where do you think I am? My humble little home in Georgia."

Georgia. Sally would have her believe it was Valhalla.

Marilyn braced for the lecture she knew would come. "Ah, how have you been?" Marilyn asked coldly.

"Okay. But forget about me. What's with you? I called your office and they said you were sick. You all right?"

"I . . . I guess I have a touch of the flu. Nothing serious. Really."

Her sister chuckled knowingly. "You see, you're letting that job get to you. It's affecting your health. It's not worth it, and someday you'll come to understand that. Someday you'll get out of the city, out of the rat race just like me. My god, the fresh air alone would . . ."

"Look, Sally, I'm really not in the mood," Marilyn interrupted.

Sally laughed. "Okay, so hurt my feelings. Anyway, what have you been up to? Got a guy, do ya? Bet you've got all those brainy bankers chasing you."

"No. Nobody special—not at the moment."

"Maybe that's what you need, a good hunk to hang on to. I think maybe . . ."

"Sally!" Marilyn snapped. "You seem to forget—I've got a job working for the President. I'm not sitting down there in some swamp counting birds or whatever you do. I've got a national economy to worry about."

"Well, pardon me, madam politician," Sally said sarcastically.

The line was silent for a moment, then Marilyn said: "Look, I'm sorry I'm so snippy. It's just that I don't feel too well. I think I need some sleep."

"I understand. Just give me a call now and then. We're all that's left, you and me. And I worry about you."

"I will—and thanks for calling."

Marilyn hung up the phone. She *was* tired. But she did not attempt to sleep. Instead, she returned to the stove and stared down at the ashes in the bottom of the pot. She had difficulty focusing her eyes and they began to play tricks on her. Out of the mass of gray and black debris in the pot came the image of Whittaker's face, his noble English face, the eyes so alert and piercing, the lips so tight and sensual. He was grinning that grin that had touched something deep inside her, that had renewed feelings she had not felt since a single daring night in high school, a night that had caused her to forfeit so much control . . .

She shook her head violently. Her hands went to her temples. "No!" she screamed, running to the medicine cabinet in the bathroom. She couldn't handle it. Not now.

6

Driving up Third Avenue, FBI agent Bill Nolan tried to remember how long it had been since he last communicated with his star informant, known in bureau files only as Confidential Source Eagle Seven. Nine or ten months, Nolan guessed—he hadn't had time to check his records. From the federal government's viewpoint, the last contact between agent and informant had not been very fruitful—Eagle Seven had called the meeting to complain about the inadequacy of his retainer. Nolan had balked at an increase, a posture he knew from experience his bureau superiors would want, but Eagle Seven was well aware of his worth. In the end, the informant's quarterly payments were adjusted dramatically upward, and Nolan secretly was pleased—Eagle Seven had been very good to him.

Even Nolan did not know why he had been chosen by the informant as his FBI contact. Sometimes, there were hints that his selection had been random. But Nolan knew his source to be too methodical for that. However the relationship had come about, it was clear the informant trusted him. And Eagle Seven, in turn, had never burned Nolan.

At 57th Street, Nolan cut over to Lexington and headed back downtown. He pulled the dark blue sedan into a loading zone and lowered the visor with its federal government identification card. The N.Y.P.D. was not above towing government vehicles—in fact, the traffic cops sometimes seemed to relish it—but Nolan knew he would be only a few minutes.

He continued on foot, dreading the next step in the rendezvous process, which Eagle Seven insisted be followed. Nolan felt silly—but Eagle Seven dictated the terms of his employment, including when and how he would conduct his exchanges. Nolan was the only agent the informant would deal with, and, thanks to the ingeniousness of Eagle Seven's self-preservation system, the barrel-chested, overweight veteran FBI agent had no idea what his pigeon looked like, who he was, or where he came from. This vacuum of knowledge, of course, troubled the Bureau's brass. Despite the flawless accuracy of Eagle Seven's information, and the clear evidence that he was not a Soviet disinformation agent, the brass wanted to know with whom they were dealing. Two years earlier they thought they had identified him as a high-ranking secretary in the Soviet U.N. Mission, but that theory faltered when the Russian diplomat left the country, while the flow of data from Eagle Seven continued.

Five blocks from where he had parked, Nolan reached Bailey's Bytes, a personal computer store. He peered through its plate glass door, and was relieved to see that this time, the store had few kids. On his last visit, Nolan had been the only adult customer among a dozen ten- and eleven-year-olds crowding the demonstration terminals to try out the latest in space and dragon games. This time, the store was almost empty.

"Can I help you, sir?" a bespectacled young clerk asked from behind the counter.

Nolan studied him a moment. A computer whiz, no doubt. Probably a gifted hacker who routinely penetrated the Bureau's own obsolete mainframes. The agent smiled. There was a widespread public perception of a huge army of well-armed, highly trained G-men, tracking homegrown radicals and foreign spies on foot in dark alleys or behind the wheel in speeding cars running red lights, employing the most advanced high technology to pierce their privacy, eavesdropping on their every conversation and communication, if not their thoughts. In truth, the agency was so strapped for manpower and the constraints on overtime were so severe that tailing the brigade of foreign agents in New York and Washington was, at best, a token effort during the week, and virtually nonexistent on holidays and weekends.

It would never change, Nolan concluded. Maybe it was time to get out. But what would a fifty-one-year-old washed-up agent with a law degree he had never used do in an age of microchips and logic flow charts?

"Can I help you?" the clerk repeated.

"Sorry. Daydreamin'," the agent said. "Think I'll just look around, if it's okay."

"Sure."

Posing as a browser, Nolan made his way slowly toward the rear of the narrow store. On his left were four small computer terminals for trying out packaged software; on his right, colorful boxes containing the programming discs were stacked side by side like books on library shelves. Nolan moved to the display unit and counted the third shelf from the bottom. He dropped into a stoop and counted to the fourth programming package from the right. There it was—upside down. Eagle Seven's sign.

Nolan removed the box and turned it over. "Savvy Spreadsheet," the software was entitled. "What the hell," he asked himself, "did that mean?"

The agent returned to the counter and held up the package. "Do you mind if I give this a try?"

The clerk waved his hand. "Forget that. It's old. We've got much better spreadsheets—and cheaper, too. Let me show you . . ."

"That's all right," Nolan protested. "I'd really like to try this. I've heard good things about it."

The clerk's feelings were hurt. His face showed disgust. "Whatever your pleasure. Take any tube. You know how to load it?"

"Yep," Nolan replied. That was about all he knew.

The agent selected the rearmost terminal and sat down. A green light showed that the computer was turned on. That was good—he wouldn't know where to begin looking for the switch. He removed the floppy disc from its sleeve and inserted it into the drive, then pushed the three keys Eagle Seven had told him would boot the computer, whatever that meant. Noises came from the disc drive; a red light flashed on. The screen flashed bright green, then went blank. Presently, the noise stopped—and the screen displayed an instruction:

"Enter today's date (m-d-y),"

Nolan, who employed a two-fingered technique in typing his reports, now used it to enter a date: July 4, 1776.

The drive once more came alive. The red light blinked. The instruction about the date, and Nolan's response, disappeared, and the screen filled with what appeared to be gibberish. There were letters, upper and lower case, random numerals, foreign symbols, and punctuation marks. To any experienced computer user, Eagle Seven had told him, the computer would appear as if it were conducting a self-test. But it wasn't a self-test. It was special programming the informant himself had hidden on the disc sometime earlier. And on the bottom right side of the screen was the information Nolan was seeking. "NW35LX1008," the screen read.

Nolan translated the code silently: his next stop would be a public telephone at the northwest corner of 35th Street and Lexington Avenue. At 10:08 a.m., that phone would ring.

Nolan replaced the disc in its package—Eagle Seven had assured him the added programming would erase itself after a single viewing—and returned it, right side up, to the shelf.

"You were right," he told the clerk on the way out. "Not very efficient. I'll be back to see you about that better stuff in a day or two."

Nolan found a brown-uniformed meter maid eyeing his car. "Leaving right now, ma'am," he said, climbing behind the wheel and starting the engine.

"Hey, mister!" she called after him.

But he paid no attention and raced away. He looked at his watch—it was almost ten. Not much time. Luckily, the lights were with him on the run downtown, and it was not until 43rd Street that he had to stop. He considered running the red light, but decided against it when he saw an NYPD patrolcar— no time now for intergovernmental relations.

As before, Nolan parked several blocks away and approached the contact point on foot. A half-block away, he spotted the telephone and was relieved to see it not one of those unenclosed units attached to a pole, but rather a booth—the better for privacy. And he was beginning to think it was his lucky day—the booth was empty. "Now if only the goddamned phone works," he said aloud, attracting an annoyed glance from an elderly woman walking her dog.

He was only a few yards away when the phone began to ring. Nolan broke into a trot. But the ringing had attracted the attention of two white-uniformed sailors. "Hey!" Nolan shouted, as one of them reached for the phone.

The sailors looked at him curiously.

"That call's for me," Nolan said, smiling, leaving it up to them to figure it out.

The servicemen stepped back, but stayed there, watching. Nolan lurched for the phone.

"Hello," he said breathlessly, reaching to close the folding door.

"Hi there, cowboy."

"What?"

"Oh, really, sailor, don't be so coy."

"Who the hell is this?" Nolan demanded.

"What's in a name?" the male voice asked back. "How would you like to . . . Hey, wait a minute here. I see you! You're not one of those sailors." There was a pause. Nolan could barely hear the next word. And the line went dead.

Nolan opened the door and partially stepped out onto the sidewalk. He began scanning the apartment buildings on both sides of the street. In one, he knew, was one pissed off Murray Hill queen with a pair of binoculars, whose fantasy of a morning interlude with the United States Navy had just been frustrated.

"I thought you said it was for you," one of the seamen said antagonistically.

"Be on your way, son," Nolan said, then closed the door again. His watch showed 10:07 a.m. In another minute, almost to the second, the phone rang once more.

"Hello?" the agent said, cautiously.

"Good morning," came the cheery response. "There is a tombstone in Concord dated July 4, 1776."

Nolan took a deep breath. "It's been awhile," he said.

"Business has been slow—until now."

"What do you have?"

"This Englishman, Whittaker. Are you interested?"

"Of course."

"Your friends were after him. The woman was Anatole."

"The Moroccan?"

"Yes."

"Holy shit!" Nolan said. Anatole was well-known to the counterespionage fraternity, but until now she was not known to have operated this side of the Atlantic. "Big league, huh? And naturally we knew all about it. Where were you, if I may ask?"

"She failed."

"I guess so. A big blemish on her record."

"She was the best."

"So I've heard. Who killed them?"

Eagle Seven hesitated, then answered: "I don't know."

Nolan felt the beginnings of a massive headache. "Can you find out?"

"You take care, Mr. Nolan."

"But . . ." The agent stopped—the connection was lost. "You, too," he said into the dead mouthpiece. "You take care."

7

Monk Ling was seated in the center of the Seventeenth Precinct squad room, where four desks had been pushed together to form an island. Across from him, two detectives, their coats off and shirtsleeves rolled up, were at work collating the dozens of handwritten and typed reports that had already been filled out by team members, detailing their initial work on the case. Most cops complained that it was an exercise in bureaucratic waste, but Ling knew better—an investigation, especially a long, complex investigation, often hinged on a forgotten detail discovered in a random flipping through the pages of a bulging file.

Ling was paging through the reports when he was interrupted by a uniformed sergeant from downstairs. "Excuse me, Monk."

"Yes?"

"These gentlemen have asked to see someone in charge, and the chief's not back yet."

There were two of them: one, a ramrod-straight, middle-aged man who had federal government written all over him; the other, a much younger, slender, and shorter man, wearing a European-cut suit.

"I'm Wainwright, with the State Department, lieutenant," the older man said. "And this is Mr. Breckenridge Collingsworth of Her Majesty's Government."

Ling shook their hands. "You've promoted me—I'm not a lieutenant."

"Excuse me?" the State Department man asked, uncomprehending.

"You called me 'lieutenant.' I'm a detective first grade."

"But . . . but you're in charge of this investigation."

"No—Chief Golden is heading the investigation, only he's not here just now."

"I see," Wainwright said, nervously tugging at his ear. "Well, in any event, Mr. Collingsworth flew over here immediately upon learning of this tragic event. I just picked him up at the Wall Street heliport. He is an official representative of the prime minister and, needless to say, Washington would be grateful for any courtesy that can be shown."

"Of course," said Ling.

The State Department man shook the Englishman's hand, then gave him his card, urged him to call for any reason at all, at any time, and departed. Ling pulled a beat-up wooden chair to the side of a desk, and proposed the Englishman be seated.

"Mr. Hollingsworth, was it?"

"Collingsworth—with a 'C.' "

"And your first name? Brecken—"

"Breck would be fine."

Ling guessed condolences were in order. "I'm very sorry about this. I mean, your prime minister has my sincere sympathy. This doesn't speak very well of New York, does it?"

"He was an ass, detective."

"Ah . . . excuse me?"

"James Whittaker was an ass. One of those semi-criminals who hover on the fringes of trouble just long enough to get their jollies and prime their bank accounts, but never quite long enough to be apprehended."

Ling rubbed his chin. "I see."

"The prime minister is distressed, naturally—he *was* her brother—but she is also well aware that he would have done anything to embarrass her and, I'm afraid, might have managed to accomplish just that in the end."

Ling hesitated, then said: "We found some playthings—a little marijuana, some suspected cocaine—but you find that in half the apartments in Manhattan. Nothing else has surfaced to suggest he was involved with any crime."

"Perhaps. But your work has only begun. Whittaker had his hands into something, or he wouldn't have come to be shot."

Ling measured his words: "What exactly is it your government wants?"

"The prime minister seeks nothing special, nothing more than your ordinary, thorough investigation. My only function is to aid you in any manner possible, and to keep her informed—that is, if you have no objection."

"I don't believe the chief will have any objection. What is it you normally do?"

"I'm a very low-ranking adviser, sir. In fact, I have no official title."

Low-level, perhaps. But connected. Ling knew the type. Young. Ambitious. Precocious. There was at least one in every circle of power; there because his loyalty, reliability, and flexible morality allowed him to perform those little dirty deeds that inevitably needed to be done from time to time. Ling had seen dozens of such surrogates during the four mayoral administrations of his police career. They were trouble—with their direct access to power, they could, if not checked, really foul-up delicate investigations.

But there was something about Collingsworth that appealed immediately to Ling. Perhaps his candor. Maybe his style. He seemed above the power-hungry juveniles from the mayor's office. Besides, he seemed to be looking at Ling in awe.

Pretenses aside, Ling knew the suave Englishman was there to watch them, perhaps to test them. And what did he know about Whittaker? About the murders? The young man had come in a rush from London at a time when just about any representative of the British consulate could have served a liaison function. Why?

Ling looked at his watch. "It's well-past noon. I guess that's about five or six o'clock your time. You must be hungry. How about a drink and some lunch?"

"Delighted, detective."

"I'll call you Breck—how about you call me Monk."

"Monk?"

"Yeah—I had a cousin that looked like me, almost became a priest."

"But he didn't?"

"Naw, he became an embalmer."

Ling stood. The Englishman hesitated, then offered a tentative smile.

In that moment, Ling knew he had him.

They started to leave, but a detective across the room, waving a telephone, shouted to Ling: "Pick up four, Monk." Ling excused himself and picked up a line.

"Hello, Monk. It's Edison. Took me four calls to track you down."

Edison W. LeGrande was Ling's father-in-law, a son of the founder of a three-man candy kitchen grown to an international packaged foods concern, with offices in seven countries. The firm had gone public, of course, but remained soundly under LeGrande's control. It was the source of the LeGrande wealth, a small sampling of which had been placed into trust for Alex, and had passed to Ling as his inheritance upon her death.

"I'm on a special case," Ling said. "It's a temporary headquarters."

"That Englishman, isn't it? I heard about that and told Nancy for sure they'll have Monk on it. You got it solved yet?"

"Working on it. In fact, we're kind of tied up with . . ."

"Now don't give me the brushoff, Monk. We haven't heard from you in weeks and you promised me an answer. I like you, you know. You're family. I want you to leave all that civil service drudgery and come aboard with me."

"I . . . I've been giving it some thought, Edison, but . . ."

LeGrande laughed. "I'm sure you have three-hundred excuses. So let's have lunch and talk about it. Come to the club at one."

"I'm afraid I can't—at least today. It's out of the question. In fact, I'm just leaving to have lunch with someone now."

"Then tomorrow. Make it around three."

"I appreciate it, Edison, but . . ."

"I'll see you then."

The line went dead. Ling held the phone a moment. He

was fond of LeGrande. The man had been very decent to him when he no longer had an obligation. But leaving the force to work under him . . . Ling didn't want to think about that—just now.

Ling replaced the phone and rejoined the Englishman. In a few moments, they were in an unmarked car, a detective at the wheel, heading down Second Avenue.

"First trip to New York?" Ling asked.

"No. I visited once as a student. I had about twenty pounds in my pocket and went through most of that in about forty-eight hours. Have you been to London?" Collingsworth replied.

"Yeah—kind of liked it, except for all the queues."

"Why was that?"

"The Army. Vowed I'd never stand in another line in my life once I got out."

"Vietnam?"

"I was there," Ling answered. "Twenty-six months."

"Bloody bad outcome, that conflict."

Ling said nothing. His fingers began toying with the strap of the Nikon hanging from his neck.

Traffic was backing up—a bottleneck at a construction site. Ling looked out the window, then abruptly ordered the driver to pull over and stop. "Be right back," Ling said, opening the door and jumping out. Dodging traffic and ignoring a chorus of horns, he crossed the avenue. Ahead of him, fifteen yards away, was a woman. The purse girl, he had pegged her. Twenty-five, maybe, wearing two dresses and an unknown number of petticoats. Her wiry, red hair stood on end as if the sidewalk against her bare feet were electrified. Her face and hands were unwashed. And around her neck, as always, were the straps of a dozen or more purses.

He moved quickly, cocking the Nikon's shutter and adjusting the focus. He waited, in the style of Cartier-Bresson, until the final instant and then, in a practiced motion too fast to be noticed, he had the camera to his eye, the shot made and the Nikon back on his chest. The purse girl paid him no attention.

Ling returned to the car.

"What was that all about?" the incredulous driver asked.

"Purse girl. Got her five or six times already. Usually find her further downtown."

Collingsworth was doing his best to conceal his confusion. "Photography your hobby?"

"It comes in handy," Ling answered, replacing the lens cap. "Look, we're only a few blocks away. Care to walk?"

"Fine."

The Englishman stepped out of the car and they began walking.

"I would say a psychiatrist could make much ado about that," Collingsworth said.

"About what?"

"Your camera, there—with that long lens."

Ling smiled. "My wife used to have a theory—something about a substitute gun."

"Perhaps. But I was thinking more in terms of all the turmoil in a police officer's day. You make these tidy little rectangular pictures, neat microcosms of the world around you. They don't change. They don't flee. They don't hurt."

Ling was wondering if perhaps the Englishman wasn't onto something.

"Then, too," Collingsworth continued, "what you are doing is stealing a slice of time. Some might say it's a bit criminal, that. And there would be an irony in that, yes?"

"So they can book me for theft of an image, if they want," Ling said.

The sky was cloudless, and the sun almost directly overhead. It was one of those rare days on which Manhattan seems to sparkle. The plate glass windows of the street-level shops acted as mirrors, reflecting the buildings opposite and giving the illusion of the wide, open space of Paris or Barcelona—but broad French avenues and expansive Spanish plazas were not to be found in New York, where every square-inch of property was seized for some profit-making purpose.

Ling stopped at a bland, red-brick, 1960's apartment building, of the type that lined the East Side for sixty long blocks. He craned his neck and looked toward the upper floor. Collingsworth, curious, did the same.

"Lost a jumper here once," Ling told him, his face expressionless.

"A jumper?"

"Suicide. Maybe ten thousand people watched. Guy flew through a window on the twenty-second floor. He did a couple of cartwheels and landed headfirst right here." He pointed to a spot near the curb.

"Got the job done, I would guess."

"He was a black homosexual hairdresser. Lost his lover and took the leap."

"Anyone attempt to stop him?"

Ling looked into his eyes. "It was me who tried. I was passing by when I saw the crowd. Talked to the kid through his apartment door for an hour. Suddenly, he opened it. I rushed in. He took a flying start toward the window. My fingers brushed his pants leg as he passed over the sill."

"I'd remember that a good long while."

Ling nodded, then looked back to the upper windows. "The sound, once you hear it, never leaves you. Like a rifle shot, the bones snapping on impact."

"And of course the onlookers were urging him to jump."

Ling laughed. "We're not quite that uncivilized, despite what they say. At least, I've never seen it. Let's move on."

Ling, feeling frustrated, studied the Englishman as they walked. Collingsworth was urbane. Normally, even the most sophisticated of visitors was taken aback by the brutality of New York's streets. Monk Ling's introductory course on New York reality, a baptism he reserved for politicians, cub reporters, and slumming academics, was having little effect.

The sunny day and the noon hour had combined to fill the sidewalks, and Ling and the Englishman had difficulty staying side by side, as they picked their way through the throngs. They passed a Korean vegetable stand. Ling looked the other way—the sweet smells of garlic and onion and moistened greens served only to remind him of Alex's fondness for such places. Ling's eyes instead focused on two young men across the street. They were clearing out an apartment, dumping horribly dirty and damaged chairs, tables, lamps, mattresses, and other furnishings into a pile on the sidewalk. Littering on that scale carried a hefty fine. But no cop would stop it—

garbage pickers would have the sidewalk cleared within an hour.

They walked another two blocks, the Englishman seemingly lost in thought, until Ling stopped again. This time he led Collingsworth into a small, standup pizza parlor.

"Monk, how the hell are ya?" greeted a short, roly-poly man with a thick gray mustache behind the counter. He wiped his hands on his food-stained white apron, then offered the right one to Ling, who took it and introduced Collingsworth. "What can I get you?" the fat man, a Greek, asked.

"Nothin' just now, Nick. Just lookin' around." He turned to Collingsworth. "Nick, here, is manager of this establishment." Then to the Greek: "How's the sugar situation?"

Nick leaned over the counter. His expression turned grave, his voice a whisper. "Worse than ever, Monk. Sugar's costing me more than the coffee. They'll put me out of business yet."

"Sugar?" Collingsworth asked.

Ling solemnly pointed toward a narrow counter against the wall where several customers were standing eating pizza slices. "Nick used to put bowls of sugar packets out there for his coffee-drinkers. He can't anymore." He turned to the Greek. "Tell 'im why, Nick."

"The goddamned addicts."

Collingsworth was still puzzled. Ling explained: "The junkies think sugar helps them through withdrawal."

The Greek chimed in: "They come in here, buy a small Coke or demand a glass of water, then they dump a dozen sugars into it. If I tell 'em no, they say they're gonna come back some night and slit my liver." He shrugged. "So I buy a lot of sugar."

Back outside, Collingsworth asked: "Will he make it?"

"Maybe. Or maybe they'll send me here some night and I'll find him dead on the floor, a butcher knife in his liver. It's too bad, too—you learn to love these Greeks. If they love you, they love you forever."

The Englishman was silent as they continued their walk. Maybe, Ling thought, his tour was having an impact, after all.

Ling stopped when they reached a corner bar a few blocks further downtown. "This is it." He held the door.

It was a typical cop bar. The Thirteenth Precinct and the Police Academy, with all the special units stationed there, were three blocks away. The bar was dreary and plain, its floor heavily scuffed to bare wood almost throughout, its off-white walls stained from tobacco smoke and badly in need of paint, its ancient mahogany bar gouged, scraped, scarred with cigarette burns and, in one spot, splintered. Smoke saturated the air, giving the long room a yellowish-gray cast not unlike that of an artillery battlefield.

To New York cops, the bar was akin to a shrine. On one wall was a gallery of dozens of small black and white photographs of cops who had passed through the Academy—and the tavern—only to die in the line of duty. Behind the bar were mementos of long-ago eras. There was a tattered poster with large red block letters reading: "FUCK THE PIGS!" Underneath, in a blue pen scrawl, was written: "Please do! You won't forget it." There was a framed portrait of Teddy Roosevelt, and an autographed studio shot of Betty Grable. There was a faded map of Ireland, with X's marking various counties—a long-ago barroom poll, no doubt. There was a Patrolmen's Benevolent Association recruitment handbill, and near by, tacked above a row of bottles, as if it was a prize scalp, was a long-haired red wig which, legend had it, had been lifted from some prematurely balding hippie during a long-forgotten trashing of Wall Street.

Ling inspected the crowded room, spotting most of the patrons as cops, in uniform and out, along with a group of technicians from the city morgue, also a few blocks away. There were three or four police groupies, women, often quite striking, who got their kicks from men with guns and were passed without protest from man to man through entire precincts. There were also a dozen young men and women who were obviously cadets, even if out of their gray uniforms. They clustered in tiny groups, their voices subdued, their postures showing a mixture of fright and humility. Someday, Ling knew, they, too, would return to the shrine and attempt—unsuccessfully—to recapture their youth and their idealism and the notion that theirs would be a job with some lasting impact.

Ling acknowledged greetings from several cops as he escorted the Englishman to a booth. Their driver, who had arrived earlier and was seated at the bar, nodded. Collingsworth, his eyes wide taking in the scene, plainly was uncomfortable.

"You might have guessed that this is kind of a police hangout," Ling said. "The food's not exactly the best in the city but the corned beef luncheon isn't bad."

"Must be the safest establishment in New York, what?" Collingsworth said, chuckling.

"Not necessarily," Ling deadpanned. He pointed to one of a half-dozen, thumb-sized holes barely visible in the many coats of paint on the tin ceiling. "Guy came off some narcotics thing last week. Said he hadn't slept in four days and nobody understood what he and his partners had to go through, not his wife, not his neighbors, not the press, not the mayor. Drank for four, five hours, then kind of went crazy. He got off a shot before they could pin him down."

"Wild West, huh?"

"Guys in here would tell you the West's full of pansies."

"They'd say that about England, too, I would imagine."

Ling hesitated a moment, then said: "Any *Irish* cop would say that, yes."

Collingsworth studied him a minute, then answered, "And you've Irish blood yourself, haven't you?"

"Very perceptive—my mother came from Wexford."

"Yet your name is, what, oriental?"

"Chinese. It's a complicated story."

Ling was spared an elaboration with the arrival at their booth of a wide-hipped, middle-aged waitress. She had a round, puffy face, with freckles and stringy red hair, and had been a fixture in the bar for more than two decades, a den mother to scared cadets who, most of them, matured into men. Her name was Maggie, and she was the shrine's resident priestess.

Without asking, she served Ling a club soda on ice. She struck an impatient pose and, saying nothing, looked at Collingsworth. Unnerved, he shifted in his seat, then meekly requested a gin and tonic.

Ling grinned. "Part of the ambience," he said when she had left.

"I gather," the Englishman said, laughing. "I saw a lady

just like her in Amsterdam once—she was outfitted in leather.''

Maggie was back with Collingsworth's drink. "Special's corned beef," she announced.

Ling looked at Collingsworth, who nodded. "Make it two, Maggie," the detective said. "And wipe that smile off your face.''

"Kiss it, Monk," the waitress shot back, then stalked away.

Collingsworth took a large swallow of his drink. "You've been testing me, haven't you?" he asked.

Ling immediately reaffirmed his initial, gut assessment of the young Englishman: Collingsworth *was* smart. The mayor's flunkies never did seem to catch on. "Look, I don't mean to insult you, but . . ."

The Englishman, annoyed, interrupted: "You should know that I've been tested before—Leningrad, Argentina, Belfast."

Ling smiled. "Okay, you've put me in my place."

Collingsworth, still showing his irritation, sipped his drink. "What, if I may ask, is the purpose of this, ah, exercise?"

"The purpose?" Ling repeated. "A little dose of reality." He cocked his head. "We get them, see, novice prosecutors, children scarcely two weeks out of law school. Or the mayor's yes-men, mama's boys usually, wanting to throw their weight around and avenge every schoolyard fight they ever lost. What they don't know is how violent and bloody this city can be, and if they don't know that, they're not going to understand what we do and why we do it." Ling leaned forward. "You read Kafka? He wrote the script. Lifted his stuff from the goddamned New York newspapers."

The Englishman laughed. "Everything's relative, yes? And just when did you become so cynical?"

Ling answered promptly: "The first homicide I came upon."

"What happened?"

"Old man was stabbed by a mugger while sitting on a bench in Bryant Park. That's over by the library, near Times Square. I was a patrolman. When I found him, he was slumped forward onto the footpath in a huge pool of blood. Another cop comes, then leaves to call an ambulance, but I see the guy's already gone and about all I can do is keep the crowd away."

The food arrived. This time Maggie was smiling. "There you go, gentlemen," she said pleasantly. "Enjoy it."

Collingsworth, puzzled, looked at Ling. The detective shrugged.

They tasted their sandwiches. "Continue, please. I'm very interested," Collingsworth said.

Ling ran a napkin across his mouth. "So this couple comes along, see. Hippies. Stoned on something or everything. They see the corpse and the blood and start this hysterical laughing. Next thing I know they get by me. They're on the grass, maybe a foot from the corpse, and he's on top of her, unzipping his pants with one hand and grabbing her tits with the other. She's laughing. It's funny, see. And later, when I started to read Kafka, I knew exactly what he was talking about."

Ling resumed eating. Collingsworth sat motionless, staring at him. By some standard, Ling knew, he was being measured. Finally, the Englishman asked: "What did you do?"

"I took my nightstick and put it as hard as I could where it would do some good." He grinned. "That was twenty some years ago—bet that kid still can't sit in one place for too long."

Collingsworth smiled. "And now you put that same energy to solving who-done-it riddles. This time it's Whittaker's riddle."

"Riddles? Yes, I guess you could call them that." Ling decided he rather liked the word. Nothing, absolutely nothing in police work followed a straight line.

"Tell me something about James Whittaker," Ling said.

"That is exactly what I intended to ask of *you*," Collingsworth said. "He's a bit of a mystery figure, really. We tried to keep tabs on him, but there's only so far you can go, him being who he is, and not a demonstrable criminal and all that."

"Was—"

"Excuse me?"

"Whittaker was—"

"Oh yes, of course. I do mean the past tense. Must get accustomed to that."

"He was some kind of a political activist?" Ling asked.

"That was a smokescreen. He lined himself up with your anti-nuclear movement with no greater goal than to embarrass your President and, in turn, put pressure on the prime minister to give him an ambassadorship, among other demands. The first we learned of it was when *The New York Times* published his letter. You can imagine how the prime minister felt, her brother calling her strongest overseas ally a 'warmonger.' The next piece of news was that he was supposed to be the featured speaker at some large anti-nuclear rally, in your Central Park, I believe."

Ling was aware of plans for the rally—organizers expected as many as two-hundred thousand people to gather in Sheep Meadow—but he had not known Whittaker had been a scheduled speaker. "Your government was watching him?" Ling asked.

"On a very limited basis. We were on him in the Bahamas but had to withdraw when he came here. A touchy situation."

"Why all the attention? The letter to the *Times* seems to be . . . What I mean is, there had to be more."

Collingsworth studied Ling's face, then leaned forward. "James Whittaker was buyable. And, at a very low price. From a security standpoint, he was a very significant risk for us."

"Buyable by whom?"

"Anyone capable of meeting his price. He circulated among many, many unsavory people at home, in the Caribbean, in Asia. It was there, incidentally—in Manila—where he lived until his sister's election."

Maggie took their plates away. Both declined coffee.

"Were they close, Whittaker and the prime minister?" Ling asked.

Collingsworth thought a moment. Then, in a labored tone, he said: "Let me say their relationship was not unlike that between any two siblings where one ends up in a very successful, powerful position. I don't mean to be rude but think of some of the brothers of your presidents. And in our case, the situation was complicated by her sex. He had difficulty handling that, especially since it was he who had introduced her to her late husband, a very prominent banker who, in turn, made the prime minister's entry into politics possible."

"So Whittaker must have felt she owed him."

"Something like that. And it got worse with his accident."

"Accident?"

Collingsworth, beginning to appear weary from jet lag, rubbed his eyes, then said: "Whittaker lost his wife in an auto accident. After that, he changed. He deteriorated, and his descent took him through virtually every layer of decadence known to mankind. He seemed to believe one gets only so many shots in life and he was adamant he was going to take his."

"And then he found New York. A perfect marriage, Whittaker and this city. A Manhattan free-fall."

Collingsworth nodded slowly. "He partook of all America had to offer, by the look of it."

"Heavy drinker?" Ling asked, the question a mere formality.

"Around the clock."

"Drugs?"

"Anything in a chemist's cabinet."

"Sexual quirks?"

Collingsworth chuckled. "Any act two or three people can do, he tried it. At least, that was the appearance. For a while, our people were keeping count of his women, then more or less abandoned that for the numbers it involved." He paused. "However, there was one relationship he had that quite intrigued us. A woman named Simpson. She lived with him a bit. Our people suspected that she was a plant from the opposition, someone to collect the dirt, provoke him toward even more embarrassing debacles. But that was pure speculation—it never was confirmed."

"What about the woman killed with him?"

"We're still checking, of course, but as of now, we know nothing about her."

Ling thanked him for the information, then summoned the waitress and paid the check. He excused himself and went to the public telephone to check in with the Seventeenth. Returning, he signaled the driver that they would be leaving, then told the Englishman: "I'm informed we now have an address for our Miss Simpson. Let's pay our respects."

8

The double-chinned morgue attendant was growing impatient—
Stanislas Lubelski had already viewed three bodies without
making an identification, and a fourth was now being loaded
onto the dumbwaiter from the refrigerated crypts in the basement. The surly bureaucrat's expression showed that he was
beginning to suspect Lubelski as another psychotic just released from Bellevue Hospital, next door. But the attendant's
feelings were irrelevant—Lubelski needed his confirmation.

The dumbwaiter clanked to a halt behind the viewing room
glass. The curtain snapped open revealing yet another dark-
haired young woman lying on a gurney pan, a sheet rolled
down past her face.

"Here's our last Jane Doe that might even vaguely match
your description," the attendant said impatiently.

Lubelski had told him he was looking for a young Pole
who had come to New York on an emergency visa to visit a
dying aunt, and had not been heard from in more than two
weeks. Polish authorities were attempting to trace her for her
desperate family.

Lubelski pressed toward the glass. The face of this victim
was disfigured by a gunshot wound but there could be no
doubt—it was Anatole.

"No, that's not her either," he said.

"Maybe you should try the hospitals."

"I did."

"Well, people from behind the Iron Curtain . . . sometimes, you know, they . . ."

"Defect? My friend, that would hardly be possible in this case," Lubelski snapped.

The attendant was taken aback. "Maybe she met a young man—that's all I meant."

Lubelski handed him a calling card. "Here's my number. Call me please if anyone resembling her turns up." Without waiting for a response, Lubelski left. His card, he knew, would flutter into a wastebasket even before he had stepped through the glass doors of the incongruously cheerful, blue-tiled building on First Avenue.

Outside, Lubelski hailed a cab for the trip to lower Lexington Avenue. A few minutes later, he instructed the driver to discharge him outside a coffee shop.

The coffee shop was perfect—he had used it as a sighting post in the past. Sitting at the end corner of the counter, one could obtain a clear view of the small lobby of an inconspicuous hotel wedged in between two office buildings across the street. The hotel was merely ten stories and of a dying class—old but clean with moderate prices and European-style service. Family owned, it was favored by foreigners, including the crews of several overseas airlines. Anatole had checked in for an extended stay two weeks earlier.

Lubelski ordered tea and a piece of pie. Except for an airport limousine discharging some stewardesses, the hotel entrance was quiet. There was no indication of police activity.

He thought of Anatole. He had never actually met her, although they had communicated on one operation. Her reputation, on both sides of the game, made her the equal of the coldest male assassin. Her weapon was her sex. Among her key victims had been a French government minister, an Italian diplomat, a Dutch banker—all brought under the spell of her magic and compromised in some useful fashion. Anatole had appeared invincible. How had she become so vulnerable? Where had she misjudged her advantage?

Lubelski stalled for a half-hour until the waitress, bothered by his claiming of a stool for so insignificant an order, slapped his check on the counter. Lubelski, banking on a possible future use of the same seat, tipped her generously.

He left the restaurant, walked to a newsstand at the corner
and bought a *Post*. Taking a position a few feet from the
kiosk, he began flipping through the tabloid's pages. His
eyes, however, were zeroed in on the hotel's fourth-floor
corner room. Anatole, under the standard procedure, had
asked for that room specifically, explaining she had occupied
it on an earlier visit to New York. Lubelski saw that the
windows on both sides had their curtains pulled open and
blinds raised just as Anatole had been instructed. In one
window, a spare purse was still resting against the glass, a
sign that the room had not been raided.

It was time to make his move. Lubelski rolled the newspaper
into a tube—a weapon, should he need one—and entered the
hotel. The lobby was an anachronism, a museum. Its deep,
authentic leather chairs were old but clean. The tables glistened from their polish. A uniformed porter was busy vacu-
uming a threadbare oriental rug. Another man was on a
ladder, painstakingly cleaning the cut glass of a chandelier.
Off in a corner were two old-fashioned brown telephone
booths. Nearby was a small cigar stand, its gray-frocked
proprietor appearing to be in his seventies. No aluminum
baggage trolleys were visible. Nor were there any engraved
plastic signs, tin ashtrays or piped-in music. The hotel's days
were obviously numbered.

Lubelski's heels clicked on the dull marble floor as he
strode purposefully to the handcarved wooden front desk.

"My sister's key, please. Four-seventeen," he said.

The clerk hesitated, inspecting him. Apparently intimidated
by Lubelski's expensive attire and air of authority, the clerk
handed over the key without question. Lubelski started away,
then stopped and turned. "Are there any messages for this
room, please?"

The clerk shook his head.

"And no one's called for my sister?"

"No."

"Thank you. We were expecting visitors."

Lubelski entered the elevator—it was automatic; one of the
hotel's rare concessions to modern technology—and pushed
buttons for both the third and fourth floors. He got off on

three, then went to the firestairs. If they were waiting for
him, someone would be posted in the stairwell to block that
potential escape route.

The stairwell was empty.

He slipped into the fourth-floor corridor. A maid was
pushing her cart. Lubelski approached her from behind.

"Excuse me, but have you made up four-seventeen yet?"

The maid was startled but composed herself quickly. "Yes,
sir—but no one had slept in the bed."

Lubelski smiled. Unless the maid was part of it, the room
had not been tossed. "We were out of town last night. Thank
you."

He inserted the key and opened the door warily, but there
was no sign of intruders, past or present. He immediately
checked the dresser drawers for the traps Anatole had been
instructed to set. The pieces of straw were undisturbed.

She had traveled lightly, and it took only seconds for him
to gather her toiletries and clothes, and pack them into her
suitcase. In the suitcase, in the top right pocket just where it
was supposed to be, was a tiny combination address book
and diary. He flipped it open. Several lines in French about
the Empire State Building and the Statue of Liberty filled a
page in the diary section; the address pages included numerous
sets of initials along with phone numbers. Lubelski smiled.
Maybe the Russian was correct—to this extent, at least,
Anatole had been a thorough professional.

Lubelski took the luggage and checked out, paying the bill
in cash and apologizing profusely that a sudden emergency
had forced his sister to change her travel plans, necessitating
she leave the hotel with so little notice. A twenty-dollar tip
won the desk clerk's sympathetic understanding.

Lubelski allowed the doorman to flag him a cab, then told
the driver to take him to Kennedy Airport. Only after they
were out of sight of the hotel did he change his destination to
his news agency's small uptown office.

Heading up First Avenue, Lubelski felt relieved—the Americans obviously had not traced Anatole's movements. The
odds were good they had yet to learn her identity.

At his news bureau, Lubelski greeted the secretary, then
went into his private office, locked the door and placed the

suitcase on his desk. He opened it and extracted the leather-bound diary, then cleared the desk top except for the book and a sheet of paper.

He worked on the telephone numbers first—in a simple transfer code, every fifth number contained a date. He was finished in minutes. He next turned to the initials Anatole had entered. Strung together, they formed a message. The message was in a book code, the key to which would be the horoscope columns for the corresponding date's *New York Daily News*.

Anatole, as with most field agents working on their own, had been trained to record in code as much of her findings as security would allow. From that ledger, if she were lost, her control still had a chance to pick up the pieces.

Lubelski reached into his desk drawer for a clipboard which contained a year's worth of horoscopes from the *News*. The decoding would not take long—she had not left much; there apparently hadn't been time.

In less than ten minutes, Lubelski had Anatole's legacy—it was basically a list of names:

—DeGrazia, convict
—Cal Thornton, stockbroker
—Whse???
—Simpson, whore

There was an added notation:

—Holmes, UK embassy, secret pact

A criminal named DeGrazia, a broker named Thornton, and a prostitute named Simpson—acquaintances of Whittaker, obviously. And someone named Holmes in the British embassy, who had had some type of clandestine arrangement, apparently with Whittaker. All would likely be easy to trace. But what was the remaining entry: "Whse?"

Lubelski decoded the entry once more to make certain he had not erred, but his original deciphering stood. Perhaps Anatole had made an encoding error. Could she have meant "warehouse"? Or "whorehouse"? Then another possibility came to him: "Whse." The White House!

Lubelski's insides stirred with mixed dread and excitement; then he mentally pinched himself—a reference to the White House could mean anything. Whittaker, after all, had been the brother of the British prime minister, and it would not have been unusual for him to have been invited to some affair at the White House.

But Lubelski's instincts told him it was more than this—that Anatole, from her temporary grave inside a refrigerated drawer at the New York City Morgue, was trying to tell him something.

Speculation, however, would have to wait. There were routine procedures to follow, and they had priority.

Lubelski picked up the Manhattan yellow pages and turned to the listings for brokerage houses. He started at the top, calling each and asking for Cal Thornton. He was fortunate—it was on his seventh call that he reached Thornton's secretary.

"I'm afraid he's not available. May I take a message?" the woman asked, in an irritating nasal voice.

Lubelski looked at his watch—it was not quite two. "Is he at lunch?"

"I'm not supposed to give out that . . ."

"Look, miss, I'm one of your firm's biggest customers and if you want to try to explain to your bosses how a discourteous secretary from Brooklyn lost them a rather large account, then don't tell me whether Thornton's at lunch or not."

He braced for her to slam down the phone. She didn't. "Yes, sir," she said, her voice nervous. Lubelski grinned—a souring capitalistic economy with its scarcity of jobs did that to people. "I didn't mean any offense," the woman continued. "Mr. Thornton went to lunch."

"Well, I'm the one he's supposed to be having lunch with and I was never informed where to meet him."

Her voice was hesitant. "There must be some mistake—he was scheduled to lunch with Mr. Gordon Bennett and Mr. . . . ."

"Do you think I'm lying to you, young lady? Do you honestly believe I have nothing better to do with my time than waste it on the phone with an imbecile?"

"The Parrot Club, sir."

"The what?"

"The Parrot Club. It's a private club in SoHo."

"What time?"

"His luncheon appointment was for one."

Lubelski hung up the phone. Thornton possibly could still be at his club. It was worth a try.

Lubelski rushed from his office two short blocks to the underground garage at the United Nations, where he parked his car, courtesy of the Polish U.N. Mission.

"Good afternoon, sir," the security guard said.

"Perilli around?"

The guard smiled knowingly. "Yes sir, in the back by the gas pumps."

Perilli, a short, fat man with thinning, slicked-back hair, greeted him warmly. "Where you been, my friend? Haven't seen you around."

"We've got a new ambassador. Have to be careful."

"What can I do for ya?"

Perilli held the wet stub of a cigar between his fingers. The collar of his white dress shirt was open, revealing a clump of chest hair. His belt barely made it around his girth, and missed one of the loops of his slacks, which, Lubelski suspected, were likely the second pair offered with an Orchard Street suit. But, despite his appearance, Perilli was smart— and trustworthy. He had to be, for the variety of services he offered. Perilli ran the U.N.'s largest horseracing and sports book, oversaw a squad of numbers runners among the maintenance staff, could produce a hooker in five minutes for a rendezvous anywhere in the city, and was a ready buyer for those staples shipped under cover of a diplomatic pouch.

"Man named DeGrazia," Lubelski said.

"DeGrazia," Perilli repeated, his hand rubbing his chin. "Brooklyn?"

"Could be."

"If it's the guy I'm thinkin' of, he's one of Little Brother Marco's boys. Don't remember his first name. Strictly small change, nickel and dime stuff. What you doin' mixed up with him?"

"I need some information, that's all."

Perilli considered the situation a moment, then said: "Try O'Grady's. It's a joint by the Brooklyn docks."

Lubelski thanked him and shook his hand. In his palm was a folded twenty dollar bill.

Perilli pocketed it. He would inspect it later. "Give my best to the ambassador, ya hear?"

Lubelski didn't answer—he was rushing to his car for a ride downtown, in search of a stockbroker.

9

She had served their drinks and was standing there, smiling lasciviously as Gordon ran his hand up and down her bare thigh.

"The most perfect body in the world," he kept repeating.

"For chrissake, Gordon," Cal Thornton said, "let her go. We've got trouble, big trouble."

Gordon's hand slithered up her body to her exposed breasts. "*You* have trouble, Thornton. Not us."

"He's right, Cal," said Steve, like the other two men, a Wall Street broker. "It was your idea and you're the one who dealt with him."

"Let her go, I said," Thornton snapped.

Gordon glared at him, then slapped the waitress's buttocks. "See you later, honey."

She left, closing the door to the private dining room.

Thornton gulped from his double scotch, silently cursing his acceptance of Gordon's proposal that they meet at the Parrot Club—while it was true the exclusive SoHo club offered guaranteed privacy for its young executive members, the waitresses, attired only in lace-fringed aprons and available for side duty in the backrooms by the hour, were too distracting.

The Parrot Club was three months old, and Thornton had been one of its charter members, delighted that he had been able to finesse an invitation from its organizers. The club was instant plush, put together in little more than a week in what had been a failed Thai restaurant. Each of the tiny dining rooms had a low hanging ceiling of acoustical tiles, to conceal the overhead pipes. The plasterboard walls were papered in red imitation velvet with plain, glossy black wooden trim. The golden rug was thin but still suggested a hint of elegance, or at least expense. On one wall was a modestly sized horizontal mirror; on the others were aluminum framed Museum of Modern Art prints. The round table, thinly padded chairs, and coarse white table linen were all standard hotel issue.

"So this dude Whittaker was your source, huh?" Steve asked.

"Damn! Watch what you say," Thornton scolded. "These walls are paper-thin."

"Well, you should have told us," Steve said.

"Why? What purpose would it have served?"

"We could have protected you from yourself. What the fuck did you have to shoot him for? He steal your lady or somethin'?"

"Up yours, Steve. I didn't kill him."

"Who did, then?" Gordon asked.

"Fuck if I know. All I know is I'm in trouble. They must have every cop in the world trying to figure out what happened, and unless I do something, they're gonna follow a trail right to me."

"Well, you do have an alibi, don't ya?" Steve asked.

"Of course. But half the population of Attica had alibis, too."

The waitress returned with their lunch. Thornton tried one bite of a two-inch-thick cheeseburger, then pushed his plate to the side.

"Just what do you want from us?" Gordon asked.

"I . . . I don't know. I'm just scared, man, that's all. You guys have got to protect me. They come knock on your door, you barely know me, you know?"

"I wish that were true," said Gordon. "I hate losers."

The word stung. Cal Thornton lusted to be a winner, one of those Wall Street boy wonders the magazines were always

writing about. The potential for wealth, power, and glory was
what had attracted him to the Street in the first place. And he
had worked hard, very hard, to get on the inside. Now, a
rotten twist of fate stood to deny him all that, to brand him as,
trouble, to slam the golden doors in his face.

Thornton cocked his head. "You fuckers talk big now, but
you're potentially as vulnerable as me."

"How?" Steve asked, somewhat apprehensively.

"Whittaker's dead. And the woman. Those are facts. Reality. And the more you think about it, it gets scary. I mean it
could be big, very big. The White House. The Russians, for
chrissake."

Gordon laughed. "Or some junkie or hooker or midnight
cowboy."

"Sure—but the timing's too coincidental. We were within
two weeks of another windfall. Maybe a million. Think of
that." Thornton rubbed his bloodshot eyes, then announced:
"I'll be gone for a while. Sudden business overseas, understand? A week, a month, whatever it takes 'til all this cools
down."

"That could be a mistake, Cal," Steve said. "It could look
like you're runnin' from somethin'."

"I am."

There was a hard knock on the door. A hefty blonde
wearing long leather boots and a wide leather belt entered.
With her, eyes cast downward and wearing a fluffy pastel
blue dress, was a petite, much younger woman. "Come on,
Gordon," the blonde said sharply. "You're keeping us
waiting."

Gordon rose. He smiled sheepishly. "See ya around the
campus, guys. Gotta go."

Steve also departed, saying he had an appointment to keep
downtown.

Thornton buried his head in his hands. The Parrot Club had
been a mistake. As had Whittaker.

The waitress presented him with the check. He signed it
without checking the amount. He'd eat it—he always seemed
to whenever the group had lunch.

10

Monk Ling had her categorized as soon as her Upper East Side address was combined with information from the luxury building's doorman; that Miss Samantha Simpson lived without roommates in a six room apartment, and was rarely home. And yes, the doorman believed, she was up there now, just returned from her exercise class.

"You can forget the announcement, Mac," Ling said, flashing his shield.

The doorman nodded.

In the elevator, en route to the twenty-fourth floor, Ling briefed Breck Collingsworth on what they were likely to find: "They come from Minneapolis and Charlotte and Des Moines, and you can spot them the instant they touch the floor of the Port Authority bus terminal or the airport. Innocent things, with suitcases full of dainty dresses they'll never wear again and letters of wisdom from their mothers that they'll never read."

"Country girls," the Englishman said.

Ling shook his head. "Not that simple. These women are special. It takes them about forty-eight hours to realize that they're what New York is all about. Within a week, they're fixtures on the disco floors. By the end of a month, they can walk into any afterhours club in the city and they pick up secrets they don't even tell their sisters. Brains, energy, good looks—I've never met one that didn't have all of them.''

"Prostitutes.''

"Again, not that simple. You can't even dismiss them as high-class callgirls. 'Multi-talented entrepreneurs' would be more accurate.''

Samantha Simpson was waiting with the door open, the doorman obviously having called up on the intercom to warn her. Ling produced his shield and introduced Collingsworth by name only. She invited them inside reluctantly.

The woman led them to a large, sunken conversation pit. Ling and Collingsworth took seats on one side of a rectangle of stuffed, armless, snow-white sofas. She sat on the opposite side, her legs curled under her, her eyes hard, her expression annoyed.

Studying her, Ling found that she indeed met his expectations: cynical, tough, and well-aware of her hidden power.

Her legs were dancer's legs, streamlined, long and muscular in a very feminine way. They would be million-dollar legs with the right agent, the right patrons, the right luck. But Ling had known even before he met her that Samantha Simpson would have no agent, her patrons would have ties to Wall Street or Park Avenue rather than Madison Avenue or Hollywood, and what luck she had she made herself.

Her hair was jet black and cut short, her eyes milky, round, and a haunting gray, her body shapely under her leotard, and her nails magazine perfect and fire engine red.

Ling had encountered many Samantha Simpsons. He had fallen for every one of them instantly. This time, he promised himself, he would know better.

"I figured you'd be around,'' she said. Her accent was Texan.

"Why's that?'' Ling asked.

"Whittaker. It wouldn't take a Dick Tracy to connect me.''

"You a friend?''

She swung her legs to the floor and reached forward to a marble coffee table to take a cigarette from a gold-plated box. "Friend . . . lover . . . mistress. Depends on how nice you are, what you want to call it.''

Collingsworth leaned over the table to light her cigarette.

"You lived with him, Samantha . . .'' Ling started.

"I hate Samantha," she interrupted.

"Hmmm . . . so he called you Sam," Ling said—a guess.

"And I called him prince. But you know that, too, right?"

"What we do know is that you lived with Whittaker for weeks, then walked out on him—and a day later he's dead."

"Who are you, Perry Mason? I'm supposed to break down now, and confess or something?"

Ling laughed. He leaned back. "Confess what? That you killed him?" He laughed again. "No—that wasn't your bit of handiwork. We know that."

She appeared insulted. "Think I couldn't do it?"

Ling leaned forward. His eyes narrowed. "I know damn well you could."

"But you don't think I did?"

"That's right."

"Why?"

Ling smiled. "Because if dear Mr. Whittaker from London had managed to piss off a Texas cowgirl like you so much that you'd kill him, we wouldn't have found his balls between his legs where we found them."

She was grinning. "And where *would* you find them?"

"In the mail, probably, sent to his mother."

"You sure you're a cop? You talk like Madison Avenue. And that camera—what the hell's a cop got a camera for? And your friend here—he's so quiet. Let me guess: he's really the undertaker, huh?" She stubbed out the cigarette in a crystal ashtray. "Well, don't expect me to pay to bury Whittaker. I mean, he was born a jerk, only dumb little me didn't know it."

"Who were you working for?" Ling demanded sharply.

"What do you mean by that crack?"

Ling stood and began pacing through the apartment. "You see, I'm at an advantage here—I know who you are and you don't know me."

"You think you know me?" She was in for the fight.

"What's your rate, five hundred a night? Or six thousand by the month, a little more for the kinky stuff, discounts for the disabled?"

"Fuck-off."

He was standing over her. "Oh, I apologize—you really *were* in love."

"Stiff like you wouldn't know the meaning of the word."

Ling returned to his seat. He stretched out his legs and slouched. "You're probably right."

"You can leave now."

"We need your alibi."

"I was home all day and all night, reading a book."

"What book?"

"Jack and Jill."

Ling shook his head. "Won't do."

She stalled. Her eyes showed sincerity; her expression turned serious. "I'd like to help you. I really would. I mean, the man is dead, isn't he?" Her voice grew softer. "Can we keep this confidential? I mean, it's kind of delicate. A reputation's at stake."

Ling was smiling. "Try me."

She turned her head away. Her tone was confessional. "I was fucking the cardinal."

"No shit! He any good?"

"Better than some turkey cop."

Ling jumped to his feet. "Have it your way, child," he said, then led Collingsworth to the apartment door.

She remained on the couch, motionless. Ling turned and shouted back to her: "Not Houston and not Dallas—probably El Paso. State university. At least one degree, probably two. Comparative literature, or art history, or philosophy. Your mother hates you. Your father kind of understands, but couldn't handle it if he knew everything. And it took a lot of work and a lot of risk, but you know how it plays now, who has the power, the money, the creativity . . ."

"You're wrong, mister!"

"How so?"

She was walking toward them. "It wasn't El Paso—that was the big time—it was a town so small it could fit in a corner of Gramercy Park. And it wasn't comparative lit or art or philosophy—it was anthropology. You know, savages, buried bones, primitive brains?"

"Which was Whittaker?"

"I was thinking of you."

Ling produced a card and wrote the Seventeenth Precinct's telephone number on it. He handed it to her. "Call me sometime."

Ling opened the door and stepped into the hall, then stopped. "Hey, Sam. You're a gambler. You know Saturday's Florida State score?"

"Fuck off, I told you." The door slammed shut.

Ling and Collingsworth walked through the deserted, rust-carpeted hallway, with its ugly glass ceiling fixtures, to the elevators.

"The Florida State score?" the Englishman asked.

"Football," Ling replied. "There was a Florida State game Saturday night." He summoned the elevator.

They rode silently. The automatic doors opened and they stepped into the garish lobby.

"What happens to them?" Collingsworth asked. "They *do* grow old, I imagine."

Ling looked at him. "Some go back home. Others develop legitimate careers, public relations or something, or move to the coast. And more than a few let their guard down just once or find themselves overmatched for the first time and then they end up in my little book." He patted the notebook in his blazer side pocket. "We find them stuffed into a trunk, thrown out some window, OD'd on a bathroom floor. Then I've got to call their mothers and try to explain that their little babies were born under stars that predestined it to be this way, that they were created to tease and seduce and excite New York, this season's maidens consumed, then thrown into the fires."

They were in the lobby. "If you'll pardon my forwardness," Collingsworth said, "it sounds a bit to me like you've had some firsthand personal experience with a few Samantha Simpsons."

Ling laughed. "I guess so," he said, not wanting to get into something he didn't understand himself. Alex, in many ways, had been the antithesis of the Samantha Simpsons. Her quest had been much different than those of the young women chasing Manhattan kicks, power, and money. She was born with her claim to a fortune, yet had forsaken it—at least temporarily—at the time Ling met her. She was hitchhiking on a desert highway in Nevada, a knapsack on her back, her one pair of jeans faded and torn. It was not for many weeks that Ling had learned who she actually was. And later, when they married, she barely acknowledged her wealth, and had dipped into it sparingly. Samantha and Alex would never have understood one another.

As they headed for the street, Ling caught a glimpse of himself and the Englishman in a lobby mirror. They made an unusual couple, Collingsworth with his Saville Row suit, razor haircut and distinctly British gait, Ling with his muscular chest, too broad for the V-cut of his blazer, his athlete's shuffle and his loosened shirt collar. Ling smiled, wondering what kind of make the street's riffraff would put on them.

They had just reached the sidewalk when Collingsworth was suddenly accosted. "Out of my way, Harry," shouted his assailant, an elderly woman at least two inches shy of five feet. She had a bird's nest of steel-wool gray hair, and fierce wide eyes that told of horrors others could only imagine. She was pounding Collingsworth's chest with a fist. Annoyed, he was backing away, trying to parry her blows.

"Hey, what is this?" Ling demanded, stepping between them.

"He's a traitor," she screamed back, taking another jab at the Englishman. "I reported him in '37."

"Now, just a minute here," Ling said. "I'm a policeman. Maybe I can help."

In mounting her assault on Collingsworth, she had dropped an aluminum ladder she had been carrying under her arm. She also had abandoned a baby buggy. Ling lifted a handful of rags from inside the buggy. Underneath, stacked like a deck of cards, were dozens of metal plates—New York street signs.

"Where did you get these, honey?" Ling asked.

"Took 'em down."

"Why?"

She leaned forward. "The Arabs! Those signs are in Arab talk. They're everywhere."

"I see," Ling said, rubbing his chin. He looked at Collingsworth. The Englishman was open-mouthed.

Ling fished out his notebook and wrote on a blank page.

He ripped out the sheet and handed it to the old woman. "This here's got the address of the Seventeenth Precinct," he said. "I want you to go up there and ask for Officer Sullivan. He's our Arab specialist. You give him all those signs, okay? He'll take care of those Arabs."

The woman studied the piece of paper. "You sure?"

"Absolutely," Ling said, biting his lip to suppress a laugh at the vision of Sullivan being presented with a baby buggy of purloined street signs.

"Okay, mister," the woman said, collecting her ladder and cart and heading uptown.

"Sullivan?" Collingsworth asked.

"Yeah—he's kind of our community relations man," Ling answered, deciding against any elaboration of how the fat, foul-mouthed Sullivan and his partner had been the first cops to arrive at the Whittaker death scene.

Collingsworth said little on the ride back to the Seventeenth Precinct. Arriving there, they found Chief of Detectives Julius Golden speaking to two FBI agents. One was a barrel-chested Irishman; the other a tall, quiet Italian. Ling recognized both—they were heavies, the best of the New York field office. Listening to Golden, they appeared solemn and worried.

The chief spotted Ling and came over. Ling introduced the Englishman. Golden, in turn, handed Collingsworth a message. He had had a call. Someone in Washington. Collingsworth excused himself.

With the Englishman gone, Golden motioned Ling to follow him into the conference room. Mickey Triano was there with an expensive leather attaché case. Triano opened it. The case was packed with cash. Dollars.

"Found it in the closet under a built-in shoerack," Triano explained.

"How much?"

"Haven't inventoried it yet—wanted it dusted first—but I'd guess two-, maybe three-hundred thousand."

"Looks like Whittaker didn't trust banks."

"Yeah. And he also had a thing about this—" Triano produced a small address book. "Had it stuffed behind some books on a shelf."

Ling flipped open the book. There were no full names—nicknames and initials only. "You're tracking down the numbers?"

"Got Telco on it," Golden replied.

Dismissed by the chief, Ling immediately moved to one of the windows overlooking the station house entrance. He spotted Collingsworth in a phone booth on the corner. Ling grinned—he had argued for years that the city's crime rate would drop by twenty-five percent if only the courts would allow them to bug the public telephones outside police station houses.

The two FBI agents were busy updating themselves with clipboards containing the case's DD-5 reports. Ling went up to them. "This must be bigger than I thought—Washington sent out the guns."

"How you been, Monk?" the heavyset agent, Bill Nolan, asked. "Haven't seen ya since that Cuban Mission thing."

"You gonna step on my toes now like you did then?"

Nolan laughed. His partner, still looking worried, chimed in: "Background. That's all they want from us."

"Then buy 'em a history book." Ling started to turn away, then stopped. "I don't suppose you have anything to help us."

Nolan, casting his eyes downward, shook his head. "Sorry."

Collingsworth was coming in the squadroom door. Ling approached him.

"Anything new?" the Englishman asked. His voice was hollow; his eyes distant. He appeared distracted, a man trying to make sense of something.

Ling motioned him to follow and led him into the side office. Ling opened the attaché case. Collingsworth stared wide-eyed at the currency. "Whittaker's?" he asked.

"We think so."

Collingsworth thought a moment, then said, "Extraordinary. The only question is—what unlawful scheme did he employ to obtain it?"

Ling closed the cover. "If you feel up to it with your jetlag and all, I've got another little errand to run. You're welcome to come along," Ling said, as they left the side room.

"Where to?"

"Whittaker's apartment. I thought you might want to see it."

Collingsworth hesitated, then said: "Yes, that would be fine."

"Oh, and Breck . . . next time you need a phone, feel free to use ours." Ling's hand swept past the squad room, with its dozen telephones, half of which had just been installed for the temporary headquarters.

The Englishman turned a slight shade of red. "That would be wonderful. I would have asked but I also wanted to step outside for some aspirin. My flight is catching up to me."

Ling smiled. "We've got aspirin, too. Government issue. The department runs on them."

They were descending the stairs. "That call I made . . . I don't want you to think I'm keeping anything from you."

"The thought didn't cross my mind."

"It was my embassy in Washington. They're a bit nervous there about all this, and they were curious for an update."

"First Secretary Holmes?" Ling asked.

"Yes." Collingsworth halted. "How did you know?"

"We had a little chat early this morning. Seems like a pleasant man."

They continued toward the door.

"Holmes is a very experienced diplomat. Highly thought of, although one would be hard-pressed to tell you anything of substance he's done. A survivor. A remarkable survivor."

And someone, Ling told himself, with an intense interest in this case.

11

Stanislas Lubelski double-parked—his diplomatic plates would likely spare him a ticket—and looked for the entrance to the Parrot Club. He passed a deli and a florist. Down the street was a dry cleaner. Was this the right street? Finally he spotted it, the name spelled out in half-inch gold leaf letters on an inconspicuous plate glass door, midway down the block.

Lubelski crossed to the other side of the street and continued walking. He glanced over to the doorway. Inside, a small television camera could be seen hanging from the ceiling. The foyer, from what Lubelski could see of it, was decorated chiefly in red.

The decor, the security, and the inconspicuous sign told Lubelski what the club was—a disguised brothel. Lubelski had found it profitable to keep current with developments in the underworld of the city, and he knew there were between two and four such clubs in existence at any one time. They were invariably formed by three or four partners, people who recognized the money that could be made from the sexual appetites of young, would-be tycoons, who had no time in their day for dinner dates, movies, and strolls through the park, but rather needed a quick fix, sex without complications, a physical release little different from that some of them got in a gym. The police looked upon these operations benignly, knowing any attempt to penetrate the club would be hampered by loopholes in the law. And besides, better the young studs romp in a controlled environment than on the streets. Ultimately, it didn't matter—the clubs consumed themselves, most often when a member did his own calculations as to how much money was being made and started his own club, stealing half the membership of the other.

What made the clubs a success, however transitory, was the safety they offered their members when exposing their own secret vulnerabilities. But this, Lubelski knew, was not always so—two years earlier, the KGB had operated one.

He went to a telephone booth on the corner and called information for the club's number, then dialed it. A sweet, sensual voice answered the club's phone.

"I'm trying to reach Mr. Thornton, please," Lubelski said. "He's dining there."

"I'm sorry, sir, but we're not allowed to interrupt."

"Please, miss. I'm his business partner and there's an emergency."

That pitch also failed but Lubelski continued his pleading. Finally, in exasperation, she asked him to hold. A moment later, she was back on the line: "I'm afraid Mr. Thornton and his party have already left."

Lubelski cursed his luck. He would have to catch up to the stockbroker at his brokerage office. The visit to SoHo need not be wasted, however.

He removed a cuff link from his right sleeve and slipped it into a pocket, then crossed the street to the club's door. It was locked. He rang the bell. A huge man with a shaved head answered. "Are you a member, sir?"

"A member? Ah . . . oh, no. I'm a guest. That is, I just had a luncheon here with Mr. Cal Thornton. He's a member, I'm sure you know. I had lunch with him and I'm afraid I dropped a cuff link." He raised his arm, exhibiting an open shirt cuff.

"Come on," the bouncer said gruffly, allowing Lubelski into the lobby. "Wait here. I'll have someone look for it."

Lubelski thanked him profusely.

The bouncer returned in a few minutes. "I'm sorry, sir, but I had the girl search your room. She found nothing."

Lubelski snapped his head away. "Oh, damn!" He turned

back to the bouncer. "It's not that valuable, granted, but it had been my brother's, my late brother's. Great sentimental value, if you know what I mean." Lubelski edged closer to the other man. The Pole glanced at his own right hand hovering next to his belt. The bouncer followed his gaze—and saw a corner of a folded fifty dollar bill. "It would mean a great deal to me if I could look for it myself. Put my mind at rest, you see, knowing that I didn't drop it here after all."

The bouncer looked around, then nodded. He held out his hand. Lubelski slipped him the bill.

The bouncer led him to a private dining room where a shapely young woman, barren of clothing except for a white French maid's apron, was on her hands and knees still searching for the lost piece of jewelry. The bouncer introduced him as the missing jewelry's owner, then left, saying he had to get back to his post at the door.

"I can't seem to find it," the woman said, rising slowly. Then her eyes caught Lubelski's face. "Say, you weren't in that party! What the hell's going . . ."

Lubelski was on her instantly, one hand gripping the back of her neck, the other cupping her mouth. Revulsion filled him—he was so, so tired of violence. "Don't worry, I'm not going to hurt you," he said. "Just listen to me." Her eyes were wide but she made no sound. "You're a business-woman; I'm a businessman." He raised his other hand to her face. Scissored between two fingers was a hundred dollar bill. Her eyes grew wider still. "A little information—that's all I want."

The woman nervously inspected the room, then beckoned him to follow. She led him through a heavily carpeted corridor, opened a door and guided him quickly into a darkened room.

As his eyes adjusted to the dim light, Lubelski made out the outlines of a king-size bed in the room's center. Above it was a ceiling mirror. Against a far wall was what appeared to be a pair of Puritan's stocks, with holes for hands and head. He moved further inside, reaching down to touch the bed and finding that it really was not a bed but rather a bench made of heavy wooden planking. As he grew more accustomed to the darkness, the walls began to show a texture. He touched one—it was stone. He moved toward the stocks and, at the closer distance, could now discern several instruments—chain devices, riding crops, and metal restraints—hanging nearby.

The woman whispered something.

"What?"

"The money."

"Oh, yes." He smiled, then in exaggerated movements, ripped the bill in half. He handed her a piece. "You'll get the other when we finish our little talk."

She looked apprehensively toward the door. "We have to hurry. They're very strict here. The rules . . ."

He hushed her. "You're wasting time."

Lubelski told her he was interested in anything—any tiny detail—she happened to have overheard while serving Thornton and his guests.

"Oh, god," she said. "I don't know . . . I mean, I don't listen in to their boring talk. It's bad enough what we do have to do to earn a buck, ya know? And anyways, I don't really understand business talk. It's so complicated, ya know?"

"Just try."

She lowered her head. "All three of them are members, I think. One of them, this guy Thornton—he was talking about going out of town. Leaving the country."

"That's good. Go on."

"They were like arguing with each other. I mean the other two were telling Thornton it was his own fault and he wasn't gonna drag them into it."

"Into what?"

She concentrated a moment. "I don't know. All I know is this Thornton, he got very upset." She looked up brightly. "Do I get the money?"

"Think," Lubelski said sternly. "There must have been something else."

She rubbed her face. "They mentioned a name . . ."

"Whittaker?"

"Yeah—that was it! How did ya know?"

"What about him?"

"Like he'd been giving him—I mean, Thornton—something."

"What?"

"Information, I guess."

Lubelski smiled. So a Wall Street stockbroker, apparently very worried and preparing to flee the country, had been receiving information from Whittaker, who, in turn, had had some sort of secret arrangement with a British embassy official.

He handed the woman the remaining half of the bill, removed the ostensibly missing cuff link from his jacket pocket and returned it to his sleeve.

The woman held the two parts together to check their match, then looked vainly for some place to put them—her apron lacked pockets.

Lubelski left her. Back in the lobby, smiling broadly, he flashed the cuff link at the bouncer. "I had the feeling I'd find it."

"Must be your lucky day," the bouncer said.

"You may be right."

Lubelski found an empty telephone booth a block away. He called a special number. A woman answered.

"I'd like to talk about my retirement account," he said. It was the code word for her to summon Petrovich.

Petrovich came to the line shortly. "This is Mr. Lincoln. May I help you?" he said in heavily accented English, his voice showing irritation.

Lubelski reached into his pocket and produced a plastic device the size of a cigarette box. He placed it against the phone's mouthpiece. It was a portable electronic scrambler.

Speaking rapidly, but being careful to enunciate clearly, he provided Thornton's name, the name of his firm, and explained that the broker would be leaving on some overseas flight, probably within forty-eight hours. "It would be helpful if he had some company."

There was silence for a moment. Then Petrovich said: "We will assist him in any way possible, sir." The line went dead.

Lubelski stood holding the phone. They would probably assign the tail to Yuri. With his red hair and flab, Yuri was more American than half the freckle-faced kids in Iowa. In prior jobs with Lubelski, Yuri had successfully posed as a plumber, a television repairman, and a house painter. This time he would probably pass himself off as—Lubelski smiled—a salesman! Yes, fat, fast-talking Yuri, who could recite the scores of every National Football League game played the previous Sunday, and list the entire roster of the 1957 American League All-Star team, would be a salesman.

12

First Secretary David Holmes pressed a button on his intercom. His secretary responded. He needed help, he told her, something strong for his stomach; it was on fire—again.

"Perhaps you have a touch of the flu, sir," the woman suggested.

"Perhaps," he said, doubling over against the glass top of his desk to ease the pain.

But it wasn't the flu irritating Holmes' stomach. It was the arrival of Breckenridge Collingsworth, the P.M.'s troubleshooter and hatchetman. A lifetime of civil service, years of sleeplessness, labor, and worry for the crown, meant nothing to the likes of Collingsworth.

It figured London would send him. And the ambitious, untrustworthy commoner would only muck things up. Still, Collingsworth had seemed impressed with the news Holmes had related to him on the phone. And it *did* seem to make sense.

The secretary arrived with a glass of bubbling bicarbonate of soda. Holmes dismissed her with a wave of his hand, then stared at the fizzing liquid, reviewing what exactly it was he had told the young fixer from 10 Downing.

The FBI had called, the director himself, with a tip, Holmes had explained. The call involved the most confidential of information. One of their New York agents, it seemed, had just been contacted by a very reliable informant. The informant—and God knows who he was—had a message that was indeed disturbing. The FBI director said he was distressed, but it was his duty to advise the British government that Mr. James Whittaker had been a target for Soviet recruitment and, unknowingly, of course, he had had extensive contact with at least one Eastern Bloc agent. It was quite clear to the informant that the Soviets had been setting up Whittaker to make a move—and perhaps had done so.

If true, the FBI director added, it was quite possible Whittaker had somehow served his purpose, and was murdered to keep him quiet.

For his own part, Holmes had told Collingsworth, he always suspected there was a foreign angle to Whittaker's activities. Then Holmes cautioned that the tip was strictly confidential and unofficial, and that the New York police had not been informed, chiefly because the director was searching for a way to establish federal jurisdiction over the case, regretting that his bureau had not stepped right in, as it would have in the beginning had it not been for two woefully inexperienced agents. Their next assignments would take them to North Dakota and Mississippi, respectively.

Reliving his conversation with Collingsworth helped calm Holmes' stomach. He had handled it well, he concluded. Collingsworth certainly had seemed receptive to the theory.

The veteran diplomat had also welcomed Collingsworth's descriptions of the detectives handling the case. This Golden, the chief, was a showboat, it appeared. A politician. And Ling, his key detective, sounded like the typical New York cop—lower class, uneducated, part thug. True, Ling had an interesting case-solving record, but even his own superiors had not seen fit to reward him. Given enough chances, even a blind man can shoot a target.

Holmes rose from his desk. His knees felt a bit shaky, but he could delay his task no longer. He told his secretary he would be back in a few minutes, that he needed a bit of fresh air and so on. He left the embassy and walked to the nearest Metro subway station. A public telephone was near the automatic ticket-dispensing machines. Holmes looked around—

except for two confused tourists and a student fumbling in his pocket for change, the area was empty.

He laid out a few dollars' worth of coins, then dialed a number in Brooklyn. The usual gruff voice answered.

"This is Washington. Let me speak to him."

"Well, he's kind of busy right now and . . ."

"Damn it! Put him on!"

Another voice presently came to the line, his voice dripping with good will. "Well, if it isn't my good friend in our nation's capital. How are you, sir?"

"You heard the news, I presume," Holmes said.

"Such a tragedy! And he was so young!"

"I'm through. I don't want you contacting me anymore."

"What? I can barely hear ya, Holmes. You in a train station or somethin'?"

"No names, for godsake. What *is* the matter with you!"

"I can't hear you."

"I said it's over as far as I'm concerned and I never want to see or talk to your people again."

The line was silent for a moment. "I'm hurt, Mr. Ambassador. I have feelings, too, ya know."

Holmes hung up the phone.

"Excuse me, sir, but could you tell me how to work these machines?" It was a young man in his twenties. He was wearing a suit, and his eyes were hidden by sunglasses. Sharp pain jolted Holmes' insides.

"I'm afraid I don't feel well," he said, pushing past the stranger and dashing into a nearby men's room. When he emerged a few minutes later, the young man was gone from the arcade. A train was pulling into the station. Holmes rushed to the electronic turnstiles. From there he could see most of the station's platform. He looked down toward the tracks. The man with the sunglasses was among those stepping onto the train.

Holmes inhaled deeply. His fear had been unfounded. He would have to beware of paranoia, of acting out of character, of sending any signal that hinted at his final plan. He had one remaining success to engineer—then he would retire.

Holmes adjusted his tie and buttoned his coat. He headed for the station exit. Work awaited him at the office.

13

A grim-faced patrolman stood outside the apartment door. A strip of yellow tape marked "Police Crime Scene" was stretched across the doorframe. Ling and Collingsworth ducked under the tape. The cop looked curiously at Collingsworth but recognized Ling and did not challenge them as they entered.

The apartment, in contrast to Ling's last visit, was eerily quiet. The windows were closed and the air was musty. Ling opened one.

"The apartment belongs to a wealthy young man by the name of Robert Crayton Samuels. We're looking for him now. Apparently, he had befriended Whittaker and was letting him stay here," Ling explained.

Collingsworth walked around the living room, inspecting the art and furnishings. "A rather plush flat, I must say."

Ling led him into the master bedroom. "The corpses were found in here; one on the floor, one on the bed." An outline of a body was rendered in black chalk on the white shag rug. A small pool of blood had hardened, turning a very dark brown. The bed linen had remained unchanged. The sheets showed bloodstains where the woman's head had rested. The odor of death seemed to linger. Ling opened another window.

The Englishman studied the area where Whittaker had fallen, then said: "I feel as though we're intruding, as if we're violating their privacy and shouldn't be here."

Ling nodded. "It happens."

Collingsworth looked at him. "One doesn't think of it, that they take away the bodies and the police go, and still there remains the bloody debris for some soul to clean up. And the regular occupant, this Samuels, how can he possibly move back here knowing what happened in this room? Or, for that matter, how could a new tenant move in?"

Ling smiled. "With the apartment situation in Manhattan, they'd step on their mothers to get their hands on the lease. Many a cop has broken up a fight over claims to an apartment, even before the morgue wagon arrives."

"You don't say?" Collingsworth asked incredulously.

Ling showed him into the huge bathroom with its sunken tub, statue of David and wallpaper featuring silhouetted couples engaged in various acts of love. Ling opened the medicine cabinet. It was jammed with prescription bottles in the name of Samuels. Ling picked them up one by one. "Uppers, downers. The boy has them all." They all bore the name of the same physician, whom Ling recognized as a no questions asked East Side healer favored by the Park Avenue crowd.

He replaced the bottles and photographed the collection, taking three shots to be sure.

Back in the bedroom, Ling moved to the wall of electronics equipment and opened one of the built-in cabinets. The upper shelves were filled with erotica: *The Story of O*, *The Kama Sutra* and other classics of eroticism, in what Ling judged to be collectors' editions. On the bottom shelf, stacked haphazardly, were hundreds of glossy so-called magazines of the type once hidden behind counters but now sold openly in Times Square. Ling gave a handful to Collingsworth, who examined their covers. They ran the gamut of fast-track sex: S&M, bondage, gay, oriental, bathhouse, Greek, salt and pepper.

"Quite a library, I must say. Do you think anything's been missed?" Collingsworth asked.

"Anything there about three-legged dogs and left-handed mermaids?"

Ling spread an assortment of the publications on the bed, then leaned over and photographed them.

He replaced the magazines and books, then moved to the large color television monitor. To the side were a half-dozen electronic decks, including two video recorders, a sound mixer, a video editing console and an audio tape player. "There's at least fifteen-thousand dollars' worth of equipment here," Ling said. "And there's another system in the living room."

He studied the rows of silver-fronted consoles in detail, noting their special features and complex wiring. The setup was sophisticated and powerful, its orderliness and efficiency similar to that found in Ling's darkroom. He stepped back and focused the Nikon on the electronics wall, snapped two quick frames, then moved in for close-ups of each individual unit. He had just clicked off his second shot when the telephone rang. Ling picked up the bedside extension.

It was Triano. "The chief told me to call. I've got those phone records, Monk. Sorry it took so long but our phone company cousins all of a sudden started worrying about warrants."

"So you got one?"

"Judge Michaels. Piece of cake."

"Good. Anything interesting?"

"You might say that. This guy had calls to the White House—dozens of them. And one call the day before the murders to a downtown hotel. We checked it out—the female victim was staying there. Registered under the name of Michelle Pilat."

"Phony?"

"I think so. Paid a hefty deposit in cash so she didn't produce any credit card. Bellboy ID'd her picture. And that's not all—seems as though some gentleman claiming to be her brother checked out for her this morning."

"Got a make on him?"

"Only a description. Kind of vague. The clerk who handled it either isn't too bright or he's stoned. Maybe both."

"What's the description?"

"Man in his sixties. Powerfully built. Glasses. Hair as white as the coke the asshole clerk was probably snortin'."

Ling thanked him and hung up.

"Something significant?" Collingsworth asked.

"Not sure, yet."

Ling told him of the White House number showing up in the billing records for the apartment telephone and how a mysterious man had appeared at a hotel apparently used by the female victim.

"What does it mean?" the Englishman asked.

"Someone was working the girl, setting up a con, maybe. Could be a pimp, but I doubt it. Or someone—"

"Preparing to buy the prime minister's brother," Collingsworth interrupted.

"The thought did occur to me." Ling waited for more. But Collingsworth's face tightened and he averted his eyes toward the floor, the actions of a man who perhaps now regretted having blurted out a theory. The Englishman said nothing.

Ling turned back toward the electronic wall. The next two cabinets revealed shelf after shelf of stereo records, audio tapes and videotape cassettes. The videotapes appeared nearly evenly divided between standard commercial films, including many classics, and X-rated editions reflecting the same wide range of interests as did the magazines. Ling photographed the collection, then noticed that one of the shelves was full of non-commercial tapes for home recording. The boxes were numbered with a black marker from one to thirty-two. Printed on each in neat block letters were the contents, television films and specials mostly, along with some cable TV sex-related shows. Three of the cassettes were devoted to news clips of anti-nuclear activities. And one in the series—number eight—was missing.

Ling pointed this out to Collingsworth, who then spotted a cassette box, labeled number eight, resting at the side of the television monitor. Ling looked more closely at the two video recorders; one was empty—the other contained the missing cassette.

"Let's see what we have here," he said, turning on the recorder and the monitor. He rewound the tape and pushed the "play" button.

The screen came to life with "Monday Night Football."

Ling and Collingsworth looked at each other. "What in bloody hell is all that?" the Englishman exclaimed.

Ling laughed. "American football."

"Those helmets, those shoulder devices—excuse me for

saying so, but they look ridiculous. We've got nothing like that in rugby.''

Ling considered pointing out that rugby also lacked three-hundred pound linemen but decided against it. Instead, he changed the subject, explaining how video recorders could be programmed to come on at a certain time on a given day.

''Is that what happened here?'' Collingsworth asked.

Ling pushed a series of buttons to check for settings stored in the machine's memory. The digital display showed that no advance programming had been entered.

''What does that mean?'' Collingsworth asked.

''Someone decided to record the last three quarters of the football game.''

''Three quarters?''

''They just flashed to the scoreboard—it showed the second quarter.''

Ling stopped the tape—he would have the entire reel reviewed for its contents later—and went into the kitchen. He returned with a pair of tongs and a plastic bag.

''This we're going to have dusted,'' he said, ejecting the cassette and carefully placing it into the bag with the tongs.

They continued their inspection of the bedroom, Ling pointing out the large collection of vibrators, dildos and other sexual paraphernalia in the dresser.

''Like a damn brothel,'' Collingsworth noted, staring in awe at the man-sized phallic floor sculpture.

''Just your ordinary run of the mill East Side apartment,'' Ling answered. ''I've seen better.'' He motioned toward the bed. ''Sit down for a moment, would you please?''

''Excuse me?''

''Have a seat,'' Ling said sternly.

Collingsworth, puzzled, sat down on a corner of the waterbed, which began undulating from his movement. With his Nikon to his eye, Ling continued to move about the room, taking shots of the fixtures and furnishings from varying perspectives.

''Mr. Collingsworth, you told me earlier today,'' Ling said, as he worked the camera, ''that your government feared Mr. Whittaker was buyable.''

''Yes, of course—that was our fear.''

Click. Click.

"Then when one of my colleagues informs us that the dead woman apparently had an accomplice, you immediately deduce that they could have been working in consort to recruit Whittaker into some kind of scheme."

"Yes. Surely it *is* possible. I'm certain you agree," Collingsworth answered, bewildered at the questioning.

Click.

"Yes I do . . ." Click. Click. Ling stopped. He looked into the Englishman's eyes. ". . . but I also have this feeling you have a little more evidence than I do from which to reach that conclusion."

Collingsworth bowed his head, thinking, then looked up, saying: "A man and a woman, working together— It makes sense, that's all."

"Except for this gut feeling of mine, this suspicion that there's a missing piece, something maybe I don't know." Ling paused. "*Is* there something I don't know?"

The Englishman lowered his eyes, then slowly nodded. "I was under orders—from my embassy. It was during that phone call from Washington."

Ling snapped off three more frames, then dropped the camera to his chest. "Perhaps it would be in *both* of our interests if you tell me all of it—now."

Collingsworth pondered for a moment, then related to Ling the FBI director's call to First Secretary David Holmes and the unconfirmed information that the Soviets indeed had sighted Whittaker as a potential pigeon.

Ling braced for the anger to rise within him—how the hell were the police supposed to conduct a homicide investigation when a key piece of information was withheld from them— but no anger came. In its place was resignation—it was not the first time New York detectives and a federal agency had fenced with each other.

"Let me be blunt with you, Mr. Collingsworth," Ling said finally. "You go to the Federal Bureau of Investigation and tell *them* you'd like to tag along with them as they chase this case. See how far 'hands across the sea,' and all that gets you with them."

Collingsworth stood. "You've made your point—and I apologize. It won't happen again."

"Is there anything else you think I ought to know?"

The Englishman turned away. A hand moved to his chin. His eyes were on the bronze sculpture. He took a step, then faced Ling again. "It's very hush, hush. The press never got on to it."

"What's that?"

"Actually, it's probably irrelevant and . . ."

"At this point," Ling interrupted, "everything is relevant."

Collingsworth returned to his seat on the corner of the bed. "It was eight years ago. Nine, actually, when Whittaker lost his wife."

"You said it was a traffic accident."

"It was," the Englishman said defensively. "But—"

"But what?"

Collingsworth pressed forward. "You must promise me you will keep this absolutely confidential—unless, of course, it somehow proves pertinent to the case. The murders are scandalous enough as it is for the prime minister without having to dredge up the bitter past."

"You have my word," Ling said with sincerity.

The Englishman looked to the blank television screen a moment, then back to Ling. "You must understand," he said, "who Whittaker's wife was."

"Nobility?"

"Quite. Purebred stock. But what I should have stated was not who she was but rather what she was."

"I don't understand."

"She was a goddess, Ling, a reigning goddess. Twenty-four when she died, I believe, and every man in England lusted after her from the day she turned fifteen. She was one in a million, one of those women innately capable of touching the very soul and spirit of a man."

"And Whittaker was jealous."

"Of course. But that was not the problem. The problem was his wife was . . . shall we say . . . a bit unbalanced."

"Emotionally disturbed."

"Yes. That's a quaint way to frame it. She was placed under treatment almost yearly. Eventually, all the psychiatric rituals seemed at last to have worked. For more than a year, she acted as if cured. And then, apparently with no warning, she tried to kill poor Whittaker.''

"How?"

"They were in this old Hillman she kept as a toy. She was driving. They were speeding. And she steered the damn thing directly into a stone wall.''

"Terrific!" Ling said, shaking his head. "That's when she was killed.''

"Yes—and more importantly, that's when Whittaker nearly died. His whole lower torso was crushed. He had surgery on seven or eight occasions. And he was never the same again.''

Ling knew well the impact of the unexpected death of a wife. "That's understandable—to a degree.''

"But there's more.'' Collingsworth glanced to the floor briefly, considering what he was about to say, then looked into Ling's eyes. "The accident—that's what we call it, an accident—it left Whittaker impotent.''

"Permanently?''

"The doctors didn't think so. They could find no physical reason for it, and they ultimately concluded that it was all in his head. But it was some time, three or four years, before Whittaker could function again.''

"And then he set out on his international odyssey of decadence and adventure.''

"Yes,'' Collingsworth said resignedly.

Ling studied him a moment, then smiled. "Thanks for your candor. It helps to understand what motivated a homicide victim." He paused. "I think we can go now.''

Ling, his mood upbeat, pointed out some of the sights as they drove back to the station house. Collingsworth, also buoyed, asked many questions and laughed heartily at a group of street mimes they watched while waiting for a red light.

Back in the squad room, Ling immediately excused himself from Collingsworth, found Golden, and briefed him on the FBI involvement. As expected, Golden went into a rage, stopping only when Dotty Levine came in to report.

Golden held her off, waving the Englishman over instead. A lecture on professional courtesies and British-American mutual trust followed, including a caution that Golden had strong ties across the Atlantic, what with his wife being a bull-headed Swede, not to mention his days with the U.S. Army in West Germany. Collingsworth took it stoically. The skin of a diplomat, Ling thought.

Finished with the Englishman, Golden's eyes searched for the two FBI agents, but both had disappeared. "Those sons of bitches come back, I wanna have a talk with them," he declared, then turned to Levine. "What bad tidings do you bear?"

"Still no line on the whereabouts of this kid Samuels, chief," she said. "His father claims he hasn't heard from him in more than a month. But intelligence had a pretty good file on him."

The file, she said, painted the picture of a very bright blue blood with an Ivy League background, who had never asserted himself in anything, until he got active a little less than two years earlier in the anti-nuclear movement. Then he became a swirl of motion: trips to Cuba, Moscow, Angola. Speaking engagements from Brooklyn to Berkeley. Black-tie fundraisers with the Central Park West crowd. A book contract being negotiated. Sudden, heretofore unknown popularity.

"Someday," Golden said, "somebody is going to tell it like it is—that half the people in these movements are nothing more than lonely boys and girls lookin' to get laid."

McKinnon and Triano also had updates. McKinnon said the stepped up canvassing had produced essentially nothing, and the fingerprints lifted from the apartment were mostly those of Whittaker, Samuels, the Simpson woman, and a maid. There was at least one set yet to be identified.

Triano summarized what had been documented about Samantha Simpson's background. His report basically confirmed what Ling had instinctively expected, and what she herself had allowed. Triano added that there was still no progress in learning the true identity of the female victim, the name Michelle Pilat having been dismissed as undoubtedly bogus.

Ling turned to Collingsworth, who had listened to it all in silence. "You said Whittaker had been pressing his sister for an ambassadorship, among other things."

"That's correct."

"Who was his contact in this country to press those demands? He must have had one."

"Secretary Holmes was designated to handle him."

"And did he?"

"Not with any more success than anyone back home."

With that, Collingsworth said that he was finding it difficult now to even keep his eyes open and thought it best that he retire to his hotel.

Ling gave him his home number. "Call for anything." He took the Englishman's arm and escorted him away from the others. "You and I, Breck—we're gonna get along."

With Collingsworth gone, Ling went downstairs to the precinct commander's office. He asked if he could use the phone. The captain, saying he would gladly do anything to help close the case and expel all the brass from his station house, readily surrendered his desk.

Ling dialed information in Washington, and obtained the number for a veteran New York newspaper reporter who had broken in on the New York police beat and moved on to politics and government. The last seven years he had spent in the capital, a fixture on the Georgetown dinner party circuit.

Ling found him at his news bureau.

"I need some background, Eddie, but strictly off the record."

"For you, Monk, anything—I have a long memory for those that helped me."

"An Englishman, David Holmes. Some kind of diplomat."

The reporter laughed. "You really find 'em, Monk. Holmes is a Washington institution. Worse than me. Been here twenty, maybe twenty-five years. Knows his way around. Keeps his job no matter what party's in power. Growing kind of cynical with age. Could be pissed off, I guess, that they've always passed him over and never given him the embassy, I don't know."

They exchanged pleasantries, and Ling promised to look him up if he ever got to Washington, a distinct possibility in this case.

Back upstairs, Ling advised Golden he would be hitting the streets.

"Give me just a tiny hint, would ya?" the chief said.

"Got a date with a young lady, only she doesn't know it."

"Who might that be?"

"Samantha Simpson. I think she kind of likes me," Ling answered. And maybe, he told himself, a few minutes' time with a Samantha Simpson was what he needed.

"Watch it, Monk," Golden called out after him.

14

"We've got to cancel it!" Robert Crayton Samuels III was screaming. "I can't go on like this, do you hear me?"

"Sit down, Robert. Calm yourself," the woman named Josie said, her voice soft and comforting.

Samuels complied, taking a seat on a small sofa in the tiny living room of Josie's two-room Greenwich Village apartment. She sat in a director's chair opposite him.

"Look, I can understand why you're upset, but we can't cancel the rally. For god's sake, it's bigger than any one person. Bigger than Whittaker. Bigger than you."

"But he was going to be the key speaker, the one the news media would pay attention to, and now he won't be there." Samuels leaned forward, the overhead track lights harshly accentuating the dark circles under his eyes. "They *murdered* him. He was going to speak out for peace and the bastards got him. Next they'll come after me."

"For chrissake, Robert, nobody wants to kill you—except me, maybe, for the phone bill you've run up here in the last two days. Do you have to call everybody in the whole goddamned world?"

"I'll pay you, Josie, you know that."

She went to the mini-refrigerator for a can of beer. "You want one?"

"Don't think I should."

"Who are you kiddin'? You're popping pills like candy. Try some beer instead."

"The doctor tells me I need that medication."

She laughed derisively. "No wonder you can't get it up."

Samuels returned to the sofa. They were silent for a while. Then Samuels said: "You know, Josie, you use people. I mean there's a lot of sincerity around, especially in the movement, but you . . . you use people."

"And I suppose you don't? Little rich boy with nothing to do, so he becomes a self-appointed expert on peace. You think all these starry-eyed kids look up to you because of your profound thoughts or something? It's your money, man. They're intimidated by it. They say they don't want it but they're in awe of it. And you're right there suckin' it up, playing the game like your old man plays polo."

He was shaking his head. "I don't believe you're saying this, Josie. I really don't."

"What about Whittaker? You didn't use him? He was your magic password to the network news. And what happened to him?"

"Stop it, Josie! I mean it!"

"Oh, go stick it, Robert. I'm sick of you, sick of your type. You're nothing but an asshole anyway. No balls."

His hands were covering his eyes. "You can't mean this. I know you don't. You're just upset, just like I am, and . . ."

"Stop your whimpering," she shouted. "You sound like a dog."

"But they killed him. James Whittaker. He's dead!"

The woman had had enough. She grabbed Samuels by the collar with one hand and began slapping his face with the back of the other. "Get the hell out of here. I never want to see you again. You or your money."

"But . . ."

There was a knock at the door.

"Now who the hell is this," she complained, "more of your dainty little bearded friends?" She moved to the door. "Who is it?"

"Police. Open up please." It was a female's voice.

Samuels jumped to his feet. He began to turn white. "Oh, my god!"

Josie opened the door. A short, middle-aged woman flashed a gold shield. Two uniformed patrolmen stood behind her.

The detective looked beyond Josie to the slender, boyish man. "Are you Robert Samuels?" Dotty Levine asked.

He nodded.

"I'm afraid you'll have to come with me, please. We'd like to ask you some questions."

Josie stepped between them. "He has a right to have a lawyer, doesn't he? And what are the charges?"

Samuels put a hand on her shoulder. "I don't need a lawyer." He looked to the detective. "Am I being charged with anything?"

"Not now. That is, not unless you force me to. If so, there's a little matter of some cocaine in your apartment."

"I know nothing about that!" he protested. "I have nothing to do with drugs!"

"And snow ain't white. Let's go," Levine said.

He reached into Josie's two-foot wide closet for his coat and pulled a small vial from a pocket. "Just let me take my pills, okay? See—it's a doctor's prescription."

"Unless and until you're booked for something, what you do is your own business, son," the detective said, stepping forward to lead him away.

"I'm sorry, Robert," Josie called after him. "I didn't mean it."

A hand was on his arm, hustling him down the stairs. Josie said she was sorry—and he knew she meant it. Behind all her feminist aggression was a core of sisterly compassion for him. And he would need her support now. All that was coming down—the bloodshed, the bullying police, the betrayal—was so frightening to him.

Josie was following them. "I'll call your father," she shouted.

"No!" he yelled back. "Anybody but him."

15

The evening was early enough, Ling suspected, that Samantha
Simpson would likely still be at home. She was—Manhattan's
night shift had yet to begin.

A new doorman was on duty. This time, Ling kept his
shield in his pocket and allowed himself to be announced,
not that she wouldn't be forewarned of his arrival, anyway.
Upstairs, Samantha was once again waiting at her apartment
door.

"My lucky day," she said sarcastically.

She was wearing tight new jeans, their color not yet faded,
and she was braless beneath a body-hugging bright red top.
She made no move to step aside from the door.

"I'm glad I caught you," Ling said.

"What do I have to do, beg for you to leave me alone?"

Ling smiled. "May I come in?"

"I was just leaving."

"Then let me buy you a drink. You must have time for a
drink."

"Oh, I get it"—she grinned; her eyes filled with disdain—
"I've got to fuck my way out of this."

Ling matched her false smile. "You don't seem to understand the significance of this, how history is being made here,
right here, at your door."

"What are you talking about?"

"Here stands the very first man Samantha Simpson has met in New York, outside of the few fags in her various circles, who doesn't want to get in her pants." His eyes, however, had done just that.

She hesitated, then shrugged her shoulders. "What the hell, come on in."

Ling didn't move. "I meant it—about buying you a drink."

"That in your police handbook?"

"It's in mine."

"Well, at least tell me your name again. I had no cause at all to remember it."

"Monk Ling."

They walked to a bar on the corner, dimly lit, barmaids with aprons, one of a hundred mock Irish pubs in the city. There was much wood, most of it laminated, and several hanging plastic ferns. The tables and booths featured red and white checkered tablecloths and candle vases tightly bound with netting, also plastic. Prominently placed on the bar was a credit card billing machine, and on the wall, a collection of fiberglass beer company displays. The men outnumbered women four to one along the bar, most of them still wearing their business suits, but with ties loosened. Advertising men, purchasing agents, insurance underwriters—all on the prowl in a communal cage that would prove productive for a very, very few.

Ling led Samantha to a booth in the rear. There was no one else near them. The bartender, who wore a vest and had garter bands on his sleeves, gave her a glance that revealed she was known—Samantha and another of her middle-aged men. He then looked at Ling. His eyes had a message: Beware, mister—watch the claws.

She ordered Scotch; he, soda water.

"Little drinkin' problem, huh?" she teased. "All you cops are the same."

"It's my legs. I get drunk, they hurt in dance class."

"Neon aerobics. Lot of that in New York. Very popular."

The drinks came.

"What is this Ling business?" she asked. "You don't look Chinese to me."

He laughed. "Oh, but I am. I speak it. I live it. There was a day, I smoked it."

"Come on, you're not oriental."

"My stepfather was."

"And your mother?"

"Irish."

Her fingers massaged her glass. "How'd that happen?"

"You want the truth?"

"Guys like you don't know the word."

He ignored the jab. "My mother lived in Hong Kong. She was a hooker." He allowed the word to hang.

"You trying to be funny or somethin'?"

"It's the truth."

"I don't believe you."

"It doesn't matter." He resumed sipping from his glass.

Her eyes were still upon him. "Well, who was your father, then?"

"My real daddy? Best guess is he was Scandinavian. From Norway."

"And your mother named you Monk?"

"Naw, she named me Ezekiel. Liked the sound of it. And it was in the Bible."

Samantha rested her elbows on the table and leaned forward. "So then she married this Chinaman?"

Ling shook his head. "No. She left Hong Kong and abandoned me. I guess I was about a month old. Ling, he was her whoremaster. He took me as his own."

"And brought you to New York and everyone lived happily ever after."

"Not quite. Ling got chased from the colony by a Tong war he couldn't win. Emigrated to San Francisco and took up every petty racket he had left behind—drugs, gambling, illegal immigrants. I grew up in a mushroom cloud of opium smoke."

"Maybe that explains it, this class act you got."

Ling smiled. "Maybe you're right."

She thought a moment, then said, "I'm still not sure I believe you."

"It's the truth."

And it was.

They sipped their drinks in silence, she gazing around the bar, Ling watching her. She looked down to her glass, then up, and their eyes met. There was an uncharacteristic mellowness to her eyes. Whether through fatigue, or the first swallows of Scotch warming her throat, she had let her guard down.

"You're running hard after something, only you don't know what it is," Ling said gently.

"What the hell's that supposed to mean?" she responded, her tone softer than her words.

"You wake up every morning and find each day the same as before. Different names, perhaps, but the same bland faces, and inside you've got this empty feeling. You wonder if there isn't more to it than this. You wonder where you missed the turn, where your dreams have gone."

"You have all the answers. Do you know the questions?"

"Too many of them."

She sat back against the booth's pseudo-varnish plastic finish. "Look, I added everything up once and figured my best shot was in public relations. So I put in an application with a big Madison Avenue firm. This asshole who interviewed me had a nice Brooks Brothers suit. Every hair was in place. He didn't stop smiling. But his hands didn't stop shaking and the whites of his eyes just about matched the yellow in his shirt."

The waitress arrived and, unasked, served them fresh drinks—probably, Ling suspected, standard procedure for Samantha and her marks. He wondered if she received a cut, but decided a percentage of the bar tabs here would be insignificant compared to the other fees she commanded. Probably just a smart bartender, confident no man in Samantha's grasp was about to object to another round.

"So this guy smiled a lot and liked his Scotch," Ling said. "What else is new?"

"Well, this Mr. Madison Avenue pours me a drink," she continued. "He tells me he got his start as a public relations flack for the city. The Department of Highways or something like that. And everytime it rained, the radio stations would be calling him at home asking about what roads were flooded. In the beginning, he'd make a few calls to find out. Then he discovered that the flooded roads were always the same. He wrote them down and taped the list by his bed. Then, whenever the radio stations would call, he'd tell them he had the latest information right there, all at the ready, and he'd read them his list. They'd go on the air and tell I don't know how many million commuters to avoid this highway and that." She leaned forward. "And that, he said, was the dirty little secret of big league P.R. I told him to shove it up his ass and walked out."

"Life's a lie, like your mother said."

She grinned. "Not the way I live it."

"You're bitter and you're deceiving yourself."

"I'm not bitter—I wallow in reality."

Ling studied her awhile, then asked: "When have you eaten last?"

"None of your damn business."

He summoned the waitress for menus. Samantha refused hers. Ling ordered London broil for them both.

"Jesus, you're pushy," she said. "You that way with your wife?"

"Haven't got one."

"Divorced, huh. Every cop is."

"No."

"Come on, guy like you marries when he's nineteen."

"I had a wife—she died."

Her eyes grew busy, bouncing from her drink to her hands to the pictures on the wall as she searched for words. "Cancer or something?"

"Childbirth."

She considered that a moment, then asked: "The baby?"

"Lost him, too."

She was looking at him suspiciously.

"Go ahead and say it," he said.

"Say what?"

"What you're thinking."

"Well, with modern medicine and . . ." She stopped and restarted: "It's not that I don't believe you; it's just that I didn't think that happened anymore."

"Neither did I."

She finished her drink, then asked: "Any other kids?"

"The boy would have been the first."

"I'm sorry."

He watched her face. The tough Manhattan hustler had softened. For an instant, her hair was long and curly again and she was wearing a pink dress and sitting on a white-painted wrought-iron bench in the community square of some small Texas town.

She read his thoughts and blushed in embarrassment. She was saved by the arrival of the food.

"What's that stupid camera for, anyway?" she asked, pointing to the Nikon resting on the table.

"I'm looking for models."

"Knew you had an angle. They always do."

She attacked the beef as if she had not eaten in a week, then noticed him watching and slowed. "You're bitter yourself, aren't you," she said.

Ling laughed. "Not me, lady. I'm collected."

She looked up from her plate. "Bullshit! You're dripping with it. Probably something to do with Vietnam. Everybody older than thirty-five seems to be hung up on Vietnam."

"So maybe I am—I was a sucker."

"How?"

Ling sat back. He didn't really want to drag it all out again. Yet he also had an urge to do just that. "They told me to work hard in high school and I'd get into a good college," he said crisply. "Then they told me to get my degree and in a lifetime I'd earn maybe half a million dollars more than a high school dropout plumber. They told me to answer my country's so-called 'call to duty' because I'd be respected and those who didn't would be ostracized the rest of their lives." He paused. "So I got good grades and went on to college and finished my degree and enlisted in the Army." He put his arms on the table and leaned forward. "And now the plumber earns more than the college graduate, and the draft dodgers not only are not branded for life as cowards, but used the four years of freedom denied me to advance their goddamned careers to where every veteran finds one of them his boss."

"Whew!" she said, shaking her head. "You're one pissed off dude."

"I thought you'd understand," Ling responded, sarcastically. "And I'm glad you do because, you see, there were very few women my age who did."

Samantha appeared confused. "I don't get it," she said.

Ling took a deep breath. "We got our leave time, see, and so I went to some of the peace rallies. San Francisco. Berkeley. Even the Chicago Democratic Convention. I was there. Listened to Hoffman and Rubin and Dellinger and the rest. I looked around. And I knew that there were three grunts over in 'Nam more sincere about ending the war for every longhair I counted. I looked around and saw 4-F's, fairies, and pubescent boys with hard-ons who found anti-war rallies a good, cheap way to get some head. And I saw all the sweet little honeys with their iron-pressed hair get all moist and worked up in this global village orgy and fall over each other to give the first phony conscientious objector, man that he was, some service."

She was grinning. "So don't scream at me—*I* wasn't there."

He stared at her. She was right, of course. At her age, how the hell could she know what he was talking about?

Ling felt embarrassed—and vulnerable. Samantha also appeared uncomfortable. Their attention returned to their plates. Again, she forked up the food lustily. Finally, between bites, she asked: "These murders, do you think you'll solve them?"

The subject was back where Ling wanted it. "Yes," he answered.

"Are you always so sure of yourself?"

"No. Very seldom, in fact."

"Why now?"

"For one thing, you're going to help me."

She put down her fork. "What makes you so certain of that?"

Ling didn't answer. He began eating his meal. She gave up, resumed her eating and finished off the plate. She patted her lips with her napkin, then asked: "Mind if I smoke?"

Ling stopped eating. He picked up a book of matches from the ashtray and lit her cigarette. Then, lifting his fork again and studying his food, he asked: "Who was paying you, Sam?"

She stared at him, then took a nervous puff from her cigarette. "What if I told you nobody?"

"You're too smart for that." Ling pushed his plate away.

"Maybe I loved the guy."

"A cowgirl like you with that Englishman?"

The waitress came for their plates. Both ordered coffee.

Samantha's eyes were on the red and white checkered tablecloth. "Samuels," she said, almost inaudibly.

Ling smiled. "You had the British fooled. They think you might have been working for their opposition party."

She looked up. "Someone like that did approach me—after I'd already hooked up with Whittaker. Said he'd pay me for anything, anything at all, about Whittaker."

"You declined?"

"It may surprise you, but I do have *some* ethics," she snapped. "Besides, I kind of liked the guy."

"Yet you took Samuels' money."

"Whittaker didn't know it."

"This guy who approached you, was he foreign?"

"Another Englishman."

"You sure?"

"Yeah—but I was hardly in a position to demand his passport."

The coffee came. Ling passed her the cream and sugar. "How did this little arrangement with Samuels come about?" he asked.

She hesitated, stirring her coffee. "Samuels set it up like an accidental meeting. It was at a dinner party. Whittaker and I hit it off, and Samuels continued to pay me. Said he wanted to keep the guy happy so he'd stay in New York, at least through this damned rally."

Ling drank from his coffee, then asked: "What was Whittaker like?"

"A hustler. That's why we hit it off so well. We were on the same wavelength. Like, I knew that he suspected Samuels was paying the tab and he knew that I knew, but we pretended otherwise." She paused a moment, then added: "His wife tried to kill him, did you know?"

"Yes, the British told me. Did he talk about it?"

"Once is all—but he went on and on for half the night about it."

Ling knew what it meant to lose a wife; he didn't know what it meant to have had that wife try to take you with her.

"You called him a hustler," he said. "He apparently had his hands in a lot of things."

She nodded. "But he was pretty good at it. Secretive. I didn't learn much."

"What *did* you learn?"

She thought for a moment. "He'd get these calls for a while. Some smartass with a Brooklyn accent. Then he'd go meet him somewhere. There was also a stockbroker. Only reason I know that is his secretary left his office number one day and I checked it out. Then there was this chick from Washington. Very brainy, but basically your number one drip. Looked like she was in her late thirties, but I think she was younger than that. Don't ask me what he was chasin' her for—only thing I know for sure is that it wasn't for her tail."

"Know her name?"

"No. He was careful not to use it—very hush, hush about that one. And if your guys find her, they'd better watch out—she'll serve up their balls."

Ling pulled out his notebook and began writing. "The stockbroker you mentioned, what was his name?"

"Thornton," she said without hesitation. "I never did learn his first name. Little more than a kid, really, but he was riding around in a steel-gray Mercedes. One of those guys who vows to make his first million by the age of thirty, and would hand over his mother to do it."

"Why did you leave?"

"Samuels told me I was off the payroll—effective immediately. He said Whittaker all of a sudden was refusing to appear at that stupid rally."

"Did Whittaker ask you to stay?"

She laughed. "Hardly."

"Why was that, do you suppose? He must have been out of his mind."

"Better merchandise showed up. The woman that was killed. One day she just appeared."

"Who was she?"

"Damned if I know. Very strange woman. European or something. Had a French accent. I thought she was kind of a psycho. But to each his own. Anyway, she didn't get far with him, whatever she was after—didn't have time, as things turned out.''

"One more thing," he said.

She looked at him.

"This Samuels, is he gay?"

Samantha laughed. "Both ways, maybe—but not gay."

"You sure?"

"He came on to me one night and insisted on testing the hired help.''

"Not too pleasant an experience, I would guess."

She smiled. "It was over in two minutes."

"Where did Whittaker hang out? What bars?"

She provided a list of more than a dozen establishments, East Side singles bars for the most part, but also some downtown spots, including an after-hours club, and a type of theater where the audience's sexual fantasies were acted out.

"That help you?" she asked.

"Yes it will. Now tell me about the cardinal."

"The cardinal?"

"Yeah—he was your alibi, right?"

Her face tightened. Her voice was harsh. "You know, I've been trying to cooperate. I mean, I could tell you to fuck off and call my lawyer. After all this help I give you, you consider me a suspect? Why would I possibly murder him?"

"Someone might say because he cut you off and kicked you out.''

"That's bullshit! I *told* you why I left!"

Ling smiled. "Of course, you did," he said softly. "Still, it would be better for the record if we knew where you were and who you were with. There'll be a grand jury on this. That jury will be mostly women. They'll resent you."

She lowered her head. "I was with a guy."

"Where?"

"The Hampstead Hotel, if you really must know."

"Who?"

"A longtime friend."

"Who?"

Samantha spit out the words: "City Councilman Jack O'Bannion."

Ling showed no reaction except to resume his note taking.

"I suppose now you'll go talk to him," she said bitterly.

"No." His eyes stayed on the notepad.

"No?"

"We won't be talking to Councilman O'Bannon."

She seemed shocked. "Why not?"

He looked at her. "Because I believe you."

Ling finished writing, then put the notebook away.

She was staring at him. "You know, you're different, aren't you. I mean you're not your normal cop," she said.

"I'm a real find."

"And all-man, huh?"

"What can I say."

She broke into a broad smile. A gleam came to her eyes. "For some reason, I like you, Monk."

As he stared at her half-parted lips, so naturally red she probably could forgo lipstick forever, as his eyes ran up and down her perfumed hair, glistening even in the subdued light of the bar, there were stirrings inside him. It wasn't fair, he told himself. She was quite aware of her power. He was tempted to seize her blatant invitation and take it to its natural conclusion. But he knew that he couldn't—and she knew it, too.

"I think I like you very much," she was saying.

Ling grew uneasy. A woman like Samantha Simpson knew instinctively when a man was low, when he was vulnerable. He could not deny his attraction to her, but was it her coyness, her intelligence and her beauty? Or was it the pathetic crying out of a man whose emotions had been beaten back by forces he neither controlled nor understood? His mind recognized the futility of learning the answer and sent up one alarm after another on how self-destructive the course was that he was steering. But he ignored the warnings, lingering instead in the warm bath of his feelings and fighting every impulse to let go.

"Why?" she asked.

"Why what?"

"Why would I like you?"

He searched for a suitable answer, something urbane and funny, then gave up. "Does it make a difference?"

She busied herself with her coffee.

"You're a weapon, Miss Simpson, do you know that? You are gifted in a way that even you, with all your experience, can't possibly comprehend. Whittaker never had a chance."

Her expression became serious. With an almost imperceptible movement, she edged back in her seat, withdrawing from whatever game they were playing. Her retreat confirmed for Ling her own awareness of how far she had taken him, of how deeply her primal magic had penetrated. Was it pity that inspired her to release her hold? Or a coldly calculated strategy?

"You don't have to fear me," she said. "I don't bite, you know."

"Neither did Eve."

Ling called for the check. The waitress said nothing as she deposited it on the table.

"Do you miss her—your wife, I mean?" Samantha asked.

"Of course," he answered in a sharp tone he immediately regretted.

"What did you do when it happened?"

"Why do you ask?"

"I'm trying to understand you, to find out where you're coming from."

"Okay—for three days I stayed in bed. In one hand I kept a bottle; in the other, my service revolver."

She showed disbelief. "I just can't picture you contemplating suicide."

"I wrote a note—then destroyed it. One day, when the sun came up, I rolled out of bed and began trying to pick up the pieces."

"Did you?"

He hesitated. "Not yet."

Her eyes were off in the distance. "My father died when I was twelve," she said. "I try very hard to remember what he was like, to remember the touch of his arm around me and the sound of his voice. But his voice is only an echo, a hollow monotone, like on an old phonograph record." Her eyes began to water. "And then I feel so very, very guilty. Inside, silently, I call out to him and apologize. I tell him how sorry I am that I can't remember. And I don't know why."

Ling reached across the table and took her hand. "See, Miss Simpson is human, after all."

She dried her cheeks with the napkin, then shook her hair and straightened her back. "This isn't healthy."

Ling stood. "I'll walk you home."

Outside, she decided instead she wanted a cab.

"You should get some sleep," Ling scolded her. "It would help you come down."

No, she protested, she wanted a cab. Ling flagged one, then held the door for her. She glanced back as she climbed in, then gave the driver directions. The taxi turned at the corner and headed crosstown.

For Samantha Simpson, the evening was young.

Ling watched the cab blend into the traffic, then found a phone and called the station house. Dotty Levine answered, and had news.

"We picked up the Samuels kid," she said.

"Where?"

"In the Village. He was staying with another activist."

"Did you get a statement?"

"Just started. The chief's got him sittin' by himself and stewin'."

"Lawyer?"

"He said he didn't do anything and therefore had no need for an attorney."

"Your kind of guy, huh?"

"Don't insult me."

Ling asked her to advise Golden he had a list of the hangouts favored by Whittaker. She returned to the line shortly, saying Golden would have O'Brien and McKinnon check them out. Ling was to take a break, the others already having done so. "Golden wants you in early to help with this kid," she said, explaining that the chief intended to release Samuels after the initial questioning, so he would have a night to contemplate his predicament. But Golden first wanted to put some fear into him, to have him return in the morning.

"I think he's already got the fear of the Lord in him, Monk," she said. "He whimpered on and off all the way uptown."

"Good. That's what we need in this country—more believers."

After dictating the list of Whittaker's hangouts, Ling walked to a bus stop. He would go home. There was film to be developed, a case to be thought through.

When he arrived home thirty-five minutes later, however, he was not up to the hard floor and caustic fumes of the darkroom. And when he sat down to consider the Whittaker investigation, he found himself unable to concentrate on anything other than his evening with Samantha Simpson. Why, he asked himself, were their never any storybook romances for Monk Ling? Women came into and went out of his life and meant nothing to him unless they were naive rich girls with pure, egalitarian motives; or power starved sirens who consumed men like tissues. Would he always be doomed?

At eleven, Ling gave up any pretense of analyzing the investigation. He put on low-cut sneakers and a sweatsuit, and stepped into the night.

He began jogging up Seventh Avenue, keeping an eye out for stoplight-running cabs and ill-tempered dogs, and he was soon into his second wind. For a while, his shoulders ached, then the muscles of his arms, but the pain passed quickly. The sidewalk began to rise and his legs started feeling tight and sluggish, seeming to delay a full second between his brain's instructions to move and their accomplishment of another stride across the concrete. The legs, he laughed to himself, were the first to go. But when he crossed over to Eighth Avenue and headed south, the downhill run chased away the stiffness. When he again reached a level sidewalk, his thighs and calves moved with the grace he had had as a college athlete, and showed the strength he had developed in Army Ranger training. Or was it an illusion?

He was perspiring and breathing heavily when he returned to the apartment. The phone was ringing. It was Samantha Simpson.

"I'm sorry to be calling so late," she said.

"It's okay."

"Are you all right? You sound like you're dying."

"I was out running."

"Oh. Anyway, you gave me your card with your home number so I thought it would be okay to call."

"It's fine."

"I just—I just wanted to thank you, that's all."

"For what?"

"For being gentle with me. You're a decent man."

Later, unable to sleep, Ling put some jazz on his stereo. He sat in his easy chair and found himself once again haunted by Samantha Simpson. Why, he asked, had she affected him so? He had to chase her from his mind, free himself from her spell. The cabin. He would contemplate the retreat he had been planning since he set aside his service revolver and bottle, and climbed out of his bed to rejoin the living.

Ling left the chair and removed a set of plans from atop his bookshelf. He spread them out on the oak table and pulled up a chair.

He would build the cabin either in the mountains of Pennsylvania or in the woods up near Woodstock. A simple house, energy efficient and self-contained, with a wood stove and a sauna. Outside would be a pool, but not an ordinary pool, kidney-shaped or rectangular, but rather one with a long, single lane for lapping, built in such a way that it could be enclosed in the winter. He would have a darkroom, large and fully equipped, and a study, its walls lined with books. He could hide there, alone but for a dog, maybe, and undisturbed, free from the department and the city and the memories.

Alex's money. Her legacy. All he had to do was say yes.

16

Stanislas Lubelski, sitting alone at a small, wobbly table, made no effort to be inconspicuous in the decrepit waterfront bar. His expensive, gleaming shoes, his tailored suit, his jewelry, his manicured hands, and the Lincoln Continental parked at the door had drawn immediate attention upon his entrance. It had also generated the deference he sought, from both the regulars and the bartender, who had come from behind the bar to take his order.

Lubelski placed his order—gin and tonic—in as close to a French accent as he could muster, enhancing the presumption that he must be a major player from Europe, in town for a deal—and who the hell knew who was behind him.

Perilli's twenty dollars' worth of intelligence had proven to be on the mark—not only was DeGrazia one of the Brooklyn bar's regulars, he was there at this very moment. Lubelski's eavesdropping on the bar talk revealed that DeGrazia's first name was Tony and he had been there for most of the day. A short, middle-aged thug, he was seated by himself at the end of the bar, his head and hands unsteady in his drunkenness.

Lubelski watched discreetly as DeGrazia slapped his shot glass in the bar's trough. Saying nothing, the bartender refilled it, reached into DeGrazia's disheveled fan of money and extracted a beer-soaked dollar bill.

Without looking, DeGrazia found the shot glass with his

fingers and lifted it to his lips, emptying it in one gulp. He followed with a sip from his beer.

Lubelski fought a smile. He knew the type—there were DeGrazias in every port city in the world.

DeGrazia undoubtedly went down to the Brooklyn docks whenever he was troubled. Boss trouble. Money trouble. Track trouble. Wife trouble. All of them sent him to this dark, drafty, mud-tracked, sweat-smelling hole where a man could huddle over a mug of beer with a chaser and curse his rotten luck, while others reverentially kept their distance and understood: understood what it feels like when everything comes down at once—and you look to the sky for help and all you see is crap and more crap.

DeGrazia's eyes were watching a television on a raised shelf in the corner, where a cheery-faced anchorwoman was detailing the latest from Beirut.

"Turn that fuckin' thing up, would ya, Frankie," he ordered. "Who wants to hear that shit?"

"Turn it up, goddamnit. I do."

The bartender looked nervously toward Lubelski, who did not react, then reluctantly complied, prompting protests from some of the other patrons, mostly hook-carrying longshoremen.

The anchorwoman's face turned grim as a black and white picture of James Whittaker, the British prime minister's brother, appeared as a backdrop behind her. "An elite team of special detectives today . . .," she began.

"Shut the fuck up!" DeGrazia shouted to the other drinkers.

". . . Chief of Detectives Julius Golden said authorities are pursuing several leads at this time, but when pressed by reporters, he refused to say whether an arrest is imminent."

The picture cut away to a taped report from the Seventeenth Precinct, where the investigation had its base.

DeGrazia emptied his mug, then slapped it down hard. "Give me another."

"What next, huh, Tony?" the bartender said as he pulled the beer tap lever. "The fuckin' queen's brother."

"Prime minister."

"What?"

"Prime minister's brother." DeGrazia smiled. "Chickenshit."

"Huh?"

"He was a chickenshit, lyin' bastard."

"You knew him, Tony?"

"Lot of people knew him."

The barkeep bent over the bar. "Business?"

"Lot of business."

"Not good, Tony, huh?"

"Bad, Frankie. Bad business all the way around."

DeGrazia did not get the opportunity to finish his beer—two young men wearing trenchcoats entered the bar and took positions on either side of him.

"Let's go, Tony," the shorter of the two ordered.

DeGrazia looked up from his mug. He glanced first to one side, then the other. Lubelski saw the unmistakable flash of fear in his eyes."

"Where to?" DeGrazia asked, his voice shaken.

"Marco wants to see you."

"What the fuck for? I mean . . ."

Both men reached for his shoulders. "The boss, he's kind of pissed, see."

"But . . ."

The three were out the door.

The tension lingered and the drinking men were silent, each busying himself with his drink, or cigarettes, or money, fighting hard to conceal the fear that somewhere, sometime it might be him getting that tap on the shoulder.

The bartender cleared DeGrazia's mug and shot glass, then pocketed the remaining bills.

Lubelski fingered his glass. He had one answer, anyway—DeGrazia, whatever his involvement with Whittaker, was now in trouble with Brooklyn's key crime boss.

Leaving a ten dollar tip on the table, Lubelski walked purposefully to a public telephone next to the men's room toward the rear. He felt every pair of eyes in the place on his back.

The call was pure theater—it would add to his air of mystery—but he also had business to conduct. Madam Celeste. Beekman Place. Most popular procuress of young ladies for the United Nations community. With the trade he had sent her way over the years, Lubelski had her number memorized. He also knew that if anyone in New York could provide a lead to Miss Simpson, the prostitute listed in Anatole's diary, it would be Celeste.

She answered the phone herself: "Stanislas, how are you, baby? . . . My goodness, but where have you been? . . . Of course, I'll try to help out . . . Simpson, Simpson, Simpson. Doesn't ring a bell. Probably a freelance . . . Sure I'll check around. Get back to me in a day or two."

Lubelski turned away from the phone. His eyes inspected the full length of the bar as he straightened his tie. Several heads turned to avoid his gaze. Adjusting and buttoning his suitcoat, he walked directly to the door and out to the rented Lincoln, which was parked illegally at a fire hydrant, in view of the bar's grimy window.

Lubelski once more had to resist a smile—whether it be Marseilles or Antwerp, Southampton or Hong Kong, an expensive black car parked outside a working man's bar by the docks was more secure than a visiting king's limousine parked at the White House.

The currency was fear.

17

The old brass clock showed a few minutes before nine. Golden would be annoyed with him again. But Golden could wait.

Ling had a problem with time. There was some bug in the circuitry of his logic and memory that made it impossible for him to judge time—or relate events to it. It was a flaw that sometimes frightened him. Occasionally, when someone asked his age, he actually had to take the year of his birth and calculate it. So it was also with his relationship with Alex. He had to work backward from her death to determine that they had been married a little over two years when she died, that he had met her three years earlier on a highway outside Stateline, Nevada, and that she was dead now almost two years.

Ling peeled off his clothes—he had slept in them—and put on a robe. He moved to his coffee table, a heavy oaken dining table whose legs had been sawed short, and picked up three books off its top: a collection of Thoreau and two treatises by the Jesuit anthropologist Teilhard. He returned them to their places in a makeshift plank and cinderblock bookcase. His stereo, which sat on the floor a few feet from his bed, had a stack of records on its spindle. The recordings were Miles Davis mostly, but also included some Gregorian chants and an early Stravinsky. Ling slipped them into their jackets.

He paused a moment and looked around. Yes, the loft *was* spartan. He had found it when Alex was pregnant. She loved it, calling it "poetic," but had been denied the time to furnish it the way they had planned. Ling was left with the few pieces they had saved for the transition and added little to it. The simplicity appealed to him—Alex had called him a born ascetic—but the other cops didn't understand. Long before, they had likened his lifestyle to that of a monk. The name had stuck. Some went beyond that, saying he lived no better than the men he sent to prison. In a way, he guessed, it was true.

He tidied up the rest of the apartment, throwing out dated newspapers, but keeping partially read copies of *Popular Photography* and a newsletter. The newsletter was called "Conservative Update" and generally arrived almost simultaneously with "The Liberal." Ling was looking for answers—neither side seemed to offer many.

He returned to the bed and pulled the top sheet up over the mattress, then dropped to the floor, his hands falling into place under his shoulders. In less than three minutes, he had completed fifty push-ups. He rolled to his back and executed fifty sit-ups. Closing his eyes, he followed with leg-lifts and assorted stretching maneuvers and bends, concentrating on the movement of his muscles and the ease with which they re-energized themselves after the dormancy of his sleep. He could sense the blood stepping up its flow, and his heart gradually thumping faster. His mind began to follow his body, cleansing itself of whatever nightmarish memories had haunted his sleep. If there had been any, he didn't recall them now.

He was breathing heavily when he finished. En route to the shower, he paused before a full-length mirror on the bathroom door. His right hand moved across his abdomen. It was ribbed with muscle, not as taut as during his football or military days but an improvement over the paunch that had been the target of so many of Alex's taunts. His frame had rolled with flab then, and his discipline, awash in alcohol, false ego, and the misguided values of a man trying to live out a movie role, had been even softer.

Showered, Ling moved to the kitchenette, poured a tall glass of peach nectar, and prepared a large bowl of bran with skimmed milk. His nostrils played tricks on him, filling the room with the smells of frying bacon and eggs, but it had been more than a year since he had had such a breakfast. He sat in a high-backed wooden chair at a small, round, oak table and sipped the juice, closing his eyes as the chill rolled down his throat. Frowning, he spooned up the tasteless bulk of the bran. As he ate, he reoriented himself to the state of his current case. The brother of the British prime minister, for chrissake! What next?

Ling rinsed the bowl and glass, then phoned the Seventeenth Precinct. Triano gave him the report he expected—a great deal of legwork had led to very little information and no key breaks.

"I'm on my way," Ling told him.

Before leaving, Ling stepped into his darkroom. It was the one area of the loft into which he had put some effort. He had installed a long, stainless steel sink and a good-sized roll dryer. The enlarger was bolted firmly to a customized counter with an easel area that for large blowups could be lowered in steps, almost to the floor. Next to the enlarger was a light-proof photographic paper safe and a digital exposure clock. In a corner stood a small refrigerator for storing film. Above it was one of the new super-fast film dryers. On one wall was a cork bulletin board on which he had tacked notes and charts with figures for calculating exposure and development times, and for mixing chemicals. The wall above the sink featured shelves containing neatly labeled brown chemical jugs. On the opposite wall was a metal cabinet for his filters, lenses, and cameras—three Nikons, a classic Pentax, a new Hassalblad and a 1950's four-by-five Speed Graphic for studio work. Ling removed the oldest of his Nikons—his favorite—and reloaded it.

Outside, Ling found traffic at a standstill. Four—no five—people were frantically attempting to flag cabs. A meter maid was writing a summons. Stationary, she looked like a buoy struggling against its tether in a current of grim-faced executives, secretaries, and clerks, streaming en masse toward the nearby subway entrances. The sidewalks had the look of a mass evacuation. Ling chuckled. Maybe that was the answer—mass evacuation.

Ling found himself lucky—a cab pulled up to his building and discharged a passenger. Ling grabbed it.

On the ride uptown, the cabbie studied him in the rear view mirror for several blocks, finally asking: "You're a cop, right?"

"Naw," Ling answered. "I sell lingerie. What do you care?"

The cabbie looked hurt. "Just tryin' to make conversation, mister."

Ling apologized, then added: "Yeah, I'm a cop. How did ya know?"

"You guys all look the same or somethin'."

Ling tipped him generously.

Inside the station house, Golden was meeting with McKinnon and O'Brien. To Ling's surprise, the chief said nothing about the lateness of his arrival.

McKinnon and O'Brien, both disheveled and extremely weary, recounted one by one the stops they had made in their survey of Whittaker's favorite hangouts. The Englishman had been well-known at all of the places, they reported, both for his heavy tipping and the striking women he always had clinging to his arm.

"Nothin' but the best, huh?" Golden said.

"Not exactly, chief," said McKinnon. "Bartender in this one place . . . let me see . . ." He checked his notes. "Harmon's Turtle. It's up on Second Avenue. Barkeep there . . . man by the name of Blackstone . . . says Whittaker's image was all but shattered a couple of months ago when he began showing up with a dog."

"I know the feeling," Golden said. "Go on."

"The bartender, he couldn't figure it, so he starts really taking a good look at the woman and then it comes to him he knows who she is. Seen her picture in the papers or on TV. Washington. Something to do with the White House. He doesn't recall her name, see, but then one afternoon, while they're sittin' there with the joint all but empty, the TV behind the bar comes on with one of those news breaks. They were showin' film from the day before . . ."

"And there she is, bigger than life," O'Brien interrupted. "In the Oval Office standing with the President and they give her name as somethin' Mason."

"Mason," Golden repeated. "Think it *does* ring a bell."

Ling recognized the name, too. An economic or budget adviser, as best as he could recall. In her late twenties or early thirties. And rather plain—at least as she appeared on television. Was she the mysterious woman from Washington whom Samantha Simpson had been talking about?

Golden began pacing in a small circle. "So we've got ourselves the brother of England's prime minister, with very high tastes in women, lowering himself to escort a wallflower who happens to be a key presidential adviser. Why?"

"Maybe entrée, a pass to the inside circles of Washington," McKinnon offered.

Ling shook his head. "He'd have that on his own name alone."

"You're right," Golden said, bowing his head in thought.

"There's more, chief," O'Brien said.

"What, she has a sister?" Golden asked.

"One of the places Ling came up with is a coke house on the Lower East Side. Rough trade. Enough dealers to fill half of Riker's. Naturally, the joint empties with the speed of light when Rosie and I walk in."

"The barkeep, he don't want to know us," McKinnon said. "So we sit there, sipping our Seven-Ups like we got all the time in the world. The douchebag finally gets the message that his cash register ain't gonna ring unless and until he talks to us."

"He gave us a name—Tony DeGrazia," O'Brien said. "Wise guy from Brooklyn. Kindergarten class. Double-digit I.Q. Seems he and Whittaker had a friendship."

"That so?" Golden said.

"Yeah—until a couple of weeks ago, they hit the place regularly," McKinnon said.

"We put a little more heat on the barkeep and he confides as how he's also seen Whittaker and DeGrazia huddled together at some afterhours place off Union Square. We went there but the guy handling the setups was so spaced out he wasn't sure what city he was in, and the bossman wasn't due in until later this morning.''

"Monk and Triano can grab that one later," Golden said. He summoned Triano, then said: "DeGrazia. First name Tony. A citizen of Brooklyn. I want him picked up."

"You got him, chief," Triano said, "but first let me tell you this: Just got a call—patrol found Whittaker's wallet."

"Where?"

"Wino had it—with the charge cards. The guy tries to buy a case of Scotch with it. Liquor store man flags down a patrolcar. They've got the guy sittin' at the ninth. Claims he found it in a trash can. Got the lab en route to pick it up."

"Won't find jack on that one," O'Brien said.

"Worth a try," Golden said. He dismissed Triano, then turned to Ling. "What you got, Monk?"

Ling briefed them on Samantha Simpson's account of calls from a man with a Brooklyn accent—possibly DeGrazia—and of Whittaker's very hush, hush affair with a woman from Washington—probably Marilyn Mason.

"I'm startin' to get a good feeling," Golden said.

"What a way to hide an affair, hitting an Upper East Side meat market," O'Brien said.

"Maybe it was just hush, hush as far as Samantha Simpson was concerned," McKinnon said.

"Could be," Golden said. He looked at Ling. "Anything else?"

"A Wall Street character. A What-Makes-Sammy-Run type with a Mercedes. Spent a lot of time with Whittaker. Last name Thornton. That's all she knew. And Miss Simpson, incidentally—she's a part-time pro. Expensive. Freelance."

"Whittaker payin' her?" McKinnon asked with disbelief.

Ling shook his head. "Not Whittaker—that kid Samuels."

Golden grinned. He nodded toward the closed door to the side office. "Dotty's babysitting him now."

"A God-fearing boy?" Ling asked.

Golden's eyes narrowed. "He came to church."

Golden renewed his pacing. "Seems like what we're getting here is some sideshow: a Brooklyn boy scout who meets with the deceased regularly up until about two weeks of the murders, a sweet-thing activist planning a rally, a hungry moneyman from Wall Street, and a hooker who gets shown the door.''

"I think you can count Simpson out, chief."

"Why? She got an alibi?"

"Yeah."

"You check it out?"

"I'll vouch for her on it," Ling said.

Golden studied him suspiciously, then said: "I don't know why, but I'll buy that—for now."

Golden summoned another detective and instructed him to check for every Thornton listed with the Department of Motor Vehicles as owning a Mercedes. He told McKinnon and O'Brien to get some sleep. Then to Ling: "I want you in on questioning the Samuels kid."

Golden and Ling were heading for the side office when the chief spotted the two FBI agents coming through the squad room door. The chief, his face flushed, his eyes afire, charged toward them.

"Fine fuckin' situation this is, when the New York Police Department has to find out from a foreigner that you assholes have your hands in this," Golden began.

The two agents, unprepared for the outburst, edged back. "Jesus, Julie, what the hell you talkin' about?" the tall, slender agent asked.

"What I'm talking about," the chief said, jabbing a finger into the agent's chest, "is a call from your director to the British embassy allowing as how one of your informants— paid more than me, no doubt—is saying the KGB was bird doggin' Whittaker."

The shorter agent, Nolan, cleared his throat. "We didn't know, chief—honest. I mean, him and me, we're low on the totem pole, the last to find out anything. . . ."

The other picked up the chorus: "And when we did find out, only this morning, we headed right over here to brief you."

Golden began wagging a finger. "I believe that and next you'll be pitchin' me pork belly futures. This *is* a homicide investigation; I think we're *entitled* to know."

"Of course, Julie," Nolan said, "and if you'll ease off one goddamned moment, we'll fill you in."

Golden calmed. The two FBI men related essentially the same account Ling had extracted from the Englishman.

"Solid?" Golden asked.

"Washington thinks so."

"Who was working him, the female?" Golden asked.

Nolan nodded. "Her name was Anatole. Top of the line. They brought her in from Europe."

"Anything else?"

Nolan shook his head.

Golden turned away with a look of disgust. "The sons of bitches," he muttered to Ling, then continued with a stream of staccato Yiddish while he led Ling to the side office.

Collingsworth stopped them at the door. "I'll understand, Chief Golden, if you decline, but I am wondering if I might possibly observe this interview."

Golden considered the request a moment, then said: "Okay— but please leave the questioning to us."

A thin, pale man in his late twenties, with the beardless face of a teenager, was sitting nervously at the table. He bolted upright with the group's entrance. Golden, in a calm but authoritative voice, introduced Ling and the Englishman, then dismissed Levine.

"Detective Ling has some questions to ask you," the chief said.

Ling sat opposite Samuels. Collingsworth moved a chair to an unobtrusive spot in a corner. Golden, still visibly seething at the FBI, moved to the window and stared blankly through the oily, gray glass at the drab buildings across the street. Ling wondered if the naked fat lady would give him the finger.

Ling looked at Samuels. "You okay?"

"No, I'm *not* okay," Samuels answered. "Would you be *okay* at the hands of the Gestapo?"

"You're entitled to a lawyer. Your father probably has several good ones."

"I told them last night I don't need a lawyer. I haven't done anything to require one. Those drugs in my apartment . . . They weren't mine. You surely know I wasn't living there."

"Have you been read your rights?"

"Damn you, aren't you listening to me?"

Ling said nothing. With the dispassionate and knowing demeanor of a psychiatrist observing a troubled patient, he spent more than a minute watching Samuels' hands and face. The scrutiny began to unnerve Samuels. His eyes darted around the room and he fidgeted in his seat. He searched for a place to rest his hands. Finally, he slid down in his chair, his hands entwined on his lap, his eyes half-closed and averted to the side. "Please, get on with it," he pleaded.

"We don't care about the drugs, Robert," Ling said softly. "Times have changed—what you do at home is your business. What we're investigating are two murders. Those we care about."

"He was sincere."

"Excuse me?"

Samuels raised his head. "Whittaker. I met him socially. He asked me what I did with my time, given my family's wealth. I told him about the movement, about how time is running out, and unless we do something, all of us, there won't be a world to live in." His voice had picked up speed and energy.

"Nuclear war," Ling said.

"Exactly. And James Whittaker was very interested. He asked what he could do. Because of who his sister was, I told him, *anything* he did would carry a major impact. The next day, I got a call from him. He said he was ready to make a statement but didn't know how to do it. I suggested he write the *Times*."

"What was his motivation?"

Samuels' eyes grew wide. "A sincere belief that we are facing doom—the same motivation we all have."

"I see," Ling said. "And the letter, he wrote it himself?"

Samuels looked to the unpolished, gray tile floor.

"You wrote it for him, didn't you?"

Samuels hesitated, then said: "Yes—but that was only because he had no experience writing such things, what, in effect, was an essay."

"Not the first ghost-written letter to a newspaper, I should think."

Samuels smiled. "I suspect you're right."

Golden turned from the windows and moved to the table, leaning against the edge furthest from Ling and Samuels.

"I don't want you to get upset, Robert," Ling continued. "This is a question we have to ask everybody even loosely associated with the two victims. We need to know where you were on the night of the killings."

"Like I told the lady officer last night, I was at group therapy, then I spent the night with a friend. You can check it out."

Ling looked to Golden, whose nod indicated Levine or some other detective was already taking the young man up on his suggestion.

"We've been talking with Samantha Simpson. In fact, I had dinner with her last night." Ling paused. "Do you know her?"

"Of course—she was shacked up with Whittaker. He picked them up like garbage."

"Miss Simpson says you were paying her."

Samuels slapped the table. "That's a damned lie! I never even met her until Whittaker introduced us and then I wanted nothing to do with her. I know her type."

Ling held up a hand. "Fine."

Samuels sulked back into his seat.

"Tell me about this rally," Ling said.

"What's there to say? It will be the biggest anti-nuclear rally ever held in this city and maybe it will help the politicians to get the message."

"Whittaker was to be a speaker?"

"Yes," Samuels said, his tone sad. "And he was writing his remarks himself. It would be more sincere that way."

"But then he canceled out. . . ." Ling left the sentence hanging.

"That's not true! Who told you that?"

"Samantha Simpson."

"She's a liar!"

Ling stood. "But, you see, I happen to believe her."

"It simply isn't so. Whittaker was ready. All the networks were going to be there. British and Australian television, too. He recognized it as an opportunity to . . ."

"Embarrass his sister?"

Samuels didn't respond. His face was sullen.

"That was his motivation all along, wasn't it? He would do anything to embarrass the prime minister."

"Of course! She deserved it," Samuels snapped.

"How's that?"

"James *made* her. She was nothing until he introduced her to his circle of friends and she met her husband. Surrounded by the right kind of people, she was able to thrive. She discovered she had this knack at politics. Then, when James' wife died very tragically, this sister of his abandoned him. He never forgot it."

"So he took his public stance on the bomb."

"That's right—but he meant it."

Ling's voice grew louder, his tone accusative. "But then someone got to him—his new girlfriend, maybe—and convinced him of the wisdom of laying low, of staying out of the press, so he would not further alienate his sister and thereby jeopardize a potentially very lucrative arrangement he had pending with a certain Soviet agent, not to mention his other business dealings that might have been damaged, had he drawn too much attention to himself." Ling retook his seat. He leaned over the table, staring into Samuels' eyes. The young man appeared frightened, shocked at the extent of Ling's knowledge. "Whittaker informed you he would not appear at your rally," Ling continued. "You argued with him but to no avail. He wouldn't change his mind. So you notified Miss Simpson her services would no longer be needed."

Samuels had the look of defeat. "So much happened so fast. I had thought him to be sincere."

"But he wasn't. And his return to true colors placed you in a very awkward position. An embarrassing position. I mean, here you had been telling the world that the British prime minister's brother was going to keynote your rally and then he doesn't show. You'd lose face unless . . . unless there was some other reason for him not showing."

Samuels was on his feet. "I didn't kill him! I couldn't do it even if I had wanted to!" He snapped around to face Golden. "I want a lawyer. I'm not saying another word until I get a lawyer."

Golden slid upright off the edge of the table. "You don't need one."

"I have a right to representation . . ."

"You may go."

It was unclear who was more surprised: Samuels or Collingsworth.

"I said you can leave, Mr. Samuels. Now. If there's something you remember that you'd think we should know, I'd appreciate a call."

His eyes darting between Golden and Ling, Samuels edged backward toward the door. Golden opened it for him—and he was gone.

"You're allowing him to leave?" Collingsworth asked incredulously.

Golden nodded.

"But you'll have him followed."

"No sense to that."

"I don't understand . . ."

Ling explained: "A lawyer comes in here, it would be useless to go on. If Samuels has something to hide, he'll go to an attorney, and the odds are better than even they'll be back in here trying to make a deal."

"But why not follow him?"

"Because it would take a half dozen of my men minimum," Golden answered. "And then what would they learn? He went to see his therapist? That boy's so scared he'll probably hide out in a closet 'til all this blows over."

There was a tap on the open door. It was the detective whom Golden had assigned to check all the Thorntons with a registered Mercedes. "Got one," he said. "A Calvin Thornton. Address is a co-op on York. Occupation is stockbroker."

"Get after him," Golden said.

"Already tried, chief—called his home. Maid gave me his office number. His secretary says he won't be available—indefinitely."

"Why?"

"He's already left the country. The Concorde. I checked—it was airborne a few minutes ago. To London."

"Damn it!" Golden pounded the table. He thought a moment, then asked the detective: "My two friends from the Bureau still here?"

"They're around."

"Good—appraise them of the situation and then ask them if they would kindly consent to have one of their men waiting for Mr. Thornton at Heathrow."

"Right, chief. Oh, and Monk—the lab just sent back that videocassette you gave them."

"Prints?" Ling asked.

"Not a one. They said it looked like it had been wiped."

"What cassette?" Golden asked.

Ling didn't get a chance to answer—there was a commotion at the squadroom entrance. Vanzi, a short, pudgy, balding desk sergeant from downstairs, came running through the door, trailed by a patrolman. Both were puffing from the climb.

"Chief!" Vanzi called out across the room. "I've got to see you!"

Golden and Ling walked over to him. "What is it, Gino? You're gonna have a fuckin' stroke."

"Nearly thirty years on the force and I've never seen anything like it."

"Like what?" Golden demanded.

"Tell him," the sergeant ordered the patrolman, then bent over in a spasm of coughing.

"Well, chief, today's the day they pick up the garbage, see, so we got all the cans lined up at the curb. Me, I'm on post outside the door and I think nothing of it when this sanitation truck comes along and empties the cans. But then five minutes later, some sanitation foreman comes runnin' up and says he's seen the truck and it isn't one of his. His truck isn't due here until later. I don't know what to think, so I send him inside to the sarge and . . ."

"The foreman makes a call, see," Vanzi, recovered, interrupted. "It turned out this goddamned truck is stolen. Missing from Queens this morning."

Golden looked at Ling. "Tell me it was some kids out for a joy ride or some psycho playin' Santa Claus. Tell me that, Monk—please."

"I don't think so, Julie."

"The carbon paper, right? Carbons from every report we've typed up in the past twenty-four hours. And that's only the beginning."

Ling nodded.

Golden turned back to the sergeant. "Any word on the truck?"

"I don't know, chief. I put out the call, then ran right up here. Figured you'd want to know about it right away."

"Keep me posted. I want that truck found."

Vanzi spoke slowly: "Sure, chief. But let me tell ya somethin'—we ain't never gonna find that truck unless, maybe, they drain Jamaica Bay someday."

"What's next?" Golden asked. "Do we start looking for microphones in the shithouse stalls?"

Ling didn't have an answer.

18

The plane, sleek with its delta wing and sharply tilted beak, was over the Atlantic and still climbing.

"You know you're on a plane with this baby," said the obese, redheaded microchip salesman seated on the aisle. "By the way, what line you in?"

"Stockbroker," Cal Thornton answered.

The salesman's ridiculous grin and ceaseless chattering had bothered Thornton from the moment the pilot had begun his taxiing. The throttling of the engines on takeoff had drowned the salesman out, but once the long plane had moved gracefully down the runway and lifted its trademark nose into the skies, the jet noise began to abate and the redheaded salesman renewed his irritating monologue: "My firm's been so successful lately that we routinely use the Concorde when there's a big deal in Europe. My boss believes it makes sense to . . ."

Thornton tuned the fat man out and breathed deeply with relief that he was on his way. He stopped fighting the plane's powerful thrust and allowed his head to rest against the back of his seat.

The aircraft began to level off.

"Fantastic!" said the salesman. He tugged at Thornton's arm. "This is my fourth Concorde flight."

All of the hundred seats were filled—Thornton had been

fortunate to get a reservation on such short notice. He looked across the aisle. Two swarthy men wearing Arab headdress were busy sharing a Saudi newspaper. Four Japanese in front of the Arabs occupied the seats in the last rows of the forward non-smoking section. In front of Thornton sat a young couple, their attention on the plane's tiny side window.

"It's worth the damn fare just for the takeoff," the salesman was saying as the aircraft entered a layer of clouds. "We're still accelerating, see, but you can't feel it." He pointed to the mach clock on the forward bulkhead. In gold digital numerals against a black background, it read: "M 0.74." "Won't be long before we break that sound barrier," the fat man effused.

Thornton was calculating: the flight would take three and a half hours or so. It would take nearly another hour to get from Heathrow into the city.

He looked through the window, but saw only gray, then glanced at the mach clock again—it was still climbing.

The man in front put his arm around the woman, who, in turn, nuzzled up to his chest, her lips caressing the lower edge of his face.

Thornton observed them through the crack between their seats, then turned his eyes away. He himself had never known such a display of genuine affection, and its very concept perplexed him. He dismissed it as the playacting of fools. He had learned early in life that associations with others, whether in bed or the corridors of Wall Street, should have a tangible purpose or should not exist at all. To pursue a relationship, however superficial, when there was no prospect of measurable reward was a waste of time and energy. That was reality—and there was no reason to feel shameful or guilty about it.

"Look!" the salesman shouted excitedly, pointing to the mach clock. "M 1.07," it read. "We broke the sound barrier! And you don't feel a thing!"

Thornton ignored him. What concerned him most just now was not the speed of the plane but the agility of his mind. The death of Whittaker had thrown Thornton's analytical powers askew. He had to get his logic back on track.

Whittaker had used him. Thornton could see that now. He

had thought the deal with Whittaker was more or less spontaneous, a chance meeting of two minds on an ingenious tactic, but all the while, the Englishman had been manipulating him like a puppet according to a carefully crafted plan. And then Whittaker had gone and gotten himself killed, out of greed probably, leaving Thornton to sift through the rubble. If only he could turn back the clock and undo it. . . .

The public address system clicked on, and a British voice from the cockpit formally announced the passing of mach one. The news produced ''ah's'' from most of the passengers. The announcement also disclosed that the aircraft was at its cruising altitude of 32,000 feet and was precisely on schedule.

One of the Japanese began furiously pointing out the mach clock to his companions. The Arabs also had their eyes on the forward bulkhead.

''The pilots have to wait to break the sound barrier until they're well out over the Atlantic because of the noise,'' the salesman was saying.

''Okay, fat man,'' Thornton said to himself. ''You want to have a conversation?''

Thornton looked to his seatmate's face. ''Friend of mine just died,'' he said.

''Oh . . . I'm very sorry.''

''What do you think it's like to feel a slug tearing through your flesh?''

''I beg your pardon?''

''They say your entire life really passes before you. Do you think so?''

The salesman looked away. ''Haven't thought about it much.''

''I doubt it, though. I think that men, when their bellies are gutted, probably don't think of their wives or their mothers or their childhoods—they think of pussy, or they think of their last fifty-foot putt, or last year's goddamned Superbowl.''

The salesman was watching him curiously through the corner of his eye. Thornton laughed to himself, then turned away.

He was, Thornton acknowledged while peering through the viewless window, obsessed with death. Sometimes, until he caught himself, he stared at a man's face, imagining what it would look like in a grimace of death, picturing that final expression of betrayal which froze on a dying man's face in the infinitely long moment when he comprehended that he had rolled the dice and lost—forever. Never to be privy even to the outcome of his battles: the soldier who would never know who won the war.

A flight attendant, wearing a dark blue skirt with white pinstripes, distributed menus. Thornton ordered champagne; the fat man, Perrier water.

When the drinks arrived, Thornton raised his glass in a toast: "To the sound barrier!"

The salesman nodded, then gulped his drink.

The attendant presently returned with their food: chilled Sevruga caviar topped with lemon, followed by roasted quail and a mixed green salad.

They ate in silence. The plates were removed and coffee poured. Thornton checked the mach clock: it showed the aircraft already beyond twice the speed of sound—1,340 miles per hour.

"That's more than the speed of a rifle bullet," he told the fat man, grinning.

The salesman's eyes began to show a trace of fear. He kept nervously tracking the movements of the attendants, an obvious precaution in the event he had to summon help.

"You know," Thornton said, "a lot of people have this image of a stockbroker as this sleazy kind of guy who sells AT&T paper to gray-haired widows." The salesman glanced at him briefly. "But not me, see. I'm not like that. I make a move, you read about it in the papers."

"I see," the salesman said.

Momentarily, the plane began its descent. The attendants distributed hot towels. The clouds had broken and Thornton could see the steel blue and gray of the ocean.

Thornton looked to his seatmate. "The tower won't keep us waiting, not this bird."

The fat man had his eyes on the Japanese across the aisle.

The pilot came on the P.A. to announce their imminent landing. The rear wheels soon eased onto the Heathrow runway. The nosewheel dropped slowly seconds later.

The passengers began lining up for the exit. Adrenaline

shot through Thornton's veins as it occurred to him that he was about to become vulnerable again, that he would no longer have the protection of a tube of aluminum high in the skies.

Someone already had been asking about him—the Parrot Club manager had tipped him off to that. And that bitch waitress telling everything she knew. Fortunately, the club management didn't trust its whores and had bugged the bedrooms to keep them from soliciting business appointments outside the club. The waitress obviously hadn't known this. The manager had fired her on the spot. Thornton would have to take care of him—in a big way.

Thornton looked up and down the plane, checking faces, but he saw no evidence that any eyes were watching him. This changed, however, after he left the plane. Reaching the terminal, he couldn't stop feeling that people were staring at him.

The gawkers seemed to look first to his face, then to the rest of his frame. Those in his way stepped aside. Was his paranoia running rampant, or was he being mistaken for an actor, or an athelete?

The customs officer was asking him questions. Why so little luggage? the government man wanted to know.

"I had to pack in a rush," Thornton answered.

"Are you on business or a holiday, sir?"

"Last-minute business. That's why the rush."

The agent waved him through—reluctantly, Thornton thought. Then he was in a taxi. Thornton looked through the rear window—there was no sign of his being followed. Or was there another taxi behind them? The passenger, wasn't it that redheaded bore from the plane?

Thornton slumped down in the seat. He was starting to see things. He was getting paranoid. Surely no one was behind him. He would have to do something about his short-circuited imagination. A good three-day binge, maybe. Or a sunset-to-sunrise trip with two or three hookers to leave him drained.

The driver, living up to the reputation of London hacks, found the hotel handily despite its sign being so tiny as not to be readable from the street. It was a small, obscure place, one that could provide Thornton the privacy he needed until he decided where to go next. The Costa del Sol, perhaps. Or maybe Sweden.

The driver's face lit up with the ten pounds Thornton handed him as a tip. Then he was at the desk, the clerk telling him that, yes, his reservation had arrived.

"How long will your stay be, sir?" the clerk inquired.

Thornton started to answer but a hand was on his shoulder. He turned around. It was a tall, husky man with blond hair who had been reading a newspaper in a chair in the lobby.

"Mr. Thornton? Mr. Cal Thornton?" the stranger asked.

Thornton nodded.

"My name's Denton. I'm with the FBI."

"The FBI? What the hell are you doing here? This is England."

"I'm connected with the embassy, Mr. Thornton. May we have a little talk?"

"What the hell about? You think I avoided the draft or something?"

"It should only take a few minutes."

Thornton thought a moment, then decided that, with his assets still sitting in the United States, he had little choice but to go through the charade. "Where do you want to do this?" he asked.

"How about your room?"

"I haven't checked in yet." Besides, he did not want to meet anywhere that wasn't public—he might need witnesses.

"There's a tiny pub next door," the agent said.

Thornton nodded.

The pub *was* small—perhaps a dozen stools along the bar, two small tables toward the rear. They stood at the bar. The agent ordered a half-pint; Thornton, a gin and tonic.

Neither said anything as the drinks were prepared. Hardly had the barmaid put Thornton's glass down than he had it to his lips, allowing the cool alcohol to ease the dryness of his mouth and throat. He lit a cigarette, then demanded: "What exactly is it you want from me?"

"What brings you to London, Mr. Thornton?" Denton asked.

"Business. I'm in stocks."

"Specifically, why are you here, please?"

Thornton didn't like the agent's insolent tone. "Look, chief, I agreed to sit down with you after you didn't even have the decency to let me check into my room. I just got off a transatlantic flight, for chrissake. And I'd like to know on what authority you think you can ask those kind of questions."

"You're an American citizen, Thornton. And I'm with the FBI."

"But you're out of the States, if you care to check your map. I can tell you to go fuck yourself. You have no jurisdiction here."

"But *I* do," said a voice from behind them.

Thornton turned. A tall, slender man in a dark gray banker's suit was displaying an oversized leather wallet. "My name is Malloy," he said. "Scotland Yard."

Thornton looked to Denton. "He with you?"

"It's a joint investigation."

Thornton took another long swallow from his drink. "I'm here partially to get away for a while, partially to check on a few potential British investments," he said, his eyes on the tumbler in his hand.

Denton removed a notebook from his coat. "What kind of investments?"

"Oh, a few things. Microchips, mainly. Nothing wrong with that, is there?"

"Does the name James Whittaker mean anything to you?"

"Of course. The prime minister's brother. He was just killed. I heard it on the news."

"That's correct. And did you know him?"

Thornton began to feel lightheaded. No, he pleaded silently, this wasn't happening. What should he do? Maybe he should stall until he could find a lawyer. But this was London, not New York. He wouldn't know how to begin to find a British mouthpiece with the savvy to handle a situation like this. In fact, he had never gotten it quite straight, the difference between a barrister and a solicitor. With his current run of luck, surely he would summon the wrong one. Then he heard himself saying: "Yes, I knew Whittaker. I met him in a bar. . . ."

19

A District of Columbia patrolcar had passed twice, the cop eyeing him suspiciously each time. Stanislas Lubelski decided to abandon the park bench if the patrolcar passed yet a third time. He looked at his watch—it was nearly noon. He had been sitting on the bench for a tedious two hours.

A map of Washington was positioned conspicuously at his side, along with a sightseeing brochure. Lubelski was merely a tourist, if anyone asked. If pressed, however, he would have difficulty explaining exactly why he had spent more than two hours sitting outside the British embassy.

Petrovich's office in New York had provided a set of photographs of Holmes. Surprisingly, their quality was very good. Lubelski had studied them until he had Holmes' features well memorized—the thin, gray brush mustache, the receding hairline, the dark-framed glasses, the long, slender neck—and then destroyed the packet. The KGB researchers also had provided a rather full background file, including the diplomat's regular schedule. That schedule called for Holmes to depart his embassy for lunch precisely at noon. Lubelski, bored and bitter at this forced assignment, his back stiff from waiting, hoped the British diplomat would stick to his habits today.

He did. At noon, on the dot, a thin, short man left the embassy. A security man at the door showed him considerable deference. A chauffeur-driven Rolls Royce pulled up. The thin man climbed in, exposing enough of his face for Lubelski to confirm that it was, in fact, Holmes.

The diplomat had an air of Oxford about him. Small, very alive eyes, and a narrow nose. His mandatory civil service mustache was so thin as to be barely noticeable. Every strand of his gray-streaked, dark brown hair was in place, and he moved in that brisk, loping style favored by British military officers. His face showed weariness, but little hint of the bitterness his KGB dossier attributed to him. Holmes was said to be a career man passed over too many times, a man with no future, a man betrayed by a system he could view only as ungrateful. The KGB file had, in fact, labeled Holmes a potential recruitment target.

With the Rolls pulling away, Lubelski quickly hailed a taxi and ordered its Vietnamese driver to follow the Rolls. The cabbie complied without hesitation—Washington drivers, Lubelski suspected, were accustomed to this sort of thing. They kept a few cars back from the Rolls through the atrocious noontime traffic, almost losing it at one of the capital's infamous circles. But the Rolls did not go far—it discharged its lone passenger outside a restaurant called Chappy's.

The chauffeur continued up the block and double-parked. Lubelski paid the cabdriver, handing him double the fare.

"I know nothing," the cabbie said.

Lubelski winked.

As soon as he entered Chappy's and saw the crowd, Lubelski recognized it for what it was—the lastest fad restaurant where those of power, wealth, or celebrity were apt to be found, their pecking order painfully advertised by their table assignments. In six more months, Chappy's would be empty except for tourists late to get the word that yet another establishment had won the in-crowd's favor. The insiders would have moved on.

Chappy's was exactly what Lubelski did not want—he would have to bribe the maître d' substantially merely to gain admittance during the noon hour, and his hopes of winning a table within earshot of Holmes were slim.

An arrogant stride and the exaggerated bearing of being someone important got Lubelski past the line of would-be

diners to the reservations stand. Some quick talking in hush
tones and a palmed twenty dollar bill won him a small table.
The table, as he had feared, was across the room from where
Holmes had joined two distinguished oriental gentlemen. It
would be impossible to overhear Holmes' luncheon discussion, but at least the diplomat would be in view.

Judicious questioning of Lubelski's waiter established that
Holmes' companions were two high ranking Japanese diplo-
mats. It became clear that Holmes was at home with this
crowd—several of the restaurant's patrons waved greetings to
him and some stopped by his table to pay their respects.
Otherwise, the diplomat's luncheon was uneventful, prompting
Lubelski to question his decision to come to Washington. But
Holmes' name had appeared on Anatole's list of key figures
in Whittaker's circle, and if Holmes was behind the double
murders, it was possible he would make a careless mistake in
his activities now.

As Holmes and the Japanese were settling down over their
tea, a woman approached their table. She appeared to be in
her thirties but was probably younger, her bland gray suit and
tired, distraught eyes adding years to her age. Lubelski, in his
survey of the room, had noticed her dining with another
woman and dismissed them as mid-level bureaucrats out to
rub shoulders with the powerful, thanks to a reservation made
by one of their bosses. But the boldness with which the
woman walked to Holmes' table made it clear that Lubelski's
initial assessment was wrong.

All three men at the table attempted to stand, but had
difficulty in the restaurant's close quarters. Holmes, whose
expression appeared to be one of concern, motioned toward
an empty seat. The woman shook her head.

As their conversation continued well past simple greetings,
Lubelski saw Holmes' face begin to tighten in what he first
thought was anger, then concluded was alarm. The diplomat
began looking apprehensively at nearby tables, as if to survey
who was overhearing the woman's words. The woman, meanwhile, began to gesture awkwardly. She appeared shaky on
her feet, as if she were about to faint. Her voice grew louder,
attracting the stares of nearby diners. Holmes had his hand
up, urging her to calm down.

Lubelski was on his feet and heading across the room, his hand brushing back his snow-white hair. He targeted the table behind Holmes' back, where a uniformed Army officer was dining with a deeply tanned and smiling companion in civilian clothes, a military hardware salesman most likely. Lubelski glanced at the officer's name tag, then said: "Excuse me, but aren't you Colonel Henderson?"

"Why, yes. Have we met?"

Lubelski went into a complicated explanation of how they had spent a wonderful hour or so chatting at a Georgetown dinner two, maybe three years ago, and how interesting had been the colonel's comments about . . .

Lubelski went on, but with a long-mastered skill, his ears were attuned to the discussion at the adjacent table. He was close enough to smell the ranting woman's common, musky perfume.

"Please, Marilyn, not here," Holmes was pleading.

"Don't try to hush me, you bastard. I *know* you were at least partly responsible. Maybe you were behind the whole thing. I'm not sure. But it doesn't matter—I've destroyed them all."

"You must be ill, my dear. I don't know what you're talking about."

"And one more thing—he knew you were planning to cut him out. That's what he said, 'Holmes is planning to screw me.' The only thing I don't know is what the deal involved— but I have a guess."

"Miss Mason, please!"

"You've got nothing to hold over my head. You remember that!" She stalked away.

The colonel was nodding his head. "Oh, yes—it's coming back to me now."

"Very nice to see you again," Lubelski said. He returned to his table. He was smiling—he had gone fishing and the waters had proven fertile. Mason. Marilyn Mason. She was a presidential aide. Anatole's diary had been on the mark— there *was* a Whittaker connection to the White House!

In his full career, Lubelski had never before come this close to the center of Washington power. He felt a surge of excitement, the pleasure of discovery that had made the game so worthwhile in his youth. In that moment, he was even inclined to forgive Petrovich, and had to resist an impulse to rush out of the restaurant and immediately convey the news to the Russian. This would prove he still had the touch, the instincts, and they would have to pamper him, give him anything he demanded.

Lubelski returned to his table and signaled for his check. As he waited, his elation evolved into a feeling of great relief. This would be his last case. He would free himself from the game. Marilyn Mason would be his liberator.

20

"All I can figure is it's magic," Mickey Triano was telling them. "Now you see him, now you don't."

Triano had spent the morning on the streets and working the phone, squeezing every source he could find, and the word was unanimous: Tony DeGrazia had vanished.

"Traced him to a bar at the Brooklyn piers where he sat most of yesterday drinkin' and mutterin' to himself," Triano said. "Then a coupla messenger boys from Little Brother Marco appear and haul him away."

"Let me see if I have this straight," Golden said. "Whittaker buys it . . . a bartender says Whittaker was a good pal of DeGrazia . . . DeGrazia gets summoned by the big bad boss and, by and by, is nowhere to be found."

"Like a fairy tale, chief."

Golden looked to Ling. "What do you think?"

"DeGrazia was operating out of school, maybe—in which case, he's probably in the river. Or he was on an authorized job and Marco figures to get him out of sight, what with all the heat."

"Either—or," Golden said pensively. "Someday I'm gonna find a road with no forks."

"That happens and they won't need us," Ling said.

"Days like this, that's fine with me," Golden said. He

then instructed Triano and Ling to visit the afterhours club off Union Square favored by Whittaker.

They took an unmarked car, Triano doing the driving.

"The disappearin' act is suddenly very popular," Ling said.

"How so?"

"My British pal, Collingsworth. We finish up with the Samuels kid and he's out of the precinct like a shot."

"I didn't notice."

"I'm getting the feeling he doesn't want to be alone with me."

"Maybe it's your deodorant, Monk. I've been meanin' to say something."

Triano pulled the car into a no parking zone on West 14th Street. The afterhours club was a block and a half away. Three street hookers on the corner of Seventh Avenue spotted them and scampered away.

Ling recognized one of them. "Porpoise, get over here!"

"Porpoise?" Triano asked.

"Rumored to be the best crotch-diver south of 72nd Street." Ling called her again.

Her face angry, the hooker, who weighed well in excess of two-hundred pounds, strolled defiantly over to them.

"How you been, Porpoise? It's been awhile," Ling said.

"Not long enough."

"How's business?"

"Does Macy's tell Gimbel's?"

Ling edged closer to her. "There's this Englishman, James Whittaker. You read the papers?"

"Never learned how."

Ling guessed the claim was probably true. Triano reached into a trash basket for a copy of the *News*.

"He bought it—uptown," Ling said. "Very heavy scene. You ever seen him around?"

Triano held out the paper with its picture of Whittaker.

She studied it a moment, then shook her head. "Only Englishman I know comes every Friday at eleven o'clock, not a minute later."

"And . . . ?"

"And he ties me to the bedposts with sheets and then does his thing."

"To each his own," said Triano.

"Who's this guy, some kind of philosopher?" she asked, nodding toward Triano.

"Forget him, Porpoise. He's just a priest," Ling said. "Tell me this, your client, was he Whittaker?"

"Naw. Trick I see got a beard. Says he's a doctor."

"Free medical care, huh?"

"Ain't nothin' free, Monk. Leastwise, nothin' I've found."

"Take care of yourself, Porpoise," Ling said, a touch of compassion in his voice. He watched her waddle away, wondering how long she had until the wrong john picked her up, or the needle took its final plunge.

The afterhours club occupied a second floor loft and was a replica of dozens of others scattered around lower Manhattan. All were bad news.

The odor of a night's worth of partying hit them even before they reached the second floor. The windowless interior had the look of a hurricane scene, with overturned tables, broken glass, and a handful of immobile casualties passed out, or nearly so, their bent backs and bowed heads in seeming supplication to the half-pint bottles of liquor poised before them as if miniature Buddhas.

An elderly Puerto Rican was making a noble effort to sweep up the soggy cigarette butts, crushed plastic containers, and splintered bottles that littered the floor.

"Where's the bossman?" Triano demanded.

The old man looked at them suspiciously.

Ling flashed his shield. The cleanup man, his eyes revealing this was a ritual he endured regularly, gestured toward a rear door.

The two detectives entered without knocking. It was a small room cluttered with paper. An old-fashioned adding machine sat discarded on the floor in a corner. The walls displayed calendars, a badly ripped psychedelic poster, and numerous sex magazine centerfolds. Bent over a beat-up wooden desk missing one of its three drawers was a man who appeared to be in his forties, with a huge belly overhanging his belt and a glistening layer of sweat that began on his forehead and traveled up into his severely balding scalp.

He looked up abruptly at their entrance, gave them a quick glance, then lowered his eyes to a pocket calculator he had been punching atop the desk.

"I already gave to the Police Athletic League," he said.

Triano looked at Ling. "A philanthropist!"

Ling took the *News* from Triano, folded it to display Whittaker's photo, and slapped it over the manager's calculator and hands.

The manager swung around, his battered wooden swivel chair emitting a painful squeak, and lifted his feet to the desk. "Isn't he the guy I seen on *Dallas*? Or was it *Hollywood Squares*?"

Triano smiled. "You been in the Army?"

The manager laughed. "Bum knees."

"That's too bad."

"Why?"

" 'Cause they'd teach you a little respect." Triano moved instantly, lifting him by his shirt and slamming him into a wall. A centerfold depicting an oriental woman draped over a hassock fell to the floor.

Ling had his Nikon to his eyes and, as Triano backed away, advanced toward the suddenly pale manager. Click. Click. Click. Ling stepped back and focused the camera on the desk. He shot another two frames, then opened a desk drawer and photographed the strewn contents inside.

"What the fuck's he doin'?" the manager demanded of Triano.

"Tryin' to control his temper," Triano answered in a stage whisper. "They suggested he take up a hobby."

"Okay! I don't need the hassle!" the manager blurted out. "The guy was in here. Kind of a regular."

"With who?" Ling asked from across the room, the Nikon still in his hands but silent.

"Lot of broads."

"One of them named DeGrazia?" Triano asked.

"Yeah, Tony was the one that brought him around. You know all this, why you roustin' me?"

"What did they talk about?" Ling demanded.

The manager shrugged.

"Listen, asshole . . ." Triano, his hands raised chest-high, began edging toward him.

"Okay, okay!" The manager ran his fingers across his dripping forehead.

"What did they talk about?" Ling repeated.

"Coke—what else?"

"You mean that little white stuff, kind of looks like baby powder?" Triano asked.

"What about it?" Ling demanded.

"A deal. They yapped on and on about a deal. Big time, they said. And a permanent arrangement. They had a pipeline and they were gonna get fuckin' rich."

"And DeGrazia, his mind not being too bright, decides to freelance this one without the blessing of Marco," Ling said.

"Oh, no," the manager said. "Marco was right in the middle of it. At least, that's what they said."

Ling and Triano looked at each other, then turned for the door.

"Hey, wait a minute!" the manager called after them. "This is confidential, right? I mean Marco would . . ."

"He won't touch ya," Triano said reassuringly.

"You sure?"

"What, with your bad knees?"

They were back outside, walking to the car.

"Free enterprise," Triano said. "Ain't it wonderful?"

"Yeah—and some kind of permanent pipeline."

"So it shapes up as a drug wipeout," Triano said.

Ling had his doubts—it was too simple.

They continued walking in silence, Ling preoccupied with their findings, when suddenly a kid jumped out of a shadowy doorway and asked them for a light. The youth's eyes were riveted on the Nikon hanging from Ling's neck.

The two detectives, expressionless, shot glances at each other. Ling began fumbling in his pockets as if looking for a lighter. Then, just as abruptly as the youth had stepped before them, Ling edged Triano aside and faced the kid squarely. "Show me your hands," he ordered.

The boy squinted, his body stiffening as he readied an attack.

"Your hands—like this," Ling said, holding his hands out palm upward. "Show them to me."

The kid, his aggression tempered by his bewilderment, hesitated, then complied.

Ling studied the kid's outstretched hands, then said, "I was afraid of that." Then to Triano: "Here, you have a look."

Triano inspected both palms. "I think so," he said, nodding gravely.

The youth looked down at his hands. "What the fuck are you talking about?"

"Nubiles," Ling answered.

"What the . . . ?"

"We're doctors, see, and those are nubiles. Bad, too."

The kid's eyes were wide. "How you get them?"

"You jerk off?"

"Uh . . ."

"Answer me. You ever jerk off?"

The kid nodded sheepishly, his face furrowed with shame.

"How old are you, anyway?" Triano asked.

"Fif-fifteen," the kid stuttered.

"I wouldn't fuck around, if I were you," Ling said. "Get your damn ass over to Bellevue or something."

"What do I tell 'em?"

"Tell them what you told me—that you jerked off and now you got nubiles."

The kid was back inspecting his hands.

"Now you can do *us* a favor," Ling said.

"Like what, man?"

Ling held up the newspaper photo of Whittaker. "Ever see this guy around?"

"Yeah, plenty of times," the youth said without hesitation. "He a doctor, too?"

"Why?"

"I just figured he was, what with him comin' here sometimes in a Mercedes."

"Alone?"

"Naw. Younger dude with him, 'cept when he come by cab."

Triano looked at Ling: "Our stockbroker, Thornton."

Ling smiled. "Let's go."

They left the kid, who had returned to inspecting his hands.

"He'll get good care at Bellevue," Triano said, laughing.

"Yeah," Ling said. "A week's worth—upstairs."

Back at the station house, Ling found Collingsworth waiting for him. "May I speak to you?" the Englishman asked.

Ling ushered him off to a corner.

Collingsworth's expression was glum, as if he were a schoolboy awaiting the wrath of a teacher. "This Miss Marilyn Mason in the White House . . ." he began. "I have reliable information from our people in London that she and Whittaker had been seeing each other socially."

"I see," Ling said, rubbing his chin. "And, if I may ask, just when did you become privy to this reliable information?"

"Now, see here . . ."

"Don't 'see here' me, goddamnit," Ling snapped. "I thought you and I had reached an understanding."

Collingsworth's voice was equally stern. "You don't understand! You may well know criminal law and the back streets of New York City, but you're out of your element in diplomacy."

"So educate me."

The Englishman lowered his voice. "It's very delicate for us. We can't be in a position of implicating one of your top government officials in the outrageous transgressions of one of our own. To put it bluntly, the cleaning of your house is your task, not ours."

"That's nice," Ling said sarcastically. "That's the same logic that's brought so much peace to the world. Take the big duck, right? And what do we get: the Falkland Islands? Vietnam?"

Collingsworth threw his hands in the air. "You're hopeless."

Ling edged up to the Englishman and cocked his head. "What you've lost sight of in all your diplomatic niceties, my friend, is that there is a murderer out there. Two corpses are already sitting in the morgue. How many more are on the way?"

"I understand that but . . ."

"And you also are underestimating Julius Golden. He's not some rickshaw coolie genuflecting to British society ladies in one of your colonies, and if I told him how you held out on us again, the entire U.S. State Department couldn't stop him from mailing you back to where you came from—express."

"Are you going to tell him?"

"No."

The Englishman touched Ling's arm. "I'm grateful."

Across the room, Golden was herding his key detectives into the side office. Ling turned to join them, then stopped. "Come on," he said to Collingsworth.

The Englishman hesitated, then smiled. He followed Ling to join the others.

Ling and Triano briefed the group on their major discovery at the afterhours club: that Whittaker and DeGrazia had discussed a very large cocaine deal in what would be the first step in a permanent arrangement, and that Little Brother Marco apparently had a hand in it.

Golden's eyes lit up. "Bullseye!" he said.

Ling added Collingsworth's confirmation of the one bartender's report that Whittaker had been entertaining White House aide Marilyn Mason.

"What else?" the chief asked.

O'Brien, refreshed after his break, advised that the check of parking tickets in the area of the Park Avenue apartment house had turned up no noteworthy names, but had, as usual, found several summonses issued to rental cars.

Golden himself related the substance of an FBI report delivered to him only minutes before: The stockbroker, Thornton, had been picked up and interviewed upon his arrival at Heathrow Airport in London. At first reluctant to cooperate, he ultimately allowed as how he had met Whittaker at a bar several weeks earlier, had been at home studying stock performance charts on the night of the murders, and was in London to research the microchip market.

Levine advised that the FBI had, as requested, expedited the searches through its fingerprint files. Several sets of prints lifted in the apartment were still being traced, she said, but there had been one noteworthy match: Miss Marilyn Mason's prints were found all over the place.

There was a tap on the door and a detective entered. "You have a call, chief."

"Get a name and number," Golden said.

"I think you'd better take it," the detective said.

Golden, irritated, left the room. He returned a few minutes later. His expression and tone were uncharacteristically serious. "One of our guys on the Brooklyn Organized Crime Task Force," he said. "They've had a wire going on Marco for months. Turns out, Marco has had a few cryptic conversations with an unidentified caller with a British accent. The calls didn't make much sense—until now." He looked at Collingsworth. "They've got a name for the caller: British First Secretary David Holmes."

Collingsworth's face showed shock. "Are they certain?"

"Marco blurted it out during a call yesterday. Must have been drunk or somethin'."

The Englishman stood. His face was white. "Please excuse me." He rushed from the room.

"We go visit Mr. Marco, you think?" McKinnon asked.

Golden contemplated a moment, then shook his head. "Not yet. Let's see what, if anything, the British come up with." He thought a few moments more, then ordered that every drug-related street source in the city be pressed for information about a large coke deal—past or future—involving DeGrazia. The hunt for DeGrazia was to go on. And the ticketed rental cars were to be traced. Golden looked at Ling. "Any of your people help us out on this drug thing?"

"Maybe," Ling said.

"I'll get to my snitches, too," O'Brien interjected. "I used to work narcotics, don't forget."

Golden nodded, then asked: "What's our situation on mug shots?"

"DeGrazia and the hooker, Simpson. Both have sheets, so theirs we have," McKinnon said.

"The girl has a sheet?" Ling asked, doubting that Samantha Simpson would ever have allowed herself to fall on a prostitution rap.

"Small potatoes. Picked up four years ago at a gambling party—her and about fifty others."

"Let's find some friendly newspaper editor to help us out with file photos of Marilyn Mason and the Samuels kid.

They've both been in the news," Golden said. "What about our friend on Wall Street?"

"Nada," McKinnon replied.

"Well, we could hit up his firm's personnel department for one but that would start talk. We already know his car was in the neighborhood, so let's leave him out of the gallery for the time being."

"What about Holmes?" McKinnon asked.

Golden looked at Ling, then decided. "Skip him, too—for the moment. The last thing we need is some kind of international pissin' contest."

The chief ordered that the collected photos be shown to all the residents and help at the Park Avenue building as well as to neighbors in other buildings, particularly the window watcher Ling had spotted.

Golden then looked to Ling: "Ever been to our nation's capital?"

"Once. Guess I'm going again, huh?"

"First thing in the morning. I'll make the arrangements. Want you to pay a couple of courtesy calls for me—one to the British, the other to the White House. And take Collingsworth with you—on Her Majesty's tab, of course."

"You think that's wise, Julie?"

Golden thought a moment. "Yes—take him. He might be able to oil the wheels at the embassy."

The chief went off to get downtown's clearance. The bureaucracy would shake at the request of a round trip shuttle ticket to Washington, but Golden would prevail—on a case like this, even the accountants couldn't say no.

A phone was ringing across the room. Ling went over and picked it up.

"Monk, is that you? It's me, Edison."

"Damn!" Ling cursed to himself. His father-in-law. He had forgotten all about their luncheon appointment. "Did I miss you?" Ling asked. "I'm sorry, Edison. It just slipped my mind. This case . . ."

"We're going to meet at three, Monk—at the club. I'm just calling to remind you."

"How about a raincheck, Edison? We're all jammed up here. Maybe next week."

"Then dinner. Tonight. Yes, let's make it dinner. Seven or so. And I won't accept any excuses. We've got to talk, son."

"But—"

"But nothing. See you at seven. Same place. Until then—"

The line clicked dead. Dinner? Well, Ling thought, he could probably make that and get it out of the way. But lunch was out of the question. He already had other plans for a lunchtime meeting—with a lady.

21

The trouble with the new generation, British First Secretary David Holmes was thinking, is that they see everything as black or white. One was for, or against. Right or wrong. Left or right. But little in this world—and especially in matters of government—fell into two tidy piles.

"If you would only calm yourself a moment," Holmes said into the phone, "you will see there are a multitude of possible explanations that have nothing to do with the dark, dreary conclusion you seem to have already reached."

"The opportunity for explanations seems to have passed, don't you think?" Breckenridge Collingsworth snapped back at him. "What I do know as fact is that it was through the New York City Police Department that I, a personal representative of the prime minister, first learned of your activities with this Italian criminal."

Holmes laughed condescendingly. "Criminal? My boy, you have seen too many American films."

"What do you mean by that?"

"Open your eyes, Collingsworth! You're not in Leeds or Stratford. Think instead of Marseilles. Or Baghdad. A maze of underworlds. One stratum of power and influence layered on another, with those at the very highest dropping tentacles to the lowest whenever it is profitable and convenient . . ."

Collingsworth sighed. "Please quit with your riddles and get to the bloody point."

"You're in America—it's one gigantic free port. The culture is pure commerce. Green currency is their god. This Italian, you say, is a criminal. How simplistic! He's a businessman! What they call a player! These Sicilians have a veil of legitimacy now. It is not at all improbable that those police inspectors you're dealing with are in his very pocket."

"Perhaps so, but I fail to see the slightest relevance of that to the crown."

"I'm a diplomat. The earth has shrunk, yes, but my mission is no different than that of my predecessors dispatched to nineteenth-century China or Burma or Bombay. My mission? To protect the interests of the crown no matter to what depths of uncivilized depravity I must lower myself." He paused.

"What are you trying to tell me, Holmes?"

"Listen carefully—"

"Get on with it, please."

"The late Mr. Whittaker was running amok. You people in London had no conception of the reach of his activities. With respect to the government, he was a walking time bomb. One false turn, one miscalculation and England would have been blackened by unprecedented scandal, her integrity eternally tarnished. Yes, Mr. Whittaker was hopelessly out of control. Certain steps had to be taken."

"Such as?"

Holmes delayed his answer, finally saying: "Not over the phone, old man. Not even with a scrambler."

"Just what, then, do I advise London?"

Holmes laughed. "Advise them to trust one of their more experienced and loyal servants."

"Will this loyal servant be filing a report?"

"God, no! They would barely have it deciphered and it would be spread through the entire foreign office. Not all of that very clubby group, you know, subscribe to the rather heavy-handed diplomacy of our prime minister. She has her enemies. They are poised to strike." He lowered his voice. "You come here, Collingsworth. We'll have tea. We'll talk."

"I don't like it, Holmes, but you leave me no choice. I'll

get there when I can. In the meanwhile, do nothing. Understand? Nothing.''

Holmes was smiling broadly as he hung up the phone. Remove the boys from their home turf and they're helpless, their fright and ineptitude directly proportional to their mileage from London.

Holmes left his desk and poured himself a Scotch from a crystal decanter. He lifted the glass into a beam of sunlight and the Scotch instantly burst into a bloom of golden yellow. It was a deep, penetrating glow, the result of experienced blending and twenty years' aging, a blossom fashioned and nurtured by time. Holmes brought the glass to his lips and tasted its mellowness, allowing the first sip to roll over his tongue, the thought occurring to him that there was something to be said for endurance, for aging.

How long now had he been in Washington? He could measure it by the crises. Put one to bed and there would be another. And rarely would there be a thank you. Now there was yet one more crisis. He would handle it, yes—Collingsworth already had been primed, as called for in the contingency strategy Holmes had long before mapped out. But an old, tiring diplomat had learned a few lessons, and one was never to sit back complacently while allowing a crisis to run its course. They rarely did—at least to one's liking. What was needed was some engineering, some altering of the course: a diversion. Holmes laughed at the thought that, in the end, an effective diplomat was in reality nothing more than a glorified sapper in top hat.

He reached for the phone and ordered his secretary to put him through to the White House.

22

She was a shapely black woman, her fine featured face filled with pride, and as she made her way along Mott Street, she carried perhaps three-thousand dollars in apparel on her back, another seven or eight thousand in jewelry. Gwen Chambers had not always claimed such riches—not in Mississippi, not in Harlem, not until she had attracted the attention of a bull-necked, fast-talking, one-time City College of New York sociology major who had put the principles of urban dynamics to work to become the biggest cocaine distributor working the East Side. He was greedy, and selfish, and occasionally brutal, but he took care of her—and, in a special way, she loved him.

The sidewalk traffic was diminishing as Chinatown recovered from its lunch hour invasion. But there was enough of a crowd left to cause her worry. Her eyes darted from face to face. She was afraid—any break in security would cost her her life—and death would be a welcome escape compared to the torture her betrayal surely would warrant. She shuddered, thinking of it.

Chambers collided with an elderly oriental woman carrying a bag of fresh vegetables. She excused herself, then ducked into a somewhat dingy Chinese restaurant. Chou Ho, the elderly proprietor, spotted her immediately, but was careful to make no show of recognition as he escorted her to a table in the rear.

A young waitress offered Chambers a menu. She waved it away and ordered a cup of won ton soup. With the spicy odors of the food being served to other diners filling her nostrils, her insides ached for some pork lo mein, with fried rice, perhaps, on the side. But she knew from past experience she would be denied the time even to finish the soup, so it would be useless to order an entrée.

Presently, Ho appeared in position at the kitchen doorway, a napkin draped over his left arm. He began staring at her, his eyes penetrating, his stone-like face suggesting mysteries she would rather not imagine. Chou Ho frightened her, and for a moment she considered bolting out the door. But she stayed, nervously dabbing her mouth with her napkin. Then the Chinese blinked twice.

Chambers pushed her soup away and walked toward the women's room. Her knees felt wobbly. She stopped at the restroom door and braced herself, then turned around. Satisfied no eyes were upon her, she sidestepped through the adjacent kitchen door, which Ho held open for her.

Saying nothing, the Chinese took the lead, escorting Chambers past a pair of large gas-fired stoves, filled with sizzling woks and steaming pots of noodles and rice, to a food storage area in the rear. He opened a narrow door next to a walk-in refrigerator and stepped aside. Chambers slid past him and took a dark wooden stairway to the basement. He followed, then took the lead again. Chambers had been through this exercise more than once but had yet to master the complicated route. She hadn't really tried. It was better that way.

What followed was a rat's maze of rooms and corridors. Two lefts, then a right, followed by a left again. Chambers had the sense of walking in circles as they made their way through the interconnected basements of Chinatown. They passed two well-lighted areas in which long, shallow trays of bean sprouts were growing. Further on, the aroma of opium filtered under a pair of doors. From another closed room she heard angry Chinese voices in what was likely a gambling dispute.

Chambers had heard all the stories of the opium dens, the

gambling pits, and the tunnels to the East River that were said to provide a route of safety to Chinese seamen jumping ship in New York Harbor. She was one of the few non-orientals to gain admittance to the darkened chambers.

Ho came to a halt outside a heavy oaken door and motioned Chambers to wait. The Chinese opened the door and entered a dark room. In a moment, he reappeared and beckoned the woman to join him. Taking her upper arm, Ho guided her to a metal folding chair. When she was seated, Ho departed, switching on a dim light as he left. Monk Ling was standing in the corner.

"Hello, Gwen. How are you?" he asked.

"Some days it rains; mostly it's sunshine."

Ling smiled.

Chambers tried to remember how long it had been since her last meeting with the detective who had saved her kid brother's life, by getting him transferred out of Attica when the leather and chains white bikers had pegged him as their number one target. Almost two years, she guessed—but she still owed this cop.

"Your brother okay?" Ling asked.

She nodded. "He's makin' it, Monk. Another three years and maybe they'll give him parole."

"Can he stay clean?"

She shrugged. "It's rough."

"I know, Gwen. That I know." Ling pulled up another folding chair and sat across from her.

"What you need, Monk? Not my man, I hope."

"Naw. That's not in the deck between you and me. What I got is an Italian from Brooklyn. One Tony DeGrazia. Small time. I thought I'd ask you as a longshot."

Her face lit up. "You rolled 'em, Monk. Him I hear lots about—all in the last month."

"Shipment?"

"So it was said. Made mucho big promises, so much my man pays attention. The dude claims he's got enough coming to dust Manhattan in white. But then come delivery time, he's nowhere to be seen."

"No delivery, huh?"

"No snowstorm from him—but we heard it from here and there that it was still comin', only postponed."

"Coming from who, DeGrazia?"

"Don't know that, Monk. There was lots of talk. Seemed like maybe Marco had his greasy fingers in it. And some foreigner."

"Italian?"

"No, Monk, don't think so. I don't know that much, ya know—I kind of got to keep my place—but what I did hear was maybe this other dude come over from London."

23

Marilyn Mason knew now she never should have accepted the call, but curiosity had defeated her self-discipline. And then, on the line, British diplomat David Holmes had been so cryptic, so mysterious.

"It will be well within your interests . . ." he had told her. She had taken it initially as a threat, and her hand had tightened on the phone, ready to slam it down. But some sixth sense stopped her. Was he making a threat? Or was he trying to give her a helpful warning?

But now, as she waited for him, she realized her agreement to meet him had been a mistake. She didn't need to be manipulated like a toy, not when she was struggling hour by hour merely to get through the day, her feet tapping out of sight beneath her desk, her eyes fastened to the second hand of the clock, her hand reaching every ten minutes into her purse to verify that, no, she had not forgotten her bottle of pills.

Damn him anyway! she silently cursed, her right palm slapping her thigh. Holmes was keeping her waiting and the delay was intentional. The shakes were returning again. She opened her purse—the pills were there. Where was there a water fountain?

She was at the Lincoln Memorial, surrounded by marble and stone. The massive bulk of the monument left her feeling so insignificant, so small. Her eyes caught sight of Lincoln's face, that sad but hopeful face that signified so much promise. What had happened to her own promise? What had happened to her dreams?

She turned and looked away from the monument, out over the reflecting pool. The sun bounced off the tops of convoys of tour buses along the tree-lined Mall. On the horizon, a jetliner was making a noisy descent into National Airport. In the distance were the Capitol, the Jefferson Memorial, the Washington Monument and, yes, the White House. Together with the Lincoln edifice they formed a cross, a pair of intersecting lines marking the center of the most powerful checkerboard of earth and concrete in the world, maybe the universe. There was a touch of ancient Rome to the panorama, and she had this fleeting image of darkness, the vast plazas and fields of grass sprinkled with the campfires of Caesar's legions, awaiting the dawn and a new day of carnage in the name of the empire; nations and peoples to be subordinated to a mystical blueprint, while veiled virgins danced in circles at the base of the intimidating, stumpy obelisk, itself fittingly symbolic of what was at the heart of it all.

Power. Global in scope. As enduring as the currents of the nearby Potomac. And she was part of it, a central part of it. She should have been able to stand there and revel in her position and deeds, the world's economy dependent to a startling degree on her. Instead, she felt fragile and vulnerable, unable to free her mind of James Whittaker, memories of the press of his hardened body against her, her legs undulating almost imperceptibly with the sensation of his touch, both of them naked, laying full-bodied on the sofa, on the bed, on the floor, he on top, the candlelight flickering off their bodies, the stereo bathing them in tender sound. . . .

One by one the scenes came to her, snapshots in an album of dreams. A carriage ride in Central Park, the pavement still wet from an early evening rain, her wearing the orchid corsage he had presented in the Plaza lobby before their dinner in a cozy corner of the Persian Room, where their legs had brushed beneath the table. A Sunday afternoon at the Rockefeller Center skating rink, Whittaker, unable to skate, clinging to her for support, both of them tumbling to the ice, laughing.

A Saturday at the Bronx Zoo, giggling so much that their sides hurt, watching the monkeys in their scatological play. They would film it, they decided. They would return with his videotape camera and record the monkeys' sexual play so they could relive the moment, so they could laugh again. But they had never gone back. Nor had they flown to Paris. Nor had they . . .

"I'm glad you came," a voice over her shoulder said.

David Holmes took her arm and led her toward the rear of the monument, away from the clusters of tourists. "It's always so beautiful here, so calm, don't you think?"

She stopped when they reached the shadows and broke his grip. She was his equal in size, and their eyes were level as she glared at him. His thin lips were drawn into that patronizing smile of his, and she wanted to slap him, rake the back of her hand across his mouth again and again, until that smug smile went away. "What do you want from me?" she demanded.

Holmes smiled. "I *want* nothing."

"Then why the fun and games?"

"I should be asking you that. I didn't appreciate that little scene of yours in the restaurant."

"I didn't appreciate your helping him set me up," she shot back.

"I don't know what you're talking about."

"Oh, don't you?"

He stepped to the side and looked off into the distance. "I'm not here to debate."

"Why *are* you here?"

He faced her again. "To tell you a story."

"I don't need any stories," she snapped.

"It happened to me twelve or perhaps fifteen years ago. I was at this diplomatic reception. The Canadian embassy, I believe it was. A prominent financier from an investment house in Montreal cornered me. There was no avenue of escape, I discovered to my displeasure, and so I was reduced to standing there and listening to his babble about venture capital and selling short and stock transfer taxes . . ."

"What do you want from me?"

"Then, out of the blue, he lowers his voice and propositions me. A strange proposition. I had never encountered it before. . . ."

She began edging away. "I don't want to hear any more!"

"It would be worth thousands to him, he said, perhaps even millions—and, of course, I would have my share—if the next time Britain devalued the pound, he had advance notice. Only a few minutes, he said, was all he needed. With the proper communications to the exchange floors in New York and London, a fellow could really take them to the cleaners. That's what he said, 'Take them to the cleaners.' "

"What has this got to do with me?"

"Of course, I advised him that despite what he might have assumed, London acted on our currency without giving the slightest forewarning to those of us in the field. His proposal, therefore, could not possibly work."

"Stop it!" she shouted, then turned her back to him and strutted away. He caught her with another tight grip on her arm.

"What information did *you* provide, Miss Mason? Currency changes? Or the Federal Reserve money supply? Or the banks' discount rate? What were you feeding him? I dare say that even budget and deficit figures before their official release could be profitable—in the right hands."

"Go to hell!"

Holmes released her. He was smiling maliciously. "How did he persuade you to do it? Promises of a wonderful honeymoon? Mexico, maybe. Or Paris? Or . . . or perhaps he had something to hold over your head?" He cocked his head. "You don't look well, dear. Your face is drawn. You look emaciated. Deathly symptoms, my dear. What's your malady, a little allergy to cocaine? Or an adverse reaction to Darvon? Amphetamines? Or maybe something exotic, like opium."

She slapped his face. "Who do you think you're talking to?"

Holmes reconstructed his smile. "I like you, you know. You're brazen and strong. I admire toughness in a woman. You have intelligence and you know how to use it."

Her lips were quivering. Her face felt numb.

"I want to help you, Marilyn. Whittaker used you. He used me. We're in the same trash bin, so to speak."

"I . . . I don't feel well." She was starting to collapse.

He helped her to a park bench. She opened her purse and began fumbling at the cap to her pill bottle. She felt panic—her hands wouldn't work!

He took the vial and opened it for her. As tears rolled down her cheeks, she clumsily accepted a single pill from him, dropped it in her mouth and almost gagged swallowing it without water.

"I have my lines out," he said softly. "I'm in touch with the New York police."

Police. She jolted at the word.

"They have learned about you and your relationship with Whittaker," Holmes continued. "They are building a file. You must be very, very careful."

Her eyes grew wide.

"They'll want to know places and dates. They'll want to know all the whys. If you allow me, I will help you. We can protect each other. All you have to do is keep your mouth shut. You see, we all have our dirty little secrets." Holmes waited.

The look on his face—she had seen that look before. It was the face of a gambler, a man who had placed his bet and now was awaiting the outcome of a roll of the dice, the dealing of a hand, the spin of a wheel.

She stood. Her legs had steadied. Her posture was ramrod straight. She straightened her hair with a defiant movement of her hands.

"I don't need your help," she declared. And she walked away.

24

They are so careless, Stanislas Lubelski thought as he watched David Holmes and the Mason woman enact their little drama at the Lincoln Memorial. Their illusion of safety betrayed them.

It was not difficult to figure out: the woman had insulted and embarrassed Holmes at the restaurant; now, after making her wait for him at a rendezvous he had demanded, he was threatening her with reprisals. His smile, her retreat, and her near collapse neatly laid out the scenario.

There were still many questions. What setup had she been talking about in the restaurant? What was he now holding over her? The answers to those, Lubelski suspected, would provide the key to who had murdered Whittaker—and Anatole.

When Holmes and Miss Mason parted, Lubelski decided this time to tail the woman. She took a taxi. Lubelski followed in his rental car.

The cab led him directly to the Executive Office Building, next to the White House. When Mason disappeared inside, he elected not to wait—penetration was impossible and the presence of a mysterious car in the area would arouse suspicion. Besides, there were other potentially more fruitful explorations awaiting him.

For the moment, he would assume that Mason intended to complete her workday at the White House. That was reason-

able. But given her state of near-hysteria, he would have to
hurry—she might approach collapse once again and depart for
home prematurely.

Traffic was congested and the drive to Georgetown excru-
ciatingly slow. Perhaps he should have taken the Metro, an
alternative that seemed even more attractive when he could
find no parking space outside Marilyn Mason's building. He
left the car in a commercial lot around the corner.

There were four floors to the building and an equal number
of names on the mail boxes. He was inspecting the lock on
the vestibule door when a young delivery man suddenly came
down the lobby stairs.

Lubelski fumbled for his keys. "Hi," he said, smiling, as
the other man stared at him suspiciously. "I'm a guest of the
Johnsons—upstairs."

The delivery man hesitated, then held the door open for
him.

The locks on Mason's apartment door—there were two of
them—were sad hoaxes. Lubelski's swift-moving pick put him
inside the apartment in under thirty seconds. The window
drapes and shades were closed, leaving the apartment dark
and him protected from any curious neighbors in buildings
across the street. A radio had been left on—an announcer was
reading the news—in what was either an oversight by a
troubled woman or a ploy to discourage burglars. Lubelski
followed the sound to the kitchen.

On the stove was a large pot, its inside charred. An
overcooked dinner? He lifted it and inhaled. He immediately
ruled out burned food—the pot had the odor of a paper fire.

He opened the doors under the kitchen sink. A trash basket
was lined with plastic. He lifted it out. Coffee grounds, some
bread crusts and ashes. He found a plastic sandwich bag, then
using a spoon, scooped a sample of the ashes into it. He
carefully sealed the bag and placed it in his pocket—Petrovich's
technicians would be able to tell him exactly what substance
had been burned.

Lubelski moved on through the apartment. The bedroom
was stark, lacking those feminine flourishes common in the
homes of most single women. No flowers, no porcelain, no
lace. The single visible photograph showed an elderly man

seated in a wheelchair. Her father? On the dresser was an old, cheap jewelry box, a souvenir from Niagara Falls. He lifted the lid and found only a few pieces of jewelry, all rather plain. There was no paper, no address book, no key.

Lubelski opened the closet. A half-dozen solid or subtly striped business suits, two skirts, both dark, and severe white blouses, mostly plain and appearing starched, a couple with ruffles. On the floor, a row of shoes was lined up with military precision, the footwear reflecting the same all-business flavor of the clothes above them. Hanging from a hook on the side of the closet were two pairs of jeans; one of them appeared unworn.

The living room, with its modern decor, echoed the sterility of the bedroom. Except for a stack of paperbacks on a side table, there was no evidence that anyone lived here regularly, that it was not a room in a motel. Lubelski lifted the books: two were psychological treatises offering counsel on how to increase one's self-esteem and assertiveness; the third pondered how a woman could excel in the business world.

A small writing desk stood in the corner below a collection of framed certificates and diplomas. There was also a black and white photograph. Lubelski removed it from the wall. The frame was black and made of plastic, a stock frame, probably purchased at a dime store. The photograph was taken in the Oval Office, and it showed the President with five young aides, one of them Marilyn Mason. "To Marilyn," the President's inscription read, "with gratitude for all your hard work and devotion."

Lubelski returned the photo to its hook and opened one of the desk's two drawers. He found one of the targets of his search—Mason's file of personal papers. But the documents were disappointing: utility bills, bank statements, paycheck stubs. Only the most recent telephone invoice was productive— it listed many long distance calls to New York, all to the number Lubelski recognized as Whittaker's. He copied the dates and times of the calls, then carefully replaced the invoice with the other papers.

He opened the other drawer. It contained a box of stationery, a stapler, and a small stack of mementos: Broadway Playbills, a pair of New York Yankees ticket stubs, a New

York subway map, and a catalogue from the Museum of Modern Art. He smiled—Marilyn Mason had a hint of human emotion after all.

Lubelski wrote down the date of the Yankees' game, and the opening and closing dates of the MOMA show.

Next to the desk was a small wastebasket. Lubelski bent down to examine it. But the wastebasket was devoid of any discarded notes, crumpled letters or other documentation that might be useful. All he found were some unopened envelopes of junk mail and a partially wrapped, withering potted plant with a card bearing the name "Bill."

Lubelski looked around—he had covered everything. All in all, the penetration had not proven very productive, at least when compared to the risk he had taken. He decided to leave. But it was not soon enough—just as he reached the small foyer, there was the sound of a key in the door.

He ducked quickly into the bedroom and hid behind its open door, his eyes watching the foyer through the crack at the hinges. The outside door opened. It was Mason. She slammed the door shut and hurled her trenchcoat to the wooden parquet floor. Her heels clicked with urgency as she moved inside. Sounds of her sitting—at the desk. A drawer opened. Something slapped on the top of the desk. The sounds of paper being shuffled, pages turning.

Lubelski edged from behind the door. He could see her back as she sat bent over the desk. He leaned further and then caught a glimpse of yellow. The Playbills! She was rummaging through her small collection of mementos. Had he missed something? Had he checked to see if anything had been concealed between the pages?

Suddenly she stopped. She stared at the disheveled stack of paper. Tears began rolling down her cheeks. Then, in an attack so violent she nearly tipped her chair, Marilyn began ripping the thin Broadway keepsakes, the ticket stubs, the subway map and the museum catalogue, shredding them into hundreds of tiny pieces until there was no fragment big enough for her to tear in half once more. Forming her hands into a pair of cups, she scooped up the remains and hurled them into the wastepaper basket atop the wilting plant and junk mail. Then, when the desk was cleared of every last shred of paper, she folded her arms on the desktop, lowered her head and began to weep.

Lubelski had to leave—and fast. Mason had come home early and there was no telling who might be arriving next. But something was holding him back. In defiance of all his training, all his experience, he was caught up in curiosity. Why was she crying? My god, he even felt a pang of sympathy for this weeping woman. Then he got hold of himself.

What was happening to him? Lubelski demanded of himself, as he eased out the door.

25

Ling's timing was perfect: his head curling under his chest, his body somersaulting, then twisting, his feet coming up together against the tiled wall of the Knickerbocker Athletic Club pool. He pushed off with power, his body surging through the cool water several meters before he resumed his stroke. He then concentrated on his slightly cupped hands as they pierced the surface once every second, the strokes and the flutter kicks propelling him forward with a smoothness that concealed his actual speed and power.

The sensation of the water streaming along his naked body and the effects of the exertion upon his heartbeat and lungs left Ling in a trance-like state. Almost as a stranger standing outside himself, he listened to his breathing, monitored the rhythmic filling of his lungs on every fourth stroke, and the air's expulsion in a steady release of bubbles underwater. For twenty minutes he swam, alternating between a sprint and a long distance pace until his legs felt as heavy as stone and his arms ached every time he thrust them over his head. He was staggering when he climbed the gold-plated ladder and accepted a large towel from the white-coated Irish pool boy.

"You'll kill yourself doing that," Edison LeGrande called from a row of poolside tables.

"Maybe," Ling said, toweling off his hair as he took a

seat across from his father-in-law. "There are times when I think that's the way to end it."

LeGrande reached around his martini to touch Ling's arm. "You still miss her, don't you, son."

Ling nodded. "More than I ever thought possible."

LeGrande, suddenly appearing older, looked vacantly toward the pool. "Me, too."

A waiter came to take Ling's order. LeGrande grimaced when he selected coffee.

"Have yourself a drink, boy. It'll do you some good."

"Coffee, please," Ling repeated to the waiter.

Other men, most in their sixties or older, pot-bellied, with toothpick legs and arms, some nude, some with towels around their waists, sat at other tables drinking or picking at huge slabs of rare prime rib. Others were settled into lounging chairs, reading the *Wall Street Journal* or the *Times*. The waiters shuttled back and forth with perspiring tumblers of martinis, Manhattans, screwdrivers, and platters barely large enough to hold the inch-thick steaks and roasts. No one swam.

Ling's coffee came—along with a refill for his father-in-law.

"It's good to see you, Monk. We don't get together enough," the older man said.

"The job, Edison. They make you live it."

"That's not healthy. And besides, you deserve better. That's what I want to talk about."

"I . . . I've given it some thought and I'm grateful, believe me, Edison, but—"

"At least hear me out," LeGrande said impatiently.

Ling stared at him a moment, then slid back in his chair and gestured for him to go on.

"My personnel man just resigned, see. A vice-president. Now that's a job where you don't have to know a whole hell of a lot. About that particular specialty, I mean. These women, they do the work for you. All you have to do is be pleasant and keep the troublemakers in line."

Ling bent forward. He toyed with the handle of his coffee cup. "I appreciate it, Edison. You don't know what it means to see the confidence you have in me. But I'm just not ready. I don't think I could do it."

"A hundred grand, Monk. And your father-in-law the big boss."

Ling smiled—and slowly shook his head.

LeGrande, unable to conceal his anger and frustration, turned his head away. He gulped from his martini glass and reached for his cigar, whose coal had died resting in the crystal ashtray.

Ling lit a match and reached over the table. LeGrande cupped the flame, then sat back, puffing.

"What is it about this police work that's got such a hold on you, son? Why do you stay?"

Ling probably would have shared his answer—if he had known what it was. He was haunted by the same question.

"It must be very frustrating—and there don't appear to be too many people lining up to say thanks," LeGrande continued.

"So, that's life, Edison."

"And that kind of statement is bullshit. It's meaningless. You've got to do better than that—for your own sake."

Ling looked down at the white tablecloth. "I need it, I guess. Just now, anyway. It's my fix."

He *did* need it—but he didn't know why. What was it, the decadence? The riddles? The preview of hell? Sometimes he suspected it was the drama that had addicted him. He had frequently caught himself acting out a role, measuring his words and actions as if he were in front of a movie camera. Other times, he thought he stayed on the job for the single reason that it was something he did well. What Ling did know was that he would not survive as a personnel director reporting to his father-in-law.

The waiter was back to take their dinner order, but neither man felt like eating. Instead, they dropped their towels and headed for a bank of steam rooms. They had their choice of four: warm and dry, warm and wet, hot and dry, and hot and wet. LeGrande announced his preference as hot and dry— "Got to sober up for the little lady." That was fine with Ling. He opened the airtight door for the older man to enter first.

There was only one other occupant, an overweight man stretched out on a high shelf, snoozing. They took seats across from one another on the low benches. LeGrande closed his

eyes. Ling allowed his chin to fall limply to his chest and his
arms to hang loosely. The heat quickly penetrated his muscles, mixing with the fatigue from his swimming to produce a
mellowness beyond that which alcohol had ever supplied him.
Bathing in his sweat, he tried to think of the case, the
puzzling death of an Englishman, consumed, long before the
fatal gunshot, by his own desperation. But Ling was unable
to keep his thoughts on the investigation—as the heat of the
chamber reached deeper within him, there came flashes from
other mellow days, images of Alex, her long, athletic legs as
she jogged along a white sand beach in the Caribbean, her
smile the moment they were pronounced married, that special
glow of fulfillment she showed even in the first few weeks of
her pregnancy . . .

"I've had enough, I think," Ling told his father-in-law.

LeGrande followed him from the steam room. "I've got to
be going, Monk," he said. "You stay and have yourself
another swim. But I want you to think about my offer. And for
godsake, start spending a little of your money." He grabbed
Ling's hand with both of his, winked and padded off to the
showers.

Ling needed something to clear his mind. He looked to the
pool, then decided against it—his muscles had abandoned
him. Instead, he entered an elongated chamber near the steam
rooms. The room had a low ceiling, with a railing running
lengthwise through its middle. At one end, waist high, was a
nozzle the size of those used by firefighters.

Ling turned a handle and a stream of water shot out on a
path parallel to the floor. He adjusted a dial to set the water's
temperature and another to fix its pressure, then grabbed
ahold of the railing, easing himself into the powerful surge,
allowing it to push him back slowly until he was midway
between the nozzle and the opposite wall. Carefully he turned
his body to permit the high pressure stream to pound his
back, chest, and abdomen, his neck and thighs—regretting he
could not turn the water loose on his mind. The water kneaded
his muscles as effectively as any masseur, its coldness hardening the tissue and re-energizing him. At last, freed by the
water's violence, he succeeded in turning his attention to the
Whittaker investigation. He thought of Whittaker and DeGrazia,

the Samuels youth, and the mysterious dark-skinned female victim.

And then he thought of Samantha Simpson.

An hour later, Ling was on the Upper East Side standing outside Samantha's apartment building, unclear as to how he had gotten there—or why. His movements since leaving the club had been mechanical, a pigeon homing in on his coop, and his thoughts had been off in that fourth dimension sphere he suspected he had somehow inherited from his Chinese stepfather. But that, given the laws of genetics, was impossible. Maybe it was a simple case of his beginning to lose touch—half the department seemed to think so.

He was watching the building entrance, stalling, his feelings in conflict.

Then suddenly she was there in the lobby, her arms around a large, blubbery man who was staggering. Even from across the street, Ling recognized him—City Councilman William O'Bannion.

Samantha was guiding him toward the door. The doorman, revulsion on his face, went to help. O'Bannion's mouth was twisted upward, not unlike that of a baying dog, and he was singing, the discordance of his drunken howling penetrating the thick plate glass of the lobby door, overpowering even the sounds of the traffic.

When they reached the sidewalk, she left him in the doorman's arms, then went to hail a taxi. Twice cabbies started to stop, then saw what awaited them and drove on. Finally, a Checker stopped—a woman driver. Compassionate, Ling guessed. One too many drunks would vomit all over her cab—then she'd learn.

O'Bannion clumsily ran a hand through his disheveled thinning hair. He started to grin. His eyes grew wide, showing both pomposity and greed, advertising his self-perceived power and the assumption that he had license to do exactly as he pleased. The folds of fat under his chin rolled as Samantha and the doorman lugged him to the cab and packed him inside. The doorman slammed the cab door. Samantha went to the front window and gave the driver an address. Ling was behind her when she turned.

"Rough night?"

"Oh, christ! Did you *have* to see this? What are you doing, following me?"

"It's a nice evening," Ling said. "I thought we could talk."

She studied him a moment, then said: "He made quite a mess upstairs."

"Then let's walk."

She shrugged. "Why not?"

The night was unseasonably warm, and the streets were crowded. Couples, mostly. Some were stepping into and out of bars. Many held hands; a few propped against lightposts or the sides of buildings and embraced. The door to one bar was propped open. From inside came the music of a live band. Ling glanced into the doorway. In the shadows, couples were dancing. There was laughter—and giggling. He resisted an urge to take Samantha's arm.

"You said you wanted to talk," she said.

Ling *did* want to talk. He *had* to talk. "It's about Whittaker," he lied. "I'm curious as to what you think."

"What do you mean what I think?"

"I mean, you knew him. You spent a lot of time with him. You must have some feeling for who might have killed him."

They were at a red light. She didn't answer until it had changed and they had crossed. "He was into a lot of things."

"What about Samuels? He seems somewhat emotional."

She stopped. "Samuels kill Whittaker? You've got to be kidding."

"The stockbroker, then."

"Him I know nothing about."

"You mentioned the woman from Washington."

"A barracuda, yes. But basically harmless, would be my guess." She looked at him as they walked. "If you're serious about wanting my opinion . . ."

"I am."

". . . then I'd look to Brooklyn. I don't know what was coming down there, but it was heavy."

"The guy who kept calling?"

She nodded. "He didn't impress me as very mellow."

They stopped now and then to look into store windows. An import shop. A custom-blend coffee store. A framing studio.

Then she announced that she would like to head back. They turned around.

"Do you miss Whittaker?" Ling asked.

"I feel sorry for him."

"That's all?"

She glared at him. "What do you want me to say, that I loved him? It was business, no more. Besides, he was in a shell, a tough shell. Hard to figure him out except . . ."

"Except what?"

"Like he was always thinking of himself. Yet he had this gift, this ability to find a woman's interest, what's important to her, and delve right into it."

"A good line, huh?"

She shook her head. "It was more than that. It was . . . a kind of magic."

Ling lagged behind half a step, his eyes inspecting her. Her dark hair glistened under the street lamps, and there was a suppleness and sway to her walk that could have hypnotized any man.

"You're staring at me," she admonished.

"I'm fond of beauty."

"So go to an art museum."

He laughed. Then they were at her building. She broke into a smile. "As I said, I kind of like you, you know." She started for the door, then stopped. "Hey, I feel like a party. You smoke grass? Sure you do. Come on up."

Ling hesitated.

She bent toward his ear. "No charge. Honest."

"I've got to catch a plane early in the morning."

"And the postman's got to deliver his mail." She edged away. "But whatever you say." She blew him a kiss and turned toward the lobby.

Ling fought it. His professionalism banned it. His emotions were too asunder to chance it. "Wait!" he heard himself say.

She held his hand in the elevator. He looked to the floor and counted the seconds, the opportunity for escape ticking away. Inside her apartment there followed a ritual: soft lights strategically placed, music, an offer of drinks, the kicking away of shoes. She was curled up on her sofa, her head slightly cocked, her eyes wide and knowing, her hips and thighs bulging beneath her too-tight skirt. She had thrown back her shoulders and, at some inconspicuous moment, had unknotted her string bow and released the top two buttons of her loose, ruffled silk blouse. "You're special," she said. "You understand me."

Ling could take no more. He left the chair opposite her and removed his coat and tie.

"Take off your shoes," she said. "Relax. I can teach you how."

Ling did as she ordered, amazed all the while at how little had to be said, at how innocent and natural they accepted one another, giving pleasure, feeling wanted. There was no awkwardness, no fumbling, no unbroken rhythm as they followed a script over which neither had any control.

The feel of her flesh took him into another world, a mystical world that he again attributed somehow to the genes of his stepfather.

Later, holding her, he began wondering what it would really be like—to be a corporate personnel director.

"You know," she was saying, "I'm not entirely the woman you think I am."

"How's that?"

She sat up and bent forward. Ling's hands went to work on the muscles of her bare back. "There was this boy, back in Texas . . ." She turned to look at Ling. "I loved him. I really did. Then he left me. Went to work on some oil rig in Mexico."

"You deserved more than that," Ling said.

"We planned to get married. And I . . . had a baby." She paused. Her lips were quivering.

Ling wanted to protest but couldn't find the words. What was she doing? They had had a moment. Why spoil it now—with a confession.

Samantha looked away. "It was a boy. A precious little thing." She stopped. Ling pulled her back to him. "He's five, now," she resumed. "Kindergarten. Lives with my mother."

"Do you get to see him?"

Her eyes came alive. She smiled and shook her head slowly. "No. My son doesn't even know me."

Ling loosened his grip on her but she pressed harder against him. Her face was on his chest—and she was crying.

"He knows you more than you think, Sam," Ling said softly. "And he loves his mother, don't ever doubt that."

"Maybe someday he'll grow up and understand," she said, stroking Ling's face. He closed his eyes. She kissed him. And Ling, for a second time, surrendered.

An hour later, Ling took a bus home, staring through the grime-streaked window at the passing couples, struggling to frame the questions he would ask in Washington, hating himself.

26

Monk Ling and Breck Collingsworth said little to each other on the early morning shuttle to Washington. The Englishman several times attempted small talk but Ling was not in the mood. Ling had not really wanted Collingsworth along, chiefly because the Englishman now had potentially conflicting goals in the case. Collingsworth was seeking the apprehension of Whittaker's killer on the one hand, while attempting to protect the political interests of his prime minister on the other.

As the plane began its descent, the Englishman, surprisingly, raised the issue directly. "You don't trust me, do you," he said in what was a statement, not a question.

"You're a professional," Ling said.

"Yes, I am," Collingsworth responded. "And it's very much in our interest that you succeed in your investigation. That's paramount."

"No doubt it is. But what happens when it develops that one of your key foreign service officers got his hands a little dirty."

"Whatever the price, we will pay it."

"Are those your words—or somebody else's?"

"Mine—and also those of the prime minister. I spoke to her this morning."

Ling let it drop. He still had his doubts—he had too much experience with politicians.

The Washington Monument and the Capitol were visible as the shuttle made its approach. National Airport was crowded and bustling with tourists, military men, students, and brief-case carrying bureaucrats traveling on government vouchers. Outside, in the confusion of taxis, limousines and government sedans, Ling and Collingsworth found the British Embassy car the Englishman had arranged.

Their first stop was the Executive Office Building. When Ling had called her, presidential aide Marilyn Mason agreed to meet with him, acknowledging that, yes, she had known James Whittaker and professing that it was vital that his murderer be brought to justice. Her cooperation had surprised him—federal officials had a tradition of slamming doors on New York cops. Ling had suggested she might consider having an attorney present, but she saw no need for that and added: "Washington is a cyclone of gossip; I'd prefer your visit to be as low-keyed as possible, if you understand."

Ling had assented and he kept his promise, withholding his shield from the White House security men, identifying him-self only as a visitor of Miss Mason's. To avoid complica-tions, he had left his service revolver in the car.

A secretary welcomed them graciously and asked them to be seated, explaining that Ms. Mason had a briefing sched-uled for the President later in the day and was busy preparing for it. They were not kept waiting, however—immediately upon the announcement of their arrival, Mason appeared at the door to her private office, bidding them to come right in.

She was tall and slightly paunchy, and her hair was pulled back into a rigid bun. As Ling made the introductions, he noticed that her fingernails were clear and trimmed short. She was wearing a charcoal gray skirt and matching jacket, with a thin black bow around the high collar of a smooth, white blouse.

"I'm afraid I'm facing a major briefing in the Oval Of-fice," she said, taking a seat behind an oversized desk. "Perhaps you'll excuse me if I seem a bit harried."

She *did* appear harried. Makeup failed to conceal dark circles under her eyes. Both eyes were slightly bloodshot. Her fingers toyed nervously with a pen except when her hands tinkered with her hair. Ling was accustomed to nervousness on the part of the subjects he questioned and she *did* have an important briefing upcoming. Still . . .

Ling thanked her for her time and, in what he said was merely a formality, reminded her that she had an uncontested right to have a lawyer present.

She laughed. "The only time I've ever retained the services of a lawyer was to probate my father's estate, not that that amounted to anything except a tumble-down house in a one-horse town in western Pennsylvania."

"I hitchhiked through Pennsylvania while a student," Collingsworth said. "A very pretty state."

"Yes—but a somewhat archaic state of mind. I'm glad to be out."

"I've heard a lot about you," Ling said. "Is it true you can multiply a pair of four-digit numbers in your head?" Golden had passed on that last-minute nugget—Ling didn't know where he had gotten it.

She laughed. "Not quite. I still need help. But I admit, I rarely use a calculator. I'm probably the only economist in the western world still using a slide rule." Her expression grew serious. "Do you have any suspects?"

"An arrest is not imminent, if that's what you mean," Ling answered. "That's why we're still interested in assembling as much information as possible about the victims."

"Oh, yes. Victims, plural. I forgot about the woman. I, of course, had never met her."

"But you did know James Whittaker."

"Yes. We had met here in Washington—I don't remember the affair, I'm afraid—but he struck me as a charming conversationalist, and he invited me to give him a call if I ever got to New York."

"And you did."

"Yes. That would be about six months ago. I went there to address a meeting of analysts on Wall Street and had some free time afterward. He met me and gave me the grand tour: World Trade Center, Central Park, Statue of Liberty, the whole works. I enjoyed it. I had never been to those places before."

"Did you see him again?"

"Oh, yes—several times. For some reason, I had a stream

of New York engagements. As I said, he was a charming host. He showed me the town.''

Ling watched her eyes. "Were you in love?''

She laughed heartily. "Goodness gracious, no. Now don't take this the wrong way, but I consider the position I hold very important. It's also very time consuming, if you do it right. There's simply no time for . . . shall we say, affairs of the heart.''

Ling nodded in understanding. "His other friends and acquaintances, did you get to know any of them?''

She thought a moment. "There were a few. Let's see if I can remember them.'' She smiled patronizingly. "Again, don't get me wrong but when you work in the White House, you meet so many people. They knock down your door.'' She began doodling with the pen on a pad of legal size yellow paper. "I did meet the Samuels boy.'' She looked up. "I assume you know about him and his involvement in the so-called anti-nuclear movement and all that.''

"We're aware of him.''

"Well, it was that relationship that unfortunately ended my friendship with James Whittaker.''

"His letter to the *Times* must have put you in a rather embarrassing position.''

"That's an understatement. I'd been escorted by a man who now publicly criticized the President. But I must say they were very good about it around here—they never said a word.''

Ling said he wanted to make certain he understood. "What you're saying is you never saw him again after his letter was published in the *Times*?''

"We had one farewell dinner—oh, I guess it was a month ago—and that was it. And no hard feelings, I might add. He was very gentle and understanding. That's why his death was such a shame, such a tragedy.'' She looked at Collingsworth. "Your prime minister has my deepest sympathy. I know she must have been very close to him despite their differences.''

"Thank you, ma'am. I will pass your sentiments along,'' the Englishman said.

"Was there anyone else?'' Ling asked.

"Yes, as a matter of fact. James appeared to have close

contact with David Holmes of the British embassy. In fact, now that I think about it, it might have been Secretary Holmes who introduced us.''

"You say their relationship was close. In what way?'' Ling asked.

"I'm not sure. It seemed they were in a collaboration of some sort together.'' She glanced at Collingsworth, then back to Ling. "The only reason I know this is one day I was having lunch with James and he cut it short in order to meet Secretary Holmes out at Dulles Airport. I was concerned—you see, James had had a few too many martinis—but then it turned out that the secretary was picking him up and they were going to Dulles together.''

"What for?'' Collingsworth asked.

She smiled coyly. "I'm afraid I was not made privy to that.''

Ling apologized in advance for his next question, explaining he could get in a great deal of trouble if he failed to ask it. The police needed to know, he said, where she was the night of the murders.

"Here in Washington,'' she answered without hesitation. "I spent that night at home. I was exhausted and went to bed even without supper. I remember it because I awoke early and heard the bulletin about the murders on the radio. Needless to say, I was stunned.''

She looked at her watch. "I'm afraid I must get back to my briefing paper—unless there is something remaining that you consider urgent.''

Ling stood. "No—nothing urgent. If you should recall anything else you think might be helpful, I'd appreciate a call.''

"Of course.''

She showed them to the door and remained there watching them leave. Ling glanced back to wave. Marilyn Mason's face had tightened and was reddening. Her eyes were drilling their backs.

"She's tough,'' Collingsworth said when they reached the street.

"A machine,'' Ling agreed. "Wind me up and watch me lead the country. Work twenty-six hours in a day. The new technocrats. Worse than the bureaucrats because they actually believe they're accomplishing something."

"And if you cross them?"

"Vengeance would be an understatement."

They were in the car headed for the embassy.

"A jilted lover, do you think?" Collingsworth asked.

"If only it were that simple," Ling said. The picture of the playboy Whittaker and the prim Ms. Mason hand-in-hand troubled Ling. At first glance, it didn't fit. But maybe she was the stereotyped lady librarian who let her hair down at night and became a tiger in bed. Perhaps Whittaker had been attracted to her undeniable intellect. And at the least, she offered entrée to the Washington power structure.

"Aren't you a bit suspicious?" Collingsworth asked.

"I'm always suspicious. And I'm also curious—about the message she was giving us."

"Message?"

Ling looked at him. "I'm wondering what she was trying to tell us about your David Holmes."

Collingsworth said nothing. He looked ahead, his expression grim, his eyes worried, the face of a man sensing unavoidable defeat. Ling, for the moment, felt sorry for him.

Collingsworth's composure changed upon their arrival at the British embassy. The power of the prime minister's special representative was evident immediately, as two security men tripped over themselves jostling to open his door.

Ling noticed a car across the street. It was stopped in traffic with its hood up. Fiddling with the engine was a middle-aged man with a full crop of white hair. Ling caught a glimpse of metal-framed glasses before the man suddenly bowed lower, concealing his face. Ling waited a moment. The man's faced reappeared. Their eyes met briefly before the well-dressed motorist abruptly dipped under the hood again. Ling had his doubts this was any ordinary motorist. Was the embassy being watched? If so, by whom? Who was this stranger with the striking white hair? "White hair," Ling whispered. It had been mentioned before. By whom? Then he remembered: It was Triano. Mickey had reported a man with white hair seen at the hotel where the female victim was registered.

With slightly exaggerated motions, the stranger slammed down the hood and quickly opened the car door. Ling raised his Nikon to his eyes and got off four frames before the car sped away.

Ling said nothing of the supposedly disabled car to Collingsworth, who was impatiently waiting for him at the embassy door.

Inside, they were greeted by a delegation led by David Holmes himself, and led to an upstairs office. It was an imposing chamber with a huge hardwood desk beneath a striking glass chandelier.

Holmes, ebullient in his welcome and hospitality, had a service of tea, coffee and pastry rolled in. Ling and Collingsworth declined the refreshments. Holmes asked the servant for a cup of tea for himself, then leaned back in his high-backed leather chair and lit his pipe.

"Bloody shame, these murders," he said. "Whittaker could be a nuisance at times, but underneath all that cloaking he was a gentleman."

"I understand you were his unofficial conduit, so to speak, back to the prime minister," Ling said.

Holmes unleashed a cynical laugh. "I had the misfortune of having to accept his various propositions and demands, if that is what you mean."

"What kind of demands?"

Holmes looked to Collingsworth, who nodded. "He wanted an ambassadorship first and foremost. Seemed to feel he had a birthright to one, given his sister's position."

"What else?"

"Oh, what you might expect—invitations to this or that, occasionally a car and driver, use of a room here at the embassy."

"Did you give him a room?"

"Of course not."

Ling decided belatedly to have coffee. He got up and went to the cart. "Did you consider him a security risk?" he asked while pouring a cup.

Holmes drew on his pipe, then answered: "A *potential* problem, yes. We were on the watch for it."

"Detective Ling has been fully briefed about the Russians," Collingsworth interjected.

"Well, there was that report," Holmes said. "It originated with your government and there was likely something behind it but—" He stopped.

"But what? Please be frank," Ling said, now back at his chair.

"If the Soviets were really after him, they were fools—his knowledge of anything useful to them was non-existent."

Ling sipped his coffee, then asked: "How did you learn of the deaths?"

Holmes grinned. "Which is a respectful way of asking what was I doing on the night in question. . . ."

Ling smiled.

"I'm afraid I have the best alibi possible because, you see, I was at a dinner at the White House. Of course, I suppose it's possible I could have sent an imposter to dine with the President. And to be honest, there were times when I wished Mr. James Whittaker were gone from my affairs, which could be viewed as a motive. But indeed I'm not your man. The First Lady herself could vouch for me and relate how I bored her with diplomatic chitchat all evening."

"I'm sure that won't be necessary," Ling said. "But there is one more area . . ."

"The Mafia?" Holmes asked.

Ling showed surprise.

"Young Collingsworth here had the courtesy to background me on that," Holmes explained.

Ling looked at Collingsworth, who appeared to be seething.

Holmes stood. He turned to the window behind his desk. "I'm not one for airing Britain's dirty laundry so publicly, but it's rather clear I have no choice." He turned to face them, draping his arms over the chair's back and working his pipe.

"Tell the detective anything there is to tell," Collingsworth instructed.

Holmes glared at him, his eyes challenging the younger man's belief that he had the authority to issue him orders. "Very well, then." Holmes returned to his seat. He placed his pipe in an ashtray and folded his hands. "Whittaker came to me

with the most outlandish proposal. It appeared that in his
continuing education he had just uncovered the fact that a
diplomatic pouch enters a nation without customs inspection.
And he had further learned that the pouch is not a pouch at all
but can be any crate or package or suitcase so designated.''

"Let me guess," Ling interrupted.

"By all means." Holmes offered him center stage with a
sweep of his hand.

"Whittaker decided that a diplomatic pouch was the perfect
setup for importing cocaine or some other contraband. It was
foolproof, and you and he could have retired for life on the
profits.''

"Exactly." Holmes retrieved his pipe and sat back. "Of
course, there would be difficulties on the other end—getting
the package properly certified with diplomatic status, not to
mention obtaining the drug. But Whittaker assured me that all
that could be worked out.''

"What happened then?" Collingsworth asked.

Holmes laughed. "I believe I broke a record in the time
elapsed in having him thrown out of here.''

"And that was the end of it?" Ling asked.

"Not quite. Whittaker was back again in a week or so. He
told me he'd made arrangements with a certain Mafia godfather,
or whatever they are, in Brooklyn. The cocaine would be
made available in Italy and the pouch would carry a forged
seal. The arrangements, it developed, were in an advanced
stage—a flight had already been selected." He paused to pull
on the pipe. "I didn't like it. It was one thing to harbor a
fantasy, no matter how incredible and unlawful; it was quite
another to get involved with the Mafia. I found myself torn
between two objectives: protecting him and stopping him. As
I saw it, they weren't quite the same. In the end, I decided to
play along.''

"But you secretly contacted Marco in Brooklyn," Ling
guessed.

Holmes nodded. "It wasn't easy. Needless to say, his
name and number are not on our blue ribbon guest list. But I
eventually did reach him by telephone." He was working the
pipe again.

"And what did you say?" Collingsworth demanded sharply.

"I informed him of my intention to place the full force of Her Majesty's government against him if that package arrived in Washington bearing cocaine."

"What did Marco say?" Ling asked.

"He said he had been led to believe that I had agreed to the plan. I told him that was ridiculous. Then he hung up on me." Holmes leaned across the desk. "You see, I thought that if the plan failed because of a breakdown in Italy, Whittaker would grow timid and drop it, and that would be one more crisis out of my hair—not that I have much hair left."

"Did the package arrive?" Ling asked.

"I'll show you." Holmes moved to the side of the room and opened a tall, wide cabinet. He reached inside and lowered a screen. On the opposite side of the room was a slide projector. Holmes turned it on, then focused the first of a series of transparencies.

"I have it documented," he said, stretching a remote control cord back to his desk. Ling and Collingsworth turned in their seats to watch. "I hired a private detective to photograph all of it," Holmes explained.

The first slide showed a view of an airport tarmac with a British Airways Boeing 707 taxiing toward the terminal. The second showed a group of four men, two of them in uniform. "A pair of U.S. Customs agents," Holmes explained. "The others are me and Whittaker going to sign for the pouch."

Another shot focused on a conveyor belt unloading cargo from the aircraft's belly. In the next, one of the uniformed officers was lifting one parcel from the procession of trunks, suitcases and packages. It was the size of a shoebox. Another frame showed the officer studying the parcel's seal and documentation. And a final view had Holmes cradling the box. The late James Whittaker was at his side, smiling broadly.

Holmes got up and switched off the projector.

"That's our version of Fellini. It developed that indeed my call to Brooklyn had succeeded—the box did not contain cocaine. One could have packaged and frozen Whittaker's disappointment when he found out. Then I aimed for the kill, lecturing him as a don would an errant schoolboy and informing him that I had it all on film, photographs that I would unhesitatingly display to his sister should any other such nonsense crop up again."

"What was his reaction?" Collingsworth asked, his words still strained but his expression curious.

Holmes stood by his desk. His eyes were twinkling. "He pledged to somehow, someday, even the score with me."

"Did he try?" Again it was Collingsworth.

"God—or more accurately, whoever pulled that trigger—denied him the opportunity."

Ling stood. He thanked Holmes for his time and assured him his statements would be treated with as much confidentiality as possible. "I was just curious about one more thing," Ling said.

"What's that?"

"The box—what *did* it contain?"

Holmes laughed. "Sugar. Pure white sugar. In fact"—he pointed to Ling's cup—"you've probably been drinking some of it today."

27

The more thought Marilyn Mason gave to the detective's visit, the greater the anger that welled within her. And why, she asked, did it have to happen now, of all times—when looming before her was her major quarterly briefing for the President.

She tried to put the entire Whittaker affair out of her mind as she bent over the charts and computer runs on her desk, searching for the words that would articulate her conclusions and recommendations for a President weak in economics. But the concentration wasn't there—she kept seeing the face of Detective Monk Ling, with his patronizing smile and eyes that told her he doubted every word she said. He had attempted to be coy—but he hadn't fooled her. No matter what unfolded, Ling was not to be trusted. He was an enemy—another one.

Just who did Ling think he was? On his appearance alone, they would stop him at the door of any of the classy restaurants of Washington. Yet there he sat questioning her as if she were a common criminal.

Sex. Why did it always have to boil down to that? "Did you love him," the cop had asked, a poorly disguised way of asking if they had slept together. She had sped to a bachelor's degree in two years of undergraduate work, opened eyes around the world with her doctoral dissertation, and lectured

at universities from London to Honolulu—and still it came
down to what she did or didn't do in bed. The leers of the
Cabinet members. The twinkle in the eyes of the Secret
Service men. Even the President. He had patted her thigh
once. Her glare had warned him away that time. The next
time she would say something. She was sick of it.

The telephone buzzed. It was her secretary on the intercom
line. Marilyn answered it and barked: "I thought I instructed
you to hold all calls."

"Excuse me, Miss Mason, but I do not believe you did."

"Well, I'm saying it now!" She started to hang up, then
stopped. "Who is it, anyway?"

"Secretary Holmes, ma'am."

Marilyn considered taking the call, then decided against it.
"Tell him I'm on my way to see the President."

"Yes, ma'am."

In fact, Marilyn Mason still had about a half hour before
her walk to the Oval Office. It was vital she gather her
thoughts. The President trusted her figures and her judgment,
and he tailored his fiscal program to her suggestions. She was
good. Everyone in the White House knew she was good. That
story of the four-digit numbers—it was just one of the tales
being spread of her mental prowess, of her stature as the
President's key economic affairs adviser, even if she had been
denied the formal title of Chief Economic Adviser. And she
loved the work. Numbers didn't betray you; they didn't change
the rules. And they gave without asking something in return,
gave her the insights into what to tinker with in the bubbling
cauldron of forces that was the national economy. Her record,
thus far, had been spectacular: near bullseyes in her projec-
tions of unemployment, inflation, and the growth rate of the
gross national project; close hits in the other major categories.

But the pressure . . . To err could cost a million jobs,
trigger a recession, or cost an election. There was no room
for outside interference. Whittaker had interfered; so too did
his corpse.

Ling and his disbelieving eyes. She could complain. That
was a possibility. She could have someone pick up the phone
and get the mayor of New York on the line. Interrupt him at
some important meeting. "Mr. Mayor, this is the White

House calling and we want a stop to the harassment of one of our aides.'' The mayor would summon the police commissioner, who would summon the chief inspector and on down the line until it reached Ling, the lowly detective who would soon learn what it was to attempt intimidation of someone in the White House. He'd end up on a foot beat and . . .

The intercom buzzed.

"It's time, Miss Mason,'' the secretary said.

She left for the White House. As she walked across the White House grounds, her stomach began to tighten, but it was a different form of tension from that which had nearly consumed her the previous two days. It was a professional's tension, the orator's jitters before a speech, the ballplayer's butterflies before stepping to the plate, the opera singer's breaking voice before taking the stage.

The usual group was gathered, gray-haired or balding men mostly, nearly all of them wearing spectacles, each in a gray or dark blue flannel suit. She positioned her charts on an easel, then waited. The tightness in her belly eased almost instantly with the President's signal for her to proceed. The rest was all downhill, the words coming to her without delay, the numbers at her fingertips, the logic of her arguments neatly packaged and delivered in a rhythm not unlike that of a Baptist preacher.

Handshakes. Smiles. Offers of "well-done'' and "congratulations.'' She bathed in the respect and was so preoccupied by it that it seemed to lift her off the blue carpet and carry her from the Oval Office.

She found herself in a lady's room, gripping a sink, staring into a mirror. Her arms were shaking so much she had to lock her elbows. She had no sense whatsoever of her legs. Her forehead was numb but not so the back of her neck, which stung as if being pricked by a million needles and nails. Her face was as white as the porcelain of the sink, and from her eyes rolled twin rivulets of tears.

"My God!'' she said, staring at the image.

She wet a towel and began patting down her face, hoping her purse contained extra makeup. She put a comb to her hair and reknotted the bun. She reapplied her lipstick and straightened the collar of her tight-fitting blouse. Then she groped in her purse for the vial. It was there—she had made certain of that. She counted the capsules. There were six—enough to get her through the work day. She took two, lowering her mouth to the faucet for water.

Marilyn stepped back and re-examined her reflection. She was much more presentable now. Thank goodness no one else had entered the ladies' room! But this couldn't go on—something had to be done. She had to stop the pressure.

Marilyn had gotten as far as she had because she was a woman of action. She reminded herself of that now. The time had come to regain control of the events shaping her destiny. A plan came to her, and she was impressed with the speed of its development.

Marilyn marched directly to the office of the White House chief of staff. As usual, he had a crowded schedule but agreed to see her.

"I hear your presentation went very well, Marilyn," he said.

"Thank you. That's why I'm here. This one was brutal. I need some time."

His eyes narrowed. There was a demanding regimen involved with working at the White House, and that was routinely made clear to every staffer. "How much time?" he asked with annoyance.

"A week, maybe. I haven't had any of my vacation."

"Why a week?"

"Like I said, this quarter's numbers were rough. They kept changing right down to the wire. I'd like to clear my head."

His tone softened. "You're not in trouble, are you?"

Marilyn was jolted by the question. Had they been in touch with him, too? Had they already sabotaged her career? Or had she somehow signaled her problems herself? "No, of course not. Why do you ask?"

"To be frank, you don't look well."

She sighed. "That's exactly why I'm here to see you. Fatigue, pure and simple. My sister has a quiet place in Georgia. She's a teacher and likes the outdoors. I thought I'd spend a few days with her."

A moment of silence, then: "Go ahead, I guess." He

already was glancing at the next name on his appointments calendar. ''But make sure we have a number.''

She thanked him and left for her office, a sense of relief filling her, the tether sliding from her neck. With luck in catching a cab, she would be on a plane within an hour.

28

Stanislas Lubelski sat at a desk in a small windowless office in the basement of the Soviet embassy. He disliked going to the embassy—all of its visitors were watched by the Americans—but he wanted an analysis of the ashes he had removed from Marilyn Mason's apartment, and he wanted the results fast. A KGB technician was in an adjacent room, conducting preliminary tests on the gray residue.

The decoded text of a wired message had been waiting at the embassy for Lubelski. It was from Petrovich in New York. The message detailed the tailing of the stockbroker Thornton on the Concorde to London and his subsequent interrogation by the FBI. The communication also related the theft orchestrated by Petrovich of the Seventeenth Precinct's garbage. As expected, carbon paper and discarded early drafts of many of the detectives' laboriously typed reports were rescued from the trash. From them came a list of persons questioned or targeted for questioning by the police. Lubelski studied the list—except for a few neighbors and building employees, there was no name on the list with which he was not already familiar.

"The fools!" Lubelski shouted in Polish, crumpling the message into a ball. Showboating—that was what the Americans called it. Risky and unwise. The odds were great that the New York Police Department was now aware of the ersatz sanitation men. The detectives would be searching not only for the stolen truck but for the purpose behind the theft. Their suspicions would be aroused, and what had been a relatively uncomplicated homicide investigation may well have already been expanded into a sticky web that would trap them all.

Lubelski shook his head in disgust. He tossed the wadded paper to the floor, then spread an open calendar on the desk. To the side were his notes of the long-distance telephone calls appearing on Marilyn Mason's recent bills.

He put an "X" on the calendar for each date on which she had called Whittaker's number in New York. A pattern was immediately apparent: there was at least one call almost every night except for weekends, when she presumably was in New York. On the weekdays, when no calls were made, Lubelski guessed, Whittaker was probably in Washington. He could, if need be, attempt to verify that from his contacts at the airlines.

The other evidence supported the pattern: the Yankee tickets were for a Sunday doubleheader, and one of the Playbills was for a rare, five performance show that ran from a Friday night through Sunday.

The telephone billings, while informative, were not current. The most recent billing period ended two weeks before Whittaker's murder. But Lubelski had a solution—he dialed the local telephone billing office.

A woman's voice answered. Lubelski gave her the Mason number, then stood by while she called up the billing history on a computer terminal.

"The problem is that I believe someone has been using the phone to call New York without permission," Lubelski said. He provided Whittaker's New York number and asked if any calls had been made to that number during the two days preceding the Whittaker murders and the day of the slayings itself.

Yes, the company representative responded, there were two calls: one on each of the first two days in question.

"But none on the third?"

"That's correct, sir."

Lubelski thanked her and hung up. He was very pleased.

The implication of there being no call on the day of the murder was significant indeed.

The office door opened and the KGB technician entered with his report. "Photographs," he said. "The ashes were full of silver. There is no doubt. Both prints and film."

Lubelski stood. He turned his back to the lab man and faced the gray wall.

Why did one burn photographs? Lubelski asked himself, the answer evident to him even before he posed the question. In the arena in which he operated, the camera was as potent a weapon as a Luger.

The revealing absence of a long-distance call on the night of the murders and the chemical analysis of the ashes, plus his witnessing her clearly unstable behavior, gave Lubelski his prime suspect—Marilyn Mason. Petrovich would be delighted. A major White House figure appeared to be extremely vulnerable at the moment. There were many potential paths to take in getting to her. They would have to move quickly, but very carefully.

Lubelski smiled. He wanted out, and he saw the outlines of a route that could, if he were bold and lucky, spirit him beyond his personal Berlin wall.

It was time to meet face-to-face again with the Russian.

29

"Where's the Englishman?" Chief Julius Golden demanded.

"He stayed in Washington," Ling answered.

"Why?"

"Said he had to arrange for the immediate recall to London of a certain long-time diplomat who, to use his words, 'had grossly overstepped his bounds.' "

"Tell me about it."

Ling briefed him on his interviews of Marilyn Mason and First Secretary David Holmes.

Golden tugged at his chin when Ling had finished. "It's getting complicated: an ugly duckling with sensitive economic information who maybe was jilted, and a crafty diplomat with an allegedly phony drug deal."

Ling picked it up: "Add to that a stockbroker who could have made handy use of the ugly duckling's information and a small-time punk who could have seen more money than he ever dreamed about at the end of a cocaine rainbow—only it turned to sugar."

"That's four," Golden said.

"Not counting a hysterical boy-activist left stranded without a speaker for his rally in the park."

Golden was shaking his head. "Count the kid out—as of this morning, his alibi's solid—he was at some kind of night therapy session just like he said."

"An honest citizen."

Golden grunted. "Then there's the hooker, don't forget. She saw a good thing end with the appearance of the female victim."

Ling started to protest.

"Oh, I forgot—you're vouching for her," Golden said sarcastically. "I think I also should tell you that we struck paydirt with that parking ticket check. Rental car. The summons was written early on the night of the murders."

"Who?" Ling asked.

"DeGrazia."

"That puts him at the scene."

"Ah . . . not quite. But he was close. The car was at a hydrant five blocks downtown."

"Have we found him?"

"Not yet. We're watching the rivers," Golden said. "What's next on your end?"

"It would help if we could verify Holmes' White House alibi, although it must be good or he's got more balls than any stuffed shirt I've ever met."

"I'll put it to our friends from the Bureau," Golden said. "They, incidentally, saw fit to inform us this morning that the French came up with prints for the female victim. A Moroccan. Certified KGB."

Across the room, O'Brien hung up a telephone. He came over to them. "How did you like that hit on the rental car, Ling?"

"Nice."

"Yeah—some of us got to do the dirty work." He turned abruptly toward Golden. "May have something else, chief. Or it could be nothing."

"Let's have it."

"Well, you know we asked Whittaker's bank to inform us if any more of his checks showed up. They got one. A custom photo lab. I looked up the address. It's down on Nassau Street."

"A photo lab, huh?" Golden asked.

"Yeah, I can hit it now, if you want," O'Brien said.

Golden thought a moment, then said, "No, let Monk handle it. He understands this darkroom crap, and like you said, you've done your share of dirty work.''

O'Brien's face turned red.

Golden looked at Ling. "Go—and take your camera."

"Why don't you come along," Ling said to O'Brien.

"Naw," the other detective said. "Fuck it."

Outside, Ling bought a hot dog with sauerkraut from a street vendor and ate it while driving downtown. He located the custom photo lab in a turn of the century firetrap, one of many along the narrow European style commercial street north of the financial district.

Ling left the unmarked car in a no parking zone with its right wheels well up on the sidewalk, the only way to park without blocking traffic. The building's street level door led to a tiny foyer and a door marked "Imports." In the rear was a narrow staircase. Ling climbed the creaky wooden steps to the second floor. The smell of hypo told him he had reached the right place even before he read the sign on the door. Ling opened the door and stepped into a small room with several oversized color prints hanging from the walls.

Despite the vibrant colors of the dye transfers, the room appeared grimy and in desperate need of paint. A heavyset, short man in his twenties, with horn-rim glasses and a blemished, oily skin appeared behind a plywood counter that looked as if it had been nailed together in an hour and then splashed with a thin coat of cheap varnish.

"Yeah?" the man asked, his tone surly.

"Are you the manager?"

"Who wants to know?"

"Watch a lot of television, huh," Ling said as he flashed his gold shield.

"So, how am I supposed to know you're a cop?"

"How am I supposed to know if you're the manager?"

"I am."

Ling smiled. "Good. We're getting somewhere."

"What do you want?"

Ling walked over to one of the prints, a horizontal shot of the Brooklyn Bridge against a red and purple sky. "Let's say someone comes in here and has you do a job, then tries to pay you by check."

"We don't take checks."

Ling faced him. "We've got a bank that says you do."

"Well . . . if we know the guy, maybe. Or we want his business bad."

"Suppose the customer is an Englishman named James Whittaker."

The manager's face lit up. "I should have known that's why you're here."

"You took one of his checks."

"Yeah. He came in with a roll of color. Wanted eight by ten's of every frame. Not even a proof sheet."

"Had he been here before?"

"No."

"But you wanted his business."

"What business? I didn't know he had a business."

"Then, why did you take his check?"

The manager squinted as if a burst of sunlight had suddenly caught his eyes. "I *knew* him. I mean, I knew who he was. The prime minister's brother. I saw him on the tube. He comes in with a good order and wants to pay by check—I figure someone like him's not gonna stiff me."

"What was on the roll?"

He shrugged. "I didn't print it."

"Who did?"

"Kevin. Kid I got helping me."

"Where is this Kevin?"

"School. He comes in later."

Ling walked to the door. "Tell Kevin somebody will be by to see him. And thanks for your cooperation—you're a good citizen."

The manager's mouth opened—but he apparently decided he had nothing more to say.

Ling left, deciding that since he was downtown, he would drop in on an old contact on Wall Street. He found a public telephone and called a man named Snow. Sure, Snow said, he would be happy to meet, only not in the office—the appearance of a cop could raise too many questions. They would meet in a bar.

Snow was the manager of a highly successful mutual fund. The fund was successful chiefly because Snow was piped into most of the inner sanctum maneuverings of Wall Street, the backroom plots, questionable in their legality, that with lightning speed could heat up or cool down a selected stock. Ling had met Snow while investigating the slaying of Snow's partner years earlier.

Ling walked the two short blocks to the bar, which was in a long, narrow building with two opposite entrances, one on Nassau, the other on lower Broadway. The bar's windows were wide and little more than a foot high, just large enough to meet the minimum legal requirements set by the city for a drinking establishment. Inside, a Formica-topped bar ran the entire length of the room and was hidden in shadows; what light there was was beamed from the ceiling to a stage that ran parallel to the bar along the opposite wall. A jukebox was blasting outdated disco. On the stage, a barebreasted dancer was on her hands and knees, grinning as a customer slipped a folded bill under her G-string.

Ling sat at the bar. A female bartender wearing an undersized deep purple leotard came for his order.

"Coke."

She grinned. "On duty, huh?"

"What can I say?"

When she turned, Ling noticed a tattoo high on her bare thigh: a heart, broken in two.

Snow and the Coke arrived simultaneously. Ling and the Wall Street man had warm greetings for one another. Snow ordered a beer.

The song ended. The dancer, perspiring now, was stooping to the stage to harvest the dollar bills that had been thrown there.

"High finance, huh?" Ling said to Snow.

"Beats the hell out of the market today. I'm glad you called—I was lookin' for an excuse to get away."

The beer came. Ling paid for it. "I'm interested in a guy who's a broker."

"Lot of brokers; most of 'em broke."

"A kid. Name of Calvin Thornton. Throws around big bucks."

"Thornton," Snow repeated. He lowered his head in thought.

"Rings a bell. But it's kind of a common name, isn't it. I could check around." He looked up. "What'd he do?"

"We're not sure. Looks like some inside information stuff. Federal figures, maybe."

"Phew!" Snow said. "Give me ten minutes' jump on the right federal numbers and I'll make you a millionaire."

"That hot, huh?"

"You shittin' me? The Feds tinker with the money supply, jerk around the discount rate, the whole market jumps this way or that. You move fast and you've collected, baby."

Ling gave him the phone numbers for his home and the Seventeenth Precinct. "Appreciate anything you can get."

Snow nodded, his eyes on the stage where a new dancer was sprawled face down, her hips undulating convincingly in rhythm with an invisible lover.

Ling left Snow to his fantasy and headed back uptown.

The second-floor squad room of the Seventeenth Precinct was abuzz with activity when Ling returned. Nearly every detective on the case was there. Golden was in the center of them, alternatingly booming out orders and shouting into a phone.

Ling walked over to the group and tapped Triano on the shoulder. "What's up?"

But before Triano could answer, Police Commissioner Hamilton Grambling appeared at the door. With him was the deputy commissioner for public information.

Golden hurried over to greet them, then escorted them to the side office. "You, too, Monk," the chief said as he passed by. He stopped and waved in his other key detectives.

"The thing hit bang, bang, bang," Golden said when they were inside the office and the door was closed.

"Usually happens that way," the P.C. said knowingly.

Golden was smiling broadly. "First thing I get home, I'm gonna kiss my big, blonde, beautiful wife who told me she had a feeling it was all gonna come down today. You tell the mayor yet?"

"First things first," Grambling snapped. "Walk me through it." Golden struggled to restrain his enthusiasm. He straightened his tie while forcing a serious expression to his face. "The first break comes when McKinnon gets back. We fixed up a rogue's gallery for him, see, and he went back to the apartment with a couple of other men and began showing around the pictures.'' He looked at McKinnon.

McKinnon listed the subjects slowly, pausing at each name to let it sink in: ''We had Simpson, the hooker . . . DeGrazia, the wise guy from Brooklyn . . . the kid Samuels from a news photo . . . and the White House lady, Marilyn Mason is her name, also from a news photo. We got hits on every one of them. All four had been seen by at least one tenant or building employee in the days before the murders.'' McKinnon paused.

''So?'' Grambling said.

''Well, sir, you see we also had this window watcher across the street. An old man. And he says he saw one of the four the night of the homicides. It was DeGrazia. The old man said he seemed to be hanging around most of the night.''

''That puts him at the scene at the right time,'' Golden emphasized. ''McKinnon gets back with that news, then we get this call. Tell him, Dotty.''

''It was this woman who lives next door to the Samuels apartment,'' Levine explained, her voice even, her tone professional. ''We used her phone at the scene, see. And of course, Rosie and the others pay her a visit with the pictures and she's no help. But later, she called to tell us she remembers seeing one of the men in the photos a couple of days earlier, out in the hallway with Whittaker, and they were arguing. About what? I ask. But she doesn't know. What she does know is that this man told the deceased he was going to get him, or words to that effect.''

''DeGrazia?'' the commissioner asked.

''You got it,'' Golden said. ''And that ain't all. We've got a car rented in DeGrazia's name ticketed in the neighborhood and O'Brien picks up something very interesting. Like I said, it all hit: one, two, three.''

The P.C. looked at O'Brien. ''I used to be narcotics, you know, so I got people feeding me all over the streets.'' O'Brien, gloating, paused for a reaction; Grambling nodded impatiently. ''Well, I get a call from one of my snitches. Street junkie, but he's reliable and he gets around. And he says this guy DeGrazia had been all over town letting out the word to the flashdancers that he's got a big cargo of coke comin' down. But then nothin' happens and when my man next sees him and asks him about when the mother lode is comin', DeGrazia says there's been some complications, but not to worry; it'll be there.'' O'Brien, smiling smugly, looked at Ling.

Ling stared back at him a moment, then nodded a salute. DeGrazia's information corroborated what Gwen Chambers had reported to Ling at their meeting in Chinatown. The word from the street seemed to be unanimous.

''None of the building help saw DeGrazia that night,'' Golden said. ''But the elevator man takes a break, and the elevators run on automatic while he's gone. Anybody who could get into the garage could take the elevator up. To get into the garage, all he had to do was wait until someone drove in or out and slide in with the car.''

The room was silent for a few moments until Golden, his voice calm now, said, ''It all fits, see. Like I told you on the phone, Commissioner, Whittaker thought he had a cocaine deal arranged with this diplomat, Holmes. But Holmes was setting him up—there was no coke. Whittaker, in the meantime, had lined up a distributor—DeGrazia. DeGrazia shoots off his mouth at every corner north of 42nd Street, and then finds out he's been stiffed. He goes to Whittaker and doesn't believe it when Whittaker says they've both been taken, that what came in on that plane was sugar, and he drills him, Whittaker, and the girl, who just happened to be there.'' Golden bent forward. ''We've got the motive. We've got the opportunity, him being placed at the scene. We've got a threat. And we've got the fact that the stupid son of a bitch runs.''

The P.C. looked to his public information man, who hesitated a moment, then nodded. ''Sounds kosher to me,'' the aide said.

Grambling turned to Golden. ''Get a warrant and we'll announce it. Let's get the word out there and put the heat on. Smoke him out.''

The P.C.'s aide looked at his watch. ''Past six already. Too late for the evening news and the first editions of the morning papers. Get the warrant, but we won't have the news conference 'til the morning.''

The commissioner stood; the others followed. Grambling extended his hand to Golden. "Well done," the P.C. said. He looked at the other faces in the room. "Congratulations to you all.''

Grambling and his aide left. Golden collapsed back in his chair. He closed his eyes. There were no cheers, Ling noted. No backslapping. There rarely was. Even when a big case was closed, the finish was usually anticlimactic.

Ling moved to a chair next to Golden. "Looks solid, chief," he said. "But the two-hundred thousand—where does that fit in?''

Golden opened his eyes. "That's a piece that hasn't quite fallen into place. Best bet is Whittaker somehow raised the cash to finance the deal and when it fell through, he kept it.''

"But that means the coke was supposedly going to be loaded in Italy with no advance payment, no exchange.''

"I know," Golden said wearily. "But Whittaker wasn't your everyday runner. They could have decided to ride with him on credit, given who he was, or else maybe he had a big-name backer, I don't know." He sat up. "When we pull him in, we'll put it to DeGrazia—if there's a bigger fish in the wings on this, maybe we'll horse-trade with him. In the meantime, I want you and Triano to go visit Marco the man and let him know where we stand with DeGrazia—and how we would be most grateful for a quick and easy collar.''

Just as Ling stood, Collingsworth appeared at the office door. His expression was somber. He moved directly to Golden and shook his hand. "The commissioner met me downstairs and told me. I would like to tell you how much my government will appreciate the news although, to be blunt, the prime minister's brother being involved in something like this is an embarrassment, to be sure.''

"There's a black sheep in every family," Golden said sympathetically. "We've certainly seen it in the White House.''

"You've never had a presidential drug runner," Collingsworth said, smiling wryly.

"I . . . I guess not.''

"Have you arrested DeGrazia, if I may ask?''

Golden shook his head. "No—but we will. Ling and Triano are off now to see our friendly neighborhood crime boss."

"May I go?"

Golden looked to Ling, who said: "Why not?"

They were heading for the stairway when a detective shouted to Ling that he had a telephone call. Ling picked up a phone. It was Snow.

"How do you find these guys?" the investment manager asked.

"You work fast. What you got?"

"One Calvin Thornton and two of his pals are nobodies, see, until about a month ago when all of a sudden they make a killing selling short. Just happens to be a day when the Fed announces its new money supply figures."

"Any idea how much they made?"

"Yeah, but only because they were putting pressure on a certain guy to kick in with them. The first deal, they told him, netted about three-quarters of a million."

Ling thanked him, then did some arithmetic: three investors plus one information source equalled four players. The two-hundred thousand found in Whittaker's attaché case times four equaled eight-hundred thousand. Eight-hundred thousand and three-quarters of a million were roughly the same. Had Whittaker gone to Wall Street for the capital to finance the cocaine?

Ling looked for Golden to pass on the information about Thornton but the chief was occupied in organizing the massive manhunt for Tony DeGrazia. "I want every cop in God's army on this," Golden was saying. Ling decided the information on Thornton could hold. Triano and Collingsworth were waiting.

Triano was behind the wheel. "It figures," he said.

"What's that?" Ling asked.

"All this ending up a run-of-the-mill cocaine wipeout."

"It is rather pitiful, isn't it," Collingsworth said. "And to think; none of it was necessary. Whittaker could have had all he wanted by doing almost nothing."

"How's that?" Triano asked. "The man wanted power and money. This was his way."

"But you see, through no doing of his own, he *was* the prime minister's brother," Collingsworth said. "No one could take that away from him. That relationship alone commanded respect. If only he'd been patient, if he hadn't been so bloody greedy, he could have capitalized on his position in some perfectly legitimate way. A corporate appointment, perhaps. His own business."

Ling could think of nothing to add.

They crossed the Brooklyn Bridge and were soon on President Street.

"The club?" Triano asked.

"Good for a try," Ling answered.

Triano pulled to a stop outside a row of stores. They got out. Ling led them past a meat market and a fruit and vegetable stand to another storefront with a fully curtained plate glass window. In red gothic letters outlined in black, a sign on the window read: "Palermo Society Social Club." Underneath, in much smaller lettering, was the caveat: "Members Only."

Ling opened the club door and strode in, Triano and the Englishman following. Several men, most of them elderly, sat at wire-legged tables that had probably come from some long-closed ice cream parlor. Two held playing cards, the stack between them indicating their game was gin rummy. Others sipped wine or espresso coffee. One younger man held a bottle of beer. It was he who came up to challenge them. Before he could speak, Ling announced: "Greetings, gentlemen. I have here Mr. Collingsworth, he being a loyal subject of Her Majesty the Queen, and on this, his first visit to America, he is interested in seeing a bona fide Mafia den."

"Up yours, Monk," the man with the beer said.

"Oh, I beg your pardon, Sal—I should have said 'organized crime den.' " He looked to Collingsworth. "There's no such thing as the Mafia."

Ling suddenly lifted his Nikon to his eyes and focused in on the face of Sal the beer drinker. Click.

He turned to the nearest table and framed three men drinking coffee. Click. All three rushed to hide their faces, one with his hands, another with an Italian language newspaper, the third with his pitifully ineffective demitasse cup.

Ling turned and began focusing on the card players, who bolted for the door.

"Enough with the fuckin' pictures, for chrissake," Sal shouted. Then, with resignation: "What do you want, Monk?"

Ling focused in on the disheveled and abandoned cards. "What's today's special?" Ling asked. Click.

Sal's face was red. "For you, sour owl shit," he said.

Triano grabbed him by his loose-fitting body shirt. "That won't do, asshole."

"Why don't you shove that camera up your ass!" came a shout from the back. A rear door had opened. In the door-frame, wearing an expensively tailored, green pin-striped suit, was Marco.

"What's the matter, Marco, all of a sudden you're camera shy?" Ling asked, focusing in on the crime boss's face.

"You want to see me or what?" Marco demanded.

"You're a winner, Marco," Triano said. "You got the winning answer."

"So we go into the back, okay?"

"Whatever your pleasure," Ling said, finally lowering the Nikon.

Marco led them through a small hallway into a backroom office. The appointments were simple—a desk, library table, and a few wooden chairs. The room was very clean and neat. Marco signaled the room's only other occupant, a burly, stone-faced bodyguard, to leave, then took a seat behind the desk.

"You look trim and tan, Marco. For a guy—what? 65?—you're in shape," Ling said. "What's the secret?"

Marco smiled. "A churchgoing wife who can cook—and plenty of retail pussy."

"Now don't go talkin' like that, Marco," Triano scolded. "This guy's from England."

Marco looked at Collingsworth. "What can I say? I have no class. Grew up on the docks."

"You read the papers, Marco?" Ling asked.

"The race page, sure. And the comics."

"What about page one—little item about the murder of one James Whittaker."

"Now let me think—he a bookie?"

"Not quite. This guy was more like an associate of Tony DeGrazia. A business partner, so to speak. We'd like to have a talk with Tony."

"Tony, I think, mentioned something about going out of town. And I don't know nothin' about this Whittaker. Honest."

"How about one David Holmes? He's an ambassador of some kind. Hear tell you and he like to talk on the phone."

Marco grinned. "You guys should know. I don't know why I don't get a bullhorn or somethin'. What do you spend on me for the fuckin' taps, anyhow?"

"If it's ten cents, it's too much," Triano said. "Maybe you just want to answer the goddamned question."

Marco looked at Ling while pointing with his thumb at Triano. "Touchy bastard, huh? And Italian, too. I've got a long fuckin' memory, and him I remember. Thought they put him out to pasture. The auto pound or somethin'."

Triano laughed loudly. "How many years was it, Marco, I put away your brother? They teach him how to read up there yet?"

Marco slammed a fist on the desk. "You want help or not? You come in here with the big mouth, and then you want Marco to give you answers?"

"David Holmes," Ling said calmly.

Marco slowly unwrapped a cigar. "Don't know the guy from nothin', then he arranges a call. I didn't call him; he calls me, see. He's got problems with this Whittaker."

"What kind of problems?"

"At first, he don't say and I'm thinkin' maybe he goes to the movies or somethin' and is callin' me on a contract to make this Whittaker disappear, like I'm a magician or somethin'."

"Can't understand that," Triano said.

"Will you tell him to shut up?" Marco demanded of Ling. Then to Triano: "Never figured I'd have more respect for a chink like this Ling here than a paisano. You really Italian? Or maybe Puerto Rican, huh?"

"Go on, Marco," Ling snapped.

Marco lit his cigar. "This ambassador, he finally tells me Whittaker has some deal lined up in Italy. Cocaine. Supposed to be put on a certain plane. The ambassador says he wants it stopped, thinks maybe I can help."

"And do you?"

"I made a call."

"To whom?"

"My cousin."

"Who might that be?"

Marco leaned forward. "Come on, Ling. You don't expect me to drag my family into this."

"You know the Florida State score?"

"The what?"

"Florida State. They played Saturday."

Marco appeared bewildered. "A score you want? Football? Sure, Monk, I'll get it."

Ling smiled. "That's all right. I'll catch it in the papers. On second thought, I'd rather not know." Ling stood and moved to the office door; Triano and Collingsworth followed. Ling stopped and said: "The bottom of the bottle is like this, Marco. They've got a warrant for DeGrazia, see. Murder. It'll be announced in the morning. Chief's got every cop that can wear shoes out lookin' for him. Another twelve hours and there'll be a lot of roustin'. Won't be anybody left alone, ya know."

Marco was on his feet. "You sit tight, ya hear. Don't get yourself excited. Wait for the doorbell, maybe."

"You take care, Marco. Avoid the pressure. Ya know what a guy told me last week?"

"What's that?"

"That it's a proven fact now that a man's born with only so many orgasms in him. You reach the end of the inventory, then that's it—the well's dry."

Ling and the others departed.

Later, in the car returning to Manhattan, Triano began laughing. "You know what, Monk? You tell him that orgasm shit . . . the look on his face . . . I think you had him counting."

3o

For the third time in an hour, FBI agent Bill Nolan calculated what his pension would be if he summarily gave the government its two weeks' notice and retired. For the third time, he came up with a figure that would mean tight living conditions for him and his semi-invalid wife if he did. But the accuracy of that assessment was questionable—against the racket of the helicopter's blades, Nolan couldn't remember the exact amount of his monthly mortgage.

Nolan was tired. He had had little sleep in the past three days. As he peered down on the city from the two seat bubble chopper, he had this feeling that something was out of control, that the bureau, so efficient on so many cases, was blowing this one—and blowing it bad. Nolan's report from the informant, Eagle Seven, that the Soviets had been massaging James Whittaker for possible recruitment had sent a shockwave through the agency. The brass wanted the case closed out with all questions answered, and if it wasn't, careers would be ended ignominiously; Nolan's included. There was a lesson in that, Nolan concluded, a built-in motivation for him to shut off his sources, to avoid stirring the soup, to notify his informants he preferred not knowing no matter what it was they wished to tell him.

Eagle Seven. Who the hell was he? There was a part of Nolan that wished he had never heard of him, that it was some other sorry, footsore, so-called G-man waiting for calls in isolated phone booths and acting foolishly in a computer store.

The FBI hierarchy had reacted to Nolan's report with an intensity he had not seen since hundreds of agents were mobilized to bring in Patty Hearst and the Symbionese Liberation Army. Every known KGB operative was placed under around-the-clock surveillance. As yet, three days after the corpses of Whittaker and the woman were discovered, the Soviets showed no sign of anything but the most routine of activities. Nolan, for the most part, was left to birddogging the city police. "Keep your eyes on things," his superior had told him. And so it had been Nolan and his partner who had had to bear the abuse when the NYPD learned, as was inevitable, that the FBI had held out on them. Nolan had thought that decision unwise and had argued vainly against it. Yes, there were occasional security leaks when dealing with local police agencies, and yes, the Whittaker case was a sensitive diplomatic matter. But when the complications were stripped away, what remained was a murder investigation. If it ever were to be solved, Nolan suspected, it would be Monk Ling and the other city flatfoots who would do it, not the British, and not the bureau.

When Nolan was not babysitting the New York police, he had been tapped for surveillance duty, which was why he was seated in the chopper tailing a long, black limousine that a few minutes earlier had pulled out of the Soviet U.N. Mission garage. Petrovich, long known to the FBI as the latest in a string of KGB station chiefs, was at the wheel. In addition to the chopper, the limousine was being tailed by four bureau cars. Twice before in the past three days, a similar procession had followed Petrovich. Both times he had led them through the Midtown Tunnel into Queens and on to the Soviet compound on Long Island. Nolan had the feeling that Petrovich was looking up at him—and grinning.

"We're on First Avenue," came a report from one of the bureau cars.

More chatter followed as the drivers arranged among themselves which of them would stay closest to the target and when each would drop off in the complicated revolving tail system they would use to try to cloak their presence.

Nolan, meanwhile, had his pilot keep the chopper slightly to the rear of the limousine, to make it unlikely the Russian would spot them through his windshield or mirrors. The normal din of Manhattan's traffic would do much to muffle the helicopter's noise.

"Approaching the tunnel," the radio crackled.

"The damn island! Here we go again," another agent piped in.

In the squeeze at the tunnel entrance, the agents in the closest car found two cabs and a semi-trailer truck between them and the limousine. There was, at this hour, two-way traffic in the tube the Russian had selected, limiting the eastbound flow to a single lane. The other three FBI vehicles fell into line further back. Nolan ordered the pilot to cross over to Queens and circle above the tunnel exit.

With the four bureau cars under the East River, Nolan lost decent radio contact and it was not until the lead car was back above ground that he knew something was wrong.

"They made some kind of switch!" an agent in the lead car shouted over the radio to him. "We're going to pass him to make sure."

Nolan watched as the plain blue bureau sedan closed its distance on the limousine, then passed it on the left.

"Shit!" the radio blasted. "It's some other bastard. The son of a bitch is waving at us."

"What the hell happened?" Nolan asked.

"The target stopped in the tunnel. The fucker just stopped. They must have had it timed perfectly. We couldn't see too well but it looked like ol' Petro jumped out and traded places with somebody in an oncoming vehicle."

"What kind of vehicle?" Nolan asked impatiently. "Maybe we can pick it up from up here."

"Yellow taxi. A Checker. Happened so fast, we missed the goddamned plate."

The pilot looked at Nolan. There were, Nolan guessed, maybe twenty-thousand cabs in the city, a quarter of them Checkers, all of them yellow. Wherever Petrovich was heading, he would get there with no representatives of the United States government on his back.

Nolan signaled the pilot to return to Manhattan and take the chopper down. It would be futile to continue the air search. Nolan would let the others explain it all to the bosses. As for himself, he would convince them of the wisdom of his returning to the Seventeenth Precinct. Better the ranting of Julius Golden than some FBI supervisor. Besides, Nolan craved a cup of coffee. And if nothing was breaking, he could find himself a quiet corner—and ponder the finances of retirement.

31

Nicholas Lubelski was on his fifth straight subway train. He had started out on the East Side IRT, taken the shuttle to Times Square, doubled back to Grand Central on the Flushing line, returned to the West Side on the shuttle and was now heading uptown, toward Washington Heights.

The changing of trains was tedious but effective—in particular the narrow Flushing platform at Grand Central offered a good view of fellow passengers, and Lubelski had seen no sign that he was being followed. The heat was on—the Russians had complained of it bitterly at the embassy in Washington—but thus far the Americans had limited their attention to the Soviets. The satellite operatives, as Petrovich had anticipated, were being left alone—the FBI simply didn't have the manpower.

Finally, Lubelski was at his destination. He left the train, lingering on the platform to allow the other departing passengers to pass him. He walked to the station escalator and found himself alone.

The escalator took Lubelski to Fort Tryon Park, high on a rocky ridge overlooking the Hudson. Nearby were the Cloisters, the walled courtyards that had been imported stone by stone from monasteries in Europe.

Lubelski rather liked his meetings at the Cloisters. The scene reminded him of the old country. Occasionally, when he had time to spare, he entered the walled monastic gardens, which were butted together into a checkerboard pattern. The atmosphere was very peaceful, and it inspired visitors to speak in whispers, if they spoke at all. There were regulars who visited the Cloisters daily, seeking a spiritual cleansing. Of these, some preferred to sit on the benches contemplating the long-dead masons' stonework, or the small shrubs and flowers, which also had been imported. Lubelski liked to wander, like a priest reading his office, and found it moving to consider that monks, their feet in simple sandals, had once paced the same stones. On Sundays, when medieval liturgical music was piped through the grounds, he could almost see the holy men in their shaved heads and robes, meditating on the mysteries of life, accepting them as divine, and, unlike himself, no longer asking why. Lubelski envied those ghosts.

The grounds outside the Cloisters had once been a popular gathering spot for pot-smoking hippies—now, on a weekday, the hilly area was nearly deserted. A few couples strolled hand-in-hand. Here and there, a tourist fidgeted with a camera. A vendor selling hot dogs had little business.

Still confident he was not being tailed, Lubelski walked to the park's bluff high over the Hudson, found a cluster of bushes and sat down. It was windy, the cool autumn breeze off the river acting as an astringent on his face. In the distance, a Circle Line sightseeing boat was heading northward. On the opposite shore, the Palisades of New Jersey sparkled in the sunshine.

In less than ten minutes, the Russian appeared.

"You weren't followed, were you?" Petrovich asked, speaking urgently in Russian.

Lubelski answered in Polish: "I was killing reactionaries with my bare hands, and not getting caught before some imbecile raped your mother."

The Russian ignored the insult and sat down. The two men stared at the gleaming river.

"Did you receive my communication about the police papers?" Petrovich asked.

"That was stupid, Petrovich, stealing their garbage. Useless. You don't understand these American police."

"What do you mean?"

"What's important is what is in their heads, not what they put on paper. Like many of your comrades, these police are semiliterate. They write down very little. What they do write is simplistic."

"Enough of your disrespect!" Petrovich snapped.

Neither said anything for a moment, then Lubelski asked: "The truck, have they found it?"

The Russian chuckled. "Their lovely white truck is sitting in an abandoned warehouse in the south Bronx. There'll be nothing left by the time the street hoodlums get through with it."

Lubelski picked up a stone and began fingering it. "Anything else?"

"The stockbroker, Thornton. It's very strange. He has made arrangements to return."

"Why?"

"We don't know. But we're not here for *you* to question *me*. I want your report."

Lubelski tossed the stone toward the water. It struck a boulder fifteen yards away and rebounded to the ground, well short of the river. "It's an irony, us meeting here, did you know that?"

"I don't understand."

"The Cloisters give it the flavor of Europe. I come here and I think of home."

"So?"

"It was, I believe, Rockefeller money that brought all this stonework here. We sit here, two Communists, and taste our motherland, taste our youth, thanks to the world's most notorious capitalist."

Petrovich looked nervously to each side. "Get on with it, would you? I have little time."

Lubelski spoke slowly, "The killer, comrade, was Miss Marilyn Mason."

Petrovich was stunned. "What? The woman from the White House?"

"Yes," Lubelski said smugly, relishing his victory.

"I had a feeling . . . ." the Russian said, staring off into the distance. His eyes returned to Lubelski. "Why would she do it?"

"Whittaker was using her, blackmailing her somehow. I'm not certain what he wanted, but I can guess."

"Go on," Petrovich said impatiently.

"Suppose France is going to devalue the franc and you had that knowledge beforehand, what would you do?"

"I don't know. I understand little of currencies."

"If you had holdings in francs, you could sell them and avoid the substantial losses that devaluation would bring."

"I still don't see the relevance."

"My dear comrade, do you really think the White House would learn of a French devaluation in the newspapers?"

Petrovich began rubbing his chin. "I see. She would have had information of that nature and Whittaker forced her to pass it along to him."

"That's my theory."

The Russian thought a moment, then broke into a huge grin. "This woman, she is in the White House. We share her secret. That makes her ours."

"Exactly."

The Russian's face grew serious. "But are you positive?"

Lubelski shook his head. "No, I am not. There is little in this life that is certain. One must take risks. Surely, in your position, you know that, comrade."

"Rational risks, yes. But—"

"Trust me, Petrovich. I will help you."

"This sudden cooperation of yours—what do you want?" the Russian asked suspiciously.

Lubelski stared at him. "If I bring you this woman, I want to be released. I want to be left alone."

"And if you fail?"

"The same thing—my price to you for trying."

Petrovich laughed derisively. "You Poles are so naive. You see, Lubelski, you have no choice. If you succeed in recruiting her, as I expect, then we will, of course, continue to require your assistance to keep her. And if you fail, then . . . Well, let me put it this way—this visit here today will be your final enjoyment of anything remotely resembling your homeland."

Lubelski looked to the cloudless sky. A jumbo jet was growing smaller as it neared the horizon. Lubelski watched it and thought of Poland. He thought of the verdant countryside, the church steeples, and the gaiety of the village people on a Saturday night; the women in their colorful, flowing skirts, the men thick-necked and strong, hard workers with simple goals, a purity that touched the collective soul of earlier generations who had labored, made love, given birth, spilled blood and returned to dust on the same hallowed land from which he himself had come.

But Petrovich was correct, of course. It had been naive to expect otherwise. Lubelski's instincts told him the woman in the White House *was* the killer, and the evidence, such as it was, supported that. If so, then she *was* ripe for potential recruitment. Thinking of it, Lubelski's stomach tightened. He had reached a crossroads in his life and would have to make a decision. His eyes stayed with the receding plane. A tear formed in the corner of his eye. Was it the wind? He reached up and brushed the teardrop away.

"What do you propose to do now?" the Russian was asking.

Lubelski lowered his face to his hands. "I'll go see Samantha Simpson." He rubbed his eyes, then looked at the Russian. "She's a whore. She's buyable."

32

Ling was too impatient to wait for the film to dry. He sandwiched the wet negative into the enlarger plate and focused carefully, for it would be a very large blowup—he had not had his telephoto lens and the motorist with the supposedly disabled car outside the British embassy had been relatively far away.

Ling lowered the easel shelf to the floor and raised the enlarger to its limit, but the subject's face still fell short of filling the eight by ten. It would have to do. He studied the reverse image on the focusing paper. The hair would print very light, almost white. He used it as the highlight for judging his exposure time, then made a print.

When the print was in the wash, he left the darkroom for his oak table, where the dozens of other prints he had made earlier were scattered. Sitting, he rummaged through them for the views of Whittaker's bedroom, selecting four long shots of the room's walls. He set aside the wall with the door, then used cellophane tape to hinge the other three together. He bent them at right angles and positioned them upright in a make-shift diorama. Then, folding his arms on the table, he lowered his head so that his eyes were level with the room's images. His eyes darted back and forth, up and down, randomly. They repeatedly returned to the electronics wall opposite the bed, zeroing in on the television screen. Nearby were the video recorder and the empty cassette box—number eight. Off to the left, in a corner of the black and white assemblage, was a tripod . . .

Wait! Ling had not noticed a tripod before. He lifted the print closer to his eyes. On the tripod was a long, narrow camera. A video camera? Somehow, he had missed it. He flipped the photo over—the penciled code told him the print had come from his first roll, the film he had shot on his initial visit to the apartment. Ling searched through the scattered other photographs, setting aside the bedroom shots he had made on his second inspection, his return to the crime scene with Collingsworth. He studied each print carefully—none showed a tripod or camera.

Triano had inspected every inch of the apartment. Ling would ask him what had happened to the tripod.

Ling returned to the darkroom and removed the new print from the wash. He had just flattened it on the dryer's stereotype when the phone rang. He left the darkroom to answer it.

His hands were still dripping as he lifted the receiver. "Yes?"

"Is that you, Monk?" A woman's voice. It sounded hollow and distant.

"Who's this?"

"Sam. Sam Simpson. You busy?"

Ling sat down on his bed. "Not busy for you. What's up?"

There was a delay, the line silent except for the faint tones of another conversation on crossed wires. "I . . ." she stammered. "I've decided to leave town and . . ."

"Why? Where are you going?"

"I'm tired. I mean, the city, it's starting to close in on me, you know? And I've got this friend . . . Well, he's kind of a sugardaddy and he's got this big place down in the Virgin Islands. Right on the water. The house faces west so you can watch the sunset. And in the morning, the little yellow birds come right up to your table and pick at the crumbs from your breakfast." Her voice trailed off.

"Sounds wonderful," Ling said. "Can two go?"

"Don't think my sugardaddy would like that."

"We could say I'm you're brother." He thought a moment. "Or your father."

She laughed. "Wouldn't cut it, Monk."

"Well, you can't leave without a proper goodbye. I'm coming over."

"No, Monk! There's no time."

Ling looked toward the darkroom. He still had other prints to make. He thought a moment, then said into the phone: "I'll be there in twenty minutes."

Her voice grew soft. "We'll do it again, Monk. I promise. But not now. Sometime when this is over, we'll . . ."

"We'll never see each other again and you know it."

"Why are you such a goddamned realist?" she shot back. "Can't you dream? Or is that a violation of department rules?"

A moment's silence, then Ling said: "Maybe you're right. Maybe that's the problem with cops—they can't dream."

She cleared her throat. "I haven't been totally honest with you," she said, her tone more matter-of-fact than confessional.

"About what?"

"About when I walked out on Whittaker—or when I was fired, however you want to look at it."

"What do you mean?"

"I took something—I figured he owed me."

"Go on."

She hesitated. "No. I'd rather not talk about it. But I've left you something."

"I'll come pick it up."

"It's . . . it's not here. I thought it best that we . . . What I mean is I left it at the desk at the Hampstead Hotel. It's in your name. Get it—then go to the Port Authority."

"The Port Authority?"

"Just . . . just a minute—there's someone knocking on the door."

A hollow thump came over the line as she set the telephone down.

"Who is it?" Samantha's voice.

An answer, barely heard and indistinguishable.

Locks being undone. The door opened.

"What do you want?" Samantha angry. "There's no reason for us to ever see each other again."

The door slammed—loudly.

"Get out of here! Now!" A pause, then: "What's that? What do you have there?" Movement. Something bumped into. "So it *was* you! I should have known." More movement.

"Sam! What's happening?" Ling shouted.

Her voice lower, measured: "We can talk. We can work this out. Just don't come any further."

A murmur. The voice, was it male or female? An accent? It was too low and indistinct to tell. Say something more! Ling silently pleaded.

A scream. Sounds of a scuffle. Glass breaking. Objects falling. Furniture crashing.

"Sam!" Ling screamed into the phone.

A shot! Unmistakable. And another. The report muffled and tinny over the line.

Dead silence.

Ling pushed the earpiece against him with such force his ear ached. Still, no sound. Then someone moving. The door opening. The door shut, this time softly, so only the clicking of the lock was heard.

"Sam, are you there?" he shouted, fighting the logic that told him she had been shot, gunned down opening her door to someone she knew. Two shots at close range. . . .

Then he heard it—a moaning. Low and throaty but continuous. Samantha was still alive!

He pushed the phone's button but no dial tone came. The connection was still there. The moaning. He tried once more, his finger frantically pressing the clear plastic knob again and again. Still, no dial tone; still, her moaning. She had called him—he couldn't disengage the line!

Ling threw down the phone. He grabbed his wallet and service revolver and raced through the door. He took the stairs—two and three steps with each stride. Through the small lobby and onto the street. The phone booth outside the liquor store on the corner. Someone using it. A kid in a leather jacket.

Ling reached out for him. His fingers grabbing the jacket,

pulling him out, the kid protesting. The emergency number—911. No coin necessary. An officious voice.

"This is Monk Ling. I'm on the job. Fast, now. Shots fired. Upper East Side. What the hell's the address?" Then he remembered it. "Send uniformed. And an ambulance. And I mean now!"

A cab in front of a restaurant. Ling bullying past the couple who had flagged it. Apologizing. Police emergency. Flashing his shield to the driver. A Filipino. His eyes wide. Scared.

Up Sixth! Forget the lights! Lay on the horn! Move!

The cab racing. Neon flashing by to the sides. A strange sensation—speed but no siren. Blocked by a bus. Goddamnit, go around! A close one, very close, running the red at Twenty-third. The hack turning pale. You're doin' fine, pal.

Crosstown. Then north again. Three blocks to go. Ling's heart pounding. His fingers wrapping the grip of his gun. Almost there. A siren in the distance, getting closer. Then, off to the right, a glimpse of snow white hair, the glint of glasses. Ling's head snapping back to look through the rear window: White hair, yes; and aviator glasses! Climbing into a cab. The man from Washington. His photograph hardly dry. Ling had to stop! But he couldn't—one more short block and he would be there.

The taxi braking. "This it?" the shaken driver asking. Ling not answering. Out of the cab. Two patrolmen in the lobby, their guns drawn.

"Up here!" Ling shouted, unholstering his weapon. "Twenty-fourth floor. One of you wait for the ambulance."

Two middle-aged men with strap purses were waiting at the elevator. Ling pushed them aside. That was luck! The elevator door was opening. He and the patrolman stepped inside. Ling pounded the "CLOSE DOOR" button. The doors responded slowly. The elevator started. Then the damn thing stopped—on four.

"Going down?" an elderly woman asked.

"No!"

Again, Ling pushed the "CLOSE DOOR" button. Again, the delay. He kicked the elevator wall, denting it.

"Easy," the cop was saying.

The apartment door, of course, was locked. But there was

only one automatic lock, the one that snapped whenever the door was closed.

Ling waved the cop away and stepped back. His kick was on the mark, just below the brass of the knob. Another kick, pain traveling up his leg. The third did it, a wide enough crack so that their bodies thrown together could finish the job.

She was there, on her back, one knee curled up, fifteen, maybe twenty feet in from the doorway. A large, soggy pool of blood on the shag rug beneath her. Her eyes open but unmoving and glazed. Her breathing short and unsteady. A weak moan. A few seconds later, another.

Ling ripped open her blouse. Two wounds, raw and ugly, one in the chest, the other in the abdomen, just below the rib cage. Too much blood. She was going fast.

The cop was standing there, his gun resting limply against his leg.

"Get a towel, damn it!" Ling ordered.

Ling fell to his knees beside her. His fingers, still smelling of hypo, caressed her forehead. "Sam," he called softly. Her eyes were fixed upward. "It's Monk, Sam. Stay with me."

The cop was back with a towel. It was a heavy, bright pink towel. Soft. Sprinkled with cologne. The fragrance of a rose. And, when it was moved, puffs of bath powder.

Ling folded the towel into a square, then laid it over the chest wound, pressing hard with both hands. A compress bandage. They had taught him in the Army. The lung cavity. Keep it closed.

Her eyes moving slightly. Her head turning.

"It's Monk, Sam. You're gonna make it. Fight, girl! Fight the darkness!"

Her lips moving. A word. What was it? Try again!

"Ruby?" Ling shouted. "Is that what you said?"

A nod. Very slight. But unmistakable.

"Ruby, who?"

Her mouth struggling. Her eyes half-closing. Distant gurgling. Then a sound. "Shoot." That's what she was saying!

"Ruby shot you. I've got it. But Ruby who, Sam?"

The word more drawn out now. The word the same. "Shoot."

"Ruby's the last name, is that it?"

But her lips did not move. Her eyes were wide once more and unfocused. The distant gurgling was renewed.

"Stay with me, Sam!" he pleaded, pressing still harder on the compress. Then, through the thick towel, he felt her body tighten. Her chest heaved upward. Her curled leg convulsed. And from inside, from deep within her, he heard the rattle, the baritone warbling that he once had thought a myth until he heard it too often in Vietnam. "Fight it, Sam!" he shouted. But the cop was pulling him away.

"Let them work," the cop said.

A paramedic in a wrinkled white smock replaced Ling. His fingers went to her eyes, then to her neck. He looked up. "She's gone."

Ling brushed away the patrolman's grip. He edged closer to her body and stood over it. He reached down and picked up her hand. It was still soft—and warm. There was a peacefulness to her face, a tranquillity, except for her still open eyes. Her eyes were inquiring, posing a question, pleading for an answer that Ling, in that moment, vowed he would get for her.

He looked at the cop. "She was tired," Ling said. Then he moved away, a burning pain eating at his belly, a rage growing within him at the waste of it all: young Indian girls thrown over the falls, adolescents bound flat on blood-stained stone altars, slender, nubile bodies with apple-sized breasts heaved to the pounding of drums into rock-bottomed desert canyons—New York had claimed another maiden.

Ling's mind went blank.

Later—it seemed like hours—he found himself in a chair. Julius Golden was stooped at his side, talking to him.

"Her arms were scratched, did you notice? And a couple of those long fingernails were broken. You're undoubtedly right about thinking you heard a struggle."

Ling nodded.

"Catch any sign of DeGrazia?" Golden asked.

He shook his head.

"The son of a bitch must have figured she could nail him. Undoubtedly the same gun. Medical examiner says it looks like a twenty-two. And I've ordered one of our own lab boys to make sure the M.E. gives him a sample of the residue under her nails. I want our own people testing this one.''

The deputy medical examiner was taking notes. The morgue men were standing by with their stretcher. A photographer's strobe flashed again and again. The lab men with their brushes and little plastic bags were swarming everywhere. From the door came the admonitions of a cop who wanted the nosy, noisy, obnoxious onlookers to step back.

"The longest running play in New York," Ling said.

"What?" Golden asked.

"Nothing."

Had he told Golden about the mysterious package she had left for him at the Hampstead?

"I've got Triano headed there now," the chief said.

Had he told him about "Ruby?" Someone Ruby. Or Ruby someone. "Ruby shoot." That's what she had said.

"She must have been delirious, Monk. Thinkin' of Jack Ruby, or her jewelry or something."

Had he mentioned the white hair and aviator glasses? The man from Washington, the man in the picture, flagging a cab, in a hurry?

"Yes, you told me, Monk. It could have been anybody, but we'll look into it. By the way, the doorman was at dinner. They didn't replace him at the door. When he's gone, visitors ring the bell. Anybody in the building could have buzzed the killer in." Golden stood. "We're keeping the lid on. No press, if we can help it. And if we can't, then no connection whatsoever with the Whittaker thing. Understand?"

Ling eased himself to his feet. He felt as if he had been through all this before, that it was just one more cruel twist to his nightmares.

"And we're going ahead with the morning news conference. I'll want you there, Monk."

Ling looked into his eyes. "It was him, Julie. The guy I saw outside the embassy in Washington. Two blocks away, climbing into a cab. The same man. I'm positive."

33

Stanislas Lubelski spotted three callgirls during his first fifteen minutes in the lobby of the Hampstead Hotel, but none was Samantha Simpson. He wanted very much to talk to Miss Simpson. He would buy her services first, of course, then put his questions to her—surely she would have some clues into Whittaker's Washington scheme and who might have killed him.

He had tried the woman's apartment but there was no answer to her doorbell and the doorman was not there to give him any help as to where she might have gone. He briefly considered breaking into her apartment, then decided, except for a possible black book listing clients, a prostitute would be unlikely to reduce to paper anything of value to him. So he headed for the Hampstead, one of the new luxury hotels popping up all over Manhattan. Madam Celeste had advised him that it was Samantha Simpson's favorite rendezvous place.

The Hampstead's lobby was two stories high, with a wall of plate glass facing the street. The decor was ultramodern, with an emphasis on the more subtle shades of gold, rose, and pink. There were few pieces of lobby furniture—to discourage shopping bag ladies and footsore shoppers—and a pair of uniformed security men eyeballed everyone entering through the three sets of revolving doors.

Lubelski bought a paper at the cigar stand, then moved to a far corner of the lobby. He scanned the paper's entertainment section, now and then looking at his watch, as if he were a hotel guest awaiting a companion.

The three hookers he had spotted thus far all had one thing in common—they did not look like prostitutes. The giveaway was their age—women in their teens or twenties on the arms of older men, their clinging a bit too much for their role as daughters or nieces. High class call girls, available only through the most exclusive of sources. Most had rates of five-hundred and up a night. Given the credentials of their distinguished clientele, the hotel had no choice but to accept the hookers. But the hotel also knew who they were.

Lubelski noticed an idle bellhop and approached him.

"Excuse me," Lubelski said as his hand very blatantly reached for his wallet.

"Yes, sir?"

"I'm interested in locating a girl . . . a certain girl."

The bellhop's eyes grew alert—the hotel frowned on staff pimping; was he being tested? "Is she a guest, sir? You could use the house phone over there to check and . . ."

"I don't believe she's a guest." Lubelski had his wallet out. He extracted a ten-dollar bill. "Her name is Samantha Simpson. All I want is to talk to her."

The bellhop's eyes were on the bill. They grew wider as Lubelski extracted yet another. The ante was up to twenty.

"There is a Miss Simpson who comes here quite often," the bellhop blurted out.

"Tonight?"

He shook his head. "Haven't seen her."

"If she were here, what room do you suppose I might find her in?"

"It changes. Depends upon who she's with. You know, I'm not really supposed to be . . ."

Lubelski folded the two bills and discreetly passed them to him.

The bellhop looked nervously about, then said: "Councilman O'Bannion would be my first guess but I haven't seen him tonight either."

"What name does he use?"

"His own. He checks in himself. Always has the same cover story—got stuck in town and can't make it home to the Bronx. Then she goes up to join him."

The bellhop was summoned by the sharp ringing of a captain's bell. The captain's experienced eyes, no doubt, had seen the passing of the money and he wanted his cut.

Lubelski moved toward the front desk. He was grinning—the bellhop was too smart to deny the transaction but the captain would be told it had involved only a deuce or maybe a fin, that Lubelski had proven to be an out-of-town stiff. Picking up a house phone, Lubelski turned to glance at the captain's station. The bellhop had his hand out displaying a palmed bill. The captain looked at it, then glared at Lubelski. Lubelski smiled back at him—on another night, he would have had some fun, alerting the captain that the tip had been a hundred and not the lousy five the bellhop had folded as a contingency before his shift began.

"Can I help you?" the switchboard was asking.

"Has Councilman O'Bannion registered tonight?"

The operator took a moment to check, then advised that no one named O'Bannion was shown registered. Lubelski thanked her and started to hang up the phone when the voice of a desk clerk caught his attention.

"Samantha Simpson, was that the name you said?" the clerk had asked.

"Yes," answered a man on the other side of the desk.

"I'll check," the clerk said.

Lubelski returned the receiver to his ear, holding it there while he studied the man waiting at the desk. He was short but broad-shouldered, with gray-streaked black, wavy hair. His off the rack suit was ill-fitting and in need of pressing. His shoes were well-worn and scuffed. His jacket was open, revealing a good-sized paunch, and his face had the rough, red complexion of a dedicated drinking man. He was leaning on the counter with outstretched arms, and there was a slight tilt to his stance which helped accent the bulge under his coat. A cop.

The clerk was back, holding an envelope. "A Miss Simpson did leave this, sir. It's supposed to be picked up by a Mr. Ling. Is that you?"

"I work with him," the man said, flashing a badge.

"Oh . . . it's okay, I guess. But I'll need you to sign a receipt."

"Whatever you say, friend."

The clerk hastily drafted a receipt. The cop signed it and accepted the envelope, then hurriedly walked to the public telephones. Lubelski followed him, stepping up to an adjacent phone.

". . . I haven't opened it, chief, but I can feel through the paper. It's a key," the cop was saying.

Through his peripheral vision, Lubelski watched as the cop removed a penknife from his pocket and slit open the envelope. He held up a heavy, round brass key.

"It looks like a locker key. She said the Port Authority, right?" There was a pause. "I'm on my way."

The cop hung up and rushed for the lobby exit. Lubelski waited a few moments, then left the same way. A line of couples, the women in furs, some of the men in tuxedoes, was formed for cabs. Lubelski went around the corner and flagged a Checker.

He told the driver to take him to the Port Authority Bus Terminal. On the ride downtown, Lubelski produced a folded beret and a pair of horn-rimmed glasses from his pocket. He put them on. He also removed his tie and opened his shirt collar. Later, when the taxi reached the terminal, he removed his topcoat and threw it over his arms.

A trio of boys, none older than twelve, fought each other to carry his luggage, then spit at him when they saw he had none. A group of Hispanic transvestites blocked his path to the doors. One stepped forward. "Carmela, she blow you good, señor."

Lubelski pushed him roughly aside.

"Stick it, you fucking faggot!" Carmela shrieked in a heavy accent.

The terminal was busy. It was also big. The cop could be anywhere. Lubelski, in step with others rushing to catch about-to-depart buses, glanced up to the mezzanine—he was in luck! A uniformed officer leaning against the railing had just been approached by the plainclothes cop from the hotel. The patrolman was pointing.

Lubelski took the escalator up, struggling to keep the two cops in sight as they melted into the crowd of travelers. He lost them once, but then spotted the patrolman's cap, just as they reached a wall of coin-operated lockers.

The plainclothesman glanced at the number engraved on the key, then searched for the corresponding locker. Lubelski spotted an unused phone across from the lockers and only a few yards away. He went over to it and inserted a coin, dialing the weather.

The two police officers found the locker. The key was inserted, but they hesitated. Lubelski overheard enough of their conversation to know they were considering calling the bomb squad.

"Fuck it," the plainclothesman said. He motioned the other cop back, then turned the key and opened the door. He reached inside and removed a long box similar to a quart of milk. The plainclothes cop removed two wide rubber bands and lifted the cover. He then raised the box to his nose and sniffed it. Lubelski heard a whistle.

"Coke?" the patrolman asked.

"It ain't sugar."

34

Ling, entering through a rear door, found the large headquarters auditorium at One Police Plaza nearly filled. Cameramen were adjusting their tripods. Light men were taking meter readings. Sound men were testing their amplitude levels. Print reporters were scattered about, notebooks ready. Two radio reporters were trying to find space for their belated entries in the forest of stainless steel microphones on the podium. Still photographers squatted on their haunches or sat on the floor between the stage and first row, staking out positions. In a side aisle, in the harsh bath of her own personal kleig light, was an emaciated, hard-faced woman whom Ling recognized as the hostess of a morning network talk show. Apparently, the network would carry the news conference to the nation live.

As he walked toward the front, Ling counted fourteen camera crews, including representatives of Great Britain, Canada, Australia, and a special European pool. Not since the formal announcement, in the same auditorium, of an arrest in the Son of Sam case had a New York police press briefing attracted such extensive and international media coverage.

Ling began to tense as the enormity of the world attention on the case became evident. He gained additional insight into what Grambling and Golden had been through, the calls from the mayor, the pressure from the State Department, a thousand questions from a seemingly equal number of reporters, the demand by the public for answers. Ling feared that they had responded by moving too fast in going public. They should have waited at least until DeGrazia had been brought in. There was still something missing, Ling thought, some angle they had overlooked. He was left with a sense of foreboding.

Golden spotted Ling and waved him to the stage.

"How ya feelin'?" the chief asked.

"Like somebody chiseled out my insides."

"Your heart, you mean."

Ling shrugged.

"I warned you, Monk. Seen it happen too often."

Seen *what* happen too often, Ling wondered. Golden was perceptive enough to know Samantha Simpson had touched off a spark in his key detective; but did he know how far that detective had allowed himself to fall?

In truth, Ling felt nothing except for the tension stemming from the upcoming news conference. Otherwise he was numb. The full impact of Samantha Simpson's senseless murder, if it were to come at all, would hit later. It had taken weeks for him to comprehend his loss of Alex. Even now, there was a part of him that still refused to acknowledge it.

"I heard from ballistics on the Simpson shooting," Golden was saying. "They confirm it was the same weapon."

"Are you going to announce that?"

Golden shook his head; he gestured toward the noisy mob of media representatives. "They're getting a bone to chew on—just enough to get the P.C. off my back, and the mayor off his."

"Mickey find anything at that hotel?"

"Yeah. Your Miss Simpson left you a key, a Port Authority locker key. Triano went there and found a nice box of purity."

"So it wasn't sugar the good ambassador imported."

Golden smiled. "This stuff even an Englishman wouldn't waste in tea."

Commissioner Hamilton Grambling arrived on stage. Golden rushed to greet him. Ling joined Rosie McKinnon and Dotty Levine off to the side.

"Where's Triano? And O'Brien?" Ling asked.

"Don't know, Monk," McKinnon said, his eyes drifting over the still growing media audience.

Levine shook her head.

A public information sergeant in a crisply pressed uniform rapped on the podium to call the news conference to order.

"Hold it!" came a shout from beyond the kleig lights where yet another television crew had just arrived. The chattering and horseplay resumed while the new crew assembled its equipment. The cameraman focused on a sheet of white paper to balance his colors, then signaled to the sergeant to proceed.

The sergeant introduced the police commissioner, who thanked the news media for coming, and effused that the case about to be detailed represented some of the finest detective work in the history of the department. He then turned the podium over to Golden, who, Grambling made note, had personally headed the investigation.

Golden cleared his throat. He shifted from foot to foot. His hands were clumsy as they unfolded his typed sheet of prepared remarks. Ling had seen the chief address audiences in the thousands; never before had he appeared so nervous. Did he share the same sense of foreboding as Ling?

"Late last night," Golden began, "detectives of the New York City Police Department obtained an arrest warrant for one Anthony G. DeGrazia. A caucasian male. Five-feet seven. One-hundred and seventy-five pounds. Scars on left side of neck and right knee cap. Date of birth: 20 December 1937. Last known address in Brooklyn, New York. Mr. DeGrazia . . ."

"Repeat the address please," came an anonymous shout.

"Brooklyn, New York."

"The street address, I mean."

"I didn't give it."

"Why not?" the questioner demanded.

"Because we don't want it on the tour bus route—not just yet, anyway."

The reporter attempted a protest but Golden's amplified voice drowned him out. "Mr. DeGrazia's whereabouts at the present are unknown and he is considered a fugitive," the chief continued. "The department has issued a thirteen state bulletin for him which will be expanded nationally when appropriate. The department has also been in contact with Interpol and other appropriate law enforcement agencies in Europe.

"The warrant alleges that Mr. DeGrazia participated in a conspiracy to import unlawful substances into the country, to wit: cocaine. He is also considered a prime suspect in the murders of British subject James Whittaker and his female companion, Miss Michelle Pilat, believed to be of Paris, France." Golden looked up. "Are there any questions?"

"Was it a mob hit?"

"How did you connect DeGrazia?"

"What was the motive?"

Golden raised his hands. "One at a time, please. In answer to your first question, no, we do not consider this your typical organized crime assassination. I will not comment at this time on what led us to DeGrazia or speculate as to a motive."

"You mentioned cocaine. Was Whittaker involved in some kind of drug conspiracy?" The question was delivered in an Australian accent.

"No comment."

"The woman—you say her name was Pilat—but who was she really?"

"As we stated before, she was a foreigner in this country on a tourist's visa," Golden answered.

"It's taken you, what, three, four days to nail this down. Why so long?"

Golden glared into the lights. "The murderer didn't leave his card."

"Are there any political connotations to the murders? Was this DeGrazia hired by somebody or some group?"

"There is no evidence whatsoever of any type of political conspiracy." There was an edge to Golden's voice.

The public relations sergeant stepped forward to rescue him. "That's it for now—you'll be updated later," the sergeant announced.

"One more question, please!"

"Come on, Julie!"

The sergeant shook his head but the reporters persisted and

he finally relented, turning to Golden. The chief returned to the microphones and the questioning continued. Triano, meanwhile, joined the group of detectives on stage.

"Where you been?" McKinnon asked in a whisper.

"Workin' my ass off. All night. Chief put me and O'Brien on a tail."

"Tailing who?" Ling asked.

"Some guy I spotted at the Hampstead last night, Monk. I see him at the hotel and the next thing I know he's on my ass at the Port Authority. I call the chief and he had me stay on him. O'Brien came to help."

"This guy, you got an I.D.?" Ling asked.

Triano pulled out his notebook. "One Stanislas Lubelski. Turns out he's some kind of Polish reporter. We tailed him back to his residence, spent the night outside there and then this morning, we just about shit when the son of a bitch leads us here—to Police Headquarters, for chrissake. He's sitting out there now." Triano pointed toward the right side of the auditorium.

Ling stared in that direction but the glare of the television lights blinded him.

"What the hell is he doing here?" McKinnon asked.

Triano shrugged. "He's a newsman, supposedly, and the P.C. called a press conference, right?"

"What does he look like?" Ling asked.

"Early sixties, I would guess. Tall guy with hands the size of Ali's. Quite a build, too, considering his age. And he's got this kind of dignified look with this white hair and . . ."

"Glasses? Aviator glasses?" Ling asked.

Triano looked at him. "Yeah, Monk. How did you know?" Before Ling could answer, Triano's face lit up. "Say, the guy at that French broad's hotel . . . He had white hair, too, didn't he?" He winced. "Shit! I should know—I was the one that talked to the clerk."

At the podium, Golden had cut off the questioning, with authority, this time. He turned to his detectives. "Where's O'Brien?" Golden demanded of Triano.

"In the lobby, covering the exits."

"Call him off. We don't have to waste any more time on that asshole."

The public information sergeant took the chief by the arm. "The P.C. would like to see you, chief." The sergeant started to lead him away.

"Just a minute, Julie," Ling called after him.

Golden turned.

"Why are you pulling them off?"

"The guy's a newsie, Monk, just one more reporter trying to play cop and solve a case on his own."

"Don't, Julie. Leave the tail on."

The sergeant stepped between them. "The P.C., chief . . ."

"Why, Monk?" Golden asked. "What do you smell?"

"It's got to be him, the guy I saw outside Samantha Simpson's apartment last night, and outside the British Embassy in Washington. By the description, he's probably the man who cleaned out the female victim's hotel room."

Golden stared at him a moment, then said to Triano: "Stay on him, then. You and O'Brien."

The sergeant led him away.

"Thanks, Monk. I needed this," Triano said, turning to leave. Ling stopped him. "Say, Mickey, that first night at Whittaker's apartment, you remember seeing a video camera on a tripod?"

"Yeah—there was one."

"Where?"

"It was in the bedroom when I got there but the lab boys put it in some closet after they finished dusting. They kept tripping over it. Why?"

"I missed it, that's all. Thanks."

Ling descended the steps of the stage. Red lights were glowing on several television cameras as broadcast reporters did their standups, summarizing Golden's disclosures. A still photographer was rewinding his film.

"Hey, Monk," came a shout from the other aisle. It was Charlie Penn, the freelance radio reporter. "Let me ask you somethin'."

"Give me five minutes, Charlie," Ling answered, moving up the aisle toward the area where Triano had said the Polish journalist was sitting. Then Ling spotted him—sitting alone off to the right. A well-dressed, white-haired man whom Ling recognized immediately as the same man he had seen outside the British embassy and the same man he had seen hailing a cab near Samantha Simpson's apartment building.

Triano had identified him as Stanislas Lubelski. Ling silently repeated the name.

The Polish correspondent was staring blankly ahead toward the stage, where Golden was huddled with the P.C. and other department brass.

"Excuse me," Ling said, cautioning himself to be very careful.

Lubelski stood. Ling introduced himself. The Pole provided his name and news affiliation, then offered his hand. Ling took it, finding a firm but not excessively strong grip.

"I have the feeling I've seen you before," Ling said.

Lubelski grinned. "Quite possibly so. Bombings. Murders. A celebrity rape or mugging now and then. I've covered many of them."

"Your readers in Poland are interested in this case?"

"Of course! They are always curious about New York bloodshed and debauchery." He was still smiling.

"I see," Ling said, rubbing his chin. "I wonder what your view is on how we've been handling *this* investigation."

Lubelski appeared to weigh his answer. His expression grew serious. "To be blunt, I wonder about the motive. You say it has something to do with drugs. I would think it might be more than that." He renewed his smile. "But I am not a professional with the reputation, for instance, of a Detective Ling. I am only a journalist, an old and tired journalist at that."

"But certainly you must have a theory."

"An armchair theory, yes."

"If I may ask, what is it?"

A twinkle came to Lubelski's eyes. "Blackmail," he said.

"Blackmail?" Ling asked with an exaggerated look of disbelief.

"You asked me my theory and that's what it is. But then, I am, as I say, a writer. And blackmail is so much more—how do you say it, sexy?—than a drug smuggling conspiracy. Perhaps it was a simple love triangle. That, too, could be sexy, yes?" The Pole's expression changed. Ling suddenly had the feeling Lubelski regretted this exchange. Why?

Lubelski reached for his coat. ''Now, if you will excuse me, I must go.'' He looked at his watch. ''My deadline nears.''

The Pole left for the rear doors. Ling watched him, then caught a glimpse of O'Brien in the lobby, as he picked up the tail.

Suddenly, McKinnon was tapping Ling's shoulder. ''Got to ride, Monk. They just got a call. DeGrazia's surrendering—at the Seventeenth.''

35

While the New York Police Department had its attention on Tony DeGrazia, Stanislas Lubelski was more interested in a woman in the White House and a prostitute who might supply a route for making the approach the Soviets expected of him. But Lubelski decided it would be unwise to search further for Samantha Simpson at either her apartment or the Hampstead Hotel. The call girl had provided the police with a key to a locker containing a fortune in cocaine—that meant she likely was either a police informant or a suspect bargaining for her freedom. It also meant she could be in protective custody, long out of the country, or on a slab in the morgue, her betrayal having caught up with her. Whatever the scenario, Simpson was now useless to him. Instead, he would have to begin closing his circle around Marilyn Mason directly.

Back in his office after leaving the Police Headquarters news conference, Lubelski concluded he would not have much time to make his move. First he would have to determine Mason's exact whereabouts. Other operatives might find this task overwhelming and call for reinforcements to establish a net of surveillance; Lubelski merely picked up his phone and dialed the White House.

"Ms. Marilyn Mason, please," he told the White House switchboard. There was a delay, then a secretary answered.

"This is Miles Milligan with the Federal Reserve in

New York," Lubelski announced. "I'd like to speak to Ms. Mason, please. It's rather urgent."

The secretary stalled, her memory for names testing the entry "Milligan." Her cautious tone suggested no match had been made: "I'm very sorry, sir, but I'm afraid Ms. Mason is off for a few days."

"Where can I reach her? As I said, it's somewhat important."

"I'm not allowed to give out any numbers."

"Well, is she in the country at least?" Lubelski demanded indignantly.

"Yes . . . she is," the secretary replied, fear in her voice. "She's in Georgia . . . at her sister's."

"If and when you hear from her, miss, I want you to pass along a message."

"Certainly, sir."

"Tell her Stanislas Lubelski, the Polish journalist, would like to ask her some questions about the Whittaker murders."

"The Whittaker murders?"

"That's correct. And please inform her that Mr. Lubelski believes the New York police are making a terrible mistake; that they're arresting the wrong suspect."

"I don't believe that Miss Mason has ever heard of a Mr. Lubelski, and how is he connected with the Federal Reserve?"

"I didn't say he was."

"I just don't know about this, sir, and . . ."

"All you have to know is how to relay that message," Lubelski snapped, then hung up the phone.

So Marilyn Mason had suddenly left Washington—apparently by herself. It was the move Lubelski had been waiting for. The woman was troubled and vulnerable, bending under the pressure and likely to make a mistake. His earlier conclusion was now confirmed—timing from this point on would be critical. He would have to move quickly, even if it meant bluffing it.

Lubelski immediately dialed another number and this time switched his scrambler on. He needed help from the KGB computer. It would be a risky call and he distrusted the security of the computer—it was U.S.-made and for all he knew, the Americans had penetrated it the day the final screw was put into place. That was the trouble with all the new technology—the KGB could monitor at will sensitive U.S. phone calls by capturing microwave transmissions, for example, but the Americans knew this and, therefore, the capability meant nothing. Intelligence had modernized itself into meaninglessness, forsaking the time proven simple tools for winning hearts and minds, the emotional and intellectual weapons that had won them the likes of Fuchs, MacLean, and Philby. If Lubelski was to capture the services of Marilyn Mason, it would be through exploitation of her greed, ego, and fear, not satellites and computer printouts.

The phone rang more than a dozen times before a clerk in the KGB's Washington research and records section finally answered.

Lubelski provided a code to identify himself, then said: "Marilyn Mason of the White House. She has a sister in Georgia."

The clerk asked Lubelski to stand by while she queried her computer terminal.

The information came in seconds. "The sister's name is Sally. Divorced. Thirty-two years old. Quit a marketing position in Boston approximately eighteen months ago. Now lives in Blakeshammock, Georgia."

"Phone?"

"None. Apparently she does not have one."

Lubelski hung up. Georgia. It had been many years since he had been to the South. He reached into a side drawer of his desk and removed a U.S. road atlas. He flipped the pages to the map of Georgia, then checked the index of cities for Blakeshammock. There was no such listing.

Perhaps he had misunderstood the clerk. Maybe he was spelling it wrong. He would call back. No, first he would search the map—it might only be a village, too small for listing with the cities.

He started at the state's northern boundary, his index finger moving back and forth across the multicolored map as he inched his way down. Soon his focus was past Atlanta, heading for the Florida border. And there it was! A tiny hamlet, judging by the miniature type. It was on the edge of a large expanse labeled "Devilsdip Swamp."

Lubelski made yet another call, this one to an airline,

securing a reservation under an alias on the earliest flight
from LaGuardia to Atlanta. He then moved to the windows
of his office and looked down.

The detectives were still there, both of them, one standing
across First Avenue at the window of a small delicatessen, the
other twenty yards away, in the shadows of a newsstand.

Lubelski had enjoyed leading them to the front doors of
their own headquarters but he would not toy with them now.
He went back to the phone and called a helicopter firm
serving LaGuardia and Kennedy airports. Yes, the clerk said,
there was a shuttle flight that could make that connection to
the Atlanta-bound plane.

Lubelski smiled. He checked his watch. There was just
enough time for him to make the necessary stop at his apartment. He was going south—he would need another set of
clothes.

He left the office and flagged a taxi, giving the cabbie his
apartment address. As the cab pulled away, Lubelski watched
through the rear window as the detective at the newsstand
jumped into a car, waited for the other cop, then slid into the
flow of traffic behind him.

Lubelski decided against keeping the cab at his apartment
and paid the driver.

Once in his residence, Lubelski hurriedly changed from his
suit into a pair of chino slacks, blue workshirt and blazer. He
replaced his dress shoes with a pair of low-cut boots, and
slipped a razor and toothbrush into his blazer pocket. He went
to the closet and pulled down a large suitcase from the
overhead shelf. He stuffed two pillows into it, plus a Manhattan phone book, then locked it. With the suitcase in his hand
and his trenchcoat thrown over his shoulder, he returned to
the street and hailed another cab for the trip to Kennedy
Airport.

The detectives were good—only occasionally was Lubelski
able to glimpse the plain blue sedan behind him—but they
were working the tail without backup and had to keep pace
with him. At the airport, they left their car in a tow-away
zone and followed him inside the terminal.

Lubelski stopped at an airline flight board, studying it until he came up with a departure time that met his needs. It was a flight to Los Angeles.

He approached the ticket counter. Yes, the clerk advised him, there were empty seats on the L.A. flight. He produced a credit card to pay for his ticket, and checked his suitcase.

Lubelski cleared the security check and began the long walk to the departure gate. Stopping abruptly for a drink from a water fountain, he spotted one of the detectives some twenty paces behind him. The other, he was certain, would be nearby.

The plane for Los Angeles had just begun loading as Lubelski reached the gate. He presented his ticket at the counter, then moved toward the entrance of the boarding ramp. He lingered there, verifying that the detectives were still behind him—they were, positioned on opposite sides of the concourse about a gate away. Lubelski studied the other Los Angeles bound passengers. Finally, he found what he needed—a harried couple with three small children who had arrived with a great amount of carry-on luggage too late for the pre-boarding normally offered such travelers. Lubelski followed them onto the ramp.

Just as he had hoped, the pair of stewardesses posted inside the plane's door moved immediately to help with the children and baggage. With their attention thus diverted, Lubelski slipped through a service door and descended a metal stairway from the ramp to the tarmac. As he moved, he reached into a sidepocket for a plastic badge reading "OFFICIAL" in large block letters with a fictitious name in smaller type below. He pinned it to his blazer. The badge, tinted a light blue with a large red band across the bottom, had served Lubelski well in a wide variety of past excursions, as it did now—several of the airlines ground personnel stared at him suspiciously a moment, then caught sight of the badge and continued about their business. One baggage handler even offered him a wave.

Lubelski looked back to the terminal. Through the tinted plate glass windows, he saw the two detectives speaking to the clerk at the counter. The clerk appeared to be protesting. She picked up a red telephone. The detectives, no doubt, were seeking to delay the plane's departure until they could contact their superiors for further orders.

Lubelski grinned—by the time the word came down the chain of command and his absence from the Los Angeles-bound plane was noted, he would already have reached LaGuardia on a shuttle helicopter, and would be boarding another aircraft, this one bound for Atlanta, Georgia.

36

Marilyn Mason had been on the road for more than an hour. Earlier, she had been caught up in the morning rush hour in Atlanta, the commuters, their eyes half-closed, speeding by her, expressionless fish in a fast-paced precision ritual that had no place for a woman whose nerves were shot. She had watched them, catching their hostile glances and wondering why they hated her. What did they know?

But the traffic had lightened the further she drove from Atlanta, and now the southbound lanes of the interstate were empty, except for some huge and frightening tractor-trailer trucks, a few local housewives, farmers, and an occasional carful of vacationers bound for the Florida coast.

She kept her eyes alternately on the speedometer and the road ahead and caught only flashes of the farm fields, forests, and wetlands to the sides. Now and then, she would glimpse the outlines of an isolated house, and would wonder about the people who lived there, what they were doing at that very moment. Gearing up for another boring day at jobs they detested, she guessed. As for herself, she didn't hate her job. In fact, she rather liked what she was doing. But she had paid a very high price to get there—in a way few could understand. James Whittaker had understood. They had talked about it and he told her he knew what she had gone through and what . . .

No, she wouldn't think of Whittaker. She would think of Sally, her sister, and the next three or four days, the fresh air and the quiet, the time and space she so desperately needed.

As the sun climbed higher, the rolling countryside began to glow in multishades of effervescent green. The peaceful terrain and the rhythm of her tires against the concrete began to lull her and she had to fight to keep her eyes open. The radio—perhaps that would help.

A search of the dial found only country music, ranting preachers, and incomprehensible farm market reports. One country and western station, however, was switching to its network news. She left the tuner there.

There was a commercial for a bathroom cleanser, then the hour's top story: "In New York today, police revealed the name of a man they say is a prime suspect in this week's murders of James Whittaker, the brother of Britain's prime minister, and his female companion.

"At a news conference, top police officials announced they have issued a thirteen state alarm for Anthony DeGrazia of Brooklyn, who has a lengthy police record.

"Authorities say DeGrazia will be formally charged with conspiracy to import cocaine, but he also has been implicated in the slayings of Whittaker and the woman, now identified as Michelle Pilat, in a plush Park Avenue apartment."

Marilyn's hands began to tremble. Her palms grew so moist she had trouble gripping the steering wheel. She slowed, then pulled to the shoulder of the highway and stopped.

The newscaster was saying something about the Mideast. Marilyn fumbled for the knob to turn the radio off, then buried her face in her hands. DeGrazia. She had met him and Whittaker had talked often of him. The police were now alleging that DeGrazia was the killer. Oh, my God! Cocaine smuggling. An arrest record. What would they say at the White House?

The car swayed as a double-bottom truck pulling two trailers sped by.

She reached into her purse for a handkerchief, removed her sunglasses and patted down her face. She had to control herself. It was okay, now—she was far, far away.

Marilyn eased the rented Chrysler back onto the highway.

She would concentrate on her driving—and look for the exit sign for the Chapman County cutoff.

In a few more minutes, she was there. She slowed the car, then exited the interstate to a two-lane road.

The county highway took her through a series of rural hamlets, each a small collection of old frame houses, a gas station, and a convenience store. Every town seemed to present the same cast of characters: an old man wearing coveralls with suspenders sitting on a porch step, barefoot kids trailed by a yapping mongrel dog, a plump woman hanging out the wash, a sunburned man wearing a baseball cap and spitting tobacco juice from the driver's seat of a pickup truck. Marilyn had to force herself to look—the memories were too painful. You could take any one of these hamlets, she decided, and find an exact counterpart in the valleys of Pennsylvania, perhaps even her own hometown where she, too, had once run barefoot—and detested it.

Leaving one town, she noticed a curling column of thick black smoke in the distance. "Must be a house on fire. Or a barn," she said aloud, feeling, for a passing instant, sympathy for the owner. Fire was a small town's greatest nightmare.

The road began a sweeping curve. When she had rounded it, the farms had been replaced by forest. Live oaks shot skyward in thick, knobby, irregular pillars, then exploded horizontally into an arboreal umbrella with branches as full in girth as the trunks of lesser trees. The roadbed began to descend rapidly and soon the mat of decaying leaves at the base of the trees became water, dark and murky. She was entering a swamp. Devilsdip, it was called. Her sister had spoken about it. Once, Marilyn had looked for it on a map. Such a curious name!

She slowed the car.

Where the oaks made no claim, equally tall but less majestic cypresses now filled the void, their tops mating with those of the oaks to form an almost impenetrable canopy, blocking the sun. The branches extended over the road, enclosing it and giving Marilyn the feeling she was in a tunnel. It was so dark she removed her sunglasses and considered putting on her headlights. But the wall of trees would be broken now and then by a shallow marsh or pond, and the sunlight would burst like a photographer's flashbulb, temporarily blinding her with its intensity. No sooner would her eyes adjust that the twisting road would enter another tunnel of darkness.

She stepped up her speed. For five, six and then seven miles the terrain remained unchanged. How big was this swamp, anyway? she wondered.

There was a partial clearing ahead. Marilyn decided to stop so she could stretch her legs. She pulled the car to the side of the road and stared through its side windows at a dark green slough. Beneath the trees, the water was interrupted here and there by spits and plugs of spongy earth, the water's surface mostly still, unbroken but for the ripples from the lily pads floating upon it like leprechauns' rafts, and the green and yellow tips of dozens of less appealing water weeds. The water rippled, too, where limpkins, white ibis, and herons waded, and where strangely shaped insects hopskipped off the surface tension.

Marilyn stepped out of the car. She was entranced by the sight. Its beauty brought her the calm she so craved. No matter what direction she looked, there wasn't the slightest hint of humanity, not even a fisherman. She took a deep breath and held it—the air was moist and fertile, tasting of life-giving chlorophyll. She exhaled, pleased she had come south, grateful for this contact with nature. But as she looked to the sky, an aftertaste lingered in her mouth. It was an odd taste, reminding her of when, as a girl, she would chew on a twig until it was reduced to a bitter mulch. That was it! Mulch. Rotting wood and foliage. Decomposition. The taste of death.

Marilyn shivered at the thought. She should leave, get on to her sister's. The village would not be far. But something was holding her back, making her reluctant to give up this moment.

She began walking along the road. The gravel of the shoulder was chewing up her loafers—but that was okay. Ahead, a tree had fallen, its insect-ravaged trunk protruding into the road. She raised her foot to step over it, then froze—on the other side of the log, in a shadow, was a foot-long lizard, dark gray with black stripes, its jaws locked on a butterfly.

Marilyn screamed and jumped back. Then she began to laugh. It was only a lizard. Some people kept them as pets.

Still, the spell had been broken. She started back for the car. She had just reached it when she was startled once more, this time by an overpowering roar coming from behind. She turned—from around a bend sped a huge truck, its trailer piled high with timber, the freshly cut pine held precariously in place by a pair of girding chains. The driver slammed on his noisy airbrakes but his speed carried the truck onward another twenty yards.

The driver, who had a beard and wore a cowboy hat, stuck his head out the window. "Anything wrong, ma'am?" he shouted.

"No!" Marilyn yelled back. "Just looking around."

The driver smiled and waved, then put the truck in gear and pulled away.

Marilyn, shaking, climbed into her car. She crossed her arms over the steering wheel and lowered her head. My God, that truck was moving fast, she thought, and he was traveling right down the center line. What if she had . . .

She shook her head. Now was not the time to dwell on what might have been. Sally was waiting a few miles ahead. Only a few more minutes and she would be there. She shouldn't have stopped in the first place.

Marilyn started the car and pulled back onto the road. And she started thinking of Tony DeGrazia again. He was from Brooklyn. Probably a member of the mob. The media would link her to DeGrazia through her relationship with Whittaker. The Mafia had penetrated the White House—that's what they would say.

Her lips were quivering. She could feel her heart pounding. "No!" she suddenly shouted, slapping her hand on the car seat. She was playing a destructive game with herself, projecting a worst case scenario that was not likely to happen. She was no ordinary citizen, no barefoot girl in a one-horse Pennsylvania farm town—she was an aide to the President! The administration would have to stand behind her. If the White House bowed to innuendo, its staff would turn over every three months. In any case, it was out of her hands at the moment. She had to steer her mind to something else.

The swamp. Her sister had written her a letter about it
once. Sally described how she had been moved by the pristine
wetlands on whose border she now lived—she always had
been a bit of a poetess—and found in it, as she put it, some
lessons in universal truth. Sally had detailed the lush beauty
of Devilsdip, but also had warned that this was deceiving,
that the swamp could be dangerous and cruel, its life fed by
the decay of death. Days in Devilsdip, she had written, were
active and noisy, the crescendo rising with the movement of
the sun and diminishing with the encroachment of darkness.
Then, with sunset, a different chorus would build with the
rumbling, lament-filled croaking of mating frogs and locusts,
rhythmic sounds pounding with a heart-like pulse, and un-
ceasing except when overpowered by the chilling shriek of an
unseen owl, the grunting of a disturbed wild pig, or the death
cry of a careless bird.

How right Sally had been! That horrible taste, after so brief
an exposure to Devilsdip, still lingered in Marilyn's mouth.
Sally, no doubt, would want to take her deep within the
swamp's bowels, on a hike, perhaps, or a canoe trip. But
Marilyn would say no—she had already seen enough of
Devilsdip Swamp to satiate her hunger for raw nature for a
good, long while.

Marilyn laughed thinking of the protests Sally would make,
her inevitable argument that women had to overcome their
dread of such things if they were ever to prove their equality
with men. "I've already proven all I'll ever have to prove,"
Marilyn said aloud, rehearsing her retort. And, she would
add, even the President had to concede that she . . .

Suddenly, Marilyn slammed her foot on the brakes. With
no warning, as the car completed a ninety-degree curve, it
was completely enveloped by darkness. Acrid, blinding smoke
surrounded the Chrysler and began seeping into the interior.
She shut off the air conditioning, then began inching the car
forward, feeling her way and hoping she would clear the
smoke in a matter of yards.

But the air didn't clear. She estimated she had traveled a
quarter of a mile, and still the smoke blinded her. She couldn't
stop for fear another vehicle—a timber truck, perhaps—would
rearend her, crushing the Chrysler with its tons of cargo. She

would have to continue forward, praying there was no on-coming traffic, hoping she herself was not across the unseen yellow line.

Then, as quickly as the smoke had appeared, it was gone, behind her now, a dark gray curtain visible in her rear view mirror. She stopped the car and rubbed her eyes. They burned. What next? she demanded, wondering what angry god was intent on her never reaching the refuge awaiting her at her sister's.

Marilyn bit her lower lip and put the car into gear, pushing hard on the accelerator. She vowed to make it. She would stop for nothing now.

As the speedometer passed sixty, Marilyn remembered the wisp of smoke she had spotted miles back. And she knew now that the smoke she had seen wasn't from a house or a barn; it was from Devilsdip. The swamp was on fire!

After a mile-long straightaway, the road curved one way, then the other, and when the Chrysler had completed the maneuver, she was in a small town. A rusting white metal sign on a rotting wooden post identified it as "Blakeshammock, pop. 137." Above the sign were a Lion's Club emblem and the circular symbol of the American Legion, both corroded with age. The weeds at the base of the signpost were knee-high.

Marilyn slowed the car and opened her side window. She had made it! Everything would be all right, now.

She passed a few houses, two of them obviously aban-doned, and an empty lot. A jeep and a pickup truck were parked outside a small country store, which had an inconspicuous sign revealing that it also served as a post office. Down the street a neon sign reading "VACANCY" blinked on and off at the Tall Oaks Motel, which more accurately was an old-style motor court, a crescent of tiny, unattached wood frame cot-tages, vestiges, she guessed, of a day when Main Street was probably a section of a U.S. highway, before the interstate.

Across from the motel was a restaurant with "Dempsey's Cafe" stenciled on the door. Sally's travel instructions had said to continue past the restaurant until the third house on the right, across the street from a boarded-up clapboard.

One, two, three, Marilyn counted, and then she was there. It was a small cottage—four rooms, Sally had said—and freshly painted in white. Marilyn pulled in front and stopped. She turned off the engine and got out, fighting an ache in her back and stiffness in her legs, feeling as if she had just survived some wilderness club's initiation. She threw back her shoulders and stretched.

A thumping sound was coming from the far side of the house. She followed it and found Sally dressed in torn jeans, boots, and a ragged lumberman's shirt, swinging a long-handled axe high over her head and down to a tree stump, the axe's flat head striking a metal wedge. A log split in two from the impact.

Marilyn watched, saying nothing, as down and down again the axe head came, her sister putting as much strength into the action as could any similarly sized man. Then Sally spotted her. She threw down the axe and ran to her, smothering Marilyn in her arms. Marilyn permitted the embrace a few seconds, then edged away, feeling awkward and embarrassed.

"Ah, come on! Let me hold you!" Sally protested. "I'm your sister!"

Sally was on her again, her arms clenching her tightly, their cheeks pressed together. Marilyn ran a hand lightly over her sister's back.

"My God! I don't believe it! You actually came!" Sally exclaimed, stepping back to inspect her. "You look pale— and tired. But don't worry—"she smiled broadly—"I'll shape you up." Sally suddenly tilted her head, her eyes on Marilyn's face. "Say, what's that scratch on your cheek? It looks deep."

Marilyn said nothing.

Sally gave a knowing smile. "Oh, I get it—a little passion out of hand. You naughty girl." She led her toward the front of the house.

"Back there," Marilyn said, gesturing toward the highway. "Bad smoke. It blinded me."

Sally laughed. "Wildfire. Comes in cycles, once every seven or eight years. Around here, they don't even bother with it."

"What do you mean?"

"They don't fight it. It's no use."

Sally explained that wildfires were usually caused by lightning from a fast-passing summer squall striking a treetop in a stand left tinderbox-dry from a lack of rainfall. The flames would travel the tree trunks to the lush undergrowth. The fire would explode like a matchhead but then begin to die down as it reached still lower, to the root systems of the trees and into the soil of the loam-like knolls that rose softly from the sloughs.

"They can burn for weeks," Sally said.

"I never heard of such a thing!"

"Neither did I until I came down here. But enough of that. Let me show you the place."

Inside, a ceiling fan revolved slowly over the combination living and dining room. The room opened at one end to a bedroom and at the other, a small kitchen with a collection of pots, pans and large utensils hanging from overhead racks. The bathroom, which featured an old style claw-footed tub, was off the bedroom.

"Sit down," Sally ordered when they had returned to the larger room. She pounded a fist on a thick wooden table. "How do you like it? I made it myself. Still needs another coat of linseed oil. Maybe I'll put you to work doing that." She moved out of sight into the kitchen, shouting back: "I ordered a table when I moved here but it was late in coming. I got mad waiting for it so I built my own." She was back with a gallon jug and two tumblers. "I also built the kitchen cabinets and the bookshelves and that firewood rack next to the wood stove." She patted the jug. "Cider. Made that myself, too." She filled the glasses, shoved one toward Marilyn, then lifted the other. "To my kid sister, the President's smartest adviser!"

Marilyn smiled. She brought the glass to her lips. The cider was warm and sweet, and its alcohol soothed her throat, helping to rid her of the aftertaste of the swamp and its smoke.

"Now," Sally said, sitting across from her, "we've got a lot of catching up to do."

37

Chief of Detectives Julius Golden was pacing the squadroom. "Where is she, for chrissake?" he demanded.

Dotty Levine glanced at the clock. "It's only been fifteen minutes, chief. Relax."

Golden swept a hand toward the side office. "With that scumbag in there, how can I relax."

Ling understood Golden's nervousness. In the makeshift interrogation room sat Anthony G. DeGrazia. The chief had elected to leave him alone in there with the hope that the futility of his position would strike home, that his tension would grow while he awaited the next move. It was a standard police ploy, but sometimes the strategy backfired, and the solitude and extra time gave a suspect an opportunity to bolster his confidence, frame his own tactics, get mad.

DeGrazia had been anything but cocky upon his arrival at the Seventeenth Precinct. The three-car caravan of Golden and his detectives had just arrived from headquarters when another car, a flashy red Pontiac, pulled up to the entrance and DeGrazia was heaved ignominiously out a rear door to the sidewalk. The unexplained delivery was, no doubt, courtesy of Little Brother Marco. Golden had DeGrazia read his rights and he was immediately hustled upstairs to sit alone in the side office.

McKinnon came rushing up the stairs. "Got her, chief. She's downstairs. And Triano's got the stand-ins ready."

"Let's go, then," Golden said. He looked to Ling: "Give us two minutes, then bring him down."

The squadroom emptied. Ling moved to a window and looked down: a crowd of cameramen, photographers, and reporters was once again gathered at the station house door. Word of the suspect's surrender had spread incredibly fast, despite there being no official announcement.

Ling went to the conference room and opened the door. DeGrazia snapped upright in his chair. "One more time, Tony, do you want a lawyer?"

"I told ya how many times already, I don't need any fuckin' mouthpiece. I didn't do nothin' and you guys know it."

"You still waive your rights, then?"

"Yeah—what do I have to do, stand on my head and sign the fuckin' paper?"

"Come on."

"Where we goin'?"

"A lineup."

"Jesus christ, I don't believe it."

Ling saw no need for handcuffs but had DeGrazia walk ahead of him downstairs. Triano and Levine were at the bottom waiting for them. They escorted the suspect into a back room where O'Brien had five other men—cops and other precinct prisoners—who would also be paraded before the witness. Three of the other men were similar in appearance to DeGrazia, who had not been told the witness's identity.

O'Brien and Triano stayed backstage; Ling and Levine left for the viewing area behind a one-way mirror. Golden and McKinnon were there with the witness, Mrs. Harriet Cunningham, the elderly widow who lived next door to the murder scene.

"Now, Mrs. Cunningham, several men will be led across that stage there," Golden said gently. "They won't be able to see you, so don't worry about that. And . . ."

"I know all about it," the woman interrupted.

"You do?" Golden asked.

"Television. These lineup things are on all the time."

Golden nodded knowingly, then said: "Well, what we want is for you to tell us which of the men is the one you saw threaten Mr. Whittaker in the hallway. Do you think you can remember?"

"I'll try."

The chief signaled for the lineup to begin. The six men paraded out, all of them grim-faced, some of them, including DeGrazia, openly surly.

They had hardly faced the front when Mrs. Cunningham blurted out: "There he is! Number five."

"Are you certain, ma'am?" Golden asked, his expression deadpan. "Look them over again, please. What we want is the man you overheard threatening the deceased, Mr. Whittaker."

She looked at Golden with impatience. "I told you, young man. It's number five. He's the one that told that poor Englishman he was going to get even."

Golden stood. "Thank you, Mrs. Cunningham." He grinned. She had unhesitatingly chosen Tony DeGrazia. "Get him back upstairs."

Ling went behind the stage to collect the suspect. O'Brien was waiting for him. "Not bad, huh, Monk?" Ling started to answer but O'Brien continued: "I mean, for an inept detective, it wasn't bad how I brought this sucker in, huh?"

"You made one mistake a long time ago, O'Brien," Ling said, his tone neither hostile nor conciliatory. "I never called you inept."

"What about now? Did I fuck it up again? You gonna go out and prove this wise guy innocent?" O'Brien's eyes burned with animosity.

Ling stared back at him a moment, then, saying nothing, went over to the sulking DeGrazia.

He escorted DeGrazia back upstairs and put him in the conference room. A police stenographer was summoned. Golden also ordered a tape recorder—he was not taking any chances.

When the stenographer was present and the recorder tested and running, Golden and Ling took seats across from DeGrazia, who sat facing sideways, his legs crossed in a gesture of defiance.

Golden announced the date and location into the microphone, then said: "Your name please?"

"Oh, for chrissake."

The chief jumped to his feet. "Face forward," he shouted.

DeGrazia, taken aback, dropped his legs and complied.

"State your name, your full name," Golden ordered.

Again DeGrazia complied.

Golden once again read him his rights and, when he continued to decline the offer of a lawyer, had him sign yet another written waiver.

Golden retook his seat and nodded to Ling.

"You're in trouble, Tony. Big trouble," Ling began.

"So what else is new?"

"Maybe you like to tell us where you've been?"

"Atlantic City."

"Why?"

"Why does anyone go to Atlantic City?"

"Because maybe Marco tells them the heat's on and to disappear."

DeGrazia said nothing.

"Monday, the night of Whittaker's murder, you were in Jersey then, too?"

"No, I wasn't in Jersey Monday. I was out."

"Out where?"

"Tryin' to get laid, what I do every goddamned night."

"Where, Tony?"

"This joint, that one—who remembers."

"A pro by the name of Samantha Simpson, you know her, Tony?" Ling asked.

"I knew a Samantha somebody. She was shackin' up with Whittaker. He called her Sam."

"She was wasted, Tony—two nights ago—by someone who didn't want her to talk."

"It wasn't me! She didn't know nothin' about what Whittaker and me had goin'. She . . ."

"You in Atlantic City *that* night, Tony?" Golden interrupted.

"Yeah—I mean, no. I was back in the city."

"Where were you?" Ling demanded.

"Home."

"We checked."

DeGrazia buried his face in his hands. "I don't know

where the fuck I was. I tied one on, see. Marco's boys, they found me this morning in some fleabag. God, my head hurts!''

Ling grinned. "Ya see, Tony, we've got at least one witness, who says he saw you outside Whittaker's building that night. Guy like you goin' uptown to get laid? You ought to know better.''

"And you should learn to park legal like other people, Tony," Golden said. "That car you rented, we've traced the summons and that puts you guess where—right in the neighborhood.''

DeGrazia leaned over the table. "Okay, okay! I'm not gonna play any fuckin' games with you. Yeah, I was up there—waiting for the son of a bitch.''

"And what happened?''

"Nothing. He never left that night.''

Ling chuckled. "I guess so.''

"But I didn't waste him. You got nobody says I was in that building. I'm not that stupid.''

"You know the Florida State score, Tony?''

"The what?''

"Florida State score. They played Saturday.''

"What the fuck you askin' that for?''

"Just figured a sportin' man like you would know the score.''

DeGrazia, bewildered, thought a moment, then answered: "Florida State won. Beat the Gators—and the spread.''

Ling looked at Golden. "I knew I should have laid a hundred on those Seminoles!''

DeGrazia eased back in his seat, showing both confusion and suspicion.

"You got cigarettes?'' Ling asked.

DeGrazia nodded.

"Go ahead and light up, if you want.''

He did.

It was Golden's turn. "You see, Tony, what we're working on here is a little cocaine enterprise that went sour. Got this man in Washington, he's some kind of an ambassador, and he tells us this tale all about Whittaker wanting him to bring in some coke in a diplomatic pouch.''

"Then we start thinkin'," Ling said, "how's this guy Whittaker going to peddle this stuff? He's an upper class Englishman, for chrissake. All he knows is growing roses and drinkin' tea. He needs somebody streetwise, Tony. He needs a pro."

Golden took over: "There's this little afterhours joint near Union Square and the fellow there, he remembers you and he remembers Whittaker and when we turn the screws, he remembers . . ."

"Okay!" DeGrazia shouted. "I'll tell ya what happened. But you guys gotta ease off. I mean, I didn't shoot Whittaker. I didn't kill nobody."

"Go ahead, Tony," Golden said softly.

DeGrazia sighed, then said: "You got part of it right. I meet this Whittaker and, after a while, he starts telling me how he's got this shipment comin' and how he wants a partner and I've got the smarts to do it. So like a stupid asshole, I tell him okay. I go out and start making the arrangements; you know, gettin' out the word so we can move the stuff and move it fast. I also make sure we're not steppin' on anybody's toes."

"What you mean is you cleared it with Marco," Ling said.

"You ain't gonna get me to say nothing about Marco, okay? Doesn't matter anyhow because comes the day the shit's supposed to arrive, this Whittaker goes to Washington. He comes back that night. I've got everything greased. And the bastard tells me we've been stiffed. He says this pouch's got nothing but fuckin' sugar. And that's it."

"What do you mean, that's it, Tony?" Ling asked. "You were outside his apartment waiting for him. We've got a witness who says you threatened him. What happened next?"

DeGrazia lowered his head. He thought a few moments, then: "I didn't believe the bastard. You know, there was somethin' about him never was right. I figured somebody's getting stiffed, all right, and it's me."

"Why were you outside the building, Tony?" Ling asked sternly.

"I knew he had the shit and sometime he had to move it. I was waiting for him."

"To waste him as soon as you had a line on the coke," Golden said.

"No fuckin' way, I tell ya. All I wanted was my half. I mean, I'd already told half the goddamned players in the city it was comin'. Tony DeGrazia's reputation was at stake."

"Ah, shit," Golden said. "You've got to do better than that, DeGrazia."

"It's the truth!"

"Who financed it?" Ling asked.

"He did. Whittaker."

"Where did he get the dough?"

"I don't know. Somethin' he had goin' on Wall Street. A scam of some kind. He never told me what."

"How much did he have to play with, you know that?" Golden asked.

"Yeah, he bragged about it. Said he had three-hundred and seventy-five thousand. This coke deal, it was gonna eat a hundred and fifty, a hundred and seventy-five, I'm not sure."

Ling thought of the two-hundred thousand dollars that had been found in Whittaker's attaché case. With another hundred and fifty added, that meant Whittaker had claimed fully half of the proceeds from his Wall Street venture, not a quarter share as Ling had initially assumed. A greedy grab like that could sit bad with the other partners.

"Was Holmes in on it? I mean, did he know everything?" Ling asked.

"Are you kiddin' me? He was the key to the delivery. And there was gonna be another."

"Another what?" Golden asked.

"Another goddamned delivery."

"When, Tony?" Ling asked.

"Today. Or maybe tomorrow. What the fuck day is it, anyhow?"

"Friday," Golden answered.

"Then it's today. The stuff is due this afternoon."

"Same script?" Ling asked.

"Yeah. Just like before. Flight from Italy to Dulles Airport. The diplomatic pouch. I figured if I caught up with Whittaker, he'd have to count me in on this one, too."

Golden nodded to Ling, who then left the room. The chief followed him to the door and called in McKinnon.

Ling raced to a phone. Collingsworth was still in Washington, arranging for the recall of Holmes. After several calls, Ling tracked him down at his hotel.

"We have reason to believe from statements by DeGrazia that another shipment of cocaine may be coming in today in one of your diplomatic pouches," Ling told him.

"That would fit," Collingsworth said. "We have Holmes in a vise and he's starting to panic. One of our top security people flew in from London this morning and we're watching every move Holmes makes, waiting for him to do something irrational."

Ling briefed the Englishman on the discovery of the cocaine at the Port Authority and how Whittaker had apparently raised money for his smuggling scheme by selling to Wall Street the inside information he had finessed out of the White House through Marilyn Mason.

"Whittaker and Holmes bypassed DeGrazia and must have dealt directly with Marco," Ling said. "But Whittaker apparently short-changed the other two and kept some of the coke for himself. That's what we grabbed at the Port Authority."

"Honor among thieves," Collingsworth said.

"Something like that."

The Englishman paused a moment. Then, with resignation in his voice, he said, "It's appears to be all falling into place."

"Yes," Ling answered. "From your viewpoint, I guess it isn't very pretty."

"It's not too pleasant. I cringe thinking of the scandal."

Ling expressed his regrets and hung up. He found the two veteran FBI agents waiting for him.

"Boss around?" the agent named Nolan asked.

"He's in with a prisoner."

The agents looked at each other. "Well, we can tell it to you, Monk," Nolan said. "We've got cable intercepts now that confirm the KGB had their sights on Whittaker."

"Did they get anywhere?"

"Didn't have time, apparently. Whittaker's sudden demise fucked it up for them."

Ling thanked them and said he would pass the information along to Golden. He then asked to speak to Nolan alone. The other agent, irritated, stalked away.

"Look, Bill, I don't mean to start trouble but the word we've got is that your informant on this KGB angle is a flake, some sell-a-secret asshole who hangs around the U.N.'s diplomatic lounge."

The agent glared at him. "Don't pull that crap with me, Monk. You're fishin'."

Ling smiled. "Give me a hint, Nolan. It could be important."

The agent looked around the squadroom. Satisfied they were alone, he said in a low voice: "Our guy they call Eagle Seven. Deals only with me. Been around for ages. Never been wrong. I could have built a career around him."

"What's he telling you now?"

"Not a fuckin' thing. He hasn't resurfaced. We figure the heat's on from his own people."

"Eagle, huh?"

"Yeah, like a goddamned bird. If it were up to me, I'd call him Mr. Univac. Whoever he is, he's been around."

"What do you mean, 'Whoever he is.' Don't you know?"

Nolan once more looked nervously around him before answering. "I've never even seen him. We have no idea who the hell he is. He sets up the meets his own way with his own rules."

Ling considered that a moment, silently questioning the reliability of an informant so anonymous the FBI had no hint of who he was.

Nolan read his mind. "Take it from me, Monk, the guy's for real."

"Okay," Ling said, "he's for real. What's he know about garbage?"

"What the hell does that mean?"

"We had a little sanitation collection here at the station house, emptied every trash can, only it wasn't the city."

The agent laughed. "I'd say you guys piqued the interest of our good friends from Moscow. They've pulled that stunt before. Better get yourself a shredder." The agent started to walk away.

"Just a minute, Bill. One more thing. There's this guy keeps showing up. We're tripping over him. Washington, New York, it doesn't seem to matter."

"Who is he?"

"So-called journalist. Polish. Name of Stanislas Lubelski."

Nolan whistled. "Big time Eastern bloc all-star. I had no idea he was in on this."

"He good?"

"Among the best. We got a file that says he might have killed thirty, forty men before he turned twenty. Russians used him a lot, here and in London, especially in the fifties. But he hasn't done much lately. To be honest, I'd kind of kissed him off as semi-retired. Your guys on him?"

Ling shook his head. "We were 'til a couple of hours ago when he shook two of our men out at Kennedy."

Nolan edged closer. "Look, Monk, I've got to report this. They find out I sat on something about Lubelski, I'm out on my ass without a pension and my pension ain't so hot as it is."

Ling hesitated, then said: "Whatever you've got to do. And thanks, Bill. About this Eagle, I mean." He turned away.

"Listen, Monk," the agent called after him. "That's strictly . . ."

"I know," Ling said. "Don't worry—I'm like a priest."

Ling turned toward the conference room, where Golden and McKinnon were emerging. Ling went to join them.

"What do you think, chief?" McKinnon asked.

"We've got him at one scene, plus a damned good motive. He can't alibi the hooker's murder. And there's a potential motive there, too. What we need is the gun."

"Good luck with that," McKinnon said.

"Let's give it a shot, anyway. Get a warrant and hit his apartment."

"What do we book him on, the drug thing?"

Golden pondered for a moment. "Yeah—and throw in Whittaker's homicide. We'll have to show most of our hand at the arraignment but it'll get the politicians off our backs."

McKinnon left to obtain the search warrant. He was immediately replaced at Golden's side by Levine. "You won't believe this, chief . . ."

"I'll believe anything today," Golden said.

"That stockbroker, Thornton, he just showed up downstairs—with a lawyer."

Golden shook his head. "Decided to do his civic duty, huh? Well, tell him to fuck himself. He can say what he wants to say to a grand jury."

"Right, chief," Levine said.

"Just a minute," Ling interjected. "Let me have a shot at him."

Golden shrugged. "Why not?"

Ling met with Cal Thornton and his lawyer in the precinct commander's first-floor office.

"You can ask him anything you want, detective, but only if I'm here," the attorney announced.

Ling ignored the lawyer. He looked at the young broker and smiled. "Been overseas, huh?"

"You should know—I mean, it isn't everybody that gets an FBI welcoming party."

"And now you're back."

"In the flesh."

"Why?"

Thornton lowered his head. "I thought about it and decided if I could be of help, I'd cooperate."

"I assume your lawyer's briefed you about your rights."

"Is Mr. Thornton a suspect for some crime?" the attorney demanded.

"In the murders, at this time, no."

"But something else?" Thornton asked.

Ling delayed his answer. "We're just wondering what it's worth."

"What what's worth?"

"Inside information from the White House."

"That's bullshit!" Thornton shouted.

"Is it? I'm sure the Securities and Exchange Commission will be interested. Possibly the U.S. attorney."

"I think . . . I think I want to go now."

The lawyer was immediately on his feet. "Mr. Thornton has nothing more to say."

Ling stood and swept his hand toward the door. Thornton, suddenly pale, moved toward it, his attorney trailing.

"Oh, by the way," Ling called after them. They stopped. "Whittaker proved kind of greedy, didn't he, I mean, demanding half the take like that."

Thornton said nothing. He didn't have to. The fury in his eyes gave Ling his answer.

38

Paley Park. Three tall, impenetrable walls, the rear one a wide waterfall. The water's roar a white sound, drowning out the jackhammers, the horns, the blasts of buses. A harbor in a hurricane on the East Side of Manhattan.

Ling purchased a cup of tea at the small refreshment stand, then claimed one of the metal tables closest to the falls. It was early afternoon. The lunch crowd had departed. Only a reader and a few couples. And the pigeons, of course.

He dropped a pinch of sugar into the tea and began stirring it, his eyes zeroing in on the miniature whirlpool inside the styrofoam cup. A whirlpool. How fitting, he thought—for at no other time in his life had Ling felt more adrift. There were so many paradoxes and contradictions: He was raised a Chinese yet he wasn't one; he had married—and loved—a blueblood debutante, yet had surrendered to an occasional prostitute programmed on a self-destructive journey to hell. A small fortune sat unused in a bank trust account, tantalizing him, yet he remained captive to a thankless, underpaid Civil Service job that threatened his sanity, his emotions and his health. He was, Ling sometimes thought, a fraud, able to bully a Marco and outmuscle a DeGrazia when pursuing a case, yet weak, selfish, and unsure of himself when it came to deciding what he ought to do with his life. Maybe it was a question of inertia. Perhaps Edison LeGrande was right and he did need a change. But what change? To cut himself loose and chase the dreams pursued by so many other men—power, money, and an unlimited supply of women—would make him no different from Whittaker. And where had the Englishman's quest taken him?

Ling threw his head back and looked up—the fall sky was pure blue. He closed his eyes, concentrating for a few moments on the splash of the cascading water, then turned his thoughts to the investigation. It all added up—and that was the problem.

"Blackmail," the fake Polish newsman had said. Was it a message? Or was it a game?

"Ruby," Samantha had uttered in her dying breath. Who was Ruby? They had forgotten about Ruby; hadn't put it to DeGrazia. Or maybe Golden had when Ling was out of the room. He would have to check with the chief.

The video camera. Ling shouldn't have missed it. It should never have been moved. He would have to find out which lab man disturbed it. That was unprofessional.

And the videotape. Number eight. It was in the recorder yet it had no fingerprints.

"No prints," Ling repeated out loud. "Not even Whittaker's."

He jumped to his feet. " 'Monday Night Football!' Why in hell would Whittaker want to tape football?" he asked, again out loud, then sprinted toward the park's gate. A couple at one of the tables looked at him with alarm. The reader's eyes left his book and stared at the obvious madman. The park's single uniformed guard watched him warily.

Ling hailed a cab and returned to the Seventeenth Precinct. Outside the station house, the newsmen were gone, crumpled coffee cups and discarded deli bags marking their earlier presence. Golden's second news conference of the day was over, the word of DeGrazia's being charged with Whittaker's murder having been flashed to the world.

Upstairs, the squad room appeared empty—Ling's colleagues either off celebrating or having accompanied DeGrazia downtown to his arraignment. The room was scattered with even more cigarette and cigar butts, partially eaten sandwiches and half-filled soda cans than usual. Ling was about to give up, passing by the door to the conference room, when he spotted Golden.

The chief was slouched in a chair at the end of the table. His shirt collar was open; his tie loose and askew. His face was drawn. He appeared exhausted—and worried.

Ling tapped lightly on the open door.

"Oh, hi, Monk," Golden said. "Come on in."

Ling took a seat across the room from him. "DeGrazia downtown?"

Golden nodded. "We'll have to build the Simpson case somehow, then nail him with that, too. But we'll hold back any charge on the Moroccan woman's death. In case everything turns to shit, we can take another shot at him with that."

"What's the D.A. say?"

"He liked what we gave him."

Golden's bloodshot eyes turned to the grimy window. Ling looked to the floor. Neither said anything for a few moments, then Ling asked: "Suppose you have a home videotape recorder and you find a football game on the tape, yet there isn't anybody in the place with the slightest interest in football. What do you think that would mean?"

"The guy probably set it to record something else on automatic but entered the wrong channel." He turned to Ling. "I do it all the time."

"But suppose you check the recorder and see that it wasn't set on automatic . . ."

"Well, then maybe the guy was recording something and forgot to turn it off. I've done that, too."

"But suppose you play the tape and the very first recorded show is 'Monday Night Football.' There was nothing recorded in front of it."

"Well, I'd have to say somebody intentionally recorded the game—lot of guys like to take another look at key plays."

"But this somebody was Whittaker. I know some Englishmen have become interested in American football, but Whittaker?"

Golden leaned forward. "Monk," he asked softly, "why are you asking me all this?"

Ling stalled. The situation was delicate. The incredible

pressure was on Golden's shoulders, not his. And Ling's hunch, his instincts, could very well prove wrong. "I've just got a feeling, Julie," he said finally.

"What you're trying to say is that there was a tape in that apartment whose contents make no sense."

"That's right."

"Was there a camera in the place?"

"Yes."

"What do you think, the crime was somehow recorded on tape and the killer erased it?"

Ling shook his head. "It could have been something else, Julie, like a tape of a deal being made or some kind of confession."

"Or somebody's indiscretions," Golden added, attacking the riddle with enthusiasm now. "But it would be hard to imagine what you could film these days that could lead to blackmail."

There it was again—blackmail. Ling was beginning to suspect the Pole, Lubelski, for whatever reason, had been trying to point him in a certain direction—and then had second thoughts. "Whatever it was, my hunch is there was something on that tape somebody wanted erased," Ling said.

"And that somebody is probably not DeGrazia because he doesn't have the brains to push a button."

Again Ling hesitated before agreeing: "I don't think it was him, Julie—but I could be wrong."

Golden leaned back in his chair. He stared at the ceiling. "Where is that tape, Monk?"

"I've got it locked up."

"Get it, then, and let's take a look."

The precinct rollcall room had a videotape recorder and a television set, which were used primarily for training films. Golden and Ling shooed a pair of patrolmen out of the room and locked the door. The screen came to life with the football game, only it began in the second quarter.

"Miss that much of the game, it means the recording began sometime around ten or so," Golden said.

"That would square with the M.E.'s estimate of the time of death," Ling said.

"What now?"

"Let me make a call."

Ling telephoned a veteran contact at the forensic lab and outlined the problem—they had a videotape on which a televised football game had been recorded, possibly to erase something taped earlier. The lab man asked Ling to hold the line, then returned with the name of a firm on the West Side that specialized in recovering accidentally erased data on computer discs and tapes.

"We've never used these guys, Monk; I only heard about this place. It would be a longshot—at best," the lab man said.

"Longshot's better than no shot," Ling responded, thanking him.

Golden was pensive during the drive to the electronics lab. Ling, driving, left the chief to his thoughts.

Then Golden broke his silence. "There was this guy I knew in the army," he said. "He was a big mother from Omaha or some other place out there in Wyoming." His voice grew more lively. "He met this hooker in a bar, see. A big, beautiful thing. Said she was Norwegian. Man, did he fall for her. So they hit the motel and it's all dark and cozy and it's not until the eighth inning that this guy from Omaha discovers that she's a fuckin' transvestite." He paused. "I should have learned somethin' from that, Monk."

"How's that?"

"Things ain't always what they seem."

They reached the lab in less than fifteen minutes. The manager, a young man with a crew cut and thick glasses, listened to their problem.

"We might be able to help you," he said. "We're just getting into that area."

"Videotapes?" Golden asked.

"Yes. We think there's a potential market out there. Folks pay a small fortune to have somebody shoot a wedding or a bar mitzvah or something, then some kid puts tape over the protector slot and uses it to record a space movie or something."

"Can you recover the original?" Ling asked.

"It's very experimental. Depends on a lot of things. And, of course, there's no way we can get the entire original recording back—not yet, anyway. At this point, if we're successful, what we get are glimpses.''

"That may be all we need,'' Golden said.

The technician led them to the back into a room crowded with electronics gadgetry. Wires, entwined like spaghetti, ran under counters along all four walls. The manager moved to one of the benches and inserted the cassette into a recorder, then sat down at a console. He pressed a button causing a monitor screen to the side to begin displaying the football game in extremely slow motion. The picture came in and out of focus as he adjusted a dial.

"All this is computerized. It's digital,'' the technician said. "If we're lucky, the second recording did not begin exactly where the first did or the recording heads were not quite aligned the same way between the two sessions. If the tape was not used very often and the erasing head was not a hundred percent efficient, we might capture enough residual information to reconstruct a frame or two.''

"What are the odds on that?'' Golden asked.

"Generally, not too good—but there's another possibility.''

"What's that?'' Ling asked.

"That the second recording had several stops in it. If so, there's a chance, depending upon the quality of the machine, that there are tiny bands in the tape that were not completely erased.''

The tape continued to roll, the vivid football scenes dissolving into white and gray snow, then returning back to full clarity again as the technician maneuvered the controls. The minutes passed. Finally, the manager turned to face them. "I'm sorry. It doesn't look good. I'm not picking up anything.''

Golden looked at Ling. "Guess it was worth a try.''

"Just a minute!'' the manager suddenly shouted. "I just saw something.''

He pressed a series of buttons and the tape began to move backward, very slowly, frame by frame. Then the screen turned entirely blank. The technician made additional adjustments and an image began to emerge, very faintly at first, but gaining definition as the computer enhanced the small block of residual magnetic information captured from the tape.

Golden and Ling put their faces inches from the screen.

There was no color and the focus was fuzzy but the frame clearly showed two naked bodies in an embrace. The faces were obscured but one thing was clear—both were women!

The manager whistled. "Nice stuff," he said. "Who are the ladies?"

Golden studied the picture. "I . . . I'm not sure," he said, more to himself than the technician. The chief looked at Ling. "Some lesbian action."

"Still subject to blackmail?" Ling asked.

Golden thought a moment. "With the right women, of course!"

"What it looks like," the technician interjected, "is somebody was recording the football game over the bedroom stuff, then stopped it. He played the tape a bit and saw that not all the bedroom stuff had been erased, so he backed the tape up and resumed taping the football."

"But he didn't reverse it enough," Ling said.

"That's right. Let's take another look."

The technician rewound the tape slightly, then played it in slow motion. The screen showed the football game until it flashed for an instant. The game then resumed—but with a slight break in the action.

"It looks like a gap in the play of about a minute," Ling said.

The technician nodded. "He would have missed some of the game while checking to see if all the bedroom stuff had been erased." He removed the tape and handed it to Ling.

Golden grabbed the technician's right hand. "You've been a tremendous help. Send us an invoice."

"No charge for you guys," the manager said. "Say, where did that tape come from, anyway? Looked like one hell of a party."

They were back in the car, Ling behind the wheel.

"A girl and a girl," Golden said.

"And somebody behind the camera," Ling quickly added.

"Whittaker?"

"He'd get my vote," Ling said.

Golden started to say something but Ling hushed him. "Just a minute, chief," he said, pulling over and stopping the car. Ling was thinking of Samantha Simpson. "Ruby shoot,"

she had said as she lay dying. Only it wasn't Ruby shoot.
Ling had misunderstood. "It was Rubyfruit!" he exclaimed.

"What are you talking about?" Golden asked.

"The Simpson girl. What she was trying to tell me was
Rubyfruit."

"I don't understand. What's that?"

"It's from the title of a book, Julie. Kind of the bible of
the lesbian movement."

Golden was shaking his head. "I'll be damned," he said.
"I never heard of it."

Ling reached out his window and slapped the red police
light atop the unmarked car, then pulled away with a screech
of wheels.

"Where are we going?" Golden asked.

"We might not have much time. Hold on."

The car, its siren screaming, raced down Broadway. They
made good time until they were blocked at an intersection just
before Times Square. A foot patrolman, shouting until his
voice cracked, helped clear a path for them.

"Should have got his shield number," Golden yelled over
the siren. "Get that boy a citation."

They flew down Broadway, past the garment center, past
City Hall, then Ling turned left. He braked the car to a
screeching halt on Nassau Street.

"Come on," he told the chief.

Ling led him up the stairs to the custom photo lab. The
door was locked.

Golden looked at his watch. "It's after six."

Ling began pounding on the door. There was no response.

"We're too late, Monk," Golden said.

Ling continued his knocking. Then, from inside, came a
shout: "What do you want? We're closed."

"Open up. Police."

"What?"

"Police. Open the door."

"How do I know you're the police?" The voice was
frightened.

"We'll kick the fuckin' thing in," Golden shouted.

A lock was turned; a chain freed. The door opened a crack.

Ling pushed his way in and flashed his shield in the face of a short, skinny kid with hair down to his shoulders. "Who are you?" Ling demanded.

"Kevin. Kevin Crane. I work here."

"You're the part-time darkroom man I heard about?"

The kid nodded. "Yeah . . . I go to school."

Ling put an arm around him. "There's nothing to be afraid of, son. Come on, let's sit down." Ling led him to the back. He spotted a small office. "How about here?"

Ling guided the kid to the room's single chair. He and Golden positioned themselves on either side of him.

"You're not in trouble, Kevin," Ling said, "and you won't be if I get some straight answers."

The kid started to stand. "If it's about that porn, I had nothing to do with it. That's . . ."

Ling pushed him back down. "There's porn and there's porn, Kevin. You can print six women making Santa Claus in a monkey cage for all we care. What we're interested in is a little job you did recently for a man by the name of Whittaker."

"I don't know the names. I never look at them."

"A color job, Kevin. One eight-by-ten of each frame. No proof sheet."

The kid thought for a moment. "Oh, yeah! I *do* remember that. Usually they want proofs, otherwise it can get expensive. I mean . . ."

"You did the printing?"

"Yeah. About half a roll. And the man picked it up. Don't think I waited on him, though; leastwise, I don't remember."

"Where are *your* prints, Kevin?"

"My prints?"

"Yeah."

"I don't know what you're talkin' about."

Ling bent down and put his face inches from the kid's. "Don't shit me, now, Kevin. You think I don't know how it is? I mean a guy comes in here and has you print a roll showing a couple of luscious babes going at it hot and heavy and you don't make yourself a print or two?"

"Well, I . . ."

"Where are they, Kevin?"

The kid stood. "I only made two."

"Get them."

Kevin went to the back. He returned with two eight-by-ten prints and handed them to Ling.

Ling showed them to Golden: two women embracing, the colors vibrant, the definition perfect, the faces clear—Samantha Simpson on the left; and on the right, Marilyn Mason.

39

An airline official handed British First Secretary David Holmes a clipboard containing a receipt. Holmes signed it, then lifted the attaché case from the Dulles Airport tarmac and began walking away from the Boeing 707. His pace was brisk—he had little time and the arrangements were complex: a quick flight to New York, delivery to Marco's man, collection of the money—then on to the Caribbean.

At long last, Holmes could put into play his carefully plotted plan. He would register at a Bahamian hotel and, later that night, deposit a monogrammed sport shirt and other personal effects on the beach. In the morning, there would be another flight, this one under an assumed name, to Rio de Janeiro. Back on the island, hours would pass before he was missed. Still more time would pass before authorities began an investigation. They would find his shirt and other possessions, and after a fruitless search of the surf, conclude that the sea had claimed him. He would not be the first Caribbean tourist to take a one-way walk into the breakers.

Still to be determined was what name he would use in Brazil. Perhaps he would call himself Whittaker. Holmes smiled. There would be irony in that. But he rejected the thought—no, he would execute his escape with no references, however subtle, to his past. Thank goodness his Whitehall sources, the lines of bureaucratic intelligence he had nurtured over so many years, had come through for him, warning that Collingsworth would soon move to ruin him. The situation called for boldness, and Holmes was prepared. Still, he had his regrets—if only Whittaker had not been killed and the cocaine pipeline they had created were still operative . . .

Holmes suddenly heard footsteps on the tarmac behind him. He turned, his stomach jolted by a shot of adrenaline. There were two of them: sunglasses, polyester suits, jackets unbuttoned and flapping in the wash of a nearby taxiing jet.

"Hold it right there, Mr. Secretary," one of them said sternly.

The other had his hand on the attaché case. "I'll take that, if you don't mind."

Holmes jerked the leather case away. "Who are you?" he demanded.

"FBI," said one, flashing an identification wallet.

"You're under arrest," said the other.

"I have credentials. This is diplomatic cargo," Holmes protested indignantly. "You have no right."

"They don't—but *I* have," came an authoritative voice from behind him.

Holmes turned—it was Collingsworth. With him was another man wearing an oversized trenchcoat.

"I'd like you to meet Mr. Tarrant. He's from Whitehall," Collingsworth said. There was no shaking of hands. "I must inform you, Holmes, that your immunity has been officially waived by Her Majesty's Government. You have no more diplomatic immunity than any other common drugrunner." Collingsworth nodded to the agents.

They took the attaché case, pinned Holmes' arms behind him, snapped handcuffs onto his wrists, then led him away.

"This is all a very grievous mistake," Holmes protested as they hustled him toward the terminal. "I was setting a trap, don't you see, and . . ."

"I suggest you save it, Holmes," Tarrant offered.

Holmes said no more.

40

Robert Crayton Samuels III was standing before a mirror, rehearsing the speech he would give at the coming Central Park antinuclear rally. He had just reached the part where he would quote from the letter.

"We must be both logical and compassionate, and for mankind's sake make the first move toward disarmament unilaterally. If humanity is to survive . . .," he was saying as Josie came through the apartment door carrying a bag of groceries.

"Is that what I think it is, Whittaker's letter to the *Times*?" she asked.

Samuels looked at her. "It is. And I've decided to read it at the rally. If James can't be there, at least his words can live."

She stared at him disbelievingly. "But . . . but Whittaker was a damned criminal, and you and I both know you wrote that letter yourself!"

He edged up to her. "They set him up, Jodie," he said in a low voice. "I can't prove it, of course, but I know it happened and I'm going to announce it to the world."

The woman walked to the other side of the room and dropped the grocery bag with a thump on a table. "You're full of shit, Robert," she said. "The government didn't set Whittaker up. If anyone did, it was the mob."

305

"You're wrong, Jodie."

"And you belong on a funny farm." She approached him menacingly. "What pisses me off about you is you're giving the entire movement a bad name. There are a lot of serious people out there marching and picketing because of something deep inside their souls, and then you come along and make a sideshow out of it with something out of left field."

Samuels turned his back to her and faced the mirror. "I know what I'm doing, Jodie. I'm going to charge publicly that James Whittaker was murdered because of his outspokenness on behalf of international peace, and that, my dear, is a very, very serious allegation." He looked at her in the mirror a moment, then smiled. "The networks will love it. You just wait and see."

"You're crazy."

41

Off to their left, the sun had dropped below the horizon, casting the sky into a fantail of fiery reds, oranges and yellows. Ahead of them, past a wide ravine, was Devilsdip Swamp, belching smoke that formed a flat, unmoving cloud of gray.

"Is it always so smoky?" Marilyn Mason asked her sister, Sally.

"Yes—but there's rarely any wind. Like now. It's so still the smoke just hovers there."

"What happens when the wind does blow?"

"Sometimes it drifts over the town; then you have to stay inside. Mostly it moves northwest, over the interstate on the other side of Devilsdip. They've had a few accidents because of it. A couple of them have been bad."

The two sisters were sitting in the small but carefully landscaped yard behind Sally's house. Azaleas, crepe myrtle, camelias. A small flagstone walkway. A checkerboard patio constructed by Sally herself from weather-proofed pine two-by-fours formed into squares. The charcoal in the stove was still smoldering and emitting a faint taste of hickory. Sally had broiled a pair of two-inch steaks. With them, she served huge baked potatoes, a garden salad, and fresh green beans. There were homemade biscuits and, for dessert, a pecan pie, the pecans collected earlier from a nearby tree.

Marilyn sipped from her glass. Scotch. She had had enough of Sally's cider and enough of the white wine. Sally had stayed with the cider.

A cardinal alighted in the birdbath. They spotted his mate rustling through the branches of a dogwood nearby. A mockingbird was perched on the very top of a pine, mimicking a bob white. The fading light caught the white tail of a fat rabbit bounding up from the ravine. Crickets, responding in unison to some unseen maestro, built their chorus, only to stop, then begin all over again.

"It's very peaceful," Marilyn said.

"I should tell you about the first time I almost stepped on a water moccasin and how peaceful it was then," Sally said, laughing.

"Please . . . spare me, okay?"

"Still squeamish, little sister?"

"Snakes and mice and budget deficits. I don't want to know about them."

They both laughed.

Sally reached for the Scotch bottle and refilled Marilyn's glass. "Hey, I don't want to get stoned," Marilyn protested.

"Maybe that's just what you need."

They drank in silence for a while as the sky continued to darken.

"It was a very big change," Sally said finally. "Leaving Boston, I mean, and coming here. But I wouldn't go back for anything now."

Marilyn had worried about her sister at the time—normal people simply did not do it, walk away from a well-paying job in an invigorating city, travel south on a route randomly chosen, and impulsively choose to stay in the first backwoods village that happened to "feel right."

"They've accepted me here," Sally was saying. "They kind of consider me special, you know. It's like a teacher to them is someone to be treasured and respected."

She had taken a job teaching eighth grade at the county's single elementary school. It was located in Darwin, the county seat, eight miles away.

"The house belonged to an elderly widow who died about four or five years ago," Sally continued. "The bank in

Darwin took it over and gave it to me for practically nothing. Mr. Remmington, the banker, said they wanted me to stay very much." She looked at Marilyn. "It's funny what you miss: cab drivers, believe it or not. And seventy-five-dollar-a-visit hair stylists. And ice-frosted crystal. And sometimes I have this feeling of incompleteness, like I mean winners are chasing winners while I'm sitting on the sidelines. Sometimes I'm jealous of you—you're a winner, Marilyn."

"I'm not so sure."

"But then, in the morning before the sun rises, I get in my little Land Rover and drive that way." She was pointing to the east. "There's a horse farm there, and the owner lets me exercise this young stallion." She put her elbows on her knees and rested her chin on her cupped hands. "The sun comes up and burns away the fog, and the dew makes everything sparkle. There's a freshness to the air you can't believe, and the horse responds to it like a puppy. You experience it, Marilyn, and you just know you're alive." She leaned back. "Daddy was right—this is where it's at. You, nature and God."

The outdoors. Their father had preached to them about it. And he had taught them: fishing in remote Ontario lakes; backpacking through the Rockies; hunting in the Midwest. Every extra dollar he made he saved for their trips. Marilyn could see his face now, creased and leathery. She could hear his voice, a stern voice, no room for challenge or compromise, the voice telling his two daughters—no, commanding them—that everyone, even a woman, had to learn the laws of nature to survive.

"Why did he do it?" Marilyn asked.

"Who?"

"Daddy—why did he make me shoot?"

"Honey, I don't know what you're talking about."

Marilyn looked at her in despair. How could Sally have forgotten. They were somewhere in the Midwest—Indiana or Illinois, traipsing through a cornfield, fall in the air, the ground crackling as their boots crushed the brittle stalks. It was Marilyn's first hunt. An explosion of sound before them as a panicked pheasant was flushed, his flight to the right and slightly ahead of them, the bird outlined perfectly against the cumulus-dotted sky, her father yelling to her, the bird sighted along the barrel of the gun, right at the bird's ringed neck and—she couldn't shoot, couldn't do it, didn't have it in her.

"That time when I didn't shoot the pheasant and when we got back to the farm he bought a rabbit from the farmer. He tied that rabbit to a tree and handed me the twenty-two and told me we were going to stay their all night, all week, if necessary, until I shot that rabbit and shot him properly."

Sally's voice was soft. "He was trying to teach you, sis."

Marilyn looked into her sister's eyes. "He said that was the way life is, that death is a part of it and until one learns that, one can never be whole. But there is a right way to kill, he said—a shot to the head, between the eyes, into the brain. Then there would be no pain."

"Hey, are you crying?"

"I did it, Sally. I finally did it. I lined that bunny up and squeezed the trigger." Sally reached over and took her hand. "And then I cried all night. I hated him. And I knew it would never be the same."

"He would be proud of you now, Marilyn. I mean, the White House! Maybe, wherever his spirit is, he knows."

Marilyn pulled away her hand. She dabbed at her eyes. "I'm sorry—I don't know what came over me."

"Let me get you some more Scotch."

They drank some more, saying little, then retired inside. Sally offered her the bed but Marilyn refused it, saying she preferred the sofa. Sally said she was tired and didn't want to forgo her riding of the stallion at daybreak, so if Marilyn didn't mind . . .

"Go on to bed," Marilyn said. "I think I'll take a little walk."

Sally went into the bedroom and shut the door. Marilyn lifted her suitcase onto the sofa and opened it. She pulled out a sweatshirt, her seldom worn sneakers, and a pair of jeans, then stepped out of her skirt and removed her blouse. She slipped off her bra and pantyhose, then kicked her loafers to the side.

Naked now, she flipped off the room's single light and moved to the window, raising its shade.

She was filled with an uneasy feeling, a sense that her life was once more to undergo an irrevocable change. She shivered, not certain if it came from her sense of foreboding or from her nakedness. She tried to close her eyes, but they wouldn't stay—that was the way alcohol affected her, keeping her alert and awake.

The bottle of Scotch. Where was it? She found it in the kitchen. She took a clean glass and filled half of it, then returned to the window overlooking the street.

In the darkness, she could see the shadowy outlines of four, maybe five houses. Small flickers of lights—from night lamps, perhaps—came from two. In one, an upstairs light flashed on for an instant, then switched off. Who lived there? What were *their* little secrets?

She took a large swallow from the tumbler, and the rush of alcohol raised goosebumps on her flesh. One of her hands involuntarily moved to her breasts. She looked down and saw the soft moonlight reflecting off her thighs. The sensation of standing before a window completely nude began to chase her anxiety, replacing it with an erotic, sensuous feeling. She spread her feet slightly, arched her back and imagined the whole world was watching, the entire Main Street of Blakeshammock, Georgia, an audience to her body and her sensuality, Marilyn Mason, the one-woman White House brain trust.

She snapped the shade down—and laughed.

Marilyn set aside the glass and put on her jeans, sneakers and sweatshirt, then she was outside, walking fast. The street was empty and quiet, except outside the cafe, where a shriveled old man was locking the door.

"Good evenin', ma'am," he said.

She returned the greeting.

She passed the motor court, where a single car was parked by the cabins, and continued on the two-lane road heading north out of town.

She stepped up her pace, extending her steps, aware that in doing so, she did not present a very ladylike figure and resembled one of those awkward, loping walkers who competed at the Olympics. It made no difference, especially with the sky growing darker as an unseen cloud moved under the first quarter moon. At times, she had difficulty seeing the pavement.

Thunder roared suddenly in the distance and diffused flashes of lightning appeared in front of her and slightly to the west with increasing frequency. The frogs and locusts stepped up their racket in the wooded areas to either side, and the squish of her sneakers against the asphalt provided their own music. The muscles in her calves and thighs seemed to revel in what was being asked of them, not tiring but rather gaining strength the longer she walked and the faster her steps came. Her breathing had synchronized itself to the pace of her feet in a slower but equally regular rhythm. The air was growing moist with the smell of incoming rain. It filled her lungs, giving her a sense of vigor she welcomed as—what would Sally call it? A celebration of life?

By the time the very first raindrops began to fall, she had walked more than a mile. She felt as though she were in a trance, an unthinking machine closing the distance on some exotic destination with each step. The rain began to fall earnestly, acquiring its own rhythm. She smiled as the drop-lets began to run off her hair in rivulets down her cheeks, cooling her in the labor of her walk, and prompting her to increase her speed to a full trot. The movement and the sounds and the rain and the almost complete blackness of the night made her feel so free that she wanted to scream, to sing, to shout, telling the humanless world around her that she was okay now, that she was safe.

"Hello, Miss Mason."

The voice came from a bush to her left and behind her. Startled, she came to an urgent halt, every muscle in her body freezing, her eyes wide and unblinking.

"Who are you? How do you know my name?" she de-manded, silently cursing the fear her own voice surely betrayed.

"Don't be frightened—I'm not going to hurt you."

"Who are you, I said!"

"It doesn't matter who I am. What matters are the ques-tions I have to ask you."

"Get away from me! I'll scream."

He laughed, moving closer. A flash of lightning brightened the sky and, for an instant, she could see his face. He wore glasses. His hair was very white. The trailing clap of thunder seemed to shake the pavement.

"You and I need to have a little talk," he said.

She was telling herself to run. He didn't appear young. She could probably outdistance him. But maybe he had a gun and . . .

"We have the photographs, Miss Mason. There was another set of prints."

"What photographs?"

He chortled. "Don't try that with me. Save it for the police. But, then, you won't have to deal with the police—not if you deal with me. I want to help you."

"Who are you?" she demanded again. "What do you want from me?"

"To be your friend. I know what you're going through. We can fix things. You can save your career. Nothing will change."

They had warned her at the White House. The many, many security briefings. The Soviets and their commissioned agents were everywhere, the impassioned counter-intelligence men had said. They could pop up anywhere, offer anything, use any lever they could find.

"Who . . . who do you work for?" she asked weakly.

A pair of headlights suddenly burst through the rainfall. The car was moving slowly. When it reached them, it stopped. It was a sheriff's patrolcar!

The car's window rolled down and she saw a uniformed officer, a young black man. "Anything wrong, miss?"

She ran to the car's side. "Somebody . . ." she started, then stopped. The photographs. The man knew of the photographs. She had to weigh her words carefully, stalling, until she had time to think. She looked back—the white-haired man was gone. She turned toward the patrolcar. "There . . . there was something in the woods. Frightened me a bit. But I'm all right now."

The officer stepped from the car. He reached back for a poncho and threw it over his head, then walked up and down the road, sweeping a powerful flashlight into the woods. " 'Fraid I don't see anything, ma'am. Probably a deer."

"I guess so," she said. "Or maybe a dog. I don't know why I'm so jumpy." She smiled and introduced herself.

"Ah, Sally's sister. She teaches my kids. Told the whole county you were coming." He extended his right hand. "I'm Sheriff Johnson. Come on, I'll drive you home."

He talked of his children and Sally, and how the entire community considered her a prize, a bright, energetic woman who had made it on her own, then decided to give something back; a woman who cared. And also, he quickly added, someone who had kin working right in the White House. "What's the President really like, ma'am?"

Marilyn provided her stock answer, that the President was indeed brilliant, and someday the country would realize how lucky it was to have his service; someday they would compare him with Jefferson and Lincoln, and the average person could not understand what kind of pressure, inhuman pressure, he was under.

They had reached Sally's house.

"I'm sorry I caused you all this trouble," Marilyn said.

The sheriff laughed. "No trouble at all. You enjoy your stay now, ya hear?"

She thanked him and went inside, closing the door and immediately throwing her back against it. Her body was shaking—where were her pills?—and something was closing in on her. Her head felt so heavy, so tight. She shook it violently, then stopped and forced herself to listen. But there was only the rumbling thunder in the distance and the splatter of the rain against the roof. Then she heard it—the laugh. It was a cynical laugh, a cruel laugh, Whittaker's laugh, the laugh she had heard when he showed her the pictures, when he ran that damned tape!

She closed her eyes—and she saw his leering, spiteful face.

42

Ling had never before seen Julius Golden so furious.

The chief was on the phone. "I don't give a good goddamn who said what or who didn't say what, lieutenant," he shouted into the mouthpiece. "All I know is me and one of my men stopped by that lab of yours tonight, found some kid doesn't even speak English, and he don't know from squat what I'm talkin' about."

Golden's knuckles grew white as his grip tightened on the phone, listening to the lieutenant's retort.

"Look, pal," Golden said, "let's leave it this way: either you get somebody who knows what he's doing down there *now*, or I'll have the P.C. call you personally." He slammed down the phone.

Golden looked briefly at the faces around him, then began pacing. "Sometimes I wonder," he said. "Got the eyes of the whole world on us and I told them specifically at the scene of the Simpson case that we wanted those tests on the matter found under the victim's fingernails expedited, then some bureaucrat comes along and puts the specimen bag on the bottom of the pile."

"They gonna test it tonight, chief?" McKinnon asked.

Golden looked at his watch. "I'm giving them an hour— then I call the P.C." He pulled a chair from a desk and sat down. "Where's Triano?"

"Ah . . . they haven't located him yet, chief," Levine said.

Ling felt an emptiness in his stomach. He looked at Golden. The chief's eyes revealed that he—like everyone else in the room—suspected that Triano was off on his own, lonely celebration.

Some cops just couldn't make it and, Ling feared, Triano was one of them. The demotions, the upstate camp, the stripping of his gun—together they had won Triano a month here, a couple of weeks there. But there was something in his makeup that precluded self-honesty. Without that, Ling knew from his own experience, it was hopeless. Drink would kill Mickey Triano.

"We can't wait," Golden said. "Listen up now."

The chief had issued an urgent call for his key detectives after the discovery of the photographs. Now, missing only Triano, they gathered around him.

"We've been given an overabundance of blessings, it seems," Golden began. "What we've got are two prime suspects, apparently independent of one another, both at the scene, both with good motives."

O'Brien, who had begun sulking immediately upon learning DeGrazia might be ruled out as a suspect, glared at Ling. "Fuckin' unreal," he said under his breath.

"What was that?" Golden asked.

"Nothin,' chief. Not a goddamned thing."

"Go ahead and say it," Ling said. "Put it on the table."

O'Brien stared at him, his eyes coming alive with the challenge. "Okay, it's like this, see—we got the case signed, sealed, and almost delivered—and here you come again with some bullshit theory at the last minute, like you're some Kojak, for chrissake."

"That's enough of that, now!" Golden snapped. "We're supposed to be professionals and if . . ."

Ling held up his hand. "I can see his point, Julie." He looked to O'Brien. "You may well be right. This could be nothing. But at least listen it out, would you?"

O'Brien hesitated, then nodded once, almost imperceptibly.

Levine took the floor: "Monk told me about the pictures but I'm still fuzzy on the sequence."

"The theory is this," Golden answered. "Whittaker's a real cocksman, right? And he finds his way into the heart of this plain jane from the White House. There's booze and there's grass and there's coke and one night she gets a little wasted; doesn't quite know what she's doin', and she ends up in a threesome with Whittaker and our Ms. Simpson, who Monk vouches for but who also probably did this sort of group partying regularly."

"And out come the cameras," Levine said.

"Yeah," Golden said. "And it was probably part of the game. I mean, nothing sneaky about it. Something like we all have a little wrestlin' match, then sit back and watch the instant replay on TV."

"Fuckin' disgusting," McKinnon said.

Golden glared at him. McKinnon apologized sheepishly.

The chief continued: "Whittaker needs Marilyn Mason to funnel him the information he's peddling on Wall Street to finance his coke deals. At first, she gives it to him readily—there's love in her heart. And maybe even she enjoys the world of big league sex he introduces her to. But things begin to sour when this French-speaking Arab shows up. As Mason sees it, a *ménage à trois*, fine, but when it grows to four, the roster's suddenly too big. They argue. She threatens to drop him. He can't afford that—he needs that inside information. So he shows her the videotape and the pictures and asks her what her White House bosses are going to say when they learn they've got a closet bull dyke advising the President."

"Classic bedroom blackmail," Levine said.

"And with a classic ending," Golden added. "She goes there one night with a gun in her purse and shoots him. The Arab, too, because she's a witness. Then our Miss Mason finds the eight-by-tens and takes them with her. She decides she can't take the videotape because, see, the box is numbered. She's an economist, a mathematician; she knows the power of numbers. She realizes that if number eight were missing when we show up, our attention would be on the videotapes and we might put two and two together. But not to worry—she simply records over it. 'Monday Night Football' happened to be on. She waits until she thinks the bedroom session is

completely erased and stops the machine. But she's cautious—
she checks it. And there were still a few minutes left of her
and Samantha Simpson playing each other like harps. She
backs the tape up, puts the machine on record again and
figures it's safe to leave.''

"But she didn't back the tape up far enough," Ling explained. "She missed almost a full frame. That's what we
captured.''

There was a moment of silence, then O'Brien asked: "So
on DeGrazia, we eat crow, huh?''

"Maybe," Golden answered. "Maybe not. This is still all
theory. But we've got to move and move fast.''

The chief began barking out instructions: O'Brien was to
get to LaGuardia immediately and try to determine if Marilyn
Mason had been on the shuttle in either direction on the day
Samantha Simpson was murdered; McKinnon was to get out
to the special security wing at Rikers and eyeball every square
inch of DeGrazia's body looking for the defense scratches
Simpson had apparently inflicted, and Levine was to hit the
phones and—the chief didn't care how—find out where Mason was at this moment.

"The scratches, I don't know how the hell I forgot about
them when we had DeGrazia here in our pen," Golden said.
He looked to Levine: "They give you trouble at the White
House, tell them it's about the Whittaker case and an emergency and all of England is interested.''

They moved into action, McKinnon flying down the stairs,
O'Brien, head bowed, following him somewhat lackadaisi-
cally, Levine moving to a telephone in the conference room.
Golden and Ling were left alone.

The chief renewed his pacing. It was the inevitable lull—
Ling had watched every commander he knew go through it. A
plane crash, you would get your units rolling and then wait
and wait for the first word of how bad it really was. Report of
a cop shot, the same frustrating delay before learning if the
report, in fact, was true; if the cop would survive, if the killer
or killers had somehow been kept within the net of blue
uniforms closing in on the scene.

"I moved too fast on DeGrazia," Golden said softly.

"You knew it and, deep down, I knew it. If we have to back off, the papers will kill us."

"I don't think so," Ling said.

Golden stopped his pacing. "Why?"

"If it's Mason and the case is solid, they've got themselves a first-rate scandal. Circulation and ratings will jump. They'll love you. In fact, half of them will think you planned it this way—as some kind of trap."

"But DeGrazia, he'll sure as hell raise a public squawk."

Ling shook his head. "Not with that coke rap hanging over his head. He's still knee deep in that, don't forget."

Golden walked off to stare out a window. Ling left him alone.

After a few minutes, Levine emerged from the conference room. The White House switchboard had given her a tough time but finally agreed to patch her call into the home number for Miss Mason's secretary. The secretary was suitably impressed with the international aspects of the emergency and supplied a telephone number in a place called Blakeshammock, Georgia. The phone was in a restaurant. Miss Mason was visiting her sister and that's how her sister took her calls.

Next came a call from McKinnon. DeGrazia had not been too cooperative until he realized it might be in his interest, then he stripped down to the nothing-nothing. There was no sign of any scratch.

"Good work," Golden said. "Now get down to the courts and call me with a phone number. You'll stand by there in case we need a warrant."

The call from O'Brien at LaGuardia followed. A quick look through the shuttle's flight manifests had found no listing for any Mason, he reported. But a male flight attendant happened to pass by and, incredibly, allowed as how he remembered Marilyn Mason being aboard a run from New York to Washington two nights earlier. He had recognized her from the news and wondered why she had paid for her ticket in cash—so few passengers did, especially government officials.

"And that's not all," Golden said, relaying O'Brien's report to the others. "It seems Miss Mason had an unsightly scratch across her cheek." Golden paused for the information to sink in, then looked at Ling and added: "O'Brien also said he thinks he owes you an apology, Monk."

Ling searched for a response but was spared one when they were distracted by the sound of footsteps on the stairs. A short, thin man in a white smock rushed toward them. "I'm Dawson from the lab," he announced. "Lieutenant told me to deliver this to you personally." He handed Golden a sheet of paper. Golden read it, then lifted it for the others to see. It was a standard lab report form.

"The substances recovered from under the deceased's fingernails included skin cells—and woman's makeup," Golden said, paraphrasing the bureaucratese.

Levine whistled. "Gotcha, girlie," she said.

43

Mickey Triano lay back against the car seat, a soaked towel wrapped over his face. Through the towel came a muffled groan, then: "I think I'm gonna die."

Ling, who was driving, looked over to him. "The stewardesses thought you *were* dead. Told me you can't transport a stiff in a seat like that, gotta put him in a box, stow him with the cargo."

Collingsworth, sitting in the back, laughed.

They had been on the road for more than an hour, en route from Atlanta's Hartsfield Airport to the hamlet of Blakeshammock. It had been Golden's decision to forgo notifying the feds or relying on local Georgia authorities to track down Marilyn Mason—and arrest her on a warrant charging her with three murders. "We're gonna bring this baby home ourselves," the chief had said, adding he would worry about niceties with the White House and the Justice Department later.

Collingsworth, arriving back from Washington late, had asked to accompany Ling. After some initial hesitation, Golden had agreed. It took Ling considerably more time to persuade the chief to allow Triano to make the trip. Finally, Golden gave his approval—then Ling had to find the troubled detective.

Triano peeled the towel off his face. "Where the fuck am I?"

"Georgia," Ling answered.

"Come on, Monk; don't play with me. It hurts enough as it is."

"You're in Georgia. We flew to Atlanta this morning. You must have been in a blackout. You looked like you were in hell."

After a moment's silence, Triano muttered: "Maybe I should be."

"What?"

"Maybe I should rot in hell."

Ling said nothing, leaving Triano to piece together himself the outline of his last eighteen hours.

"Where did you find me?" Triano asked finally.

"The late James Whittaker's favorite afterhours joint."

Triano buried his face in his hands. "Shit!"

Soon, Ling heard him snoring.

"Will he shape up, do you think?" Collingsworth asked from the back.

"He'll come around," Ling answered.

The miles passed. Ling noticed a dark blue Buick had been on their tail for almost twenty minutes. Ling slowed the rented car. At first, the Buick slowed with him but the driver ultimately pulled into the left lane and passed. Ling studied him closely. He was dressed in a short-sleeved white shirt with a loosely knotted tie. His sportcoat was draped over the empty passenger's seat. He was sleepy-eyed and holding a container of coffee.

"A normal guy with a normal job and a normal wife living in a normal house . . .," Ling said, his voice trailing off.

"Bullshit," Triano said, suddenly stirring. "The poor bastard's probably slaving away at some canary farm, a broad for his boss, and then goin' home to some piece-of-work wife who can't be bothered unless it's a Saturday night after payday."

A large tractor-trailer passed them with a roar. Triano shuddered. "We've gotta stop, Monk," he said. "I've got to call my wife."

"I already spoke to Maggie."

Triano considered that a moment, then asked: "Is she pissed?"

"She was worried."

Triano returned to his thoughts. Another mile passed. Then he asked: "The chief know?"

"Don't worry about it."

"Does he know, Monk?"

"It doesn't matter. You're on the job, right?"

Triano clumsily reached for Ling's arm. "I'm sorry, Monk. Didn't mean to let you down. I thought the case was over."

"So did the rest of us."

Triano tried to sort it out, then: "What are we doin', anyway?"

Ling explained it to him.

"Feel like you missed a chapter, huh?" Collingsworth asked good-naturedly.

"I feel like I missed the whole goddamned book, like it was upside down or something."

"I've known the feeling," the Englishman said.

"Your prime minister, how is she taking it?" Ling asked to change the subject.

"I spoke to her again late yesterday. She's no longer surprised at anything, and she's a tough old bird. Of course, the press and the opposition are playing it for all it's worth. It's no little scandal, the prime minister's brother and a top officer of the foreign service in a drug conspiracy."

"Will she survive?"

Collingsworth hesitated, then said: "I frankly do not know."

They were at the Chapman County cutoff. Ling left the interstate for a county road that quickly narrowed to two lanes. Oaks lined both sides, with their moss-draped branches covering the roadway in a ceiling of impenetrable gray and green. The air grew heavy and muggy, dispelling any notion that fall had arrived. Much of the terrain was uninhabited, except for an occasional tin-roofed shanty. Along one grassy stretch in the distance they spotted a rare bald eagle, its wings spread majestically as it circled a tall, scraggly pine containing its nest. The nest was huge—larger, it occurred to Ling, than some New York apartments.

After ten or eleven miles, the road switched from concrete to asphalt. Slash pines began to appear among the oaks and cypress. They passed a small, rock-filled creek, then a shallow pond, its stagnant water covered with a film of deep green algae.

"Look!" Collingsworth said suddenly. "Off to the left—smoke."

Ahead and slightly to the left of them was a wide column of coal-black smoke.

"Probably a forest fire," Triano said.

The road evolved into a sweeping curve which ended in a village. Ling spotted a gas station and pulled in. A long-haired teenager with grease up and down both arms left his work at the ramp and walked briskly toward them. Ling ordered a full tank, then asked the kid: "That smoke ahead, what is it?"

"Wildfire, sir. Devilsdip Swamp. Been burnin' seven, eight weeks."

"Can't they extinguish it?" Collingsworth asked.

The youth shrugged. "Why bother?"

"How far to Blakeshammock?" Ling asked.

"You see the smoke, that's Blakeshammock. Y'all got another fourteen miles."

The kid's judgment proved accurate: the odometer had just clicked off fourteen more miles when they came to a sign declaring the village limits of Blakeshammock. As they approached the town, a wind had kicked up, sending the smoke from the swamp billowing over the village. The sky began to darken above them.

Ling drove slowly. A man was standing at the door of a house trailer, attempting to light a cigarette in the newly gusting wind. At a frame house badly in need of paint, a woman was polishing a streaked bay window with a filthy rag. The door to another house was open, and two teenaged boys were struggling to move a large chair through it. A country hamlet crawling along at its own subdued pace, Ling concluded, the people seemingly without a care except for deciding what they would watch on television that night.

Ling pulled the car into a diagonal space outside a restaurant. "Let's get some coffee," he said, reaching to the seat for his camera. They climbed out of the car, Triano staggering a few steps before getting his bearings.

The restaurant was in a white clapboard structure with

peeling paint. One of its cornerposts showed a powdery evidence of termites and a fist-sized hole made moot an overhead gutter. At least three of the cross-hatched windows were disfigured by diagonal cracks and one pane had been violated by a head-high shot from a BB-gun. Ling paused at the door, then stepped back and snapped a frame with his Nikon of the restaurant's ramshackle exterior and its quaintly lettered sign reading: "Dempsey's Cafe."

It was a small diner with a six-stool counter, four booths and five square tables. Hanging behind the counter was a five-year-old calendar with a picture showing the sun setting behind a range of snow-capped mountains. Nearby was a framed dollar bill, apparently the first earned by the establishment. Propped behind a four slice toaster was a yellowing poster announcing a church auction held two years earlier. Above the counter, a ceiling fan rotated silently, attempting—with no appreciable effect—to stir the thick, humid air, which smelled of tobacco and bacon.

There were two other customers, both grizzled elderly men. Regulars, Ling guessed—probably bachelors unmoved to attempt their own cooking.

"Mornin'," said a man in a white shirt and food-stained apron who appeared to be owner, cook and sole waiter. He was a short and slender man in his late sixties, Ling guessed, with unkempt thinning hair and tired eyes. His narrow shoulders were rounded and his back was slightly stooped, probably from four decades of bending over a stove. On one forearm was an anchor tattoo; on the other, a box-faced mermaid whose once taut hips had wilted with the tattoo-bearer's age to resemble a stubby accordion.

They returned the greeting, then took places at the counter.

"Passin' through, are ya?" he asked.

Ling nodded.

"Well, I could show y'all a menu but ain't changed it in years. You name it an' I can whip it up. Ham and eggs, maybe, with grits?"

"Sounds fine," Ling said.

"What are grits?" Collingsworth asked.

The proprietor looked at him suspiciously as Ling explained it to the Englishman.

"None for me, please," Collingsworth said.

The proprietor, still looking askance at Collingsworth, was pouring their coffee, which was just short of boiling. Ling stopped him before he had filled a third cup. "You have any orange juice?"

"Squeezed fresh."

"I'll have that, instead."

Ling also merited a stony glance from the owner-cook, who appeared to be bracing himself for the next sacrilege.

"And I'll have tea, if you please," said Collingsworth.

The proprietor stared at the Englishman, then dumped one of the coffee mugs into a sink. The other he pushed in front of Triano.

"Make it regular," Triano grunted.

The cook, his tolerance nearing its breaking point, put his hands on his hips. "That *is* regular, sir," he said. "Regular coffee. We got Sanka, too. You want that, all you got to do is ask."

"He means he drinks it with cream," Ling explained.

The proprietor considered that a moment, then moved down the counter, retrieved a small metal pitcher and, saying nothing, handed it to Triano.

Shaking his head, the old man filled a tall tumbler with orange juice for Ling, then turned to the grill behind him and began cooking the ham and eggs. "We got sweetrolls," he said over his shoulder. "Or toast, if you'd prefer."

"Give me an English," Triano ordered, not too pleasantly.

Ling broke into a grin in anticipation.

The proprietor abandoned the grill, where the ham and eggs were already sizzling, and faced Triano. "I've been halfway 'round the world," he declared. "In the Navy, I was. But I have to admit I don't know what you mean when you order this here 'English.' "

"English muffin," Ling explained.

"That I ain't got," the proprietor hissed. "But there's some day-old cornbread."

"Make it toast," Triano said in defeat.

Ling watched the proprietor as he worked. His hands moved with the deftness of a surgeon and the efficiency that came from juggling a dozen orders at once in an earlier, more prosperous time. "Are you Dempsey?" Ling asked.

"That's true, sir. That's who I am." He flipped the ham on the griddle with one hand while the other reached for the toast. "Where're you folks from?"

"New York," Ling answered, steeling himself.

Dempsey placed their food in front of them. The platters were heaping with scrambled eggs and half-inch cuts of ham. Ling's and Triano's also featured a huge serving of grits, a pat of butter melting on top.

"Been to New York but once," Dempsey said. "Back in '44. Had myself some little party in Times Square."

"I expect you'd find it quite different today," Collingsworth said.

He shook his head sadly. "Ain't nothin' the same anymore, sir. Them days is gone forever."

Another elderly patron entered and went to one of the booths. Dempsey left the counter with a steaming mug of black coffee for him. Dempsey also provided a saucer. "Here ya go, Spud," he said.

The other man nodded, then began pouring the coffee from the mug to the saucer and back again, cooling it.

Dempsey returned to the grill, cracked a pair of large eggs over it and threw on some bacon. "Looks like it's gonna be a mighty fine day," he said. "Not so humid."

Ling guessed the weather was probably the number one topic in Blakeshammock.

"We'll never see it with all that smoke," Collingsworth said.

Dempsey looked at him. "The preacher says he thinks God sends us these wildfires when they're needed as a kind of reminder of eternal damnation. As I see it, though, one of those hot summer nights when the air conditioner's broke can serve just as well for us sinners to see what's awaitin' us."

Dempsey finished the bacon and eggs, then delivered them to the newcomer and sat down to join him. Ling and the others ate in silence. Dempsey was back when they finished. Standing, Ling handed him a ten-dollar bill, then accepted the change, sensing that to leave a tip would be perceived as an insult.

"Could you tell us how to get to the sheriff's?" Ling asked.

"That would be in Darwin, the county seat. Another eight miles up the road."

They thanked him again and started to leave but stopped when Dempsey said, "Ya know, it's kind of funny."

"What's that?" Ling asked.

"Y'all being the second people from New York here in that many days."

"There was someone else?"

"Sure was, sir. Not today but last night. Fella come in, ordered himself some shrimp—we got shrimp, fresh shrimp straight from the Gulf."

"What did he look like?"

"Can't tell ya much about that. To be honest, I was kind of busy an' I didn't pay too much attention. 'Cept he had this hair white as paper. Kind of guy in the Navy we'd call Whitey."

"Glasses?"

"Yeah—you know him?"

Ling shook his head. "Just a guess."

Triano had suddenly perked up. He and Ling exchanged glances.

"Where did this guy go?" Triano asked.

"Ol' Carl—Carl Livingson, that is; he owns the motel—he come in for his supper later and says the man checked himself in. Carl was thinkin' of notifyin' the sheriff. Said he smelled something, that maybe that Yankee was up to no good. Drugs or somethin'. They're pickin' 'em up everywhere, these mari-juana smugglers, I mean. It kind of made sense."

"Did he call the sheriff?" Ling asked.

"No, sir. Don't believe he did. Said it would probably behoove him to mind his own business and all."

Ling and the others left.

"The Pole?" Triano asked.

"Sounds like it," Ling said. "He's had his hands just about everywhere, it seems, but up his mother's skirt."

"Maybe there, too."

They were back in the car. In the equivalent of a city block, they were out of Blakeshammock. Ling stepped up his speed. The road resumed its twists and turns, pressed on both sides by dense pine stands.

They reached Darwin in less than ten minutes, finding it almost a replica of Blakeshammock, only bigger. On its single main street—again a continuation of the county road—they had no difficulty finding the white-painted county courthouse. To the side was a small one-story block building marked, "Office of the Sheriff."

A young woman seated at the reception counter was speaking into a table microphone. She was overweight, with arms bulging from beneath the short sleeves of her blouse. But her face was wholesome and attractive and she had a feminine quality that seemed to Ling an anachronism from the fifties.

Over a tinny speaker came the voice of a deputy in the field requesting a coffee break.

"Ten-four," the woman said, then swiveled in her chair and greeted them with a smile.

Ling displayed his shield and identified himself. He asked to speak to the sheriff.

"Sheriff Johnson's in there, folks. Just go right on in," the woman said.

They found a young black man in a crisp, tailored tan uniform seated behind a desk and leafing through a pile of forms. "They never told me about the paperwork." he said, looking up. "If they had, I'd have stayed a civilian." He stood, offering each his hand.

Ling made the introductions.

"Ah, the NYPD," the sheriff said. "You takin' good care of my alma mater?"

"You went to school in New York?" Collingsworth asked.

"N.Y.U. On scholarship, of course. Then came back home. I was born in a house not a mile from here."

Ling studied him. No hick here. Educated. He would have advanced fast in the New York Police Department. Instead, he went back home.

Ling explained their purpose, handing the sheriff the warrant.

"Big case," Johnson said. "Been reading all about it. Who'd ever think it'd end up in our little backward Georgia county." He looked up from the warrant. "This Mason woman, she works at the White House, right?"

"She's an aide to the President," Ling answered.

Johnson whistled. "That makes it kind of heavy." He stood. "In view of that, I trust you wouldn't mind if I made a phone call to verify this." He waved the warrant.

"Don't blame you," Ling said. "Man in charge is Chief of Detectives Julius Golden."

The sheriff left his office to use the dispatcher's telephone. He was back momentarily. "This guy Golden says you're the best," he told Ling.

"I owe him money."

The sheriff smiled, then announced: "I've seen her."

"Marilyn Mason?" Collingsworth asked.

He nodded. "Had to pull patrol myself last night—I've only got three men besides myself. Found her out runnin' in the rain. She claimed something jumped out of the woods and spooked her. A deer or a dog. It *could* have happened. Anyway, I drove her back to her sister's."

Ling rose from his seat. "Sheriff, could it have been a man who jumped out of those woods?"

"A man? She didn't mention anything about it being a man. But I guess it could have been. You have somebody in mind?"

"I can explain on the way."

44

Marilyn Mason, her arms fully extended, swung the axe in an arc, beginning high over her head, and slammed its flat end onto a wedge. But her mark was off. The axehead caught the edge of the wedge and was sent glancing off to the side in an itinerant path that took the blade within inches of her sneaker. She caught her balance and leaned her weight upon the axe handle. Then she laughed—she could not believe she was doing this; chopping wood.

She drew her breath sharply, raised the axe once more and slammed it down, this time with even more force. The metal head hit its mark, driving the wedge several inches, and the hardwood log split neatly in two. With two more quick strokes, she had it in four pieces, which she collected and stacked in the woodpile behind her.

Sally stuck her head out the window. "My sister, the woodsman," she taunted.

"Woodswoman," Marilyn shot back. "And besides, anything you can do, I can do better."

Sally, busy baking bread, disappeared behind the curtain. As Marilyn stooped to pick up another log, she thought of her sister fondly. Sally had been right: fresh air and exercise were what she needed. She was overtired and filled with false worry, even imagining things, like the man in the woods. It was all an illusion. There had, of course, been no one there. She had had too much to drink. And she was so weary.

Marilyn positioned the wedge in a crack on a new log, this one thicker than the first. Perhaps, she thought, she would tell her sister how James Whittaker had betrayed her, what he had orchestrated in his apartment. Sally was in touch with herself— she would understand what it meant when you were pushed to the wall by someone trying to control you, trying to strip your dignity, to gut your soul.

Her axe strokes were even and accurate now, and in less than two minutes, the split pieces were in place on the woodpile. She prepared to split another, then caught a glimpse of a green and white patrolcar stopping in front of the cottage. Behind the patrolcar was another car, a nondescript sedan. Men were stepping out of both. Marilyn recognized one of them as the kind sheriff who had aided her the previous night. With him in the patrolcar was a man who was not in uniform. She squinted, then froze. It was that New York detective! What was his name? Ling.

Marilyn dropped the axe. They had followed her all the way to Georgia! Would they never leave her alone? Her heart was pounding. Her head felt as if it would explode. Acid etched her insides. She was backpedaling, shaking her head violently in an attempt to chase what surely was no more than a bad dream. But still they came, four of them, led by that smirking detective. She had to get away!

She was sprinting, the ground falling away from her as she raced down the hill toward the ravine and the cool, shaded waters of Devilsdip Swamp. They would never find her in there.

"There she is!" Triano shouted.

"She's headed for the swamp!" said Collingsworth.

The four men ran to the side of the house. Suddenly, a woman bolted out a rear door and stood defiantly in front of them. She was cradling a shotgun. "What's going on here?" she demanded. "What are you doing to my sister?"

Johnson stepped forward. "They're police from New York, Miss Mason," he said gently. "They've got a warrant."

"A warrant for what?"

"A warrant for murder," Ling answered. "Your sister is very disturbed—she's killed three people."

"That's insane!" Sally looked at the sheriff. "You sure these people are who they say they are?"

Johnson nodded. "I made a call. It's legitimate."

Sally's eyes turned to the side. She was thinking, struggling to digest the news that her sister was about to be arrested.

In the distance, Ling caught a glimpse of Mason. She had reached the ravine and crossed it. Dodging boulders and fallen trees, she disappeared into the thick green foliage of the swamp. Ling stared at the sister. "Give me the gun, Sally," he said, advancing.

Her eyes snapped forward and she pulled the shotgun's butt to her shoulder. Ling looked into the barrel—it was zeroed in on his chest.

"Easy now, Sally," Johnson said, inching forward, his palm raised. "We don't want to do anything we'll all regret."

"But this is crazy, sheriff," the woman responded. "Some kind of frameup or something. My god, Marilyn couldn't kill anyone—she's afraid of guns."

The sheriff moved another step. "You're probably right, Sally, and I believe you. But they've got a warrant. It's official. Marilyn will have an opportunity to clear herself in court."

Sally, her eyes panicked, switched the aim of the shotgun to Johnson. "Please, sheriff. Don't come any closer. I need to think. I mean . . ."

"Give me the gun, Sally," Johnson said, still closing the gap between them. Then he was within arm's reach. He held out his hands. She stared at him, her eyes frightened and disbelieving. Then she handed over the weapon.

"Let's go," Triano said, breaking into a sprint.

Ling stopped him. "What's in there besides bush?" he asked the sheriff.

"Nothing but an old gator hunter's cabin and only one easy way out," Johnson replied.

"What's that?"

"An old clay road comin' in from the other side."

"Can you get help and block it?" Ling asked.

"I'll radio my deputy to meet me there. We both know that area well."

Ling thought a moment. "Good. The rest of us will try to follow her and flush her out."

Johnson gripped Ling's arm and pointed toward the swamp. "You see that clump of pines over there, maybe fifty yards in?"

"Yeah. What about it?"

"There's an airboat there. Belongs to one of the local men. You know how to use one?"

Ling nodded. "Tried one once or twice at Fort Benning."

"Go ahead and take it, then. You won't need a key."

Sally was sitting on the ground against the foundation of her house, staring ahead, saying nothing.

"I'm very sorry, Miss Mason. I really am," Johnson said, then rushed to his patrolcar.

The swamp was still afire but Marilyn saw no flames. Instead, the smoke belched upward from tiny volcanoes, jagged crevices or gopher-like holes in the brackish, loamy soil.

She ran unimpeded, feeling power in her legs, and did not stop until she encountered a fence, then stepped gingerly through the rows of barbed wire, as she had done so often while hunting with her father. Soon, she was in an open field of sawgrass, the footing soft yet secure. But the land continued to slope in the direction she was moving and after another hundred yards, she began to encounter pools of murky greenwater, lily pads appearing like stepping stones among the patches of wide-bladed eel grass. She stopped to think— her intelligence would have to save her. The trick would be to find a land bridge through as much of the water as possible. She knew it would not be easy—there would be spits of dry land that would appear clear pathways for great distances but would end at an impassable body of water. Steps would have to be retraced and another route attempted with a prayer that it, too, was not a false start.

Marilyn resumed her running. For the next quarter mile,

nature gave her a break—the land rose slowly until it was well above the water line. She entered a copse of mangrove trees. The green ceiling formed by the treetops shaded the undergrowth so much that only ferns, soft moss and thin, sickly fieldgrass survived. Her feet made no noise on the mangrove bed, leaving her breathing as the only sound. Then she thought she heard something else. It was in the distance. She cocked her head and soon recognized what it was—the droning of an engine. Behind her, somewhere, was an airboat.

The boat hummed over the water, the airplane propeller humming loudly in its circular cage behind them, the ride smooth as a toboggan on snow. The pontoons hurdled the plugs of land with ease and turned at the slightest change of Ling's touch upon the wheel.

Despite their movement, the air hung heavily, and Ling, tasting it, recalled other pursuits through swamps, in the bowels of Vietnam.

Triano was seated beside him, while Collingsworth squatted to the rear, clinging to the seat support, the wind crossing their faces harshly, the passing scenery a green and brown blur.

In the air's rush, Ling's eyes began to water, clouding his vision. There was a danger in traveling so blindly, so fast—a half-sunken rock could rip the boat in half—but he kept the throttle fully open and taxed the stability of the craft with wildly dodging turns.

They had to find her.

Marilyn's temples were pounding. Her eyes, though smarting from the smoke, remained wide and darting as she recorded the scene, her brain registering every detail. Her sense of smell came alive and her nostrils, strangely, found the wildfire smoke, once so distasteful and acrid, now had the flavor of hickory; a sweet, moist mellow sensation not unlike the smoke of a gentleman's pipe. Her ears were tuned to both the threatening buzz of the airboat and the crackling of the brush as she beat a path through it. Her skin felt tight and flushed with blood, the hair follicles on her arms pushing outward like a million tiny sabers, her abdomen hardening as if preparing to accept a blow. And her hands . . . her hands were steady.

Through the scrub, she caught glimpses of a slough off to the side and below her. The land began to drop and soon it was level with the water. Facing a thicket abundant with nettles, she edged toward the water line, her sneakers noisily fighting the suction of the mud. Then the buzz of the airboat suddenly exploded into a roar—they were coming right at her!

She dove for dry ground, ignoring the pricks and slashes of the brambles, and curled up in the protection of a cage of interwoven, inch-thick vines. She pressed her face to the ground and held her breath as the boat's racket drew closer and through a break in the wall of her cell-like cubicle, saw a pontoon as the airboat sped by—less than a dozen yards from her.

Marilyn closed her eyes and exhaled. Damn them! Who did they think they were, anyhow. Wait until she complained to the White House. She would . . .

Her legs began to feel warm. Then a pain began to travel from her ankles up to her calves. She looked down to her shoes. They were jammed into the side of a yard-high anthill! Fireants! Sally had warned her about them. Their bites stung. Enough bites could kill a cow.

Marilyn jumped to her feet and began swatting her jeans. There were hundreds of the ants, maybe thousands! An entire army was advancing up her legs. She frantically pulled up her pantlegs and began beating away the ants with both hands and then they were on her arms. She began crying—not knowing what to do. Then she remembered the water. She leaped toward the slough, then dove into the few inches of water and began rolling, hoping the water would wash the ants away. It did.

She lay still a moment, then struggled to free herself from the muck and slowly made it to her feet. She was dripping water and slime and the bites, the hundreds of bites, grew even more painful. They burned. Her soaked jeans clung to her and felt as if they were made of lead. But she had to move on.

Marilyn looked around, clumsily pirouetting in the ankle-deep sludge, searching for a way out. But all she saw were faces, faces of men, sneering faces, faces filled with hate. Ling and Holmes. Collingsworth and DeGrazia. The President. And Whittaker, his the most hateful of them all.

Marilyn turned away from the water and forced her legs to take a step. She would make the faces disappear. She would defeat them—and by their own rules. They would laugh at her no more, she vowed.

She searched the ground until she found what she wanted, a thick, recently fallen cypress limb. She picked it up and tested its grip, as if it were a softball bat. Then, using the limb as a machete, she began hacking her way through the nearly impenetrable scrub.

Soon, the brush began to thin and was replaced by eel grass and clover. She was able to move in a near-trot. Blood dripped from the bramble cuts on her face and arms, and the ant bites grew into tiny, white-headed pustules. But she had shaken much of the mud and water from her jeans and a breeze had kicked up, clearing much of the smoke. Fallen trees sometimes blocked the way, rotting and fast-turning into pasty sawdust through the work of insects and mildew, but she was in her second wind, her body lightened and refreshed. Her feet moved automatically in an almost unbroken rhythm, freeing her mind to think. She looked inside herself for some hint of fear or confusion, doubt or indecision. But there was none. She knew what had to be done.

Ling was trying to read the terrain, searching for the most likely route of escape. But he couldn't visualize one. Perhaps there wasn't any. Johnson had said there was a road—but Ling could see no sign of it. Would Mason find it? If so, the sheriff and his deputy would be waiting for her.

Then there was the cabin. Did Mason know of it? Was she heading for that?

Ling looked at Triano. Triano's face was red. He appeared sick, ready to vomit. Damn, Mickey, Ling said to himself. Fight it. We can't stop now.

●　　●　　●

Marilyn spotted a clearing ahead. She raced for it and stopped. On the opposite side of the clearing was a rusting tin roof. Atop the roof was a crude stone and mortar chimney. A cabin! Sally had mentioned a reclusive swampman—perhaps it was his.

Marilyn moved toward the clearing, then froze—hanging from a branch less than a yard away was a thick, black, cylindrical object. The white of its mouth betrayed it—a cottonmouth water moccasin. She edged away from it, her heart thumping, then looked down to find she had stumbled upon a well-beaten path.

, She took it. The trail followed a bend, then ended at a large, oval lagoon. Across the water was the cabin. She stopped, weighing the alternatives: The cabin appeared deserted. Inside was probably a gun. A swamp hermit would have a gun. With the sound of the airboat moving closer, her jeopardy was growing. A gun could drive them away, send them out for reinforcements. She would have time, then— time to plan her route to freedom. She looked to the sky. A pair of black turkey buzzards were circling above her— scavengers in search of a carcass. Marilyn snapped her eyes away.

The lagoon water was different from that she had encountered earlier. It wasn't murky and filled with suspended algae and weeds; it was grayish and transparent and appeared to have a slight current. She stooped and broke the surface with her fingertips—the water, probably spring-fed, was cold.

She stepped into it slowly. The drop was gradual. For the first ten yards, the water remained below her knees, then the bottom began to descend more abruptly. The waterline rose two or three inches with each step, the frigid wetness climbing her body. When it reached her waist, she began to hesitate before each step, fearful of a sudden drop. The water rose still higher. When it was level with her shoulders, she began to worry. She knew how to swim—but in water this cold and her being fully dressed and another fifty yards at the minimum ahead of her, she wasn't sure she could make it. The water soon reached her shoulders and began to encircle her neck. Shivering, she tilted back her head. The ripples from her movement began lapping at her chin.

As she neared the middle, a cloud of mist suddenly appeared. It was a gentle sight, remindful of her first glimpse, years earlier, of a mist hovering over a peaceful Canadian lake. She breathed deeply, intending to bathe her lungs in the soothing moisture, but her breath was broken violently by a hacking cough—it wasn't mist; it was smoke. The wind had died abruptly. The smoke of the wildfire was settling. In mere seconds, it thickened so much that she lost sight of the shoreline, both before and behind her.

Marilyn pulled off her workshirt, bunched it and held it against her mouth and nose, the soaked fabric serving as a breathing mask.

She was advancing slowly, her visibility cut to a few feet. Suddenly, she stopped. There was a log floating across her path. No, it wasn't a log—it was moving slightly, disturbing the water. The ripples grew larger. An alligator, perhaps. At least four feet from head to toe, it was riding low on the water.

The gator was two or three yards away and seemed to be floating toward her. She began to edge back. The gator twitched. Or had it? She wasn't sure. The ripples seemed unchanged. Maybe it was the natural play of the water. The gator moved again, bending at the middle. Its head lifted out of the water. And its tail. Then, from the tail came a locust-like sound she recognized at once—it wasn't a gator; it was a rattler! A long diamondback with a girth equal to the trunk of a dogwood tree.

Marilyn froze, then screamed. Her mind raced for options— but no action was needed.

The snake, its rattling stilled with its tail back in the water, slithered away in panicked rush.

She watched the diamondhead disappear in the smoke, then forced herself to continue onward through the water. In the distance, the airboat throttled back abruptly to a low hum. The hum lasted a few seconds, then the machine was unleashed again at full force, its direction altered. The boat was closing in on her—very fast.

The water level dropped rapidly as she stepped up her pace, and she was at the shore almost before she saw it through the smoke. The cabin was only a few yards away. She struggled up the bank, water dripping off of her. She stood with her feet apart, her eyes scanning the lagoon as the irritating rasp of the airboat grew still louder. Except for the boat, it was deadly silent.

Twice Ling thought he had glimpsed her but each time he lost the sighting in a pocket of smoke and, blinded, was forced to cut the engine.

The air partially cleared and Ling steered toward what appeared to be an open body of water. But as they entered a bay, the smoke once more intensified.

"Jesus, that stuff burns!" yelled Triano.

Ling eased the airboat ahead, hoping there would be no fallen tree, no rocks. Then, as if a curtain had been parted, they could see. They were twenty, maybe twenty-five yards from shore. There, on high land, was a cabin. Outside the cabin was a figure.

Ling cut the engine. Instinctively he reached for his gun. But he was too late—from the figure on shore came a flash followed by the crack of a gunshot! Next to him, Triano was jolted backward. The airboat was rocking wildly. There was a splash as Collingsworth fell overboard.

Ling looked to Triano. Triano was draped backward over the seat, his stomach red with blood.

"Mickey!" Ling screamed, bending over him. Triano gritted his teeth and grimaced. Ling pulled him to the deck of the boat. "Hold on, Mickey. I'll get you out of here," he said.

"Goddamn but it hurts, Monk!"

Ling ripped open Triano's shirt. The shot had opened a huge hole in his lower abdomen. He was bleeding badly.

Ling reached overboard and dipped his hand into the water. He raised his fingers to Triano's mouth and allowed the cool water to drip onto his lips.

"Is it bonded?" Triano asked weakly, attempting a smile.

"Yeah—and aged," Ling replied.

Triano struggled to sit but Ling took him by the shoulders and eased him back.

Triano's eyes opened wide. "Maggie," he called out.

"There's nothing to worry about," Ling said. "She'll be proud of you."

"Maggie," Triano called out again, his voice a hoarse whisper.

And then he was gone.

Ling stared at Triano's motionless body a moment, then looked to the water. Collingsworth was struggling to keep afloat. Ling snapped his eyes toward the shore. There, advancing toward the waterline, barechested with the stock of a deer rifle pressed to her shoulder was Marilyn Mason.

She was calm. She was confident. She was in control. Her father would have been proud of her—the shot had been true, square into the gut.

Two targets remained—and one of them was locked in her sights, the one in the water. In her peripheral vision, she could see the man on the airboat. It was Ling. He had his pistol in both hands. It was aimed at her. But he was hesitant. He wouldn't shoot until she did, until she planted a new round between the treading man's eyes. She would fall prone with the kick of the rifle, minimizing her exposure, and then she would take the last bastard out. Her lips stretched into a smile—it was getting easier.

"Shoot her!" Collingsworth was screaming to Ling. "For god's sake, pull the trigger!"

Ling felt the steel curled against his finger. He was dead on target. His finger began to tighten. Then, suddenly, he loosened his grip. He slowly pointed the muzzle to the side.

The arm was across her throat, its thick bulk choking her. She could hardly breathe. He had his hand on the rifle barrel and she fought to prevent him from pulling it away. She tried to bite him, kick him in the groin. But his hold on her was expert. She was helpless. And then the gun was ripped from her arms.

He released her neck and replaced it with a tight grip on her forearm, then spun her around. Her eyes were on his face. A stranger. Or was he? A broad-shouldered man. Glasses. White hair.

45

Stanislas Lubelski rested his back against the termite-scarred cornerpost of Dempsey's Cafe and watched the sun drop toward the horizon. The smoke from Devilsdip had died down and the twilight sky was cloudless. Down the street, Marilyn Mason sat in handcuffs in the back of a sheriff's patrolcar. The suspect's sister, Sally Mason, was seated with her, the sheriff having allowed them a few moments together.

The news media had already invaded the town—the major networks had used helicopters to ferry in their equipment—but most of the correspondents had left to meet their deadlines. Only a handful of print reporters and one or two still photographers remained.

A half-dozen FBI agents, rushed from Atlanta and Washington, were clustered outside the general store—sulking.

Down the street, Detective Monk Ling was watching somberly as a black body bag containing Mickey Triano's corpse was lifted from the back of a jeep into a hearse from some nearby larger town. The attendants closed the hearse door. Ling walked to the jeep and violently kicked a rear tire.

Nearby, the Englishman was stretched out on the backseat of the detectives' rented car. He had been complaining of feeling faint. The white-aproned cafe owner came through the restaurant door carrying a cup of hot tea. He walked over to the sedan and passed it through the window to the appreciative Englishman.

All afternoon, Lubelski had watched the authorities at work, clearing everybody out of the swamp, recovering the dead man's corpse, interviewing Marilyn Mason in the back of the restaurant and giving answers to frenzied reporters who suspected they were probably on the biggest story of their careers.

Earlier, the sheriff, clipboard in hand, had asked Lubelski his name but Ling stopped any further questioning. After a hushed conference with the New York detective, the sheriff returned to advise him that there was no need for him to remain in Blakeshammock and, because of all the media present, it might be in his best interest to be on his way.

But Lubelski didn't want to leave. He wanted to witness the picking up of the pieces. It would, in a sense, be his final chapter.

He pulled out a white handkerchief and rubbed his eyes, which still smarted from the wildfire's smoke. He then ran a hand through his hair, noting how it was getting ever thinner. Wisdom, it was said, came with age. Lubelski wondered. No longer were his choices so black and white as they were in his youth; no longer did he use deduction to thrash out those choices. Instead, he was given to following ill-defined and wavering gut feelings, as he had that very day. The sorting out would come later—if at all.

Ling, a camera hanging from his neck, left the hearse and began walking toward him. The detective was sweating. He looked tired.

"Let's take a walk," Ling said.

"I beg your pardon?"

"You and me. Let's take a stroll."

Lubelski shrugged, then joined him in a walk down the center of Blakeshammock's Main Street.

"I'm very sorry about your partner," Lubelski said.

Ling grimaced. "I notified his widow myself. She seemed to expect it."

"Your suspect, she has a marksman's eye."

Ling nodded. "Apparently her father taught her how to shoot, and taught her well." Ling looked at him. "I think you're entitled to know that she gave us a complete statement. Admitted everything.''

"I thought she might.''

Ling went on to detail Marilyn Mason's confession, which contained no element Lubelski had not himself already put together, except for the videotape Whittaker had made as a backup to the still pictures.

"She was a troubled young woman,'' Lubelski said.

Ling stopped walking. He looked the Pole in the eye. "I would have had to kill her if you hadn't been there,'' the detective said.

Lubelski looked down to the pavement's cracked and crumbling asphalt.

"I should ask you who you really are but I think I already know,'' Ling said.

Lubelski suspected Ling indeed knew his secret. The detective could not know, however—not even imagine—the indecision that had consumed him for the past five days, his guessing game over which route would lead to his freedom. In the end, even his ambivalence had proven meaningless with the realization that neither alternative would have brought freedom, neither would have taken him home.

"You didn't have to show yourself,'' Ling continued. "You could have slipped away.''

Lubelski, still silent, resumed his walking. Ling stayed with him. In the west, the sun had dipped below the treetops.

"I've already talked it over with Collingsworth, the Englishman,'' Ling said. "Neither one of us will be saying anything about what happened in that swamp today. And the sheriff will have no mention of you in his records. I thought it would be best for you that way.''

Lubelski glanced at him. "It doesn't matter.''

"What will they do to you?'' Ling asked.

Lubelski didn't answer—he knew very well what Petrovich would attempt to do, but the Russian was so incompetent. . . .

There was a sudden racket above them. Both men stopped and looked to the sky.

"Chimney swifts,'' Ling said.

There were perhaps a dozen of the tiny birds, all flying the same circular path, which took them directly over the roof of

Sally Mason's cottage. Periodically, a single bird would leave the tornado-like swirl and dive down the cabin's chimney. One at a time, the others followed, dipping out of sight behind the stone and mortar. At last, a single bird was flying, staying to the same precise course but ignoring the chimney. Lubelski started counting. Four, five, then six times the bird completed his aerial laps. Finally, the straggler also disappeared from view but not into the chimney—chirping defiantly, he flew beyond the trees into the distance and did not return.

"A loner," Lubelski said.

Ling moved to within inches of his face. The eyes of each drilled the other's. "A loner," the detective repeated. "Odd man out. You and me, Lubelski. We understand that. Two solitary birds. Me, that chimney swift there. Small stuff. But you . . . you fly dangerously. Higher stakes. Let's call you . . . an *eagle*. Yes?" Ling's head was cocked. His face was stonelike but there was an unmistakable twinkle in his eyes.

Lubelski thought a moment, then winked. Instantly, a strange sensation came over him. He was perspiring from the lingering heat, his mouth still tasted of smoke, and a foul residue of the swamp still clung to him. Yet somehow he felt cleansed.

He turned his back on the detective and began walking away, heading for the Tall Oaks Motel. It was time to settle his account.

"Lubelski!" Ling called after him.

He turned. The detective had his camera to his eyes, his fingers at work focusing its long lens.

"Take care of yourself," Ling said.

Lubelski hesitated, searching for a response, but found none that meant anything. He stepped off for the motel again, thinking of an FBI agent whose voice had revealed that he, too, was weary, that he, too, wanted out. His senses alive, Lubelski listened to his boots, their thump against the pavement the only sound to be heard in the quiet of the hamlet until, from behind him, came another sound:

Click.

Lubelski laughed. He laughed long and loudly, his laughter piercing the still of the encroaching Georgian night.